刘洪涛 [美]戴维斯-昂蒂亚诺 杨明晨(执行) 主编

今日世界文学

Global

第八辑
The Eighth Volume

Literature

Today

中国社会科学出版社

图书在版编目(CIP)数据

今日世界文学. 第八辑 / 刘洪涛,(美)戴维斯 - 昂蒂亚诺,杨明晨主编. —北京：中国社会科学出版社,2023.9
ISBN 978 - 7 - 5227 - 2194 - 1

Ⅰ. ①今…　Ⅱ. ①刘…②戴…③杨…　Ⅲ. ①世界文学—文学研究　Ⅳ. ①I106

中国国家版本馆 CIP 数据核字(2023)第 145207 号

出 版 人	赵剑英
责任编辑	郭晓鸿
特约编辑	杜若佳
责任校对	师敏革
责任印制	戴　宽

出　　版	中国社会科学出版社
社　　址	北京鼓楼西大街甲 158 号
邮　　编	100720
网　　址	http://www.csspw.cn
发 行 部	010 - 84083685
门 市 部	010 - 84029450
经　　销	新华书店及其他书店

印　　刷	北京明恒达印务有限公司
装　　订	廊坊市广阳区广增装订厂
版　　次	2023 年 9 月第 1 版
印　　次	2023 年 9 月第 1 次印刷

开　　本	710×1000　1/16
印　　张	21
插　　页	2
字　　数	305 千字
定　　价	109.00 元

凡购买中国社会科学出版社图书,如有质量问题请与本社营销中心联系调换
电话：010 - 84083683
版权所有　侵权必究

编委会

主　　编：刘洪涛　戴维斯-昂蒂亚诺　杨明晨（执行）
英文编辑：王国礼

编　　委（按姓氏音序排列）

　　曹顺庆　陈众议　Robert Con Davis-Undiano
　　方维规　黄运特　金　莉　梁　展　刘洪涛
　　刘树森　陆建德　聂珍钊　Daniel Simon
　　宋炳辉　Jonathan Stalling（石江山）　苏　晖
　　Karen Thornber（唐丽园）　Nicolai Volland（傅朗）
　　杨金才　姚建彬　张清华　赵　勇　朱　萍

目　录

卷首语（代新版《今日世界文学》发刊词）……………………（1）

世界文学理论研究

星丛化世界文学 ………………………………… 黄　嵭（3）
理论旅行的流通机制与世界文学的诗学问题 …………… 李孟奇（29）
世界文学面临的危险 ………………………… 威廉姆·阿特金森（43）
以本土性求全球化：对世界文学
　教学的反思 ……………………………… 伊曼德·米尔穆塔哈里（51）

区域文学研究

心灵的反讽：诺瓦利斯诗学接受史 ………………… 陆浩斌（61）
《天空落幕时》中的后人类肯定伦理与
　共同体渴望 ………………………………… 郑松筠　张生珍（74）
奈恩·诺梅兹与其对新冠的诗意化呈现 ………… 基斯·埃利斯（90）
浅议智利诗人艾薇拉·赫尔南德斯 ………… 苏利达·马兰比奥（119）
除恶务尽：铲除白人
　至上的执念 ………… 法比安·卡诺尔著　艾利森·安德森译（127）
我们的复仇行为会成为孩子的笑柄 ………… 菲利普·梅特斯（134）

跨文化与跨媒介研究

迷狂与开悟：论巴塔耶与铃木大拙的关系 ………… 张历君（155）

框内的时间
　　——法斯宾德电影姿势研究 ………… 林晓萍（173）

种族、历史和身体：展演中的人性 ………… 马修·谢诺达（189）

让文字发声：作为集体转换的
　　索克语翻译 ………… 麦克斯·桑切斯著　温迪·考尔译（194）

中国与世界

【晚清民国中西知识交互中的现代性】专题

《新文化辞书》试释 ………… 李欧梵著　杨明晨译（201）

震惊、祛魅与规训：晚清大众媒介中的火车经验书写
　　（1902—1911） ………… 张春田　韩雨薇（219）

想象中的文化雅集：作为民国上海媒介文化景观的
　　"咖啡"与"茶" ………… 韩竺媛（234）

世界文学创作

我们约会吧！一部关于婚恋网站的
　　独幕剧 ………… 罗伯特·肯·戴维斯－昂蒂亚诺著　朱萍译（261）

飞蚊症 ………… 詹妮·斯卡拉格斯著　徐燕译（288）

诗二首 ………… 沙西拉·沙里芙著　程文译（295）

诗四首 ………… 玛荷莉·亚葛辛著　程文译（298）

书　评

"等级制度"与"宇宙种族"
　　——评戴维斯－昂蒂亚诺《归乡吧，梅斯蒂索人！》 …… 张艺莹（305）

征稿启事 ………………………………………………………（313）

Contents

Foreword ··· (1)

Theory of World Literature

Constellating World Literature ···················· Yu Huang(3)
The Circulation Mechanism of Traveling Theory and the Poetics
　of World Literature ···························· Mengqi Li(29)
The Perils of World Literature ············ William Atkinson(43)
The Local as the Global: Reflections on Teaching
　World Literature ···················· Emad Mirmotahari(51)

Regional Literature and Area Studies

Irony of Mind: The Acceptance History of
　Novalis Poetics ································ Haobin Lu(61)
When the Sky Falls: Posthuman Affirmative Ethics and the
　Eagerness for Community ········ Songyun Zheng, Shengzhen Zhang(74)
Naín Nómez and the Proper Poetic Treatment of
　Covid-19 ······································ Keith Ellis(90)
The Insolent Gaze of Chilean Poet Elvira
　Hernández ···························· Soledad Marambio(119)

Contents

Déchoukaj'Uprooting the Fetishes of White
　　Supremacy ················ Fabienne Kanor, trans. Alison Anderson(127)
Our Revenge Will Be the Laughter of Our
　　Children Philip ·································· Philip Metres(134)

Transcultural and Transmedia Studies

Ecstasy and Satori: On the Relation of Georges Bataille and
　　Daisetz Teitaro Suzuki ························ Lik-kwan Cheung(155)
Time in the Frame-A Study of Fassbinder's
　　Film Gestures ···································· Xiaoping Lin(173)
Race, History, and the Body: Humanity
　　on Display ···································· Matthew Shenoda(189)
Giving Voice to Words: Translation as Collective Transformation
　　in Zoque ················ Mikeas Sánchez, trans. Wendy Call(194)

China and the World

Special: Modernity of Late Qing Dynasty and the Republic of China in Knowledge Communication Between China and the West

Xinwenhua cishu(An Encyclopedic Dictionary of New Knowledge): *An
　　Exploratory Reading* ······ Leo Ou-fan Lee., trans. Mingchen Yang(201)
Shock, Disenchantment and Discipline: Train Experience Writing
　　in the Mass Media of the Late Qing Dynasty,
　　1902—1911 ························ Chuntian Zhang, Yuwei Han(219)
Imaginary Genteel Gatherings: "Coffee" and "Tea" as
　　Cultural Landscape within Popular Media in
　　Republican Shanghai ······························ Zhuyuan Han(234)

World Literary Works

Meet Up! A one-Act Play About Dating
　　Stites ················ Robert Con Davis-Undiano, trans. Ping Zhu(261)

Floaters ·················· Gianni Skaragas, trans. Yan Xu(288)
Two Poems ·················· Shahilla Shariff, trans. Wen Cheng(295)
Four Poems ·················· Marjorie Agosín, trans. Wen Cheng(298)

Book Review

"Casta System" and "Cosmic Race": On the *Mestizos Come Home*!
 of Robert Con Davis-Undiano ·················· Yiying Zhang(305)

Call for Paper ·················· (313)

卷 首 语

(代新版《今日世界文学》发刊词)

  1827 年歌德"世界文学"(Weltliteratur)的提出成为联结文学经验与世界经验的重要遗嘱。无论是世界的文学或是文学的世界，都在后世的想象与实践中被不断赋形，"世界文学"也成为各民族文学相互交流、对话、竞争的重要场域空间。在当下媒介技术与全球流动方式的空前革命中，北京师范大学与美国俄克拉荷马大学时隔八年再度携手，重新推出改版后两校合作的《今日世界文学》(*Global Literature Today*，简称 *GLT*)学术辑刊，以期用新的眼光观察世界文学的发展，用新的姿态回应世界文学的议题，用新的行动参与世界文学的建设，在跨国别、跨语言的交流中达成文明互鉴的"今日世界文学"。

  北京师范大学文学院比较文学与世界文学研究所是新版《今日世界文学》的主要编辑和运行平台，该所承袭 20 世纪 50 年代穆木天先生、彭慧先生所奠基的精神，在积极了解和译介外国文学的他山之石中，寻求重新认识本民族文学的攻玉之道。合作方俄克拉荷马大学主要以该校在美国本土主办的英文文学期刊《今日世界文学》(*World Literature Today*，简称 *WLT*)为此次合作的依托。*WLT* 创刊于 1927 年，主要刊载当代世界文学评论和各国优秀作家的最新作品，其以对世界文学最新潮流的敏锐把握和引领，获得了崇高的学术声誉和广泛的世界影响，并被列入 A&HCI 国际学术期刊评价体系。*WLT* 对中国文学的关注可以追溯到 1935 年，而与北京师范大学的渊源始自 2007 年，双

卷首语

方在联合主办过多次国际学术会议的基础上共同促成了《当代世界文学（中国版）》（*Chinese Edition of World Literature Today*）在2008年的创刊，后改名为《今日世界文学（中国版）》。该刊在出版七辑后于2014年因故暂停，现经双方商议，对原有的《今日世界文学（中国版）》进行改版后重新推出，对辑刊的名称、编委、语言、栏目、风格和定位均做出改变。改版复刊后的《今日世界文学》（*GLT*）除了依然选编或译介 *WLT* 上的部分评论和作品，主要刊发中外原创学术论文，并接受中英双语来稿，但同时，为了突出两校、两刊多年合作的珍贵历史传统，卷号依然延续之前的成果，《今日世界文学》第八辑由此得以与读者见面。

本辑共刊登了22篇稿件，按照《今日世界文学》改版后的常设栏目进行编排，这些常设栏目是：世界文学理论研究、区域文学研究、跨文化与跨媒介研究、中国与世界、世界文学创作、书评。其中有10篇稿件由主编挑选自 *WLT*，其余12篇皆为从海内外学者来稿中挑选出的优秀论文或创作。

"世界文学理论研究"栏目主要刊载以"世界文学"核心概念为议题的理论反思，本期四篇文章涉及"世界文学"的认识论哲学基础、研究范式、运行机制、当下困境以及教学探索等不同议题。黄峪《星丛化世界文学》和李孟奇《理论旅行的流通机制与世界文学的诗学问题》两篇论文以概念的辨析、渊源的追踪和权力的批判，对世界文学的历史与意涵进行了理论化探讨；选自 *WLT* 的两篇评论体文章——阿特金森《世界文学面临的危险》和米尔穆塔哈里《以本土性求全球化：对世界文学教学的反思》，则以日常实践经验对世界文学宏观议题进行了案例化展示。

"区域文学研究"栏目旨在刊发以世界各国、各民族、各语言的文学文化为研究对象的论文，本期六篇文章在呈现多元化区域文学的同时，也展示出历史与当下的碰撞。陆浩斌《心灵的反讽：诺瓦利斯诗学接受史》通过爬梳18世纪德国著名诗人诺瓦利斯的接受史，揭示诺瓦利斯浪漫主义诗学在后世的构建，借此重访其诗学问题中重要的

"心灵"概念。接下来三篇文章讨论的对象紧跟当下最新的文学创作，兼及不同国家与语种，包括英国作家菲尔·厄尔2021年出版、2022年获奖的小说《天空落幕时》（郑松筠、张生珍《〈天空落幕时〉中的后人类肯定伦理与共同体渴望》），智利诗人奈恩·诺梅兹于2020年针对新冠疫情所写的诗歌《荒芜的大地》（基斯·埃利斯《奈恩·诺梅兹与其对新冠的诗意化呈现》），智利作家艾薇拉·赫尔南德斯的儿童诗歌创作（苏利达·马兰比奥《浅议智利诗人艾薇拉·赫尔南德斯》）。其中埃利斯对诺梅兹《荒芜的大地》的分析建基于与20世纪经典现代主义诗歌艾略特《荒原》的对读，这一视角本身就是历史与当下的贯通。上述苏利达·马兰比奥的文章和本栏目最后两篇文章皆选自 WLT，法比安·卡诺尔《除恶务尽：铲除白人至上的执念》与菲利普·梅特斯《我们的复仇行为会成为孩子的笑柄》并非对作家作品的分析解读，而是出自作家视角的现实政治探讨。他们分别从具体的人物和事件出发，描绘评论了美国的非裔歧视问题、英国政权与北爱尔兰之间的权力压迫，是文学与政治的相遇。

"跨文化与跨媒介研究"栏目旨在跨越国别、语言、文化与媒介的界限，颠覆话语实践中的固有区隔和对立，重新联结不同领域之间的意义关联。本期四篇文章所探讨的对象和问题丰富多样，历史时段涵盖从20世纪前期到当下。张历君《迷狂与开悟：论巴塔耶与铃木大拙的关系》通过追溯和钩沉法国文艺理论家巴塔耶对日本近代禅宗思想家铃木大拙佛学思想的接受，不仅对巴塔耶"迷狂"概念的形成和意涵做了重新理解，更揭示出东西方跨文化交流对促成现代先锋艺术理念的重要意义。林晓萍《框内的时间——法斯宾德电影姿势研究》接续前卫艺术现象，但聚焦于当代德国电影人法斯宾德的电影语言，对现代技术化媒介叙事的反思可以为文学研究提供启发。马修·谢诺达《种族、历史和身体：展演中的人性》和麦克斯·桑切斯《让文字发声：作为集体转换的索克语翻译》选自 WLT，前者从当代博物馆实践中重新反思展示或展演的权力，后者探索小语种索克语的翻译限度以反思语言媒介本质及其转换问题。

卷首语

"中国与世界"栏目的设定意在反思中国在世界文学和文化体系中的位置意义。本期三篇论文构成了特定专题"晚清民国中西知识交互中的现代性"，晚清以来中国现代性的生成无法脱离与西方经验的复杂对话、摩擦与融会，在此过程中所充斥的好奇、震惊、愉悦与创痛体验被转化为多种形式的文学与文化表征，并在当时借助于现代印刷媒介形成"新知"。李欧梵《〈新文化辞书〉试释》通过聚焦于中国现代一部重要百科全书——1923年商务印书馆出版的《新文化辞书》，而重新绘制其时知识分子接受和理解现代西学的丰富知识景观。如果说李欧梵所探索的"新知"是由精英知识分子所着意发起，那么张春田《震惊、祛魅与规训：晚清大众媒介中的火车经验书写（1902—1911）》则更多转向晚清市民社会中的知识想象，普通人对西方工业革命的感知落地为日常生活中的火车经验，形成小报等大众媒介上的火车书写风潮。而韩竺媛《想象中的文化雅集：作为民国上海媒介文化景观的"咖啡"与"茶"》中探讨的民国"雅集"现象，则是联结起民国时期精英知识分子与市民大众的典型案例，现代西方的沙龙与咖啡馆文化介入中国文人雅集的传统中，形成中西融会的现代文学与文化想象空间，并通过报刊等现代大众媒介的表述在作家、知识分子、市民大众等群体中产生广泛影响。

"世界文学创作"与"书评"栏目分别刊登世界各国的新近文学作品和书评，《今日世界文学》希冀在致力于学理研究的同时，也向读者直观展示世界文学风貌、分享海内外优秀学术著述或文学作品的书讯。本期的文学作品包括三种体裁：独幕剧（戴维斯-昂蒂亚诺《我们约会吧！一部关于婚恋网站的独幕剧》）、短篇小说（詹妮·斯卡拉格斯《飞蚊症》）、诗歌（沙西拉·沙里芙《诗二首》、玛荷莉·亚葛辛《诗四首》等），作家来自美国、希腊、加拿大，涉及肯尼亚裔、智利裔等少数族裔。其中戴维斯《我们约会吧！一部关于婚恋网站的独幕剧》是本刊首发原创文学，其余三篇均挑选自 *WLT*。作为本刊主编之一、*WLT* 社长的戴维斯-昂蒂亚诺，长期以来关注少数族裔文学，并在美国高校进行文学研究的同时身体力行尝试文学创作，而本期张艺莹所撰写的书评也是对戴维斯的学术著作所展开的评读。戴维斯在2016年出版的《归乡吧！梅斯蒂索人》一书，聚焦于作为北美混血族群的"梅斯蒂索人"（"mestizos"），通过重新发掘他们的历史档案、社会处境、文化传说、文学书写以反思美国神话，张艺莹的书评介绍了书中的重要问题、方法、观点和亮点。

复刊后的各位编委给了《今日世界文学第八辑》以莫大的支持和鼓励，西北师范大学的王国礼教授担任本期的英文编辑，做了部分英文翻译与校对工作，北京师范大学文学院比较文学与世界文学专业的博士生周天玥、硕士生魏可心和于子淳承担了部分本刊的排版与格式编辑工作，在此一并向他们表示感谢！本刊编辑部在此以卷首语代新版辑刊的发刊词，愿在今天召唤百年前郑振铎所吁"文学的统一观"的幽灵，以世界文学之梦想再造巴别塔。

世界文学理论研究

星丛化世界文学

黄 崤

【摘要】 本篇文章旨在为将星丛范式运用于世界文学研究提供理论基础。文章第一部分对"星丛"这一概念在天文学/占星学、认识论和文学阐释学中的使用做出跨学科考察；文章第二部分对当前世界文学研究中认识论转变做出理论探究；文章第三部分详细说明星丛化世界文学如何围绕三个关键因素进行运作，即不同出发点（points of departure）、视域转换（horizon changes）和普世诗学（universal poetics）；最后，作者认为星丛化范式不仅是有益的理论工具，还能为面临全球化和民族主义危机的世界文学研究提供解决之道。

【关键词】 星丛范式；世界文学；阐释学；东西方文学研究

Constellating World Literature
Yu Huang

Abstract: This paper aims to lay the theoretical groundwork for the con-

---

* 【作者简介】黄崤，女，法国里昂大学跨文化研究博士，曾任广州中山大学国际翻译学院副教授，现任香港岭南大学环球中国文化高等研究院发展统筹主任，《棱镜：理论与现代中国文学》英文学刊执行编辑。研究方向为中法比较文学、世界文学理论。

本文英文原稿标题为"Constellating World Literature"，最初发表于 Neohelicon 2013 年第 40 期。中文版于本刊首次刊登，作者略有修改，由作者和马文康共同翻译而成。

stellation paradigm in world literature studies. The first section conducts an interdisciplinary investigation of the concept of constellation in astronomy/astrology, epistemology, and literary hermeneutics. The second section presents the current theoretical explorations for an epistemological alteration in world literature studies. The third section illustrates how constellating world literature operates with three key factors, i. e. points of departure, horizon changes, and universal poetics. Finally, the author concludes that the constellation paradigm serves not only as a useful theoretical tool but also as a remedy for world literature studies under the threats of globalization and nationalism.

Key words: Constellation paradigm; World literature; Hermeneutics; Literary studies East and West

如果世界文学成为可能的那一时刻终于到来，那么它也将同时、彻底地变为不可能。我希望，我们每个人都能够对这种不可能有所体认。

——艾田蒲，"是否应当重新审视世界文学这一概念？"

世界文学（Weltliteratur）一直是众多比较文学学者倡导的理想。[1] 这一概念暗示着文学间存在亲缘性和普遍价值，是文学研究的基石[2]；并且意味着文学研究从单一国族视野到承认和重估文学多样性的转变。[3] 在现代语言学会（MLA）和美国比较文学学会（ACLA）等专业

---

[1] See J. W. Von Goethe, *Conversations with Eckermann: Being Appreciations and Criticisms on Many Subjects*, trans. J. Oxenford, Honolulu: World Public Library Association, 2010, pp. 173 – 175; R. Wellek, "The Crisis of Comparative Literature", in S. G. Nichols, ed., *Concepts of criticism*, New Haven: Yale University Press, 1965, pp. 287 – 295; and R. Étiemble, "Faut-il réviser la notion de Weltliteratur?", in R. E'tiemble, ed., *Essais de littérature (vraiment) générale*, Paris: Gallimard, 1975, pp. 15 – 36.

[2] G. Steiner, *What is Comparative Literature?: An Inaugural Lecture Delivered Before the University of Oxford on 11 October, 1994*, Oxford: Clarendon Press, 1995, pp. 5 – 6.

[3] C. Guillén, *The Challenge of Comparative Literature*, trans. C. Franzen, Cambridge, MA: Harvard University Press, 1993, pp. 37 – 45.

协会的支持下，许多学者在世界文学集册编选和教学实践方面做出了诸多努力。在一份关于现代语言学会和美国比较文学学会标准的十年报告中，伯恩海默（Charles Bernheimer）追溯了自1950年以来比较文学的转变，新的后战争时代下的跨国族视角为文学研究提供了更广阔的视野，文学研究转而开始关注国族和语言身份。但是，这种新视角对比较文学提出了三项重大挑战，即比较文学研究的精英化、跨学科研究项目的增多，以及较共时性研究而言重历时性研究。针对这三项挑战，伯恩海默提出了相应的解决方法：引入新的阅读方式；用跨学科、跨文化的议题拓展研究的疆域。[1] 四届美国比较文学学会报告以喧哗的众声（multivocality）体现了德国唯心主义者所说的差异和非差异的同一（unity of difference and nondifference）。[2] 对于苏源熙（Haun Saussy）而言，歌德的"世界文学"（world literature）听起来更像是一种分配策略（distribution strategy），而非一个学术领域或一套研究比较文学的方法。[3] 与其寻找合适的**对象**（object），比较文学学者应当重新关注领域内的不同**项目**（projects），后者使得多种多样的对象得以相遇。[4] 在这个以单极化、不平等、学术机构转型以及信息化为特征的时代里，比较文学系的愿景与使命应当是跨学科的"将对某些议题的侧重转化为一种理性（rationale）的努力，解释学科内部的讨论究竟关乎什么内容"[5]。

过去的二十年里，以不同路径分析世界文学的学术研究日益增多，但都遇到了认识论和方法论上的挑战。如果采取一种世界主义而非欧

---

[1] C. Bernheimer, *Comparative Literature in the Age of Multiculturalism*, Baltimore: Johns Hopkins University Press, 1995, pp. 39 – 48.

[2] H. Saussy, ed., *Comparative Literature in an Age of Globalization*, Baltimore: The Johns Hopkins University Press, 2006, p.1.

[3] H. Saussy, ed., *Comparative Literature in an Age of Globalization*, Baltimore: The Johns Hopkins University Press, 2006, p.6.

[4] H. Saussy, ed., *Comparative Literature in an Age of Globalization*, Baltimore: The Johns Hopkins University Press, 2006, p.23. 英文原文中的斜体部分在中文译文中以加粗表示。

[5] H. Saussy, ed., *Comparative Literature in an Age of Globalization*, Baltimore: The Johns Hopkins University Press, 2006, pp. 35 – 36.

洲中心主义的视野,"文学世界"将包含体量过于巨大的文学文本,从而变得难以把握。在国际文学经典化的过程中,由于经济—政治权力关系上的不平等,文学的自主和平等尚未实现。试图将文学作品按主题进行分类的方法可能会导致对于文学作品的分析失去历史的维度。① 对于达姆罗什(David Damrosch)而言,书写世界文学的历史面临三个主要问题:为世界文学下定义、设计书写方法、确定书写目的。这些挑战源于世界文学的突出特点,即"它的多变性:不同的读者会着迷于不同的文本构成的星群(constellations of texts)"②。世界文学的全球化(the globalization of world literature)使得文学作品呈爆炸式增长——文本无穷无尽、无从把握,并且导致了这样一个事实,即全球范围内的世界文学(global world literature)可能根本没有什么历史可供书写。为这样一种世界文学书写历史意味着要扩大范围,提供"一种类型学(typology)而非一种历史叙述"。达姆罗什提出了一种新的模型,这是一种"双重的努力"(a double enterprise)——模型为读者提供有效纵览与宏观框架,读者可以在其中填入自己选择的文学作品。这一做法已经被牛津大学的苏美尔文学电子文本语料库(Electronic Text Corpus of Sumerian Literature)证实确实可行。③

在讨论世界文学选集的编选策略时,汤姆森(Mads Rosendahl Thomsen)提出了星丛范式(constellation paradigm)——"在创作时间和空间上可能相去甚远的不同文学作品中寻找共性、发现规律"④。这是一种基于维特根斯坦(Wittgenstein)"家族相似性"(family resemblance)的复合策略,其目标是"寻找具有重要意义的作品、技巧和流派的集合;对过去几十年里已经在世界范围内被奉为经典,或者

---

① C. Prendergast, ed., *Debating World Literature*, London: Verso, 2004.
② D. Damrosch, *What is World Literature?*, Princeton: Princeton University Press, 2003, p. 282.
③ D. Damrosch, "Toward a History of World Literature", *New Literature History*, No. 39, 2008, pp. 482 – 489.
④ M. R. Thomsen, *Mapping World Literature: International canonization and transnational literatures*, New York: Continuum, 2008, p. 4.

当下正取得巨大成功的作品,寻找它们的家族相似性"[1]。汤姆森还提出布罗姆(Harold Bloom)著作中实际上使用的模式就是星丛范式,"围绕十个不同的主题集合,将不同时期和文化的作者集结在一起"[2]。汤姆森从这种实验性的世界文学研究范式中总结出了四项优点:实际、创新、多元、给人以教诲(didactic)。实际指的是能够从流派、形式、作者和作者作品(works within authorships)等多个层面选取经典文本;创新指的是它提供了一种新的面向,能够跨越流派、国族、语言、年代,在相去甚远的作品中找到连接点,用一系列特征定义作品之间的联系;这一范式从两方面体现出多元的取向,其一是它在国族和国际两个层次联结起经典化程度不同的文本[3],其二是它提供了一种颇有前景的阅读模式,可以与其他范式产生互动,从而允许多元的阐释方式;从教学方面看,运用这种范式,教师可以将世界文学呈现为有着诸多历史细节的世界文学系统,而不再只是依照一系列重要作品的书目。[4] 在运用星丛化策略图绘世界文学时,分析者必须首先承认"世界文学分化为当代文学(contemporary)和经典文学(canonical)这一正在进行的过程",舍弃"固执的、浪漫化的将作者视作天才的观念"[5]。

要进一步探究星丛范式,就要回答三个问题:(1)将星丛化作为一种文学研究方法是什么意思;(2)与其他分析手段相比,这种范式有什么特点;(3)它对于世界文学研究有什么优势和意义。这篇文章

---

[1] M. R. Thomsen, *Mapping World Literature: International canonization and transnational literatures*, New York: Continuum, 2008, pp. 58 – 59.

[2] M. R. Thomsen, *Mapping World Literature: International canonization and transnational literatures*, New York: Continuum, 2008, p. 4.

[3] 达姆罗什用三个独创的术语,也就是"超级经典"(hypercanon)、"反向经典"(countercanon)和"影子经典"(shadow canon)来描述经典化的动态过程。See D. Damrosch, "World Literature in A Postcanonical, Hypercanonical Age", in H. Saussy, ed., *Comparative Literature in an Age of Globalization*, Baltimore: The Johns Hopkins University Press, 2006, pp. 43 – 53.

[4] M. R. Thomsen, *Mapping World Literature: International Canonization and Transnational Literatures*, New York: Continuum, 2008, pp. 139 – 142.

[5] M. R. Thomsen, *Mapping World Literature: International Canonization and Transnational Literatures*, New York: Continuum, 2008, p. 59.

旨在为将星丛范式用于世界文学研究提供理论基础。文章第一部分对"星丛"这一概念在天文学/占星学、认识论和文学阐释学中的使用做了一番跨学科的考察；文章第二部分对当前世界文学研究中认识论的改变做了理论探究；文章第三部分详细说明了星丛化世界文学如何围绕三个关键因素进行运作，即不同出发点（points of departure）、视域转换（horizon changes）和普世诗学（universal poetics）；最后，作者认为，星丛化范式不仅是有益的理论工具，还能为面临全球化与民族主义危机的世界文学研究提供解决之道。

一 理解星丛：占星学含义和阐释学辩证法

对于星丛的观察和解读，属于现代学科划分中天文学的范畴。占星学（astrology）[①]在硬科学和人文科学间摇摆不定，被普遍认为是一门"弹性（resilient）学科"[②]和一个"有争议的话题"[③]。古代占星术可追溯至第一个千年早期美索不达米亚文明，祭司们最早绘制出十八个星座的星图作为推测季节变化和星体运动的参照点。在公元前3500年前后，古巴比伦的占星师们形成了一种技术和哲学工具——将黄道划分为360度，以便更加准确地呈现行星系统。到公元前6世纪，希腊人绘制了黄道十二星座，并创造了关于十二星座的神话。[④]在之后的时间里，除了对部分星座的命名存在争议外，西方占星术[⑤]大致沿用了希腊化时代黄道十二星座的划分及其拉丁名称，如白羊座（Ari-

---

[①] 此文中的"占星学"定义来自Campion的著作："一个雨伞概念，涵盖了一整批理念、想法与实践，都认为天空上的不同模式类型与地面上的生活在某种程度上有所关联。"Campion进一步表明，astrology这个源自希腊语的名词在其他文化如印度、日本和古巴比伦文化中找不到相对应的表达。See N. Campion, *What do Astrologers Believe?*, London: Granta Books, 2006, p. 3.

[②] T. Barton, *Ancient Astrology*, London: Routledge, 1994, p. 1.

[③] N. Campion, *What do Astrologers Believe?*, London: Granta Books, 2006, p. 5.

[④] N. Campion, *What do Astrologers Believe?*, London: Granta Books, 2006, pp. 12 – 16.

[⑤] 在我看来，"西方占星术"指的是从巴比伦、埃及和希腊传统中生成的占星术。其他文化传统中的占星术士对于辨认星丛和设定不同星座符号有不同的做法，比如说，中国占星术士以五行元素来命名天上的二十八个星宿。

es)、金牛座（Taurus）、双子座（Gemini）、巨蟹座（Cancer）等。①

我们可以将占星术中的星座划分与文学经典化（literary canonization）进行类比。② 与个人观星者颇为相似的是，普通读者正如弗吉尼亚·伍尔夫（Virginia Woolf）所描述的那样，是"为了个人的乐趣阅读，而非为了传授知识或纠正他人的观点"。伍尔夫认为，读者的想法和观点可能"本身无足轻重"，但是它们仍然"能够促成很重大的结果"。③ 与个人读者不同，文学评论家需要回答诸如定义对象、对比体验、评判价值这样的根本问题。④ 对纪廉（Claudio Guillén）而言，这种认识论上的困境来自"特殊与一般之间的张力"，或称"同一性与多样性之辩"（debate between unity and multiplicity）⑤。对这一问题的回应涉及知识的有效性问题，其在庄子与惠子的濠梁之辩中有所体现：庄子告诉惠子他知道鱼的快乐，而惠子对这种说法提出质疑，因为做出这番断言的并不是鱼自己。张隆溪认为这次辩论体现了知识的相对性，迁移到跨文化研究中，我们应当反思性地理解差异，避免对"真实性"（authenticity）和"他异性"（alterity）进行机械的二分。⑥

怀疑主义与知识的辩证关系在本雅明（Walter Benjamin）1928 年发表的教授资格论文（Habilitationsschrift）⑦《德意志悲苦剧的起源》

---

① J. V. Stewart, *Astrology: What's Really in the Stars?*, New York: Prometheus Books, 1996, pp. 55 – 58.

② Karl Popper 也将天文学与社会学在长期预测与宏观预测方面进行比较："如果天文学能够预测日食月食，社会学又为何不能预测革命呢？" See K. Popper, *The Poverty of Historicism*, London: Routledge, 1961, pp. 31 – 38.

③ V. Woolf, *The Common Reader: First Series*, New York: Harcourt Brace & Company, 1984, pp. 1 – 2.

④ I. A. Richards, *Principles of Literary Criticism*, London: Routledge, 1995, p. 1.

⑤ C. Guillén, *The Challenge of Comparative Literature*, trans. C. Franzen, Cambridge, MA: Harvard University Press, 1993, pp. 12 – 13.

⑥ L. Zhang, *Allegoresis: Reading Canonical Literature East and West*, Ithaca: Cornell University Press, 2005, pp. 2 – 43.

⑦ 在德国学术系统中，获得博士学位者应当准备一份"教授资格论文"（Habilitationsschrift），也就是"一篇结构完整的文字，并用以打动读者"，which is "a full-scale text, ready for impression, and submitted to the appropriate faculty of a university for public examination and judgment", See George Steiner, "Introduction", in W. Benjamin, *The Origin of German Tragic Drama*, trans. John Osborne, London: Verso, 2003, p. 8.

(德文标题为 *Ursprung des deutschen Trauerspiels*①，后文称《起源》）中也有所讨论。本雅明发现，不同于其他类型的戏剧，德意志巴洛克戏剧被否认"与历史有所共鸣"，因为"不管是德意志传奇还是德意志历史，它们在巴洛克戏剧中都没有一席之地"②。他接下来说道，"由于受到诸多偏见的影响，文学界注定不能对巴洛克戏剧做出客观的评价"③。本雅明所做研究的目的在于，"从一开始就放弃对于整体的把握，保持一定距离观察对象"，从而找到德国巴洛克悲苦剧独有的艺术特征。④ 在《起源》前言中，本雅明使用了"星丛"（constellation）这一隐喻来解释"对于真实的表征"（representation of the truth）⑤是如何进行的：

> 理念（ideas）之于对象（objects）正如星丛（constellation）之于群星（stars）。这首先意味着，理念既不是对象的概念（concepts）也不是对象的法则（laws）。理念不增进对于现象的知识，对象也不能作为评判理念是否存在的标准。现象之于理念的意义仅限于作为理念的概念要素。诸现象依其存在（existence）、其共同之处、其差异决定着包含着它们的概念的范围和内容。但现象与理念的关系却截然相反，是理念——对于现象，或说对于现象的要素的客观阐释（objective interpretation）——决定了要素彼此之间的关系。理念是永不过时的星丛，各要素可被视为星丛中的点，现象因而被细分，同时也

---

① 德文单词 Trauerspiel 本意是哀悼戏剧，这个词用来表示现代的巴洛克悲剧，与古典悲剧（Tragödie）有所不同。See "Translator's note", in W. Benjamin, *The Origin of German Tragic Drama*, trans. John Osborne, London: Verso, 2003, p. 6.
② W. Benjamin, *The Origin of German Tragic Drama*, trans. John Osborne, London: Verso, 2003, pp. 48 – 49.
③ W. Benjamin, *The Origin of German Tragic Drama*, trans. John Osborne, London: Verso, 2003, p. 51.
④ W. Benjamin, *The Origin of German Tragic Drama*, trans. John Osborne, London: Verso, 2003, p. 56.
⑤ W. Benjamin, *The Origin of German Tragic Drama*, trans. John Osborne, London: Verso, 2003, p. 28.

被解放出来。概念的作用就是使这些要素从现象中显现出来，如此，这些要素因在非常极限的状况下而显得尤其清晰突出。①

在上述引文中，本雅明使用了"星丛"隐喻来说明"理念"（idea）与"对象"（objects）和"现象"（phenomena）②的关系。根据斯坦纳（George Steiner）的理解，本雅明的"理念"结合了柏拉图式的"理念"（Idea）隐喻和语言实在论，指的是"实体中的那个瞬间（that moment in the substance）和一个词的存有（being of a word）"③。本雅明对星丛隐喻性的使用提出了一种"柏拉图—莱布尼茨式的方法"，用于解决文学研究中的历史—哲学问题："何以可能存在一种普遍的（general）和普遍化的（generalizing）处理艺术—文学对象的方法，而艺术—文学对象明显是特殊的。"是否有可能摆脱历史相对主义或历史主义空洞的教条，同时又忠于时代的特殊性，甚至忠于作者作品中难以再次经验的部分？阐释者能否"外在于"（outside）自我和所处的时刻进行阐释？在我看来，第一个问题是认识论问题，因为其涉及知识的对象；第二个问题是方法论问题，因为其回应了实证主义唯科学论（positivist scientificism）；而第三个问题挑战了知识生产者作为观察者或阐释者的"客观性"（objectivity）。以上三个问题可以归结为一个问题：我们如何缩小知识与经验之间的差距？为了回答这一问题，此处使用了阐释学循环（hermeneutical circle）来说明人类理解过程在时间顺序上的整体性："只有当我们意识到所注目的各项事物的重要性时，或说当我们意识到各项事物是如何相互关联时，理解才会发生。"④

---

① W. Benjamin, *The Origin of German Tragic Drama*, trans. John Osborne, London: Verso, 2003, pp. 34 – 35.
② 在康德哲学中，现象（phenomena）指的是构建我们经验的表象（appearances）。
③ See Steiner, "Introduction", in W. Benjamin, *The Origin of German Tragic Drama*, trans. John Osborne, London: Verso, 2003, p. 23.
④ See R. Bontekoe, *Dimensions of the Hermeneutic circle*, New Jersey: Humanities Press, 1995, pp. 2 – 4.

在阐释整体与部分的关系时，本雅明使用了第二个隐喻——莱布尼茨的单子概念。本雅明强调了单一理念与相互关联的复数理念的区别。作为单数时，理念从三种意义上可被视为一个单子。第一，它是整合的（integrated）："每一个理念都以某种不甚明确的方式包含着其他所有理念。"① 第二，它能够容纳表征："现象的前稳定状态下的表征就位于理念中，正如其在对现象的客观阐释中。理念的层级（order）越高，表征就越能完美地包含其中。"② 第三，理念是无所不包的（all-inclusive）："每个理念都包含着世界的图景（the image of the world）。"③ 作为复数时，理念指的是包含（incorporate）了现象并且在功能上成为现象法则的"现象客观、实质上的安排（objective virtual arrangement）"④。本雅明在悲苦剧（Trauerspiel）中找到了这种整合的相互关系。悲苦剧作为一个整合的、包含性的单子与"文艺复兴悲剧"（renaissance-tragedy）、殉道者戏剧（martyr-drama）和中世纪宗教戏剧等历史上其他戏剧类型有着共同的特性。⑤ 尽管悲苦剧与其他悲剧类型相互关联，本雅明也指出悲苦剧明显根植于历史，而悲剧则源于神话。两者在形式元素（formal elements）方面还存在很多差异，例如，悲苦剧中的合唱更加繁复，但是相较悲剧，与剧中人物的行为举动关联更少。⑥

在论及历史（history）和时间性（temporality）之间的张力时，本雅明区分了起源（Ursprung）和形成（Entstehung）："起源一词不是指

---

① W. Benjamin, *The Origin of German Tragic Drama*, trans. John Osborne, London: Verso, 2003, p. 47.

② W. Benjamin, *The Origin of German Tragic Drama*, trans. John Osborne, London: Verso, 2003, pp. 47-48.

③ W. Benjamin, *The Origin of German Tragic Drama*, trans. John Osborne, London: Verso, 2003, p. 48.

④ W. Benjamin, *The Origin of German Tragic Drama*, trans. John Osborne, London: Verso, 2003, p. 34.

⑤ W. Benjamin, *The Origin of German Tragic Drama*, trans. John Osborne, London: Verso, 2003, pp. 60-78.

⑥ W. Benjamin, *The Origin of German Tragic Drama*, trans. John Osborne, London: Verso, 2003, pp. 121-122.

存在者开始出现（come into being），而是指在变化和消逝过程中存在者的浮现（emerge from the process of becoming and disappearance）。在形成之流中，起源就是一个旋涡，将用以形成过程的质料卷入涡流中。"① 本雅明坚持认为，历史不应追溯起源，而应揭示理念的形构（configuration of the idea）：

> 哲学意义上的历史、有关起源的学说，是从最极限的状况和明显过剩的发展过程中揭示出理念的构成——即全体有意义的极限状况的并置。在一个理念所包含的所有极限状况被彻底探索之前，一个理念的表征就不能说是成功的。②

通过使用星丛隐喻，本雅明阐明了如何处理文学研究中时间性和普遍性间的复杂关系。对斯坦纳而言，本雅明运用星丛隐喻具有方法论意义，"对于过去作品的重估能够增进我们对于未来的了解"，因为他展示了"对于巴洛克的研究不只是对古籍、档案的爱好：它反映、预测并且帮助我们理解黑暗的当下"③。吉洛克（Graeme Gilloch）认为本雅明使用星丛隐喻不仅"表明了通过概念将现象模式化（patterning of phenomena）的重要性，也指出了这一过程的特点"。这一过程"转变了我们对于现象的理解，这种转变在瞬间发生且不可逆转，那就是现象既保有自身的完整性（individual integrity），也具有相互之间的关联性（mutuality）"④。换言之，虽然它们在时间、空间或文体风格上有所不同，每篇文学作品或每种文学类型都相互关联。

---

① W. Benjamin, *The Origin of German Tragic Drama*, trans. John Osborne, London: Verso, 2003, p. 45.
② W. Benjamin, *The Origin of German Tragic Drama*, trans. John Osborne, London: Verso, 2003, p. 47.
③ Steiner, "Introduction", in W. Benjamin, *The Origin of German Tragic Drama*, trans. John Osborne, London: Verso, 2003, p. 24.
④ G. Gilloch, *Walter Benjamin: Critical Constellations*, Malden, MA: Polity Press, 2002, pp. 70 – 71.

二 对世界文学研究认识论转变的呼吁

大约四十年前，艾田蒲提出问题，讨论世界文学的概念是否应该在 20 世纪有所改变。艾田蒲作此建议的前提在于，世界文学为文学研究者提供了一个调整思路的机会，呼应歌德认为世界文学是追求文学整体之美，批判各类民族主义的重要观点。更进一步而言，艾田蒲指出，如果世界文学这个概念被理解为各种国家文学之总集的话，实际上指称的也就是一种没有任何形容词的"文学"。要研究这个兼容并包的主题，也就等于说是要对这个宏观大类中每篇文学作品开展独立的历史、社会或批判研究。与此同时，还需要开展比较文学研究方法（comparatist method），其中可以细分为不同的次学科研究，比如说比较文学历史、比较文学社会学、类型理论、美学理论、文学研究等。在此意义上，比较文学可以做的，就是推进世界文学的理念，而非与其类同。为了促进世界文学的发展，学者们应该对自己的局限有所了解，否则他们将一事无成。[①]

近十年来，有不少学者都致力于呈现世界文学系统的整体状况，也采用了新的分析方法来编撰世界文学历史。达姆罗什撰写了一部极为重要的著作，名为《什么是世界文学?》，其中就给出了关于世界文学定义的三重描述，尤其强调此概念的动态发展：

第 1，世界文学是国家民族文学的椭圆形折射。
第 2，世界文学是在翻译中有所增益的书写。
第 3，世界文学不是一套固定的文本经典，而是一种阅读模式：让我们能够以超然姿态参与自己时空之外不同世界的一种形式。[②]

[①] Étiemble, "Faut-il réviser la notion de Weltliteratur?", in R. E'tiemble, ed., *Essais de littérature (vraiment) générale*, Paris: Gallimard, 1975, pp. 15–34.

[②] D. Damrosch, *What is World Literature?*, Princeton: Princeton University Press, 2003, p. 281.

在以上的第一点定义中,达姆罗什对"国家"(nation)概念进行拓展,从领土主权拓展到在地与民族的形构。他用双重椭圆形折射这个科学意象来描述任何一篇世界文学作品中的互动跨文化协商过程,还借用了《怪医杜立德》(*Doctor Doolittle*)故事中的双头动物"普斯米普育"(pushmipullyu)来描画这个多元文化协商互动的过程。第二点定义基于文学语言的内容和形式特点。部分具有高度语言文化可译性的在地化文学作品成为世界文学,而其他作品则无法进入国际读者视野。与此同时,文学文本的流通也取决于译者的阐释角色和读者的互动反应。以上这两点意在通过将这些文学作品放置在不同的民族和文化群组中,以此巩固世界文学的概念,从而使其得以超越跨文化与跨语言界限,保留文学作品的普世价值。而第三点则引入了时间因素,使得以上这两点所构成的定义更为动态。达姆罗什这样写道:"在任何时间,都会有一批数量时有增减的外国文学作品在某种文化中积极流通,这批作品中的一部分可能会被广泛分享,被誉为经典,但同一个社会中的不同群组,任何群组中的不同个体,都会创作出独特的作品集合体,将经典著作和非经典著作融合成实质上的微经典著作(microcanons)。"[1] 这种状态与物理学布朗运动过程中分子的随机漂浮极为相似,需要采用新的研究模式对此运动状态进行描画分析。为了分析世界文学作品在不同层面上的互动,达姆罗什建议读者阅读外国文学文本时采用超然姿态参与(detached engagement)的策略。作为读者,我们能够以世界文学作品的时空"起源"(origin)为出发点,从一定距离之外观察自身,正如达姆罗什所说:"将我们自身现状与我们身边和之前出现的大量具有不同性质的文化相连,构成三角并置关系。"[2] 他在此书结尾处,绘出了一幅图画,描写的是拿破仑1798年远征埃及时,随军的法国科学家测量埃及吉萨金字塔的大斯芬克斯像的场景。在达姆罗什看来,这幅图画表征着"定位既非当下,也非在

---

[1] D. Damrosch, *What is World Literature?*, Princeton: Princeton University Press, 2003, pp. 297-298.
[2] D. Damrosch, *What is World Literature?*, Princeton: Princeton University Press, 2003, p. 300.

古代埃及的一段历史",也正可以被理解为一种象征,"代表着打开了一个世界文学的世界:这曾经是在历史和地理意义上都有所限定,相对更为欧洲化和男性化的领地,而现在则变成一片更为辽阔与新奇的疆域"①。在这本书中,达姆罗什指出世界文学或比较文学研究领域的重点和规模方面都发生了变化,但此书未对时间多样性所带来的重要范式转换作进一步探讨。

卡萨诺瓦撰写了一部关于世界文学共和国的研究专著,影响深远,她试图以此"带来一种视角变化:'从某个优势定点'来描述文学世界;也展示这个奇特庞大文学世界的各种运作规则,这个世界充满竞争、挣扎与不平等"②。她意在"重新建立文学、历史与世界之间失落的连接,但也保存每篇文学作品无法整齐划一的独特个性"③。她并没有处理世界—文本之间的关系,而是指出两者之间存在"世界文学空间"(world literary space)一个协商之地——"一个平行领地,和政治领域相对独立,生成于某种文学特质的相应问题、辩论与发明"④。这种文学空间存在的证明首先是诺贝尔文学奖遴选过程中的"国际文学祝圣",这被认为是一个"为了定义文学普世性而设计的实验室"⑤;第二个证明就是对文学时间的特定测量方式,比如说,对美学意义上的现代性的评估已经成为文学评论中的运作机制。在这种审美时间的斗争之中,某些文学作品被归入陈旧或"过时"之列,而其他作品则超越时间淘汰,被尊为经典。⑥ 世界文学空间具有相对独立性。一方面来说,文学空间中的不同事件并非取决于政治—经济权力关系,例如欧洲商业中心和文化中心并非完全一致,拉美文学作品蓬勃兴盛,而该地区经济尚待发展。另一方面而言,这个文学空间仍被语言、文

---

① D. Damrosch, *What is World Literature?*, Princeton: Princeton University Press, 2003, pp. 300 – 301.
② P. Casanova, *The World Republic of Letters*, trans. M. B. DeBevoise, Cambridge: Harvard University Press, 2004, p. 4.
③ P. Casanova, "Literature as A World", *New Left Review*, 2005, p. 71.
④ P. Casanova, "Literature as A World", *New Left Review*, 2005, p. 72.
⑤ P. Casanova, "Literature as A World", *New Left Review*, 2005, p. 74.
⑥ P. Casanova, "Literature as A World", *New Left Review*, 2005.

学与政治这三个主要形式主导。① 通过揭示世界文学系统中不平等权力关系，卡萨诺瓦指出文学研究实践很有必要做出改变。正如罗尔（Sarah Lawall）指出，在大多数的世界文学教学模式中，都存在着文学意义上的格林尼治时间，以此划分所谓的"西方和其他地方"框架。而实际上，每个国家都有它自己"关于其他地方的理解，也对传统意义上的中心和边缘地区有着不同的概念"②。

莫莱蒂（Franco Moretti）在讨论他对世界文学的构想过程中，描画了"形式的物质主义概念"③，并提出文学历史的三个抽象结构模式。④ 他也建议应该转换概念，将世界文学视为一个问题（problem），而非某个特定对象（object）。莫莱蒂重新审视了涵括世界文学庞大整体的各种尝试，也对研究此文学体系的意义进行了反思。他引用了韦伯（Max Weber）的社会科学方法论，建议将世界文学这个概念视为另一个类型，关注不同问题之间的概念相连关系，而非各种实物之间的具体关联。在此意义上，莫莱蒂进一步阐明，世界文学是一种文学研究新范式的起点："……世界文学不是一个对象，它是一个**问题**，是一个需要用全新批判方法处理的**问题**：在此之前没有任何人能仅通过阅读更多的文本来解决它。这并不是生成理论的方式，理论的生成需要一次跳跃，一个赌注——一个假说，才能起步。"⑤ 莫莱蒂进一步表明，文学运动发展取决于三大变量：某种文学类型的潜在市场、其整体形式化过程及其语言运用。⑥ 与此同时，也取决于"**我们将比较文学视为一面我们观看世界的镜子**"⑦。

---

① P. Casanova, "Literature as A World", *New Left Review*, 2005, pp. 71 – 90.
② S. Lawall, "The West and the Rest: Frames for World Literature", in D. Damrosch, ed., *Teaching World Literature*, New York: The Modern Language Association of America, 2009, p. 18.
③ F. Moretti, "Conjectures on World Literature", *New Left Review*, No. 1, 2000, pp. 54 – 66. See also F. Moretti, "More Conjectures", *New Left Review*, No. 20, Mar. -Apr., 2003, pp. 73 – 81.
④ F. Moretti, *Graphs, Maps, Trees: Abstract Models for a Literary History*, London: Verso, 2005.
⑤ F. Moretti, "Conjectures on World Literature", *New Left Review*, No. 1, 2000, p. 55. "Problem"一词在英文原文中为斜体，在中文译文中"问题"一词作加粗处理。
⑥ F. Moretti, "More Conjectures", *New Left Review*, No. 20, Mar. -Apr., 2003, p. 74.
⑦ F. Moretti, "More Conjectures", *New Left Review*, No. 20, Mar. -Apr., 2003, p. 81. 这句引文在英文原文中为斜体，在中文译文中作加粗处理。

为了研究文学历史,莫莱蒂建立的三个抽象模型是"统计图形、地图和树木这三种人工造物的三合一,其中文本现实经历了精心计算的简化和抽象过程"。在莫莱蒂看来,这三个模型恰好对应于三个学科,而这些学科"和文学研究几乎没有互动关系:统计图形对应量化历史,地图对应地理学,而树木对应进化论"[1]。

三 星丛化世界文学:不同出发点、视域转变与普世诗学

与以上提到的不同分析理论相比,星丛范式提出可以对翻译中的世界文学采取一种另类的"行星思维"而非"地图阅读"。[2] 这种范式也为应对在编纂世界文学历史中出现的三个挑战,也就是定义、设计与目的[3],提出了一个全新的思路。那么,要撰写一部世界文学历史,就是要拓展规模,提供"一种类型学,而非一段历史"。[4] 正如奥尔巴赫(Erich Auerbach)所说,"一种兼具学术性与合一性的世界文学(Weltliteratur)语文学"[5] 会"对时髦的智性发展浪潮采取开放独立的合宜态度",从而整合"历史和与文学研究"。[6] 要编写这种历史的话,我们就需要找到一种新的范式,使得"在地与普世,单一与众多之间的对话可能发生,而这种对话从生成之日直到此时都能够使出类拔萃的比较研究焕发生机"[7]。

---

[1] F. Moretti, *Graphs, Maps, Trees: Abstract Models for A Literary History*, London: Verso, 2005, pp. 1 – 2.

[2] G. C. Spivak, *Death of A Discipline*, New York: Columbia University Press, 2003, pp. 73, 87.

[3] D. Damrosch, "Toward A History of World Literature", *New Literature History*, No. 39, 2008, p. 489.

[4] D. Damrosch, "Toward A History of World Literature", *New Literature History*, No. 39, 2008, pp. 481 – 495.

[5] E. Auerbach, "Philology and Weltliteratur", trans. Maire and Edward Said, *The Centennial Review*, Vol. 13, No. 1, 1969, p. 7.

[6] E. Auerbach, "Philology and Weltliteratur", trans. Maire and Edward Said, *The Centennial Review*, Vol. 13, No. 1, 1969, p. 10.

[7] C. Guillén, *The Challenge of Comparative Literature*, trans. C. Franzen, Cambridge, MA: Harvard University Press, 1993, p. 40.

在我看来，世界文学星丛范式通过三组要素运作：第一，不同出发点（points of departure），预设了不同世界的多元维度；第二，视域转换（horizon change），在文学作品的流通和翻译过程中得以实现；第三，普世诗学（universal poetics），也就是超越时空限制，令跨文化理解与沟通可行的共同主题与价值观念。

在苏源熙看来，开展与世界文学相关的对话的潜在危险，在于"**平面化**"（**platitude**），而这种平面化所指的并非仅仅是平庸性，而是认识论意义上的扁平性，"也就是说，认为文学能够被地图化为二元维度，或者说仅仅是一个平面，通过这种做法来提炼文学最为重要的特质"①。苏源熙的见解和歌德的观点相似，后者认为"对一个有限环境的生动诗意描述将某种特定之物（'ein Einzelnes'）提升为一种虽有限但亦无穷的宇宙（'All'），因此我们会相信自己能够在一个狭小空间中看到整个世界"②。在这里，"世界"（world）有两层不同含义。一方面，它可能指代的是不同的文学世界系统，其中包括象征意义资本与制度化市场上进行的文学生产、流通与经典化过程。③ 另一方面，它也生成了一个乌托邦式的宇宙，或者说是一种普世性的诗学，其中包含"关于文学的性质、特点、价值与组成部分的一系列基本问题，而并非世上不同传统中所出现的全部批判性观点的无限无穷无法掌握的整体集合"④。这里提到的各种文化在地性（cultural localities）也在歌德小说《威廉师傅的旅游年》（*Wilhelm Meisters Wanderjahre*, 1829）的尾声中有所强调，歌德认为"家中虔诚"（house piety）为"世界虔诚"（world piety）奠定了基础，普世性（the universal）从而被奠基，

---

① H. Saussy, "The Dimensionality of World Literature", *Neohelicon*, No. 38, 2011, p. 289. 在英文原文中，"platitude"一词采用斜体表示强调，在中文译文里加粗表示。

② J. D. Pizer, "The Emergence of Weltliteratur: Goethe and the Romantic School", in J. D. Pizer, ed., *The Idea of World Literature: History and Pedagogical Practice*, Baton Rouge: Louisiana State University Press, 2006, p. 38.

③ E. Apter, "Literary World Systems", in D. Damrosch, ed., *Teaching World Literature*, New York: The Modern Language Association of America, 2009, pp. 44 – 45.

④ L. Zhang, "The Poetics of World Literature", in T. D'haen, D. Damrosch and D. Kadir, eds., *The Routledge Companion to World literature*, London: Routledge, 2012, p. 357.

也必须与在地性（the local）相互渗透贯通。①

通过强调不同的出发点，星丛范式可以处理平面化的问题。不同研究者可以从自己独特的文化背景出发，首先把自己定位在某一个"出发点"（Ansatzphänomen），这里已经有了一个"对此问题的预设倾向"。② 然而，研究者也不应该将自己只限于这个立场，因为如果要找到"一个部分能够被理解，有所限制并切实存在的现象"③，就需要采用几个不同的出发点。对于奥尔巴赫而言，一个好的出发点必须具有这样的特质："切实、准确，有潜力构成一个能够提供更为开阔视野的向心放射圈（centrifugal radiation）。"④ 奥尔巴赫强调，在地文化和语言对于构成切实的出发点尤为重要："在任何情况下，我们的语言家园是地球：它不再是国族。语文学家最为珍贵，无可替代的财富仍然是他自身国家民族的文化语言。"类似的观点也见于周作人1923年为同乡大白先生的诗集《旧梦》所写的序言，其中提到普世与在地的互通之处：

> 我于别的事情都不喜讲地方主义，唯独在艺术上常感到这种区别。……不过我们这时代的人，因为对于褊隘的国家主义的反动，大抵养成一种"世界民"（Kosmopolites）的态度，容易减少乡土的气味，这虽然是不得已却也是觉得可惜的。我仍然不愿取消世界民的态度，但觉得因此更须感到地方民的资格，因为这二者本是相关的，正如我们因是个人，所以是"人类一分子"（Ho-

---

① J. D. Pizer, "The Emergence of Weltliteratur: Goethe and the Romantic School", in J. D. Pizer, ed., *The Idea of World Literature: History and Pedagogical Practice*, Baton Rouge: Louisiana State University Press, 2006, pp. 18 – 46.

② L. Zhang, "The Poetics of World Literature", in T. D'haen, D. Damrosch and D. Kadir, eds., *The Routledge Companion to World Literature*, London: Routledge, 2012, p. 357.

③ J. D. Pizer, "The Emergence of Weltliteratur: Goethe and the Romantic School", in J. D. Pizer, ed., *The Idea of World Literature: History and Pedagogical Practice*, Baton Rouge: Louisiana State University Press, 2006, pp. 18 – 46.

④ E. Auerbach, "Philology and Weltliteratur", trans. Maire and Edward Said, *The Centennial Review*, Vol. 13, No. 1, 1969, p. 14.

marano）一般。我轻蔑那些传统的爱国的假文学，然而对于乡土文学很是爱重：我相信强烈的地方趣味也正是"世界的"文学的一个重大成分。具有多方面的趣味，而不相冲突，合成和谐的全体，这是"世界的"文学的价值，否则是"拔起了的树木"，不但不能排到大林中去，不久还将枯槁了。①

通过运用星丛化范式，博览群书的读者能够跟从观星者的步骤来构建属于自己的文学星丛。在浩如烟海的文学作品中，读者能够提炼出一套共同的主题，从而构成他们独特的参考支点，以此从自己的出发点来辨识出不同的星丛。与此同时，这样的观星之举也能够帮助读者更好地欣赏自己的家乡文化与生活经验。举例说明，廖炳惠对台湾小说家王文兴的现代主义作品《背海的人》（下集）进行分析，提出四种形式的现代性：第一、另类的现代性（alternative modernity）；第二，单一的现代性（singular modernity）；第三，多元的现代性（multiple modernities）；第四，压迫性的现代性（repressive modernity）。②

即使出于不同历史背景，东西方文学研究者对于世界文学的各种讨论观点都在传递同一个信息——那就是文学价值在于超越地理、政治、语言或意识形态界限而对人类进行普世性表征（universal representation），而这种跨文化的普世性也能够从多极文明中总结归纳得出，免于以国族名义或以任何想象的、或者历史上存在的狭义共同体之名义被统一化。这种世界文学的本质与理念存在于其普世诗学之中，这种普世诗学"必须具备可比性，涵括超过一种国族或地区传统，也应该帮助我们更好地、更加深刻地理解和欣赏世界文学"③。这种世界文学诗学所包

---

① 周作人：《旧梦》，载周作人《自己的园地·雨天的书·泽泻集》，岳麓书社1987年版，第117页。
② 廖炳惠：《台湾文学中的四种现代性：以〈背海的人〉下集为例》，载廖炳惠《台湾与世界文学的汇流》，台湾：联合文学2006年版，第50—72页。
③ L. Zhang, "The Poetics of World Literature", in T. D'haen, D. Damrosch and D. Kadir, eds., *The Routledge Companion to World Literature*, London: Routledge, 2012, p.357.

含的"世界精神"(weltzeit)是这个经典化过程的指导原则。由此,星丛范式呈现出本雅明《德国悲苦剧起源》中所讨论的普世(universal)与特一(particular)之间的辩证关系。在此,"世界"象征着同一性(unity),正如钱钟书所言,"同时之异世,并在而歧出"。[1] 这并不能仅仅用"时代精神"或者"地域影响"来草率概括:

> 学者每东面而望,不视西墙,南向而视,不见北方,反三举一,执偏概全。将"时代精神"、"地域影响"等语,念念有词,如同禁呪。夫《淮南子·氾论训》所谓一哈之水,固可以揣知海味;然李文饶品水,则扬子一江,而上下有别矣。知同时之異世、并在之歧出,于孔子一贯之理、庄生大小同異之旨,悉心体会,明其矛盾,而复通以骑驿,庶可语于文史通义乎。[2]

星丛化范式能够有效地统合世界文学的维度性(dimensionality)和普世性(universality),大量的文学作品能够被视为不同天体的总量集合,其中部分作品受到其同代读者的认可,被视为最为闪亮的经典作品,部分作品在后世评价过程中逐渐获得经典地位,而部分作品则从未进入读者视野,也无从成为经典。在此意义上,这种范式对世界文学[3]项目设计与教学策略也大有裨益。派泽(John David Pizer)在教授"现代世界文学导论"课程中采用了一种原理论的方法,并得出结论:"只有通过平衡普世与特一两者关系的辩证阅读,才有可能去除这种感性认知的极端表现。"[4] 他要求学生们想象自己是世界文学课程

---

[1] 钱钟书:《谈艺录》,中华书局1998年版,第304页。
[2] 钱钟书:《谈艺录》,中华书局1998年版,第304页。此段引文原文为繁体,在此保留繁体原貌。
[3] 派泽用大写的 World Literature 名称来指代教学计划,而用"Weltliteratur"一词来指称歌德和其他学者所宣扬的世界文学概念。见 J. D. Pizer, "Teaching world literature", in J. D. Pizer, ed., *The Idea of World Literature*: *History and Pedagogical Practice*, Baton Rouge: Louisiana State University Press, 2006, pp. 1 – 17。
[4] J. D. Pizer, "Teaching World Literature", in J. D. Pizer, ed., *The Idea of World Literature*: *History and Pedagogical Practice*, Baton Rouge: Louisiana State University Press, 2006, pp. 138 – 149.

的教师，以此选择自己想收入这个课程的各种文本。在此之外，他也为学生们给出七种可能的类型，包括"杰出作品"、"经典作品"、举世闻名之作、全球流通的作品等。学生们对世界文学有不同看法，主要分歧在于如何理解"经典性"与"永恒性"，从而也引出了这样的结论："世界文学（weltliteratur）与大写的世界文学并非自证自明的概念，而它们却曾经是，而且仍然是自相矛盾的话语和教学理念的讨论对象。"① 在这个课程上，学生们采用另一种方式来阅读英国文学历史上的某些作品，更加强调作者所生活的时代里英国与其他国家之间的跨文化与跨语言互动。② 其他美国大学教师也给出了教授世界文学导论课程中的成功案例，他们采用的方式"具有反思性、对话性，并考察文本背景"③，将学生放在他们自身的文化背景中，从而"在本土中找到全球"④，将文学视为以主题式研究方法来解答一套普世问题的"进行中的全球文化对话"⑤。

为了拉近个人经验与一般知识之间的距离，视域转化极为重要。伽达默尔（Gadamer）运用"视域"（horizon）这个概念来阐释理解（comprehension）如何进行。所谓"视域"，也就是"视觉上的范围，其中包括从某个定点能够看到的一切事物"。在思维模式意义而言，视域可以被收窄或拓宽，而新的视域也可能被打开。⑥ 如果我们长期停留在一个立足点上，知识就会被"封闭视域"局限。但当我们四下

---

① J. D. Pizer, "Teaching World Literature", in J. D. Pizer, ed., *The Idea of World Literature: History and Pedagogical Practice*, Baton Rouge: Louisiana State University Press, 2006, pp. 142 – 144.

② J. D. Pizer, "Teaching World Literature", in J. D. Pizer, ed., *The Idea of World Literature: History and Pedagogical Practice*, Baton Rouge: Louisiana State University Press, 2006, pp. 145 – 146.

③ G. Harrison, "Conversation in Context: A Dialogic Approach to Teaching World Literature", in D. Damrosch, ed., *Teaching World Literature*, New York: The Modern Language Association of America, 2009, p. 206.

④ M. E. Rhine and J. Gillespie, "Finding the Global in the Local: Exploration in Interdisciplinary Team Teaching", in D. Damrosch, ed., *Teaching World Literature*, New York: The Modern Language Association of America, 2009, pp. 258 – 265.

⑤ C. Ayers, "The Adventures of the Artists in World Literature: A One-semester Thematic Approach", in D. Damrosch, ed., *Teaching World Literature*, New York: The Modern Language Association of America, 2009, pp. 299 – 305.

⑥ H. G. Gadamer, *Truth and Method*, New York: Continuum, 2010, p. 300.

走动，关于过去的视域就会有所变动，从这样的视域之中"形成了全体人类的生活，并以传统形式存在"。① 对于伽达默尔而言，时间性（temporality）和理解力（understanding）紧密相连于"不同视域的融合"（a fusion of horizons）——"理解力总是这些独立存在的视域之间的融会"。② 视域转化也可以被用于展示历史学中的空间变化，比如说苏轼著名诗作《题西林壁》中就描写到庐山与观者的关系——"横看成岭侧成峰，远近高低各不同。不知庐山真面目，只缘身在此山中。"③ 在张隆溪看来，诗中的庐山意象比喻说明的是"历史学并非仅是记录，也与阐释有关，牵涉到的层面远比这个具体的庐山比喻要多，因为这还包含了历史学家的参与投入，因此也牵涉到视域和视野的局限性"④。因此，要构建一段世界文学的历史，需要我们从自己的立足点出发，进入具体的不同时空，以实现视域转化与融会。以香港文学历史研究学者陈国球所主持的香港文学大系丛书编撰过程为例，陈国球提出，在构建香港文学历史的过程中，必须采用多元视野角度，整合语文学研究方法和本体论探究：

> 从"香港文学史"的角度而言，了解"境外"的观点其实是有其重要意义的。因为"香港文学"根本不容许一个画地自限的论述，如果我们不希望把香港文学史写成"地方志"中的"艺文志"或者"风土志"的话。"流动"与"越界"是香港这个城市以至香港文学的重要特色，有必要从内在与外缘的诸种因素去观测其构成与意义。⑤

---

① H. G. Gadamer, *Truth and Method*, New York: Continuum, 2010, p. 303.
② H. G. Gadamer, *Truth and Method*, New York: Continuum, 2010, p. 305. 英文原文中斜体强调部分在中文译文中用加粗体现。
③ L. Zhang, "The True Face of Mount Lu: On the Significance of Perspectives and Paradigms", *History and Theory*, No. 49, February, 2010, p. 58.
④ L. Zhang, "The True Face of Mount Lu: On the Significance of Perspectives and Paradigms", *History and Theory*, No. 49, February, 2010, p. 69.
⑤ 陈国球：《台湾视野下的香港文学》，《东亚观念史集刊》2013 年第五期。

更进一步而言，星丛范式处理的是历史学家必须面对的三个基本问题："存在于艺术作品和其目标读者的阅读期望之间的，认识论与伦理学视域之间的距离；意识如何拉近这一距离；以及每篇艺术作品可能具有的影响，这种影响有助于转换文学经典化意识的旧有与现有形式。"[①] 为了建立重写新的文学历史的系统方式，使其成为"在接受性的读者、反思性的论者与不断创作的作者身上实现的，审美接受与生产的过程"，姚斯（Hans Robert Jauss）举出七种观点：其一，"文学作品必须被理解为对话的创建过程，语文学学术研究必须建基于持续的文本重阅过程，而非仅仅基于事实"；其二，建立文学参考框架结构的客观能力必须基于对某个文本的阐释性接受；其三，某篇文学作品的艺术特性取决于它对某批读者产生影响的性质与程度；其四，通过重构期望视域，语文学家们能够探究文学作品存在于遥远过去的原本意图；其五，美学理论也要求我们将个别文学作品置于其"文学系列"之中；其六，一段新的文学历史应该在历时性与共时性的结构语言学分析模式基础上建立；其七，文学历史的任务不仅包括将文学作品置于共时性与历时性维度，也在于将其置于"一段特别的历史，它与一般历史有所关联"。[②] 我有充分信心认为，星丛范式将有助于构建这种富有新意与动感的文学历史。

四 作为结语：在全球化时代星丛化世界文学

在以上几节中，我在世界文学研究的普遍范围内探讨了星丛范式，它所面对的三个主要挑战来自语文学、方法论和意识形态视野。从本雅明对星丛概念的论述，我们可以看到这个概念从阐释学的角度清晰阐明了一与多、普世与特一之间的辩证关系。我所提议的星丛化世界

---

① H. White, "Literary History: The Point of it All", *New Literary History*, Vol. 2, No. 1, 1970, p. 179.

② H. R. Jauss and Benzinger Elizabeth, "Literary History as a Challenge to Literary Theory", *New Literary History*, Vol. 2, No. 1, 1970, pp. 7–37.

文学模式通过三个关键元素而得以运作：第一，不同出发点（points of departure），预设了不同世界的多元维度；第二，视域转换（horizon change），在文学作品的流通和翻译过程中得以实现；第三，普世诗学（universal poetics），也就是超越时空限制，使得跨文化理解与沟通切实可行的共同主题与价值观念。

在论证了采用星丛范式研究世界文学历史的可能与优势之后，我们还需要思考一个问题：如果世界文学是一个无法被理解掌握的无边星际宇宙，而它的历史牵涉星体与其观测者之间的多元对话，那么我们为何还要构建这样一段历史呢？达姆罗什并没有就此问题提供答案，而是以另外一个问题来应对之：这样的一段历史所反对的是什么？他认为有两个重要反对目标，也就是"狭隘受限的国族主义，以及无边无息的全球主义（a narrowly bounded nationalism and a boundless, breathless globalism）"①。实际上，这两个目标紧密相连，是现代社会中互为支持的同一结构。最近一项对国族主义和全球化关系的跨学科研究表明，国族主义概念来自某段特定的欧洲历史时期（1870—1945），"国族性"（nationality）出现于19世纪，作为有效工具，在全球范围而非本地范围巩固国家统治。当前对于国族主义的研究理论关注的对象不再是"民族—国家"（nation-state）和主权，而是转为20世纪出现的关注超越国境前线的泛国族主义（pan-nationalism），同时也关注在21世纪变得极为重要的三大进程：全球资本主义的转换性传播、民族—国家在政治意义上的持续性、美国军事霸权。作为文化解决方案，我们也许可以合并特一性和普世性的思维进路，从而在一个全球化的世纪里对文化进行概念化理解。②

---

① D. Damrosch, "Toward a History of World Literature", *New Literature History*, No. 39, 2008, p. 490.

② D. Halikiopoulou and S. Vasilopoulou, "Nationalism and Globalisation: Conflicting or Complementary?", in D. Halikiopoulou and S. Vasilopoulou, eds., *Nationalism and Globalisation: Conflicting or Complementary?*, London: Routledge, 2011, pp. 186 – 199.

国族主义和全球主义之间的复杂关系体现的是普世/特一悖论（universal/particular paradox）的社会政治层面。今时今日，我们正在面对一种更为先进的新殖民主义形式，这种新殖民主义对世界文学研究构成威胁。在2011年的美国比较文学学会年会上，达姆罗什与斯皮瓦克开展对话，指出"世界文学研究很容易与全球资本主义最差趋势成为共谋，文化失根、语言破产，并且成为思想上的同流合污"[1]。在这些考量之外，他还提出这个问题："我们如何在这种新殖民主义形势之外有所进展……当教授世界文学实际上已经变为方法上幼稚，文化上失根，语言上被损，而理念上成疑的举措？"达姆罗什建议我们采取这样的解决方式：引入更多语言研究、更多合作学术研究与教学，还有"大量的多元主义"。[2]

如果我们要寻找的是世界文学的单一化且权威化的整体，那么星丛范式则并不适用。这种范式更加适用于为苏源熙所预测的全球多元文学世界重绘地图："一种世界文学的模型，为数之不尽的文学世界创造空间，这个模型具有相对论性质（relativistic），而非决定论性质（deterministic）。但这也会被构建为任何一种想象空间：换言之，由各种差异性、暗示性、规则和排他性所组成。"[3] 与其将世界文学展现为封闭系统，或者将其描述为一个问题，不如将它视为舍恩（Donald Allan Schön）所说的"行动中的反思"（reflection-in-action）。在这种反思中，整个过程"对于实践者用以巧妙应对不确定性、不稳定性、独一性与价值冲突情况的'艺术'尤为重要"[4]。在这个意义上，作为反思性行动而创造世界文学历史，意在抵抗任何类型的文学偏狭主义，认识论的独特单一性，性质同一的身份认同，这些都是奥尔巴

---

[1] G. Spivak and D. Damrosch, "Comparative Literature/World Literature: A discussion", *Comparative Literature Studies*, Vol. 48, No. 4, 2011, p. 456.

[2] G. Spivak and D. Damrosch, "Comparative Literature/World Literature: A discussion", *Comparative Literature Studies*, Vol. 48, No. 4, 2011, pp. 461–463.

[3] H. Saussy, "The Dimensionality of World Literature", *Neohelicon*, No. 38, 2011, p. 293.

[4] D. A. Schön, "From Technical Rationality to Reflection-in-action", in D. A. Schön, ed., *The Reflective Practitioner: How Professionals Think in Action?*, Aldershot, Hants: Avebury, 1991, p. 50.

赫警告我们要避免的。① 这种范式邀请我们"走出文化的封闭圈"②，拥抱从个人独特体验与视域出发的诠释多元主义。由此，我认为这是对深受全球化趋势与国族主义威胁的比较文学和世界文学研究的良方解药。

总结而言，星丛范式为纪廉（Guillén）所设计的世界文学范式提供了极好的例证，后者"从某些国族文学而兴起——从而使在地与普世，一与多之间的对话得以成为可能"。③ 如果要宣扬世界文学概念，促进其发展，我愿意向更多同道推荐星丛范式，望能有助于构建从各自视域出发的全球规模文学历史。文学研究学者可以致力在世界文学的众星体系里寻找更多的星群。在文学教学上也可以从当地文学出发，以此作为从本土角度观察的世界文学起源。个体读者可以在其跨文化阅读过程中寻找相似性，作出反思性观察与重构。这是人文学科最终的发展目标——为人类发展需要服务，帮助每个人找到独特但并不排他的身份。更为重要的是，任何全新范式的提出与合理化都不能否定其他的思维模式。有鉴于此，我将引用莫莱蒂关于文学历史模式的新颖全面论著的最后一句话，为此文作结：

> 当然，关于这些各异模式的兼容性，还有很多尚待探究，这些模式之间也还能够建立解释性的从属结构。但在此刻，开拓全新的概念可能，要比从每个细节上论证之，显得更为重要。④

---

① E. Auerbach, "Philology and Weltliteratur", trans. Maire and Edward Said, *The Centennial Review*, Vol. 13, No. 1, 1969, pp. 1 – 17.

② L. Zhang, "Out of the Cultural Ghetto: Theory, Politics, and the Study of Chinese Literature", *Modern China*, Vol. 19, No. 1, 1993.

③ C. Guillén, *The challenge of comparative literature*, trans. C. Franzen, Cambridge, MA: Harvard University Press, 1993, pp. 33 – 34.

④ F. Moretti, *Graphs, maps, trees: Abstract models for a literary history*, London: Verso, 2005, p. 92.

理论旅行的流通机制与世界文学的诗学问题

李孟奇[*]

【摘要】 在世界文学研究中，世界文学理论的流通与接受机制往往很少受到相关学者的关注。结合萨义德的理论旅行概念，对理论旅行的过程、应用、变异、抵抗、经典化、本土化等多个方面进行分析，可以发现作为全球化进程产物的世界文学理论畅想，虽然在一定程度上推动了非西方文学的全球流通，但是在涉及世界文学的理论构建与文学经典的评价标准等问题上却依然具有西方中心主义的倾向。同时，针对世界文学理论的东方旅行，对从泰戈尔、郑振铎到当代中国学界的理论接受情况及相关学者的世界文学观念构建进行宏观性的考查，则可以得出结论：非西方世界的世界文学研究只有在诗学层面上能够达到与西方世界分庭抗礼的程度，才能够真正摆脱西方中心主义的束缚。

【关键词】 萨义德；理论旅行；世界文学；世界诗学；郑振铎

The Circulation Mechanism of Traveling Theory and the Poetics of World Literature

Mengqi Li

Abstract: In the study of world literature, the circulation and accept-

---

[*]【作者简介】李孟奇，北京师范大学文学院博士。主要研究领域为后殖民理论、世界文学理论。

ance mechanism of world literature theory has often received little attention from relevant scholars. Combining Said's concept of traveling theory and analyzing its process, application, variation, resistance, canonization and localization, we can find that although the theoretical conception of world literature as a product of the globalization process has promoted the global circulation of non-Western literature to a certain extent, it still tends to be Western-centric in issues related to the theoretical construction of world literature and the evaluation criteria of literary classics. At the same time, with regard to the oriental travel of world literature theory, by examining macroscopically how Tagore, Zheng Zhenduo and contemporary Chinese academy accept it and what world literature concepts relevant scholars construct, we can conclude that the shackles of Western-centrism can be rid of only if the poetics put froward in the study of world literature in the non-Western world can stand up to that from the Western world.

Key words: Edward Said; Traveling theory; World literature; World poetics; Zhenduo Zheng

一 理论旅行的流通机制

虽然《旅行中的理论》("Traveling Theory", 1982) 被收录至达姆罗什主编的《世界文学理论》(*World Literature in Theory*, 2014), 但是目前学界关于理论旅行的世界文学维度分析还缺少针对性, 这或许和理论旅行只涉及诗学层面的流通机制, 却缺少对文学文本流通的分析不无关系。同时, 在世界文学理论层面的相关探讨中, 也确实存在只关注非西方文学书写, 却鲜少涉及非西方文学理论这一现象, 正如瑞易瓦兹·克里希纳斯瓦米(Revathi Krishnaswamy)指出: "一个普遍的假设是, 理论是独特的西方哲学传统的产物。从这个角度来看, 非西方可能是异域文化生产的来源, 但不可能是理论的场所。我们被告知，即使非西方产生的理论——后殖民主义理论——也只是对西方的一种回应。"① 可见，即便是非西方世界拥有《舞论》《朵伽比亚姆》《文心雕龙》《沧浪诗话》等丰厚的文论遗产，却并不代表东西文化交流之间具有平等的理论阐释空间，就连以反抗性著称的后殖民理论也主要是以西方理论来反对西方的文化霸权，却无法在东方文论的资源中形成和西方理论双峰并峙的文化思潮。为了改变这种不平等的理论交流机制，关于理论流通的问题应该与文学文本的流通机制一样，引起一定的重视。

  如果说在文学研究中，萨义德以世俗批评的境况性分析来代替以新批评为代表的封闭式阅读，那么萨义德对理论旅行的理解则主要反对以封闭的视野看待理论，并强调在对理论进行评述时要将理论传播的社会、政治、历史等境况性因素考虑在内。可见，在《旅行中的理论》中萨义德已经将文学批评与接受的现世性维度上升至跨文化理论阐释层面的情境性考量，这种分析模式与萨义德在《东方学》中所论述的西方中心视域下的东方主义观念一脉相承。萨义德将理论旅行主要限定于四个步骤：首先是观念产生的条件与境况；其次是理论从甲地到乙地的时间与空间转换中所要经过的不同语境；再次是包含着赞同与抵抗的特定接受条件；最后是在新的地点与时间被接受与使用的理论，必然要涉及对理论的挪用与再阐释。② 然而，在文学批评领域却一直存在着方法论上的分歧，为理论旅行设置了障碍，一种是以文本性为基础的文学内部研究，另一种是包括社会历史等因素在内的文学外部研究。当文学研究局限于文本内部，文学批评就成了一种充满稳定性与专业性的阐释领域，而原本与文学研究关系密切的思想史等交叉学科也在新的学科空间中变得泾渭分明，不再干涉文学批评，这样，广义上的文学概念与文学研究就被狭义的文本研究取代，关于经

---

① Revathi Krishnaswamy, "Toward World Literary Knowledges: Theory in the Age of Globalization", in David Damrosch, ed., *World Literature in Theory*, Oxford: Wiley Blackwell, 2014, p. 135.
② [美]萨义德：《世界·文本·批评家》，李自修译，生活·读书·新知三联书店 2009 年版，第 401 页。

典性的问题也会在此基础上退居为保守主义的建制派倾向。萨义德认为，只有当这种文本性与经典性的权威被打破之时，同质性的阐释空间才能够包容异质性的他异因素，从而赋予理论旅行完整的意义，并在境况性的文本阐释背景中加以分析。

为论述理论旅行在不同历史与社会境况中的意义阐释、应用界限、理论接受等问题，萨义德以卢卡奇（György Lukács）的《历史与阶级意识》（*History and Class Consciousness*，1923）为例，论证了卢卡奇在不同时空中的理论接受情况。在《历史与阶级意识》中，卢卡奇在马克思关于商品拜物教分析的基础上，对物化现象进行了详尽的解释。卢卡奇认为，现代资本主义的劳动分工一方面使劳动成为一种高度机械化与重复性的工作，另一方面使时间量化为可以被计算的劳动定额，这致使心灵与人格被彻底地客体化，以便在商品经济中归入计算的法则。同时，人在这一劳动过程中并不表现为劳动的支配者，而是作为被机械化这一整体支配的一部分服务于这一生产流程。于是，在资本主义的生产法则下，物就成为人的主宰，而"主体日益退隐为消极的、私人化的观照，并且渐渐地、愈益脱离了现代工业生活那势不可当的碎片化现实……从而进入了终极消极状态"。① 萨义德认为，卢卡奇的目的在于对资本主义物化世界进行描绘的基础上以阶级意识锻造反抗性的可能，从而在政治上对资产阶级赖以生存的物化世界进行颠覆性的打击，这样理论就被赋予了带有革命色彩的现世性特征，而"无产阶级是他笔下的一个形象，它代表着意识挑战物化、心智维护其驾驭物质的权力、意识宣称它假定在只有客体的世界之外的一个美好世界的理论权利"。②

然而，卢卡奇的门徒吕西安·戈德曼（Lucien Goldmann）在《隐蔽的上帝》（*The Hidden God*，1955）中对卢卡奇进行引证的过程中，阶级意识却成了"世界图景"，从而失去了反抗性的维度。萨义德认

---

① ［美］萨义德：《世界·文本·批评家》，李自修译，生活·读书·新知三联书店2009年版，第408页。

② ［美］萨义德：《世界·文本·批评家》，李自修译，生活·读书·新知三联书店2009年版，第412页。

为，造成这种理解偏差的原因在于卢卡奇与戈德曼迥异的境况性处境。卢卡奇的《历史与阶级意识》是为1919年匈牙利无产阶级革命而作，而戈德曼只是索邦大学的一名教授，正是这种写作情境的差异使戈德曼将卢卡奇的反抗意识与战斗热情转变为相对温和的理论阐释。可见，理论是对情境的一种回应，而理论的旅行则是一个使理论在流通中进行变异的一个过程。当然，萨义德并不认为一切对理论的解读都是一种误读，这样的理解既引起了对理论的盲目照搬，又否认了批评家的职能，相反萨义德重在透过理论旅行的过程强调对历史、社会等因素进行批判性的考量。

在卢卡奇物化观念的理论旅行问题上，萨义德尤为看重雷蒙·威廉斯（Raymond Henry Williams）对戈德曼与卢卡奇的分析。威廉斯在《唯物主义与文化问题》（*Problems in Materialism and Culture*，1980）中一方面使卢卡奇的《历史与阶级意识》恢复了革命性的批判锋芒；另一方面则针对卢卡奇物化理论的总体性困境对理论接受问题进行了批评性的反思。在威廉斯看来，从总体性的角度思考问题其悖论性在于著述者本身也是总体性的一部分，这使得任何关于理论的反思都处于内在的方法论困境之中，即便这种理论本身是一种具有创造性的实践。在卢卡奇的《小说理论》中，这种困境得到了集中的显现，致使卢卡奇在书中失去了《历史与阶级意识》的批判锋芒。出于对戈德曼的尊敬，《唯物主义与文化问题》并没有对戈德曼的卢卡奇接受进行直接的批判，而是在字里行间表明理论的阐释并不是一种不加批判与节制的重复，正如萨义德指出："某种观念一旦由于它的显而易见的有效性和强大作用，而开始广泛传播开来，那么，在其流布过程中，它就完全有可能被还原、被编码化、被体制化。"[①] 在对卢卡奇物化理论的接受问题上，萨义德的看法与威廉斯一致，一方面对卢卡奇的批判精神表示认可；另一方面认为物化与总体化并不能主宰一切，这恰

---

① [美]萨义德：《世界·文本·批评家》，李自修译，生活·读书·新知三联书店2009年版，第419页。

恰表明理论的旅行是一种有限度的阐释与接受。正是在此基础上，萨义德认为对于人类智识空间的阐释既需要理论本身与理论旅行，又要认识到没有任何理论能够囊括一切境况性因素，所以对理论的运用形成批判性的认识就变得尤为必要。

针对理论旅行的诸多问题，萨义德提出了颇具建设性的反思性意见，具体可以归纳为以下五个方面：一是理论接受的前提在于认识到理论本身的不完备性；二是理论的解读并非客观中立，而是某种立场的产物；三是理论必须置身于理论起源的时间、地点等情境中才能得到明确的把握；四是批判意识既是对理论的一种抵抗，也是使理论得以"向着历史现实、向着人类需要和利益开放"的一种方式[①]；五是理论的封闭[②]既会使批判性的意识丧失殆尽，也会使理论的阐释因缺乏多维度的审视而走向贫瘠。值得指出的是，正是认识到了理论的局限性与对理论进行抵抗与重塑的重要性，萨义德在《旅行中的理论》中认为福柯（Michel Foucault）的知识与权力分析过于强调权力的支配性，致使其论述缺乏反抗性的精神，忽视了对于权力进行抵抗的可能性，而这样的理论建构一旦被学院派加以权威化，其弊端在于理论"可以轻易地变成独断的教条……它们不断孳生的危害则在于，它们起初的源头——即它们的对抗的、对立的派生理论的历史——就会使批判意识变得麻木迟钝，使这种意识相信，原来是叛逆的理论对于历史依然是叛逆的、生动的、敏感的"[③]。回顾《东方学》一书，萨义德在对福柯的理论加以运用的基础上确实忽略了对东方主义进行抵抗的可能性分析。从这个意义上讲，《旅行中的理论》标志着萨义德超越了知识与权力结构的固有局限，并在后续的《文化与帝国主义》、《关于流亡的反思及其它文章》（Reflections on Exile and Other Essays）、《人文主义与民主

---

① ［美］萨义德：《世界·文本·批评家》，李自修译，生活·读书·新知三联书店2009年版，第424页。
② 具体例证为新批评封闭式阅读。
③ ［美］萨义德：《世界·文本·批评家》，李自修译，生活·读书·新知三联书店2009年版，第431页。

批评》等多部著作中强调对位式的政治与文化反抗。在《理论旅行再思考》("Traveling Theory Reconsidered"，1994）中，萨义德再次重点强调理论旅行在新的环境中可以使理论获得新的生命力与批判性的阐释空间，并继续以卢卡奇的理论旅行为例论述法兰克福学派领军人物西奥多·阿多诺（Theodor Wiesengrund Adorno）《新音乐的哲学》（*Philosophy of New Music*，1949）及后殖民理论先驱弗朗茨·法农（Frantz Omar Fanon）《全世界受苦的人》（*The Wretched of the Earth*，1961）对卢卡奇的批判性继承。这表明，正是通过理论的旅行与对理论的批判性继承，理论的优势与局限得以同时暴露，并在新的境况性阐释中收获超越本土的价值与意义，从而启迪新的理论创建。

二 世界文学理论旅行的诗学问题

萨义德的《旅行中的理论》涉及理论旅行的过程、应用、变异、抵抗、经典化、本土化等多个方面，为学界考察世界文学的理论接受及其诗学问题提供了有益启示。针对世界文学的理论旅行，王宁指出：

> "世界文学"本身就是一个旅行的概念，但是这种旅行并非率先从西方到东方，而是其基因从一开始就来自东方，之后在西方逐步形成一个理论概念后又旅行到东方乃至整个世界。因此它不同于赛义德所谓的"理论旅行"，因为后者一开始就是从西方旅行到东方，并在旅行的过程中发生了某种形式的变异，最终在另一民族文化的土壤里产生了新的变体。应该承认，理论的旅行很少体现为双向的旅行，然而世界文学的旅行却是个例外。[①]

借助萨义德的理论旅行概念，王宁的论述强调了世界文学观念产生的东方背景。正是在中国传奇的启发下，歌德提出了世界文学这一

---

① 王宁：《比较文学、世界文学与翻译研究》，复旦大学出版社2014年版，第260页。

概念。可见，世界文学的双向旅行可以理解为以下四个阶段：首先，发轫于东方作品在西方的广泛传播；其次，歌德与马克思、恩格斯将这一文学文本的流通与接受现象概念化为世界文学；再次，后世学者将世界文学这一概念进行不断深化；最后，作为西方产物的世界文学观念又经由理论的旅行传播至非西方世界。可是，这种从东方及至西方的双向文化传播并非理论的双向旅行。从东西文学交流的角度看，只有文学的交流是双向的，而文学理论的旅行往往只是单向的。这样，西方在世界文学的问题上就仍然牢牢掌握着理论的话语权，卡萨诺瓦、达姆罗什、莫莱蒂等学者则成了永远无法越过的学术高峰，而非西方世界的作用往往只体现在推动西方理论的经典化。这表明，文学研究的去中心化倘若无法上升至诗学层面的平等对话，那么这股关于世界文学的理论热潮是强化还是削弱西方中心就仍然是一个值得玩味的问题。针对这一问题，张隆溪在《结语：世界文学观念的变化》（"Epilogue: The Changing Concept of World Literature", 2014）中针对世界文学的诗学问题提出了极具建设性的分析。在张隆溪看来，从歌德、马克思、卡萨诺瓦到达姆罗什的世界文学观念主要是西方观念的产物，这说明世界文学要超越欧洲中心主义与种族中心主义的局限，就不能仅仅通过阅读非西方文学来实现，而是要在理论层面上打破东西界限。因此，在世界文学的理论问题上张隆溪认为：

> 我们需要建立一个将西方与东方视为平等贡献者的公平竞争环境，世界文学的诗学应该是一组探究语言与表达的本质、意义与理解、阐释与审美价值、诗歌与文学的起源、艺术与自然的关系等问题。在不同的文学传统中，这些问题被提出和回答的方式肯定是不同的，但正是这样的基本问题及其答案构成了世界文学中的文学理论，不同的例子和批评的表述丰富了宝贵的见解。[①]

[①] Zhang, Longxi, "Epilogue: The Changing Concept of World Literature", in David Damrosch, ed., *World Literature in Theory*, Oxford: Wiley Blackwell, 2014, p.521.

张隆溪的阐释提出了世界文学研究中往往被忽视的理论问题，也充分表明如果世界文学仅仅关注文学文本的流通、翻译与阅读等问题，却忽视在理论层面上构建东方与西方的平等对话机制，那么世界文学的多元文化畅想将只是实践意义上的空中楼阁。倘若无法在观念上打破西方文化与理论的支配地位，那么非西方文学资本将仅仅是世界文学舞台上的异域风格装饰，却无法撼动西方中心的话语根基。在此基础上，张隆溪指出世界文学的诗学同样涉及萨义德的理论旅行问题，即"对位并置"（contrapuntal juxtaposition）层面上的文学创作与文化实践。通过阅读《旅行中的理论》，张隆溪认为萨义德的理论旅行与世界文学的诗学问题主要有以下几个方面的相关性：一是全球化时代的理论旅行不再遵循中心与边缘的单一结构划分；二是理论的域外传播与应用是一个适应与归化的实践过程；三是任何世界文学选集与理论的全球视角都无法做到绝对的价值中立，所以"世界文学在实践中总是本土化的，选择不同的作品进行研究和批判性的评论，以不同的文化和理论视角处理不同的问题，并具有不同的兴趣"[①]。可见，世界文学的理论畅想作为全球化进程不同阶段的产物，虽然在一定程度上推动了非西方文学作品的全球流通，但是在涉及世界文学的理论构建与文学经典的评价标准等问题上依然是一种西方话语的角力场。在这场没有硝烟的理论论争中，非西方学者既要通过西方话语来迎合西方中心的学术思维，又要承担边缘话语与非西方文论资源难以进入西方主流学界的尴尬境遇。从这个意义上讲，世界文学的理论旅行及其诗学问题事关东方与西方能否在理论的争鸣与文学经典的构建中创立平等的话语机制，这也表明对非西方学者关于世界文学话语的代表性文献进行宏观性的把握是极其必要的。

三 世界文学理论的域外旅行

回顾世界文学观念发展的不同阶段，来自非西方世界的理论创建

[①] Zhang, Longxi, "Epilogue: The Changing Concept of World Literature", in David Damrosch, ed., *World Literature in Theory*, Oxford: Wiley Blackwell, 2014, p. 522.

在不同程度上推动了世界文学的诗学构建。在东方世界，最早对世界文学观念进行回应的学者很可能为泰戈尔（Rabindranath Tagore）。据斯皮瓦克（Gayatri Chakravorty Spivak）考证，泰戈尔在《世界文学》（"World Literature"，1907）中出于孟加拉语的语境考量把英语"比较文学"翻译成孟加拉语"世界文学"[1]，这种误译或许也从侧面说明了比较文学的发展方向即是世界文学的理论畅想。泰戈尔从人类心灵的角度出发论述了文学对于重塑精神世界、展现人性光辉、塑造完美人格的重要意义。与歌德的世界文学观念类似，泰戈尔认为文学的重要意义就在于其非功利化的实践目的与普遍性人性的共通性表达，而出于功利化目的撰写的文学文本则只会在历史的淘洗中被淘汰。作为以"沟通东西方文化的桥梁"著称于世的东方作家，泰戈尔强调作家的世界意识，即"只有当作者的内心意识到人类的思想并在作品中表达人性的痛苦时，其作品才能被置于文学的殿堂"[2]。可见，泰戈尔的世界文学观念并不致力于讨论文本流通的过程性，而是主要抓住了文学文本自身的普遍性特质。在随后的散文随笔中，泰戈尔则以具体的实例论述了民族文学何以成为世界文学。在《爪哇通讯》（1927）中，泰戈尔认为穆门辛格县的民间诗歌之所以能够跻身世界文学，就在于这些诗歌表达了具有人类共通性的快乐与痛苦。[3] 在《东方和西方》中，泰戈尔指出孟加拉文学之所以能够取得成功，并出现了以般吉姆·钱德拉为代表的伟大作家，原因就在于孟加拉文学打破了民族文学与世界文学的界限，能够"毫不困难地吸取西方文化与思想的精华，为己所用"[4]。可见，泰戈尔世界文学观念的核心要义就在于在表

---

[1] Gayatri Chakravorty Spivak, *An Aesthetic Education in the Era of Globalization*, Cambridge: Harvard University Press, 2012, p.464.

[2] ［印］泰戈尔：《世界文学》，王国礼译，载大卫·达姆罗什、刘洪涛、尹星主编《世界文学理论读本》，北京大学出版社2013年版，第62页。

[3] ［印］泰戈尔：《爪哇通讯》，白开元译，载刘安武、倪培耕、白开元主编《泰戈尔全集：第二十卷》，河北教育出版社2000年版，第176页。

[4] ［印］泰戈尔：《东方和西方》，潘小珠译，载刘安武、倪培耕、白开元主编《泰戈尔全集：第二十三卷》，河北教育出版社2000年版，第146页。

达人类共通情感的基础上推动不同民族文学间的相互交流与借鉴。

在中国,世界文学的观念旅行已逾百年。据刘珂考证,在中国"世界文学"一词最早由黄人于《中国文学史》(1907)中提出[①]。然而,从引起广泛影响的层面讲,郑振铎的《文学的统一观》(1922)无疑对于理解中国的世界文学观念与实践具有先导性意义。在文中,郑振铎对文学研究中以国别划分研究界限的现象表示不满,认为应该以"文学的统一观"来整合全球范围内的文学资源。相较于分散的国别文学研究,文学的统一观可以有效地探求民族文学之间的相互影响与共同起源,把握不同民族的普遍人性与精神特质,并在方法论上形成对文学发展与进化的整体观念。同时,为解决文学的统一观在文学研究的语言、体量、翻译、鉴赏等层面面临的方法论困境,郑振铎一方面承认文学作品的可译性;另一方面认为文学研究的最高境界并非为文学鉴赏,而是以进化的视角审视全部文学作品的起源、渊源、情感等诸方面。在对西方世界文学观念的接受上,郑振铎所受到的直接影响来源于理查德·格林·莫尔顿(Richard Green Moulton)《世界文学及其在一般文化中的位置》(*World Literature and Its Place in General Culture*,1911)。经过跨越东西的理论旅行后,郑振铎并没有盲从于莫尔顿的世界文学观念,而是以文学的统一观对莫尔顿在文学研究中以一国文学为出发点的做法予以驳斥。这样,郑振铎就在理论旅行的批判性反思中形成了自身的世界文学观念建构。值得指出的是,郑振铎对于世界文学的热情不仅体现在观念层面的讨论,还见诸实践意义上以文学的统一观撰写《文学大纲》与主编《世界文库》,为推动中国的世界文学研究贡献了不世之功。

进入 21 世纪,世界文学的理论复兴也带动了中国学界的世界文学研究。但是,相较于西方学界对于理论建构的热情,中国学界关于世界文学的研究主要停留在以下三个层面:一是对卡萨诺瓦、达姆罗什、

---

① 刘珂:《中国的"世界文学"观念与实践研究:1895—1949》,中央民族大学出版社 2016 年版,第 44 页。

莫莱蒂等学者的理论研究；二是以中国文学海外传播为代表的文学文本流通研究；三是世界文学与相关交叉学科及学术概念的关系探析。关于世界文学的诗学建构则是少之又少。这其中，王宁作为佼佼者做出了重要贡献。在《"世界文学"：从乌托邦想象到审美现实》（2010）中，王宁根据达姆罗什的世界文学定义与中国文学的发展历程提出了自己的世界文学概念。他指出：

（1）世界文学是东西方各国优秀文学的经典之汇总；
（2）世界文学是我们的文学研究、评价和批评所依据的全球性和跨文化视角和比较的视野；
（3）世界文学是通过不同语言的文学的生产、流通、翻译以及批评性选择的一种文学历史演化。[①]

与达姆罗什的世界文学概念不同，王宁的世界文学定义既强调了文学文本在跨界流通中所衍化的文化现象，又对世界文学的经典性特质与文学研究的全球视角予以重视。同时，在判断一部文学作品能否成为世界文学的标准中，王宁的见解无疑也比达姆罗什的跨国文本流通更具系统性。他指出："一，它是否把握了特定的时代精神；二，它的影响是否超越了本民族或本语言的界限；三，它是否收入后来的研究者编选的文学经典选集；四，它是否能够进入大学课堂成为教科书；五，它是否在另一语境下受到批评性的讨论和研究。"[②] 面对欧洲中心主义的桎梏，王宁承认文学作为一种意识形态，其评价标准带有一定的相对性，这造成任何基于普适意义的考量都无法平衡不同民族在文化、历史、地理等诸方面的巨大差异。所以，在王宁看来世界文学标准的第三与第四个定义并不具备普遍性，反而带有一定的人为干预因素。从王宁的世界文学定义到世界文学的评价标准分析，似乎都

---

① 王宁：《比较文学、世界文学与翻译研究》，复旦大学出版社2014年版，第208页。
② 王宁：《比较文学、世界文学与翻译研究》，复旦大学出版社2014年版，第209页。

预示着世界文学的讨论必然要上升至东西诗学层面的平等对话才能够摆脱文学研究的知识与权力话语，而王宁正是在有鉴于以中国为代表的诗学体系难以在世界文学的诗学舞台上施加重要影响力的前提下提出"世界诗学"这一概念。在《世界诗学的构想》（2015）中，王宁认为世界诗学首先要建立在东西方诗学的相互比较之上，并在认知诗学的基础上形成普适性的理论构建。从王宁对孟而康（Earl Miner）与鲁文·楚尔（Reuven Tsur）的批判性继承来看，王宁的世界诗学理论重在强调文学研究从文化批评向文本研究的回归，这表明王宁有意在文化理论衰落的后理论时代以世界文学为契机调和文化批评与文本研究的结构性矛盾，并以世界诗学的理论畅想整合东西方的文学理论资源，从而使世界文学的诗学能够以跨语言、跨边界、跨学科的视角走出西方中心主义的泥淖。

除王宁外，刘洪涛在分析中国的外国文学教材在结构与观念演变的基础上提出了"'同心圆'的世界文学观"。刘洪涛的世界文学观念强调以中国为中心，具体表现在其主编的《世界文学作品选》中并没有中国文学作品入选，然而中国"却是这个同心圆关系结构的枢纽、标准、尺度，因此它又无处不在"。[①] 在选集的编选上，刘洪涛强调以洲际文学为单位，同时兼顾国籍与民族属性存在混杂性的流散、族裔、语系文学，而在选集分册的顺序上则以中国与其他洲际文学关联与影响的先后强弱关系为基础，分为"亚洲文学卷""欧洲文学卷""美洲文学卷""非洲、大洋洲文学卷""流散、族裔、语系文学卷"。[②] 刘洪涛的贡献在于将世界文学研究从理论反思与重建的基础上提升至文学选集的编选与实践，同时在编选结构上打破达姆罗什主编《朗文世界文学作品选》时的历史分期体例，带有鲜明的中国特色。

时至今日，世界文学的理论旅行在世界范围内已经引起了广泛的回应与学术争鸣，而从泰戈尔到中国学者的世界文学阐释与反思则代

[①] 刘洪涛主编：《世界文学作品选》第一册，高等教育出版社2021年版，第2页。
[②] 刘洪涛主编：《世界文学作品选》第一册，高等教育出版社2021年版，第3页。

表了非西方学者为打破东西文化隔阂，推动全球文学交流与重建世界文学经典秩序所做出的努力。然而，非西方世界对世界文学话题的讨论尚没有形成足以与西方进行分庭抗礼的诗学体系，正如达姆罗什在论述理论旅行时指出："受后殖民研究的启发，理论向西方以外的世界开放已经进行了几十年，但它仍然是一个不完整的项目，尤其是因为'理论'仍然主要来源于欧洲和北美……就像古老的伟大经典一样，理论经典赋予欧美理论全球适用的特权，而非西方理论主要用于讨论其文化起源。"[1] 在中国，一个尴尬之处在于中国学界虽早已经将达姆罗什等的理论建构加以经典化与权威化，却缺少实质性的批判性反思与理论重构。这样，世界文学的理论旅行就面临与萨义德所论述的福柯理论接受相似的风险，即一个立足于批判性与反思性的理论构建由于在理论的域外接受过程中缺少了批判性继承的维度，致使原著原有的批判性锋芒在域外经典化的过程中被消耗殆尽。综上所述，世界文学的诗学构建确实具有现实的指导与实践意义，当然这样的工作并非一朝一夕能够完成，只有经过时间的淬炼与不断的打磨推敲才能够铸就"通古今之变，成一家之言"的理论构建。不过，正如张隆溪指出："我们有前辈学者为榜样，有他们已经取得的成就为基础，加之我们自己的使命和抱负，只要不断努力，就总能够在问学的道路上，向前迈进一步，对普遍性的诗学和文艺理论，做出我们的贡献。"[2] 在治学的道路上，经过前辈学者的开疆拓土与学术后浪的薪火相传，中国学界在不久的将来于世界文学领域足以形成独具特色的理论构建。

---

[1] David Damrosch, *Comparing the Literatures: Literary Studies in a Global Age*, Princeton: Princeton University Press, 2020, p. 145.

[2] 张隆溪：《什么是世界文学》，生活·读书·新知三联书店 2021 年版，第 196 页。

世界文学面临的危险

威廉姆·阿特金森

The Perils of World Literature

William Atkinson

World literature not only has a venerable journal devoted to its discussion, it is also taught to undergraduates-and very extensively taught. According to Peter J. Simon, vice president and editor at W. W. Norton, world literature surveys enroll at almost 75 percent of the American literature survey totals. In the United States, survey courses are mostly taught as part of the general education core; those teaching them usually have graduate training in what they teach. The instructors for a survey of British literature from the romantics to the present will have taken graduate courses in much of the period and have written a dissertation or a thesis on a particular feature of the period.

It cannot be the same with the world literature surveys taught within the core. I am not aware of any universities that grant doctorates in world literature,

---

* 【作者简介】威廉姆·阿特金森（William Atkinson），阿巴拉契亚州立大学（Appalachian State University）英语系教授，主要教授与研究世界文学和20世纪英国文学。

原文为评论体，没有摘要、关键词和分节。

that prepare candidates to teach in any given year *Gilgamesh*, the *Odyssey*, *Sakuntala*, *Tang dynasty poetry*, *and selections from the Mahabhärata*, *the Tale of Genji*, the *Divine Comedy*, *Don Quixote*, and *The Story of the Stone*.

World literature is a subject of study but not a discipline whose protocols can be easily determined. What exactly is this subject that so many of us teach? I would argue that a discussion of the nature of world literature both as a disciplinary and pedagogical entity, is particularly timely because it has changed very considerably in the past few years, metamorphosing from Western literature in disguise to something more genuinely representative of most of the world's literary cultures, and thereby it has come to embody some of the academy's core values.

First, I want to address the question of who might have the authority to define world literature. In a recent collection of essays, *Debating World Literature* (2004) most of the American contributors are associated with language and comparative literature departments, and the contributors from England look as if they would find homes in such departments were they to leave Cambridge. The editors of *The Norton Anthology of World Literature* look like a very similar group, although they usually have a designated association with a particular language. None of them appears to be a specialist in world literature as a whole but rather in one or two literatures of the world. Their authority comes from their being specialists in the literatures of particular languages. The authority of the contributors in *Debating World Literature*, on the other hand, comes from their being comparatists.

For comparatists, world literature has a history, and it begins on January 31, 1827 when Goethe remarked: "National literature is now rather an unmeaning term; the epoch of world literature is at hand, and every one must strive to hasten its approach" (Conversations 165 – 66). Goethe seems to have been thinking of a state of literary affairs that was yet to come. An independent, or national, literature might be defined as the product of writers within particular boundaries in conversation with one another across space and time, but Goethe was looking forward to a time when writers from all over the world would become aware of one another's work. In 1828 he wrote to the Society of Natural Philosophers in Berlin:

> If we have dared proclaim the beginning of a European, indeed a world literature, this does not merely mean that the various nations will take note of one another and their creative efforts, for in that sense a world literature has been in existence for some time, and is to some extent continuing and developing. We mean, rather, that contemporary writers and all participants in the literary scene are becoming acquainted and feel the need to take action as a group because of inclination and public-spiritedness. (Essays on Art and Literature 225)

Goethe is calling for an imagined community of all the world's writers.

There was something of a pan-European literature by the beginning of the twentieth century, if not earlier, and it was swiftly carried to all those parts of the globe where European guns and money prevailed. But while Tanizaki Junichirō, the early-twentieth-century Japanese novelist, read Joyce, the compliment was not returned. World literature was becoming Europeanized. By the second half of the last century, however, the formal and informal empires were writing back and being read throughout the world.

The existence of an international group of writers who are more or less aware of one another's work might be taken to constitute a truly world literature, a community of readers and writers not defined by nation. This development could well be part of the reason for the current interest in the subject. But at about the same time that Goethe was first talking about world literature, another meaning of the word *literature* was evolving and literature as a subject of study began to emerge. In about 1800, *literature* meant little more than what was being written at the time. Over the course of the nineteenth century, *literature* came increasingly to refer to an archive of writing already written, an archive waiting to be studied. In this process, Stefan Hoesel-Uhlig sees the development of literary historiography as crucial because it offered "a novel, retrospective focus for cultural self-understanding" (46). The key to the culture is to be found in its literature, and because the nineteenth century was much preoccupied with national cultures, the study of literature became deeply imbricated with the development of national consciousness and patriotic values.

In Europe, elite education had long concentrated on the Greek and Latin classics. Free universal education could not aspire to such heights, but it is by no means certain that it would have wanted to. After all, Virgil was not an Englishman, nor a German nor even an Italian. So all English children read Shakespeare, Germans read Goethe, and Italians read Dante. All these men were, as is well known, universal geniuses! At the same time, they were also often said to represent the genius of their nations. If the teacher's charges thus went away thinking that their particular nation had a monopoly on universals, there were many teachers who would not wish to disabuse them of such a view-or so the history of Europe in the first half of the twentieth century would suggest.

The idea of a literature representing its culture is now considerably problematized with the increasing perception of nations as multicultural entities. Until quite recently, a fairly limited number of largely white male writers were allowed to speak for most of the nations of Europe and North America. Around the middle of the twentieth century, world literature began to appear in North American course offerings. But the American idea of world literature was far from what Goethe seems to have had in mind. As short a time ago as 1995, the standard *Norton Anthology of World Masterpieces* was made up almost entirely of European and North American texts. World literature in

American colleges meant European literature in translation.

The first such Norton anthology appeared in 1956. A comment from the preface to the 1995 expanded edition still represents midcentury thinking on why American sophomores needed some familiarity with the European literary tradition.

> Whatever our individual or ethnic associations may be, if we live in the United States it is important to understand the moral and intellectual sources of the country that we inhabit and that in some inescapable sense inhabits us…So far as our collective life in this country has roots these are to be found in the Western tradition, whose influence in the fabric of our everyday existence is best discovered byimmersion in its recognized masterpieces of drama, poetry, and fiction. (xxxii)

The dominant culture of America has evolved from European origins, runs the argument, and these origins still "inhabit us." This claim is even stronger than Hoesel-Uhlig's "retrospective focus for cultural self-understanding." By the late twentieth century, however, it was well accepted in the academy that the United States was not so fully European as it had been convenient to think, so some African and Asian material was included in the new canon of world literature in order to answer the needs of those Americans who were inhabited by different "moral and intellectual sources" and needed a different "focus for cultural self-understanding."

The *Norton Anthology* notwithstanding, by 1995 the academy had been living with the Other for a couple of decades, and the Other needed to be heard. The editors of the expanded *Norton Anthology of World Masterpieces* acknowledged its call.

Still, our central objective in this Expanded Edition is to encourage exploration of other traditions as well. As in the forest world the effect of roots is the production of spreading leaves and branches and the effects of spreading leaves and branches is the invigoration of roots, so in our human world the vigor of cultural traditions thrives rather from reaching out than from closing in. All over the planet there flourish faiths, fears, arts, and aspirations; needs and markets, likes and dislikes; racial, genderand ethnic tensions-matters that our shrinking planet of airplanes, television, computer networks, and long-range nuclear missiles has made it materially important for us to know about as well as intellectually and spiritually foolish to ignore. Hostilities at all levels are usually first gener ated and then exacerbated by xenophobia ("fear of the stranger") and by the ease with which the unfamiliar book, picture, food, custom, costume, or skin color can be demonized. For this phobia the only cure is frequent and prolonged exposure to what is different from ourselves until the unfamiliar becomes familiar, the unaccustomed perspective brings more generous ways of seeing, and we discover how much there is still to learn about ourselves. (xxxiii)

By this account, studying world literatures is a desensitizing procedure, while the claiming of all benefits material, intellectual, and spiritual-tries to appeal to everyone and thereby risks directly touching no one. Interestingly, the paragraph closes with a very similar claim for the value of the study of non-Western literature as had been made for the studyof the Western tradition: a better understanding of ourselves. It comes back to us and what we need. Otherness is thereby at risk of being erased by becoming part of us.

The transition from world literature = *Western literature to world literature* = *the literatures of most of the world* was remarkably sudden. When the world literature course consisted entirely of Western textsthere was no great difficulty in finding fairly well-prepared people to teach it. After all, half the texts could be English, and how weird can Dante be? He was, after all a Christian. Of course, no one with a historicist background would say any such thing today. And here is the source of the double bind in which the world literature course now finds itself. In the days when everyone was a basic formalist, all texts from all places from all times could, in principle, be treated much the same. I say "in principle" because specialization has, in factbeen with us for a long time. But the valorization of the universal has also been around for a long time and in nonacademic reviewing and Norton introductory materialis still very much with us. If a text is dubbed universal, it can, supposedly thereby speak to and for all of us. And if we find it possesses universal valuesit has spoken to us so we are the determiners of the universal. But most new Ph. D. s come with a roughly historicist training and therefore value the contingency and specificity of texts. Shakespeare lived in a particular place at a particular time, and it is necessary to know a good deal about that time and place if we are to understand what is going on in his texts. Our new critical assumption is that roots cannot survive once extracted from their soil. The valorization of difference and specificity has led to the kind of world literature anthologies we now have, but it has also made it both theoretically and practically impossible to teach the new world literature. A proper understanding of a cultural artifact requires an appreciation of the culture's difference from our own. But what individual could possibly have sufficient preparation to do justice to so many texts from so many moments and so many places? Yet unless students are introduced to these different cultures through their texts, the cultures will remain objects of, at best, indifference or at worst suspicion and contempt.

In contrast to the 1995 *Norton world literature anthology*, the preface to the sixth edition of the *Norton Anthology of English Literature* (1993) makes no elaborate claims for its offerings. The first sentence describes the volumes as designed for courses that "introduce students to the unparalleled excellence and variety of English literature." Such courses, they say, are "indis pensable" (xxxv), but the editors offer no justification for the adjective. Seven years later "indispensable" is gone and the editors restrict themselves to a comment on the "joys" associated with the literatures "abundance" (7th ed., xxxiii). But the abundance is increasingly plural. Few scholars would now accept the earlier view of a British literature that constituted a single literary tradition. The literatures of the British Isles are multiple, and to judge by the contents of the anthologies, *British* is becoming a convenient term subsuming anything written in English that does not originate from the United States.

Similar moves are afoot in American literature. The editors of the fifth edition of the *Heath Anthology of American Literature* (2005) regard American literature as a chorus of voices. "Heath," they write, "maintains its emphasis on the multiple origins and histories of the cultures of the United States." And they "are increasingly interested in the ongoing conversations among these cultures... and just how these conversations have come to define America as plural complex, heterogeneous-a chorus, perhaps, rather than a melting pot" (Lauter and Leveen).

It might be argued that the editors of British and American anthologies are simply climbing onto the globalizing bandwagon. Universities and colleges are going through a fresh round of core curriculum reform, and the word international is nearly always somewhere in the mission statement. And while to some people globalization means Americanization, the academy, on the whole is committed to a worldview that values plurality, heterogeneity, and difference. Whereas, fifty years ago, the course offerings in American or British literature might be assumed to communicate the core values of our West ern culture, today, if literary studies communicate any significant values at all, these values are most securely established in the world literature course.

以本土性求全球化：对世界文学教学的反思

伊曼德·米尔穆塔哈里*

【摘要】 本文强调改变世界文学课程的重要性，即从对世界文学的"调查"转向对组织世界的知识分类本身的质疑。这种转变最好伴随着对少数文学的凸显，并且从本土的家园经验出发。

【关键词】 世界文学课程；少数文学；在地经验

The Local as the Global: Reflections on Teaching World Literature

Emad Mirmotahari

Abstract: The following essay argues for the importance of shifting world literature courses away from "survey" and toward the interrogation of categories of knowledge that typically organize the world. This is best accomplished by foregrounding minoritized literatures and beginning from "home."

Key words: World literature course; Minoritized literature; Local experience

---

* 【作者简介】伊曼德·米尔穆塔哈里（Emad Mirmotahari），宾夕法尼亚州匹兹堡杜肯大学（Duquesne University）的英语与非洲研究教授，主要研究方向是非洲小说、世界文学思想与实践。

In recent years I have been searching for strategies to demystify the unruly idea of "world literature" for a general undergraduate student population in a North American university. Although this search relates to specific concerns with college pedagogy, the insights it yields can be useful beyond my particular context. Upon taking up a teaching position in 2010, I was informed by my new colleagues that while I would teach advanced undergraduate courses on world/postcolonial literatures for English majors and graduate courses, I would also teach large numbers of non-English majors seeking to fill the university's "diversity" requirement. Only recently did I realize that these circumstances and curricular conditions are, in fact, the natural habitat of world literature, where it has the most reach and can do the most work.

Initially, as a newly minted Ph. D., I was zealously committed to the imperatives of world literature on its own terms and for its own sake. Admittedly, I have not foreclosed on my early goals of producing readers of literary texts who are curious about the different and the distant and, with a little luck, inspiring them to go on to become polyglots and literary scholars. I now see my job, for the most part, as a very different one: less cloistered and more student-oriented in the broadest sense. As a teacher of world literature, I am accountable to all students, and not to English majors exclusively.

Realizing that my world literature course may possibly be the only one of its kind that many students will take, my challenge as a new professor was configuring a one semester course that maximizes the intellectual rewards of world literature. It is still quite common to encounter the "great books" model, the idea that world literature is an aggregate of what Margaret Cohen calls the "great unread". The peril of this approach is that it turns world literature into the instrument of some perfunctory "multiculturalism" that requires little mental labor from students, reducing them to impassive cultural tourists. Instead of this approach, world literature courses at the introductory and general level must unsettle students by making them "unthink" their worldviews, or at the very least be conscious of them. World literature must show them the synergies between the local, national, regional, and global.

To this end, world literature courses can, and perhaps must, begin at home, which for my students and myself is Pittsburgh, Pennsylvania, USA. This way, students see how the local, the proximal, and the familiar are coordinates of this thing called the world; the world is not something exotic, menacing, and inhospitable but an accretion of what they consider home, a larger community to which they are native. More specifically, I have found that local literatures produced by minoritized writers are especially conducive to fostering an understanding of the traffic between the local and the global. This is one of the ways in which the conversations around "world" and "postcolonial" literature are finding confluence as categories of inquiry, where world literature takes valuable lessons from the enterprise of postcolonial studies. The latter insists that power and the way one is socially situated affect how one reads and writes the world, an idea that informs the way educators use world literature as a means of encountering and learning from difference.

Foregrounding local and minoritized literatures as an entry into world literature does have a historical antecedent. Johannvon Goethe, widely credited with naturalizing the term "world literature" (*Weltliteratur*), famously declared, "National literature is now a rather unmeaning term; the epoch of world literature is at hand, and everyone must strive to hasten its approach." Less famous but related to this declaration was Goethe's attention to local and regional literatures, or "subnational literatures." I do not mean to ascribe to Goethe some vanguard iconoclasm against the established literary aristocracy, but it is clear that he pondered possible roles that literatures in the crevices and peripheries of the "nation" could play in deprovincializing literature, releasing it from the straitjacket of the national frame of reading. "Ethnic" and "postcolonial" literatures, which only tentatively belong to any national literature, are coming to occupy a special place in the conversations on world literature. They do not necessarily disperse the idea of "national" literatures, but they distress the critical practices around them and demand their rereading. They occasion thinking about literary canons in ways that converge with larger conversations about (un) belonging in lived social communities and how these communities are produced and policed.

I realize that beginning a world literature course in the United States, even with minoritized literatures, appears like a retrenchment of American and anglophone exceptionalism, but the alternative is to feign innocence of occasion and the way we are positioned in the world. Literary texts, like pedagogical situations, are "never from nowhere." Therefore, an intellectually candid and responsible world literature course must acknowledge and grapple with those default positions and ideological latencies that will inevitably shape course structure and intellectual temperament. The craft and storytelling of Pittsburgh's greatest literary son, August Wilson, has had an inestimable impact on me. So much so that being in Pittsburgh made sense to me after I read his *Pittsburgh Cycle*. Though not a native Pittsburgher or a black American, I recognized my own yearnings and anxieties in this work. Wilson's cycle also centered me as an educator given how organically (but intrepidly) it thrusts itself upon the world. While anchored to a specific place and time, the cycle is culturally agile, navigating and calling attention to the relationships among the local, regional, national, and global. Wilson's cycle might not appear to be the most germane illustration of the local-as-global. This is because black American literature—unlike other "ethnic" and immigrant literatures, which readily give way to and summon other places and cultures—has primarily been understood as discretely American in its being and deeds. In recent years, however, literary scholarship has reimagined and reconstituted minoritized writings in the United States as voices of the "global south," a larger conglomeration of communities that resist their silencing in national and linguistic contexts.

The Pittsburgh Cycle is comprised of ten dialogue-driven plays, each of which takes place in one twentieth-century decade as experienced by black Americans. Nine of them are set in Pittsburgh's Hill District where Wilson grew up, but the cycle also looks toward Chicago, an epicenter of the blues, a genre serving as a comprehensive philosophy of life for Wilson and his characters. In *Ma Rainey's Black Bottom* and *Seven Guitars*, Chicago is even extolled as a place of deliverance for black Americans. The cycle also looks back to the American South, a place of untold and unfinished stories and gaping wounds, the ghosts of which freight Wilson's characters. Many of Wilson's characters are immigrants in all but the legal sense. They move from one cultural sphere to another in search of better prospects, even though they do not cross a geopolitical frontier. But like international immigrants, Wilson's characters harbor a desire for "return." For Boy Willie in *The Piano Lesson*, to give one example, the South is the only place where black Americans can be rooted, whole, and sovereign because they have a claim to the land itself.

Africa also looms large in the cycle. Largely imperceptible and irrecoverable, it is an absent presence that is known only through its effects. It makes only furtive appearances, as in *The Piano Lesson*. Boy Willie and Berniece's ancestral piano is the play's extended metaphor, and "its legs [are] carved in the manner of an African sculpture ... mask-like figures resembling totems." The Middle Passage haunts the plays that are set in earlier decades like *Gem of the Ocean*. It is the beginning of the African odyssey in North America, the chapter that sutures the West Africa of bygone centuries to modern Pittsburgh. The Middle Passage also explains Aunt Ester's (a homologue for "ancestor") salience. A three-hundred-year-old persona who embodies a history mired in slavery and its aftermaths, she is either present or invoked in almost all the cycle's plays. Aunt Ester is a healer and sage who intuits other characters' woes, making those who are world-weary and lost "right with themselves" by transporting them to the "City of Bones" in the middle of the Atlantic Ocean. There she awakens them to the injuries of a history that is felt and lived but not always understood, what Wilson called "blood memory".

The Pittsburgh Cycle is even conversant with the diffuse yet generative organism known as the African diaspora—a macrocommunity of peoples of African descent living outside of a common reference territory. In *Seven Guitars*, the putatively mad Hedley channels a larger trans-and international black consciousness that exceeds the experience of being of black in Pittsburgh and the United States. He sees the expanse of the black world as his heritage, a cultural repository from which he freely draws to make sense of his historic conditions. Whether summoning the Queen of Sheba, Marcus Garvey, or Toussaint L' Ouverture, Hedley does so to defy his elementary school teacher's declaration that he will "amount to nothing [and] grow up to cut the white man's cane".

The cycle ends with *Radio Golf*, which is set in the 1990s against the quandaries posed by urban decay and renewal. Harmond Wilkes sacrifices his lucrative real estate career and mayoral aspirations to block the demolition of 1839 Wylie Avenue, Aunt Ester's long-standing house. He makes this decision in part out of deference to Ester, who moored the black community to the Hill District and who signified "African survivals" for black American culture as it came into its own. Saving Aunt Ester's house would mean saving the legacy of a person who represented continuity in a history of disruptions and disinheritances.

Readers of Wilson's plays will notice an unmistakable sense of disquiet in most of the characters, which is caused by spatial and cultural impermanence. One of the reasons Wilson sets his plays in hyperlocal and domestic spaces like kitchens, backyards, living rooms, cafés, and diners is because these spaces are sancta from the uncertainty and tentativeness of their lives as minoritized people who belong everywhere and nowhere, who are and are not American, who are and are not African, simultaneously rooted and itinerant. But they inhabit rings of communities that go out like concentric circles, from their local communities outward toward this thing called the "world".

World literature has its critics, of course. While I refuse to think of world literature defensively or apologetically, I always feel impelled to acknowledge these criticisms in academic forums, many of which invite productive discussions that can only strengthen world literature as an idea and an educational resource. They include the charge that world literature, like area studies, is a form of surveillance and that the reliance of undergraduate world literature curricula on translation sterilizes and domesticates other literatures for American consumption, erasing the very difference that makes them valuable (this view rests on unsound qualitative ideas about translation). Other critics argue that world literature poaches literary texts from elsewhere but grafts a critical apparatus and nomenclature onto them that are alien to the conditions of their own production. Older criticisms of world literature include the observation that it is Eurocentric. While this might have been true, "Eurocentric" is itself a category of diminishing returns because of its own vast omissions. Eastern and central European literatures hardly figured into that "Eurocentricism," nor, for that matter, did a lot of "western" European literary traditions (Norwegian, Dutch, Belgian, etc.). This is why the euphemism "NATO literatures" came to be. These criticisms may be dour and a little heavy-handed, but they are not patently wrong. Starting with the local is a way of allaying some of these concerns, if for no other reason than the fact that students will be conscious of their cultural bearings and the ways these will inform how they read their way outward, like Wilson's plays, toward and through the world.

In the past three decades, the world has come to be characterized by prefixes like inter-, poly-, multi-, hetero-, trans-, etc. World literature should be at the forefront of unpacking these prefixes and confronting their social implications. World literature has to marshal the tools and dispensations of literary education for all students, especially those students entering business, the sciences, or law. Those students, no less than we who make our life's work the reading and weaponizing of literature, will face the pitfalls of not possessing the cultural literacy literature can offer. World literature is neither an additive to the canon nor its abolition. It is a critical practice with targeted intellectual outcomes. It may not change the world, but it has the potential to reshape the way the world appears to a student. Teaching world literature does admittedly come with perils; it courts premature optimism by inviting students to trend toward "we're all the same after all" based on what they feel to be universals in the texts they read. But this is only a beginning. If students feel that they can at least sense the Other—to "imagine precisely", in the words of Amitav Ghosh—it can only lead to good things.

区域文学研究

心灵的反讽：诺瓦利斯诗学接受史

陆浩斌[*]

【摘要】 诺瓦利斯研究，甚或说德国浪漫主义美学研究自黑格尔以降至克罗齐，一直被置于"费希特—反讽"这一心灵剖析的谱系之中；而到了狄尔泰、卢卡奇时期，诺瓦利斯研究视域中开始鲜明地囊括了现代性这一维度，但同时又开始还原耶拿浪漫派尤其是诺瓦利斯思想的真相，被误读为唯情和断片的诗学得到了更理性与整全的发现。解读诺瓦利斯和耶拿浪漫派的心灵问题自身折射出了多重反讽。浪漫主义常被理解为了一个自立为与广义古典主义对观的自我立场，并且开启了现代主义的文学新浪潮。究竟浪漫主义是现代性混乱与自大的开端，抑或浪漫主义是结合了古典理念的对现代性的反思，这需要我们以严谨的态度向上回看，溯洄从之，在厘清德国早期浪漫派特别是诺瓦利斯诗学研究的接受史基础上回到事情本身。

【关键字】 诺瓦利斯；浪漫主义；反讽；心灵

Irony of Mind: The Acceptance History of Novalis Poetics

Haobin Lu

Abstract: The Study of Novalis, aka the aesthetic study the Germany

---

[*]【作者简介】陆浩斌，北京大学文学博士，山东大学文学院比较文学与世界文学研究所助理研究员。研究领域为莎士比亚、经典阐释与现代批评、比较文学与比较文化、政治哲学与思想史、跨学科研究等。

romanticism, from Hegel to Croce, is always included into the genealogy in mind analysis of "Ficite—Irony"; but during the period of Dilthey and Lukács, the vision of Novalis study begin to include modernity. Romanticism was always read as an anti-position of Classicism, and the beginning of modernism. But is romanticism the chaos of modernism or the reflection of modernity with classicism? Through the history of acceptance in Novalis study. The conception of early Germany romanticism becomes clear to thing itself.

Key words: Novalis; romanticism; irony; mind

18世纪末19世纪初的耶拿浪漫派诗人哲学家诺瓦利斯，正如每一位浪漫主义者那样，被人们评头论足而又绝少为人们所真正阅读与理解。浪漫主义似乎设立了一个与广义的古典主义对观的自我立场，同时又开启了现代主义的文学新浪潮。但事情是否果真如此简单地一分为二，则仍需更深入的研读与反思。要理解诺瓦利斯，我们当然首先要弄清楚我们已经理解了多少诺瓦利斯，其中又误解了多少和不理解多少诺瓦利斯。为此，一条路是通过他本人的生平著述，另一条路是通过后人对他的阐释研究。这两条路本应该是同一目的，而不当以现代人的骄傲自大误以为能够比作者更好地理解作者。退一步说，即便是站在历史的彼岸用后见之明宣扬比作者更理解作者，那前提依然是以作者的原义去理解作者，何况我们这里所说的不是随随便便的哪个作者，而是那些思想之复杂深刻会导致我们一不小心就误入歧途的真正的作家们。以严谨的态度向上回看，通过后见者的阶梯慢慢溯洄从之，我们才可能目击道存——回到事实本身。

诺瓦利斯的研究当从其同时代人说起。这里合适的开头，应当是诺瓦利斯的两位挚友蒂克与弗·施莱格尔在1802年最初编辑的两卷本诺瓦利斯作品选集（1846年又增添了第三卷）。最初的这版诺瓦利斯作品选集的主要问题所在是蒂克。蒂克的编辑与评价稍显随意而过于诗性。比如作为遗著出版的未完成小说《奥夫特尔丁根》，蒂克私自为第二部拟定了情节的发展并根据诺瓦利斯笔记编写了梗概附在后面。

蒂克的"编辑"很"浪漫",但其学术价值颇值争议。①

之后被编辑出版的诺瓦利斯作品选集还有 C. Meisner 与 Bruno Wille 的 1898 年版、E. Heilborn 的 1901 年 3 卷本和 J. Minor 的 1907 年 3 卷本。《海因里希·冯·奥夫特尔丁根》由 J. Schmidt 在 1876 年出版过单行本。J. M. Raich 在 1880 年编辑出版过诺瓦利斯的通信集。

再接着便是诺瓦利斯作品选集核心德文文本了,即 *Novalis Schriften*: *Die Werke Friedrich von Hardenbergs*。该文集由 Richard Samuel、Hans-Joachim Mähl 和 Gerhard Schulz 所编辑,并以六卷本形式出版于 Stuttgart: Kohlhammer Verlag。该版本简称"HKA",因为这一版本又被称作 Historiche-kritische ausgabe,也就是历史—批判版本的意思。这一版本亦一波三折,经历了数次编辑与再版,笔者目前所能搜集到的乃以相关研究最常引用的 1965—2005 年版次为准。HKA 第一卷内容为《诗作》(*Das Dichterische Werk*),第二卷为《哲学作品Ⅰ》(*Das philosophische Werk Ⅰ*),第三卷为《哲学作品Ⅱ》(*Das philosophische Werk Ⅱ*),第四卷为《日记、通信、同时代人的评议》(*Tagebücher*, *Briefwechsel*, *Zeitgenössische*),而第五、六两卷为 Hans-Joachim Mähl 最新取得并增补的相关材料。这一堪称标准的历史—批判版《诺瓦利斯文集》超越了前此所有的版本,之后有关诺瓦利斯研究的著述大部分都沿用这一版本。

比如 *Das Allgemeine Brouillon* 一书,此书的单行本便是从 HKA 第三卷的第 242—478 页抽取出来的,编者和正文前的导论作者仍为 Hans-Joachim Mähl。该单行本出版于 1993 年的 Hamburg: Felix Meiner Verlag。而 2000 年在 Paris: Allia 出版的法译本 *Le Brouillon général* 与 2007 年由 David W. Wood 翻译并出版于 State University of New York Press 的英文版 *Notes for a Romantic Encyclopaedia*: *Das Allgemeine Brouillon* 也毫无意外地以上述德文版本为底本。

---

① Géza von Molnár, *Romantic Vision*, *Ethical Context*: *Novalis and Artistic Autonomy*, Minneapolis: University of Minnesota Press, 1984, Introductory Remarks, xxxi;伍灵斯:《〈奥夫特尔丁根〉解析》,林克译,载刘小枫编《大革命与诗化小说——诺瓦利斯选集卷二》,华夏出版社 2008 年版,第 188 页。

HKA版本前的诺瓦利斯研究很难说有什么系统与整全可言。追本溯源，我们应当从黑格尔生前的上课讲义即死后被编辑出版为《哲学史讲演录》（1833）与《美学》（1835）开始说起。黑格尔在辩证地肯定了费希特返回自我意识的思想之后，又否定其自我的"空虚"、"有限性、个别性、非自在自为"，并谈到"精神"（Geist）的下一阶段应该充满自觉的精神性内容，而"自觉的自我与它的内容的统一，也就是仅仅直观其自觉的生命和直接知道这种统一即是真理的精神"。黑格尔又谈道："这种统一或精神后来在各种诗意的和预言式的、仰望式的倾向里，以夸大的形式表现出来，这些倾向都是从费希特的哲学里引申出来的。"① 这里，黑格尔谈的也就是德国早期浪漫派了。在点出浪漫派是夸大版的费希特思想之后，黑格尔从施莱格尔出发，点出了浪漫派对费希特主体以及超出主体的理论与实践——"讽刺"（Ironie，又译滑稽、反讽），这是施莱格尔自我定义的关键词，也是黑格尔评价早期浪漫派最重要的关键词，他自己做的解释如下：

> 主体知道自己在自身内是绝对，一切别的东西在主体看来都是虚幻的、由主体自己对正义、善等所作出的种种规定，它也善于对这些规定又去一个一个加以摧毁。主体可以嘲笑自己，但他只是虚幻的、伪善的和厚颜无耻的。讽刺善于掌握一切可能的内容；它并不严肃对待任何东西，而只是对一切形式开玩笑。②

在谈到诺瓦利斯时，黑格尔显然将诺瓦利斯的"蓝花"理解为一种主观性的"美的灵魂""对一个稳定的东西"的"想望仰慕之枕"。黑格尔认为这种主观性、内在性的"在自身内纺纱织布"会将主观性强调过头以至于"每每达到发狂的程度"，而"如果这种过度的主观

---

① ［德］黑格尔：《哲学史讲演录》第四卷，贺麟等译，商务印书馆1978年版，第335页。
② ［德］黑格尔：《哲学史讲演录》第四卷，贺麟等译，商务印书馆1978年版，第336页。

性是停留在思维里，那么，它便被束缚在反思的理智里绕圈子，而理智是永远对自己采取否定态度的"①。黑格尔肯定了前期浪漫派对古典艺术的赞扬与扬弃，并且认可了他们对于理念的接近，但总体说来还是认为早期浪漫派只是对费希特哲学"消极方面的片面引申"。② 黑格尔的"反讽"是真的很反讽了，这种反讽连带着可以将谢林的艺术哲学也一道推翻。然而谢林后来对黑格尔反讽自己"理智直观"（intellektuelle Anschauung）的回应却恰恰在于认为黑格尔的"逻辑学"有些过头，其逻辑学是无法顺利过渡到自然哲学的。③ 这可能也跟黑格尔将理智理解为"对自己采取否定态度"的否定哲学观相关。不过如果站在黑格尔主义的立场上来说的话，又可以认为他的精神是一种"具备形体的精神"（Embodied Spirit）。④ 这个问题很重大，因其直接关涉浪漫派哲学和唯心论哲学的内部之争以及后来受影响而衍生的诸多对浪漫派误解的观念。

这里首需认识到的便是黑格尔"反讽"观的深远影响了，后来的学者即便是没有直接读过黑格尔相关美学观点的，也或多或少具有类似的批评观。与黑格尔死后的授课讲稿出版同时，海涅便出版了德文版的《论浪漫派》（1833，1836）。⑤ 在是书中，海涅一反斯达尔夫人（其文《论德国》同样具有很深广的思想史意义）的观点，在开篇便提到"德国浪漫派与在法国人们用这个名称所表示的含意是迥然不同的，德国浪漫派的倾向也完全不同于法国浪漫派的倾向"，接着他便非常武断地说道，德国浪漫派并不是别的，就是"中世纪诗情的复活"。⑥ 他首先肯定了耶拿浪漫派的"新的美学训条"，亦即在美学批评上的

---

① [德]黑格尔：《哲学史讲演录》第四卷，贺麟等译，商务印书馆1978年版，第338页。
② 朱立元：《黑格尔对费希特和浪漫派的批判》，《学习与探索》1998年第1期。
③ [德]谢林：《近代哲学史》，先刚译，北京大学出版社2016年版，第151—197页。
④ [英]斯蒂芬·霍尔盖特：《黑格尔导论：自由、真理与历史》，丁三东译，商务印书馆2013年版，第255—287页。
⑤ 《论浪漫派》最初以《德国文学现状，继斯塔尔夫人论德国》为题发表在法文杂志上。《论浪漫派》中译本有张玉书、孙坤荣、薛华三种，兹取薛华译本《浪漫派》为准，该翻译比较新，且注释详尽。
⑥ [德]海涅：《浪漫派》，薛华译，上海人民出版社2003年版，第10—12页。

巨大功绩——"从评论过去的艺术作品和给未来的艺术作品开药方开始"①。在谈到诺瓦利斯时，他将其与霍夫曼作了比较，他肯定了诺瓦利斯是"真正的浪漫派诗人"，至于霍夫曼，"真正有学识和有诗才的人都无意向他领教什么，他们觉得诺瓦利斯可爱得多"，不过，他也同时承认霍夫曼抓住了"地上的现实"，诺瓦利斯"却总是带着他的理想形象在蔚蓝太空漂游"。②海涅还独具慧眼地点出了诺瓦利斯的《奥夫特尔丁根》这部具有象征意味的长篇"诗作"、"片段"、小说和但丁的《神曲》一样，"意在赞美天上地下的一切事物"③。而海涅由诺瓦利斯的"病态"引发的诗学结论更是值得思考：

> 但是我们有权这样来评论吗？我们，我们这些人自己不也不太健康吗？特别是现在，文学界看起来就像一处大病院？或许诗情就是人类的一种疾病，就像珍珠本是可怜的贝壳患病的产物？④

关于19世纪的"论（耶拿）浪漫派"也许同样需要提到的还有克尔凯郭尔的《论反讽概念：以苏格拉底为主线》（1841）。也许是囿于博士学位论文阶段尚未脱出黑格尔影响的原因，这部博士学位论文并没有后来卢卡奇早期的那种克尔凯郭尔化的黑格尔主义风格，倒毋宁是一篇黑格尔主义化的克尔凯郭尔文章。在此文中，他认为费希特的无限性虽然解放了思维，却是"消极的""毫不具有有限性的""毫无内容的"无限性，如审美无限性就是"为创造而不断创造"。总之，"康德缺乏消极的无限性，而费希特缺乏积极的无限性"⑤。当然，费

---

① ［德］海涅：《浪漫派》，薛华译，上海人民出版社2003年版，第31页。当然我们也可以看出来与黑格尔的区别，海涅承认对未来的艺术的展望，而黑格尔自然是抱着"艺术终结论"的观点去考量的。
② ［德］海涅：《浪漫派》，薛华译，上海人民出版社2003年版，第164—167页。
③ ［德］海涅：《浪漫派》，薛华译，上海人民出版社2003年版，第168页。
④ ［德］海涅：《浪漫派》，薛华译，上海人民出版社2003年版，第167页。
⑤ ［丹］索伦·克尔凯郭尔：《论反讽概念：以苏格拉底为主线》，汤晨溪译，中国社会科学出版社2005年版，第220页。

希特后来其实摒弃了自己的这种观点，但这种早期费希特立场与德国早期浪漫派的反讽确实紧密关联。而且费希特构建的世界是系统的构建，而克尔凯郭尔认为施莱格尔与蒂克却想"无中生有地创造一个世界"。这种过分的作为"主观性的第二个因次"的主观性是不合理的，"黑格尔对他的态度是理所当然的"①。克尔凯郭尔并没有直接提到诺瓦利斯，这有点儿意思。到了19世纪末，另一位黑格尔主义者鲍桑葵的《美学史》（1892）便直接从黑格尔谈到叔本华，浪漫派美学直接化作了第十二章"客观唯心主义——谢林和黑格尔"中关于黑格尔论述艺术类型的"浪漫型"这一小段落了。②

历史进入20世纪。我们要从另一位黑格尔主义者克罗齐的《美学》（1902）说起。强调对浪漫主义嚆矢先声的维柯是克罗齐的巨大洞见之一。在《美学的历史》中的第九章"唯心主义的美学"中，克罗齐区分了"席勒的审慎和浪漫主义者的不审慎"。③ 他也非常黑格尔—克尔凯郭尔—鲍桑葵式地将浪漫派美学置于费希特—反讽这一谱系之中。克罗齐认为费希特"并没有使幻想和艺术活动即美学问题发生关系"而只是让审美领域介于认识和道德的中间领域，"从一开始就作为表象和伦理理想表象的完满性消融在道德论之中了"④。而在滑稽说阐释覆盖下的耶拿浪漫派中，克罗齐将诺瓦利斯归为费希特的"信徒"，并说他"竟热望有一个魔幻的唯心主义，一个以自我极短暂的行为创造和实现我们梦幻的艺术"。有一笔非提不可的是，克罗齐认为只是在谢林那里，"才真正出现了浪漫主义的和美学中重新复活的有意识的新柏拉

---

① ［丹］索伦·克尔凯郭尔：《论反讽概念：以苏格拉底为主线》，汤晨溪译，中国社会科学出版社2005年版，第222页。
② ［英］鲍桑葵：《美学史》，张今译，商务印书馆1985年版，第446—448页。
③ ［意］克罗齐：《美学的历史》，王天清译，商务印书馆2015年版，第140页。克罗齐的《美学》全名为《作为表现的科学和一般语言学的美学》，该书分为两部分，第一部分为《美学原理》，曾由朱光潜翻译并于1958年出版于作家出版社，第二部分为《美学的历史》，即上书。
④ ［意］克罗齐：《美学的历史》，王天清译，商务印书馆2015年版，第143页。如此一来，费希特的美学思想被克罗齐完全置放在了前《判断力批判》的水平面上，这其中大有问题，可予以进一步分析。

图主义的第一次伟大的哲学肯定"①。这真正出现的浪漫主义与新柏拉图主义的肯定到底是什么,我们在此先发一问。还有,克罗齐的神话、直觉等观念在这个部分也许也是不充分构成克罗齐美学史观的。

狄尔泰的《体验与诗》(1905)以其独创的精神科学入手分析莱辛、歌德、诺瓦利斯与荷尔德林。他认为荷尔德林埋头于古希腊文化,诺瓦利斯和蒂克埋头于中世纪,两者看似并不同道,荷尔德林也非浪漫派团体,可我们却发现,荷尔德林所复制的新柏拉图主义的希腊文化,恰好同中世纪有很近的亲缘关系。如此说来,荷尔德林同后二人的关系是不会比施莱格尔兄弟同后二者的关系更疏远的。在1770年至1800年的德国文学与哲学运动中,狄尔泰将康德和莱辛归为第一代,歌德、席勒、费希特归为第二代,耶拿浪漫派和黑格尔、谢林归为第三代(荷尔德林应当也是这一代)。而在第三代里,我们需要在"进一步确定的意义上使用浪漫派这个流行的名称来标志这种世界观,如果我不想干脆摆脱这个名称而彻底结束半个多世纪以来对这个名称的滥用的话"。是对自然的探讨、对基督教思想的变形、对澄清"在歌德、康德和费希特之后的一代人中出现的世界观的若干最重要的动机"将狄尔泰引向诺瓦利斯,引向使许多人动心的希望。②而他正确地看到了诺瓦利斯一生"以诸学科和诗艺为基础"的方向,并全面地点出了诺瓦利斯将思想交流、爱与宗教普遍综合为魔法、神话与科学观的做法,而且诺瓦利斯和谢林两人都在用费希特的体系的眼睛看自然:"相同的条件使他们产生了相近的泛神论的形式",而诺瓦利斯"关于诸精神科学的思想具有杰出的原创性"。③狄尔泰提醒我们浪漫派并非铁板一块,其内部的方向有可能完全是言人人殊的。这无疑具有以差异性乃至延异性来解研究浪漫派中过度强调共同性之毒的功效④,而且对于一个强调精神科学史

---

① [意]克罗齐:《美学的历史》,王天清译,商务印书馆2015年版,第143—144页。
② [德]狄尔泰:《体验与诗:莱辛·歌德·诺瓦利斯·荷尔德林》,胡其鼎译,生活·读书·新知三联书店2003年版,第223页。
③ [德]狄尔泰:《体验与诗:莱辛·歌德·诺瓦利斯·荷尔德林》,胡其鼎译,生活·读书·新知三联书店2003年版,第227、237—238、250—251页。
④ 而比如到了韦勒克时代,洛夫乔伊的唯名论又将问题进行了反转。

的思想家来说，狄尔泰的这种不拘泥的研究反省力是值得我们敬佩的。在"他的世界观的形成"这部分，狄尔泰开头便点出了本书所要发挥的思想："哈登贝格要在一部百科全书里让已经获得的全部观点服从于当代哲学的基本思想。这是他同时代的哲学家内心深处的热切要求……哈登贝格的笔记包含着这样一个整体的思想萌芽。"① 沿着这一方向，我们可以看到施莱尔马赫、叔本华，又特别是谢林与黑格尔。诺瓦利斯的笔记是断片的，但其思想绝非仅仅如此。狄尔泰可谓前 HKA 时代最敏锐的诺瓦利斯研究者，我们自然可以怀疑这是否是狄尔泰的诗性史学使然，但在怀疑之前，我们也当先怀疑我们本身对耶拿浪漫派而尤其是对哈登贝格本人又了解几何。这里用狄尔泰本人评述诺瓦利斯的一段话来总结我们关于诺瓦利斯研究学术史的第一个至关重要的路标吧：

> ……他对刺激、激动和冲动之间的比例关系进行实验，他较深地触及错觉对于我们的意志的历史的意义；他认为，满足是对一个虚妄的问题的解答，"一种错觉的自焚"。他密切注意关于这些错觉的意义的想法，却不赞同悲观主义的结论，叔本华后来从他那里引出了这样的结论。一篇短小的优美的对话反倒包含着对立的浪漫派的结论。应像看待一种美好的天才的错觉、像看待一部戏剧那样去看待生命；接着，在充分意识到有时间性的错觉（此即生命）的情况下我们已经想到了绝对兴致和永恒。②

当然，历史并不会因为个别人的洞见而瞬间被改写，另一位著名的文学史家勃兰兑斯的《十九世纪文学主流》（1906）给我们的印象便是如此。皇皇六卷本的《十九世纪文学主流》中的第二卷便是《德国的浪漫派》。通过与丹麦文学的比较，勃兰兑斯肯定了德国文学中

---

① ［德］狄尔泰：《体验与诗：莱辛·歌德·诺瓦利斯·荷尔德林》，胡其鼎译，生活·读书·新知三联书店 2003 年版，第 249 页。哈登贝格是诺瓦利斯的本名。

② ［德］狄尔泰：《体验与诗：莱辛·歌德·诺瓦利斯·荷尔德林》，胡其鼎译，生活·读书·新知三联书店 2003 年版，第 255—256 页。

生活多于艺术，其以浪漫主义开端而活跃在最深沉的情绪之中，陶醉在种种感觉里面，努力想解决问题，不断创造着随即加以破坏的形式。笔者这里所取的是他比较温和的说法。浪漫主义当然是雅努斯的两面体。一方面，德国浪漫派有着反驳启蒙主义过度理性主义的功用（后来的以赛亚·柏林将之发扬），不过总体而言，勃兰兑斯是比较倾向于另一方面海涅式地将德国浪漫主义视为极端倾向于个人无限性的过度放纵与感伤的。而作为纯粹之王的死亡诗人诺瓦利斯当然是勃兰兑斯首要攻击对象。但是比如勃兰兑斯对诺瓦利斯的数学观的固化看法本身就是误读。诺瓦利斯处处彰显的两极恰恰是围绕着匮乏的圆心而画出一个个无限直径的圆周，现实与理想、个人与集体等。德意志浪漫派当然更重视思想、意志、直观而非英法之行动，但文学不就该兼收并蓄吗？况且恰恰在诺瓦利斯这里，事情的两极达到了最大的分裂与综合。重复一遍，分裂，然后综合、同一，如谢林，似黑格尔。勃兰兑斯还是近乎精确地指出了德国浪漫派的关键词的，即"心灵"（Gemüt，心绪）：

>……我们将会看到，这种心灵在浪漫主义时期具备什么性质，它在浪漫主义者中间那个首先称得上心灵诗人的人身上，即在诺瓦利斯身上，具备什么形式和气质。
>
>德国人所谓的"心灵"（Gemüt），简直无法用别的语言来传达。心灵是德国人的领域。它是内在的炉火，内在的熔锅。……
>……
>
>而今在浪漫主义者身上，心灵发生了这样的变化：歌德所谓的"灵魂的热"变成了达到沸点的炽热，用烈焰烧光了一切坚固的形式、形象和思想。浪漫主义诗人的光荣就在于他内心燃烧着的最炽烈、最激昂的感情。诺瓦利斯做任何事情，总是倾其全力以赴。最深沉、最放纵的感情就是他的原则。①

---

① [丹]勃兰兑斯：《十九世纪文学主流（第二分册）：德国的浪漫派》，刘半九译，人民文学出版社1981年版，第179—180页。

之所以说勃兰兑斯"近乎精确",是因为还有人更精确,那便是卢卡奇的《心灵与形式》(1910)和《小说理论》(1916)。在这里,卢卡奇运用的"心灵"乃 die Seele 而非 das Gemüt。后者在勃兰兑斯这里与思维、意志无关而强调感觉、感情,而前者在卢卡奇这里更体现出心灵、灵魂的精神的一面,虽然也有情感因素,但又与思维、意志互为一体,在我看来倒是更接近耶拿浪漫派尤其是诺瓦利斯这位诗哲本人的气质的。这里我们有幸遇到了深受狄尔泰精神科学与现代阐释学影响的、尚处在克尔凯郭尔化的黑格尔主义者阶段的卢卡奇。卢卡奇对诺瓦利斯的评价处处回荡着将心比心的理解:

> 诺瓦利斯是浪漫派中唯一的真正的诗人,唯有在他一人身上,浪漫主义的全部精神化作了歌,只有他表现了那种精神。其余的人,如果还算是诗人的话,也只是浪漫主义诗人;浪漫主义给了他们新的主旨,改变了他们发展的方向或丰富了它,但是,在他们完全脱离了浪漫主义之后,他们也还是诗人。诺瓦利斯的生活和作品——没办法,这是句老生常谈,但是这是切中要言的唯一表达——形成了一个不可分割的整体,作为这样一个整体它们是浪漫主义的一个象征;似乎它们的置入生活、迷失方向的诗在被生活所解救后,又一次成为纯净、清澈的诗。在他的作品里,浪漫主义的临时起跑道仅仅是起跑道,浪漫派对于统一的意愿必定总是停留在断片形式的一个意愿,再没有什么地方有比诺瓦利斯的作品中的这种意愿更断片化的了,但就在他刚刚开始创作自己的真正作品之时,他却要命归黄泉了。尽管如此,他是唯一的这样一种人,其生活留下了美丽如画的一堆碎石,人们从中挖出了美妙的断片,并满怀惊奇地问,这些断片构成的建筑原貌是什么样子。他所有的途径都通向一个目标,他所有的问题都得到了解答。每一个幽灵、每一个浪漫主义的 Fata morgana 都获得了坚固的肉身,只有他不受磷火的引

诱陷入无底的沼泽，因为他的双眼能把每一簇磷火看作是星光，他还能展开双翅去追随它。他遇上了最残酷的命运，只有他才能在这场斗争中成长起来。在所有搜寻对生活的控制力的浪漫派人物中，他是唯一实际的生活艺术家。①

本段起到为全文点题张目的性质，全段摘录是有必要的。这里至少体现了卢卡奇对诺瓦利斯洞见的以下几点：1）诺瓦利斯是唯一或者说首要体现德国早期浪漫派精神与心灵的诗人；2）诺瓦利斯的生活和作品构成的整体及其"蓝花"是浪漫主义的不二象征；3）浪漫派是流于断片形式的，而诺瓦利斯本可以或者说正在超越断片形式的构筑建筑过程之中；4）诺瓦利斯的道路和问题构成了一个全面的系统或者说架构，而不只是星群，或者说恰恰是星丛；5）诺瓦利斯在其命运中寻求控制生活与实际操作的路径，用一定意义上身为卢卡奇的老师狄尔泰的话来说，要么不用浪漫派或浪漫主义去概括，非要如此概括的话，必要首先理解诺瓦利斯的"心灵与形式"不可。

诺瓦利斯同施莱格尔兄弟一样，是理解最早的浪漫主义文学运动不可或缺的一位，他与施莱格尔兄弟的同一与差异是最开始的浪漫主义心灵的反讽。至20世纪初叶，前 HKA 时代的诺瓦利斯研究，可以概括为黑格尔嚆矢先声、狄尔泰栉风沐雨、卢卡奇筚路蓝缕②，余则

---

① ［匈］卢卡奇：《心灵与形式》（选译），载《卢卡奇早期文选》，张亮、吴勇立译，南京大学出版社2004年版，第180—181页；Georg Lukacs, *Soul and Form*, trans. Anna Bostock, Cambridge: The MIT Press, 1974, pp. 53 - 54。

② 关于卢卡奇，在陈恕林的《论德国浪漫派》中，他代表了批判卢卡奇强调启蒙运动与浪漫派"对立论"的阐释立场，这种立场是很可以理解的。因为卢卡奇在《理性的毁灭》（1954）等较后期西方马克思主义化的著作中确实有越来越强的早期就具有的批判浪漫派非理性的倾向，而且卢卡奇本身就认为浪漫派是一个较为消极的派别，何况卢卡奇在这个阶段所谈的浪漫派乃一个包含了诺瓦利斯—早期浪漫派—全部德国早中晚期浪漫派的三重大集合，那自然另当别论。而笔者这里拈出卢卡奇来专论，也是为了强调精神科学与现代阐释学烛照下的一种20世纪初新兴解读耶拿浪漫派之诺瓦利斯其人的转向。参见《卢卡契文学论文选》第一卷，范大灿编选，人民文学出版社1986年版，第48—63页；陈恕林《论德国浪漫派》，上海社会科学院出版社2016年版，第141—155页。

可圈可点而又有所偏差,反讽地解读诺瓦利斯与耶拿浪漫派的心灵过程随后又遭到了心灵问题本身在进一步还原中所绽开的反讽折射。这一作为心灵的反讽的诺瓦利斯诗学接受史旅途颠簸,至于后来的 HKA,则是玉汝于成了。①

---

① 在狄尔泰与卢卡奇等的诺瓦利斯研究视域中,无疑已经开始鲜明地囊括了现代性这一维度。20 世纪之后的诺瓦利斯研究以本雅明、高尔基、韦勒克等诸家各自迥异的观点为代表,而诺瓦利斯在中国的接受史也十分具有思考价值,限于篇幅与论旨的考虑,笔者将对此相关的进一步探讨放在其他文章之中。

《天空落幕时》中的后人类肯定伦理与共同体渴望

郑松筠　张生珍[*]

【摘要】 当代英国童书作家菲尔·厄尔的小说《天空落幕时》的故事发生在第二次世界大战期间，战火中充斥着对立、毁灭和无望，然而作者却通过对动物园、园中人和留守银背大猩猩的书写，刻画出特殊生命力与普遍生命力的联结，探求未来的希望之光。本文参照哲学家布拉伊多蒂后人类批评理论中的肯定伦理，探究小说中人与非人在动态生成的当下生命宽度的拓展，以及书中人在面对战争冲突的劫难，从消极封闭向积极创造的转变过程。小说通过后人类语境的构建，挑战了霸权、独尊和自以为是的思想，并在直面冲突黑暗、寻找光明前路时，迸发出构建肯定、积极、开放共同体的渴望。

【关键词】《天空落幕时》；后人类；肯定伦理；共同体

When the Sky Falls: Posthuman Affirmative Ethics and the Eagerness for Community

Songyun Zheng, Shengzhen Zhang

Abstract: This article examines the posthuman writing of Phil Earle's

---

[*]【作者简介】郑松筠，女，上海交通大学文学博士，北京语言大学博士后、上海海事大学外国语学院讲师。研究领域为英国文学、比较文学、翻译研究。张生珍，女，山东大学文学博士，北京语言大学英语学院教授。研究领域为英美文学、外国儿童文学和文学翻译等。

When the Sky Falls in which it depicts a story happened during World War Two. A story permeated with a feeling of hopelessness and dominated by dualistic opposition at first glance, it actually presents Earle's exploration of an interconnected *bio* and *zoe*, thereby seeking the hope even in the utmost melancholic situation through his portrayal of the zoo, its keepers and the silverback gorilla living there. This article, by referring to the affirmative ethics elucidated by Rosi Braidotti in her discussion of posthuman critical theory, explores the life extension of both human and non-human which, being interdependent, live in a present that is dynamic and becoming, and illuminates how people enable a positive transformation from negativity to creativity even when confronting with disasters like wars and conflicts. The posthuman discourse constructed by Earle challenges the hegemonic, exclusive and privileged thinking, and articulates an eagerness for a community with a shared future, which is affirmative, positive and open-ended and is regarded as a hopeful possibility which can replace the unpleasant reality tormented by binary and splitting forces.

Key words: *When the Sky Falls*; Posthuman; Affirmative Ethics; Community of a Shared Future

菲尔·厄尔（Phil Earle）为英国当代著名儿童文学作家，被卡内基奖得主、著名儿童文学作家麦高恩誉为最优秀的童书作家之一。厄尔的作品《天空落幕时》[1] 荣获2022年英国图书奖最佳儿童小说，而他曾经的工作经历也为这部巅峰之作的完成提供了灵感和动力。厄尔曾为戏剧治疗师并接触过很多患有阅读障碍的儿童，其作品《小心空隙》[2] 的排版、字体和纸张更是专为阅读障碍儿童特别设计，其初心为希冀能让更多儿童走入阅读的空间。《天空落幕时》不但继承了这

---

[1] Phil Earle, *When the Sky Falls*, London: Andersen Press, 2021.
[2] Phil Earle, *Mind the Gap*, Edinburgh: Barrington Stoke, 2017.

种包容性，书写了一位阅读障碍儿童主人公约瑟夫的故事，更在战争的背景下模糊了人与动物、儿童与成人的界限，呼应着意大利哲学家布拉伊多蒂后人类视角下的共同体之探，以及"世界现在需要什么"的发问。① 小说中的动物园，对约瑟夫而言如父如友的银背大猩猩阿多尼斯，这些看似与"人"无关的事物却在二战法西斯消泯不同性的炮火下，反衬出后人类肯定伦理（affirmative ethics）中对世界为共同整体之反思。

《天空落幕时》原作的英文题目为 When the Sky Falls，若从直译的角度而言，则为"当天塌下来的时候"②，这一表达恰可用来形容布拉伊多蒂言下"人"的焦虑。其中有面对人类纪时代如气候变化、核威胁等危机心生的恐惧以及情绪间充斥的疲惫与无望③，正如在厄尔小说的开篇，男孩约瑟夫面对战乱中城市的疮痍，同样感慨"没有希望"④，也让这部仿佛书写过去的小说与当今的焦虑形成呼应。读到书中人、动物、一切在战争中承受的伤痛，《儿童图书中心会刊》评论员贝里林德感慨这是一部"深度忧郁"的小说，其中弥漫着遗弃、霸凌与不幸⑤。然而，恰恰是厄尔笔下硝烟中的动物园，成就了主人公约瑟夫的后人类认知，帮助他实现了对自我和世界认识的一步步改变，并从以自我为中心的封闭观念中、非此即彼的敌对中走出来，在人与动物融合的一元整体里实现与自我的和解，在对战争的抨击中迸发出强烈的共同体渴望。主人公约瑟夫从封闭排他到开放包容的转变，让故事中的压抑、分裂、焦虑转化为释然、凝聚与希望，在人对自我主

---

① Rosi Braidotti, "Affirmative Ethics and Generative Life", *Deleuze and Guattari Studies*, Vol. 13, No. 4, November 2019, p. 464.

② 小说 *When the Sky Falls* 中文译本的题目为"天空落幕时"，本文沿用该译名，同时，从"when the sky falls"的英文含义来看，原题目也透露出德军空袭、战争残酷、暗无天日的含义，犹如天塌下来一般。

③ Rosi Braidotti, "'We' Are in This Together, but We Are Not One and the Same", *Journal of Bioethical Inquiry*, Vol. 17, No. 4, December 2020, p. 465.

④ ［英］菲尔·厄尔：《天空落幕时》，胡雪婷译，中信出版集团2021年版，第8页。

⑤ Natalie Berglind, "*When the Sky Falls* by Phil Earle（review）", *Bulletin of the Center for Children's Books*, Vol. 75, No. 8, April 2022, p. 248.

体认知"质的飞跃"中描绘出联结所有生命的共同体,在后人类的转向中通过"创造力和能动的伦理关系","让人性重新以肯定方式更新自我"①。

本文围绕主人公约瑟夫的三重转变,从布拉伊多蒂后人类肯定伦理的视角探究小说中"当下"、"陌生化"与"我们"的内涵,说明约瑟夫与银背大猩猩阿多尼斯关系从敌到友再到亲人的转变,体现出厄尔在面对灾难、战祸、离散等人类纪的焦虑时对共同体的肯定与渴望。

一 "愚蠢的猴子":消极与积极的"当下"

从表面上看,厄尔小说中的"当下"(present)具有很强的不确定性,深陷二战的人们需要每日面对不可预知的变化,或许这一秒的当下在下一秒的空袭中就会灰飞烟灭。在这样仿佛极端无望的现实中,厄尔则通过动物园的存在阐明了"当下"更深层的内涵。12岁的约瑟夫在父亲入伍出征两个月后,从约克郡来到伦敦,与其祖母年轻时照顾过的病人法雷利夫人一起生活。法雷利夫人在战火纷飞中守护着家族经营的动物园,同时肩负起约瑟夫监护人的责任。因食物短缺、空袭频繁,动物园中留下了少许无法转移的动物,其中就有被约瑟夫称为"愚蠢的猴子"的银背大猩猩阿多尼斯。阿多尼斯与约瑟夫一样,承受着家人离散的痛苦,但约瑟夫听完阿多尼斯的遭遇后,却无法将其与自身联系起来,"愚蠢"之论发乎于当时的约瑟夫以"人"或自我为中心理解事物的执拗偏见。根据他当时的理解,人与动物间的关系是封闭僵化的,而他对"当下"的理解同样如此。在初到这座城市的约瑟夫心里,"当下"是固执、静态的存在,反衬出约瑟夫面对失去家人与离开祖国双重创伤下的消极与被动,以及深陷自我封闭空间中的迷茫。回顾过去,他看到的是父亲出征、母亲弃己而去、祖母的嫌弃,眼前则是陌生的监护人、寒冷的冬天、短缺的物资和随时都可

---

① [意] 罗西·布拉伊多蒂:《后人类》,宋根成译,河南大学出版社2016年版,第288页。

能响起的防空警报，他本人夹在过去与当下之中，在无处可寻认同感的迷茫中陷于分裂的空间里，心中溢满着对自我、对他人、对一切的"消极激情"（negative passion）。

"消极激情"的概念源自布拉伊多蒂对肯定伦理对立面的论述，其特点是禁锢、封闭，具有道德上、认知上和情感上的"强烈乏味性"，能够损害自我与其他人和事物间建立内在联系的能力，降低自我与世界之间的关联。① 需要说明，布拉伊多蒂所述的"消极"并非与心理学上的情感直接相关，同理，她所提出的肯定伦理虽然又名"快乐伦理"（joyful ethics/ethics of joy）②，但其中的"快乐"不可单纯理解为心理学意义上的情感，而是强调后人类视角下横贯的、非人的力量所产生的积极影响。③ 这种消极激情与虚无相连④却与真实无关，因为正如英国哲学家默多克所言，真实之人的爱体现在对不同性的尊重中，而消极激情所带来的仅是对立与封闭下否定一切的敌视。或许，身在1941年、备受战火和离散煎熬的约瑟夫，作为一个12岁的孩子憎恨、抗拒眼前的一切是可以理解、可以原谅的。他每日几乎都与愤怒和抗拒为盟，断定身为大猩猩的阿多尼斯"显然不太喜欢他"，就像"生命中的其他人"一样厌恶他。⑤ 在伦敦的第一个晚上，约瑟夫感觉自己的房间像一个"钉死的棺材"⑥，而他本人也在否定一切的封闭循环中以憎恶回应周围的一切，甚至在消极激情的裹挟下，尝试以麻木不仁的方式对待眼前的战争和生命。

---

① Rosi Braidotti and Maria Hlavajova, *Posthuman Glossary*, London：Bloomsbury Publishing, 2018, p. 222.
② 在布拉伊多蒂与赫拉瓦乔娃合编的《后人类词典》中，收录了一条"ethics of joy"，周伟薇和王峰在《朝向共同体的后人类快乐伦理》[《华东师范大学学报》（哲学社会科学版）2022年第3期]一文中，将其翻译为"快乐伦理"，此处沿用该译名。
③ Rosi Braidotti and Maria Hlavajova, *Posthuman Glossary*, London：Bloomsbury Publishing, 2018, p. 221.
④ Rosi Braidotti, "Affirmative Ethics and Generative Life", *Deleuze and Guattari Studies*, Vol. 13, No. 4, November 2019, p. 468.
⑤ [英] 菲尔·厄尔：《天空落幕时》，胡雪婷译，中信出版集团2021年版，第29页。
⑥ [英] 菲尔·厄尔：《天空落幕时》，胡雪婷译，中信出版集团2021年版，第15页。

然而，厄尔创作的张力就体现在小说对动物园和阿多尼斯的书写中。这并非一般意义上的动物园，而是因战争被迫关闭、随时可能受到空袭、其中的生命随时可能遭到死亡威胁的一个场域，换言之，是常人眼中备受迫害、饱经灾祸的存在。布拉伊多蒂评述称，当年荷兰哲学家斯宾诺莎就是在风雨飘摇、生活艰难的背景下创作了《伦理学》，该书不仅为法国哲学家德勒兹的肯定主义之源，同时也极大影响了她本人对后人类理论的阐释。肯定伦理中的要义之一是，其并非为了理想化而将现实涂上浪漫的色彩，而是在直面苦难、暴力和伤痛的过程中，在二元对立模式之外，思索处理灾祸、苦难的可能性，探寻将心中憧憬的理想转化为现实的前路。伤痛、灾难仿佛是17世纪的斯宾诺莎彼时面对的当下，然而从肯定伦理的角度可以看出，若能从困苦中憧憬未来，在困难中探究前路，当下就不是一个被动、既定的概念，而是处于动态生成之中。在《肯定伦理与生成生活》一文里，布拉伊多蒂重墨探讨了"当下"的含义。从肯定性思维的视角来看，当下为一个生成的过程，是时间连续体的一部分[1]，无法与过去完全割裂开来，与未来的可能性之间也存在关联。当下有两种不同的性质，其一为"现实"（the actual），其二为"虚拟"（the virtual）。现实的当下指明我们是什么、我们不再是什么，而虚拟的当下则指向我们能够生成什么，这也让当下的概念不再平面，而是拥有了多层、多向度的特征。[2] 正因如此，哪怕身处灾难、困苦中，若能以积极、肯定的态度认知当下，就有改变现状的可能性。

理解了当下的内涵，就不难明白，为何厄尔当年听到二战中曼彻斯特动物园的故事后无法释怀，甚至将其拓展为一本小说。厄尔笔下的约瑟夫善良、聪慧，却因身患阅读障碍症长期承受着他人平面化的解读，被动地接收着别人为他贴上的"懒""笨"标签，他自己也在委屈、无

---

[1] Rosi Braidotti, "Affirmative Ethics and Generative Life", *Deleuze and Guattari Studies*, Vol. 13, No. 4, November 2019, p. 465.

[2] Rosi Braidotti, "Affirmative Ethics and Generative Life", *Deleuze and Guattari Studies*, Vol. 13, No. 4, November 2019, p. 465.

助和失望中放弃了在当下寻求转变,反而以敌对的姿态看待一切。换言之,小说伊始约瑟夫理解的当下,并非真实也并非虚拟,因为他根本不了解真正的自己,也从未用发展的眼光展望自我未来的模样。战争从五官感觉和心灵寄托两方面让他无所适从,而厄尔则通过将动物园引入战争的背景中,帮助约瑟夫打开认知当下的心门。战争为一个特别的场域,其中人和非人的界限因杀伐、武器、残疾而变得模糊,同时,当提及战争中失去的生命,这"生命"二字的指涉对象通常是人,但当人在战争中守护动物园,则受威胁、受保护对象的范畴则进一步扩大,包含人和动物在内的所有生命。书中对生命的诠释呼应着布拉伊多蒂《后人类》中的论述,即生命不是某一物种的专属财产①,而是互动开放的过程。从这个意义上可以认为,书中银背大猩猩阿多尼斯的重要性并非约瑟夫可以比拟,因为约瑟夫正是在与阿多尼斯相识、相知、亲近最后相互守候的过程中,才逐渐开始理解自我,也是阿多尼斯的信任让他敞开心扉,探寻他之前从未思考过的、感到心灰意冷的未来。

　　因此,阿多尼斯对于约瑟夫而言,不仅是一位朋友,更像一位亲人。它能让约瑟夫思绪混乱时平静下来,在他遭受同学欺凌时伸出援手,在他父亲牺牲后抚平他的伤痛,甚至在最后空袭战乱中守护在男孩身边,承受了将其视为"野兽"的人类射来的所有子弹。作为孩子,约瑟夫对母亲的遗弃难以释怀,而父亲入伍离开则让他的爱转化为愤怒和绝望。作为父亲,阿多尼斯在二战中经历了孩子夭折,妻子因战乱被迫离开的苦楚,每日在自己的巢穴中"暗自伤心"。② 两人相似的经历,让他们成为彼此的依靠,也燃起了约瑟夫在面对黑暗时在当下寻觅希望的勇气。因此,是阿多尼斯的出现、行为和爱让约瑟夫逐渐超越了消极激情,让他在肯定的观照下逐渐变得积极、怀抱希望,甚至能够"从废墟中……汲取灵感,继续前行"。③ 然而,这种积极激

---

① Rosi Braidotti, *The Posthuman*, Cambridge & Malden: Polity Press, 2013, p. 60.
② [英]菲尔·厄尔:《天空落幕时》,胡雪婷译,中信出版集团2021年版,第65页。
③ Rosi Braidotti, "Affirmative Ethics and Generative Life", *Deleuze and Guattari Studies*, Vol. 13, No. 4, November 2019, p. 470.

情却来之不易，若要打破现有观念、实现积极可能，其中一个重要决定因素在于能够让自我与看似理所当然的认知保持距离。这种与主导视界保持的批判性距离，布拉伊多蒂称为"陌生化策略"（strategy of defamiliarization）。约瑟夫在与阿多尼斯的相处中，经历了对自我所持偏见的一次次陌生化，在超越原有认知的过程中，反思自我和他人作为"人"的盲目傲慢，也在后人类的语境中形成了新的认识。

二 "大猩猩是真的想帮忙吗？"：将优越感陌生化

从"愚蠢的猴子"的诟骂到"大猩猩是真的想帮忙吗？"的思索，反映出约瑟夫心理的变化。这种改变的发生伴随着两种相向而行的转变，即"人"对自我和对其他生命存在的重新认知。之所以说相向而行，是因为人对自我的认知是逐渐从傲慢降为谦虚，而对其他生命的认知则从贬抑提升为尊重。在厄尔笔下，实现这种相向而行、双重转变的桥梁，是阿多尼斯与约瑟夫之间关系的变化。在约瑟夫与阿多尼斯相互了解的过程中，小男孩目睹了很多不可思议的情景，如法雷利夫人在给阿多尼斯喂食时，仿佛化身大猩猩，在模仿阿多尼斯的声音、动作甚至是情感时与周围的环境融为一体。另外，她会只身一人清理阿多尼斯的巢穴，却没有任何意外和危险发生。看到阿多尼斯与他人的互动，了解到大猩猩与自己相似的丧亲之痛，约瑟夫逐渐放下了心中的固执，实现了对阿多尼斯从憎恶到理解的转变。

这种转变与消极激情相对，是固有静态观念与动态生成现实之间相互碰撞的火花，而约瑟夫意识的蜕变也呼应着"陌生化"的精髓，即"对旧的思维习惯的扬弃"。[1] 陌生化策略被布拉伊多蒂称为其后人类批评理论的"黄金法则"之一。[2] 厄尔笔下的动物园，是战争混浊硝烟中的一束光，代表着对僵化封闭、不可一世"中心主义"思想的

---

[1] Rosi Braidotti and Maria Hlavajova, *Posthuman Glossary*, London: Bloomsbury Publishing, 2018, p.341.

[2] ［意］罗西·布拉伊多蒂：《后人类》，宋根成译，河南大学出版社2016年版，第241页。

挑战。布拉伊多蒂认为，应对人类中心主义的关键在于陌生化，而无论是后殖民研究、女性主义研究还是族裔研究，都是在知识论层面对于人文主义中根深蒂固的欧洲中心主义的挑战。布拉伊多蒂在探讨陌生化时，常会提及后殖民理论家。在这位意大利哲学家看来，若要突破陈旧观念，寻求创新性的别样选择，需要进行"积极的去辖域化"（active deterritorialization），进而为"创新性的选择铺平道路"。① 布拉伊多蒂源引如萨义德、吉尔罗伊等提出的后殖民理论，认为其中直指人文主义的硬伤，颠覆了内嵌欧洲中心主义的知识论。② 她将萨义德对欧洲中心式人文主义的批评视为肯定式的人文主义批评，因为萨义德在批判欧洲话语所构建的东方主义模式的同时，并未否认人文主义的价值，而是塑造出另一种人文主义。③ 吉尔罗伊的《后殖民忧郁症》（*Postcolonial Melancholia*）中对"寰球"（planetary）的探讨，也被他视为陌生化策略的例证，是对"全球性外套掩盖下帝国主义特性"④的挑战。吉尔罗伊的陌生化也并非以否定和解构为绝对主导，而是在反思帝国性、殖民性所塑造的排外人文主义的同时，探求如何能在这越发分裂又越发趋同的世界中，培养人们与不同性共处的能力。

这种冲破陈旧观念的否定性，在陌生化中探寻新可能的特点，同样体现在小说表层的"毁灭"与深层次"联结"的对比中。厄尔让小说表层以"空袭"贯穿始终，却在小说深层通过对人类中心主义的陌生化，凸显了合作与联结。从后人类的角度来看，在空袭这个仿佛要炸开一切、炸断一切联结的场域内，动物园的存在却将人与非人联系在一起。在泯灭希望的战争黑暗中，是阿多尼斯与约瑟夫之间的相互扶持，将消极激情转化为积极希望。这种从消极转向积极的创新性选择，同样呼应着布拉伊多蒂的肯定伦理。若要实现人与动植物等"非

---

① ［意］罗西·布拉伊多蒂：《后人类》，宋根成译，河南大学出版社 2016 年版，第 129 页。
② Rosi Braidotti, "The Contested Posthumanities", in Rosi Braidotti and Paul Gilroy, eds., *Conflicting Humanities*, New York: Bloomsbury Academic, 2016, p. 16.
③ ［美］爱德华·沃第尔·萨义德：《人文主义与民主批评》，朱生坚译，胡桑校，中央编译出版社 2006 年版，第 13 页。
④ Paul Gilroy, *Postcolonial Melancholia*, New York: Columbia University Press, 2005, p. 4.

人"间的积极联结，需要清除以自我为中心的个人主义以及人类中心主义设下的二元对立壁垒。其中涉及一个重要的纽带，也是布拉伊多蒂在探讨陌生化时经常提及的概念普遍生命力（zoe）。[1] 布拉伊多蒂认为，普遍生命力可以理解为生命概念向非人类的延展，具有生成的活力，能够联结那些被分隔的物种、类别和范畴[2]，因此可以被视为一座桥梁，联结起后人类主义与超越人类中心论，也让人在关注"非人"生命的过程中实现生命宽度的拓展。

厄尔在书中不止一次提及约瑟夫的固执，然而却通过构建小说的后人类语境，帮助约瑟夫在固执的外壳上打开了一扇门，让他从禁锢中走出来，走向后人类的联结。约瑟夫首先看到了在阿多尼斯面前，法雷利夫人生命的延展。她能够模仿阿多尼斯的体态、动作、声音和神情，在相互信任中完成喂食，而阿多尼斯则以拍打法雷利夫人的头顶作为感谢。此时的法雷利夫人，绝非仅关注以人类为中心的特殊生命力（bio），而是关注与非人相关的普遍生命力。这样的转变同样体现在约瑟夫身上，而且从一个孩子的角度而言，学会为阿多尼斯喂食，得到它的信任，实现与它零距离接触，让约瑟夫之前的憎恶与恐惧逐步转变为关爱与尊重，甚至对阿多尼斯的爱胜过对自己和亲人。"这不是给我或者我的家人的，这是给我的大猩猩的"[3]，这是约瑟夫在战乱中的菜市场为阿多尼斯讨要蔬菜时的话。然而，在卖蔬菜人耳中，物资都难以满足人们在战争年代的温饱，约瑟夫却将大猩猩视为最重要的人，甚至高于自我和其他"人"，简直不可思议。根深蒂固的物种优越感，让阿多尼斯在动物园遭受空袭时，哪怕拼尽全力保护了约瑟夫的生命，却依然被视作"野兽"并惨死于士兵的枪下。当法雷利夫人发出让士兵帮忙找兽医的呼喊，士兵脸上的疑惑也照映出卖菜人

---

[1] "普遍生命力"一词沿用了布拉伊多蒂专著《后人类》的译者宋根成对"zoe"的翻译，对布拉伊多蒂而言，"zoe"可以被视为动物和其他非人类的生命，见 Rosi Braidotti, "A Theoretical Framework for the Critical Posthumanities", *Theory, Culture & Society*, Vol. 36, No. 6, November 2019, p. 35.

[2] Rosi Braidotti, *The Posthuman*, Cambridge & Malden: Polity Press, 2013, p. 60.

[3] [英] 菲尔·厄尔：《天空落幕时》，胡雪婷译，中信出版集团2021年版，第186页。

当时心中的不解,因为从以人类为中心的角度来看,这些仿佛都是无理取闹、匪夷所思的要求。

卖菜人、士兵的不解归根结底是因为他们的认知中仅有特殊生命力却无普遍生命力,这也恰好印证了布拉伊多蒂所言,"人"只有彻底放下唯我独尊的想法,彻底将自我重新定位,才能践行以普遍生命力为中心的平等主义,而实现重新定位的最佳路径为陌生化策略[①]。厄尔在书中也将人与动物的概念陌生化,呈现出二者间流动的疆界,而凸显这种流动性的本质则在于对人类中心主义中"理所应当"的质疑。"笼子的里面和外面都有动物"[②],这句话是伯特父亲所说,而伯特正是欺凌约瑟夫的男孩,也是阿多尼斯为了保护约瑟夫,隔着笼子用手抓住的男孩。伯特的父亲不顾儿子欺凌约瑟夫的事实,试图用自己理解中"动物"一词的含义侮辱约瑟夫和阿多尼斯。厄尔通过"笼子"和"动物"两个意象,模糊了人与动物的边界,在后人类的语境下思索人类中心主义的局限。书中的笼子是一个无法延展的空间,伯特的父亲将约瑟夫视为"动物",然而事实是他自己却一直生活在狭隘、偏见的牢笼中,固执地认为被冠以"人"的名号就是勾销所有劣迹的通行证。伯特作为"人"霸凌、殴打约瑟夫,而伯特父亲口中"危险的野兽"却在伯特拳头即将落在已经受伤的约瑟夫身上之时,救这个眼睛已经被打肿的小男孩于水火。

在这样的场景中,传统意义上"人与动物的界限开始崩塌,二者间不再有物种上的差别,而仅有程度上的区别"[③],也将"人"这一长久以来与权力和特权关系密切的词汇陌生化。这一点在阿多尼斯与伯特父亲的对比中体现得尤为明显,甚至可以认为,伯特及其父亲的行为更像野兽,而阿多尼斯更具人性。从霸凌者手中获救的约瑟夫,向阿多尼斯说出了"谢谢"二字,这是他"不常想到,更很少大声说出

[①] Rosi Braidotti, *The Posthuman*, Cambridge & Malden: Polity Press, 2013, p. 88.
[②] [英]菲尔·厄尔:《天空落幕时》,胡雪婷译,中信出版集团2021年版,第156页。
[③] Andy Miah, "A Critical History of Posthumanism", in Bert Gordijn and Ruth Chadwick, eds., *Medical Enhancement and Posthumanity*, Berlin: Springer, 2008, p. 82.

口"的两个字。① 在后人类的语境下，在生成的当下中，约瑟夫对自我和自我之外其他生命的认知朝着积极方向发展。他感受着生命宽度的拓展，亦如从阿多尼斯的角度而言，与约瑟夫和法雷利夫人的相处，也让它的生命向着更广阔处延伸。

  书中也通过对阿多尼斯的书写，将空袭的威慑力陌生化。可以说阿多尼斯的存在，让黑暗的硝烟中开出了一道缝隙，在人与动物融为一体的联结中凸显出正义和希望。在约瑟夫眼中，阿多尼斯的英气与"野兽"二字毫不相干，它伸张正义时的怒吼犹如雷鸣，"比纳粹能扔下的任何东西都更迅速、有力"②。德军空袭的炸弹可以摧毁房屋和生命，却远不如孩童眼中救自己于水火的阿多尼斯的怒吼有威力。被空袭蹂躏的城市如地狱一般，炸弹的猖狂与阿多尼斯的威严，城市的灰暗与阿多尼斯的英气在约瑟夫眼中碰撞。在与阿多尼斯的联结中，约瑟夫体会到那些看似恐怖的威慑力，只是充斥破坏、否定、僵化的黑暗，是割裂、毁灭的牢笼。相反，阿多尼斯的威严"直冲天际"③，让天空投下的炮弹都显得暗淡无光。阿多尼斯的怒吼是划开"理所当然"的利剑，他身上的正义之气，是心存傲慢与优越感之人所感受不到的，却让约瑟夫震撼、难忘，而身为孩子的约瑟夫，从消极憎恶这个世界到积极感受其中正义的转变就昭示着希望。

  "阿多尼斯"（Adonis）这个名字的含义为"美少年"，其中"美"本身就是开放、生成、动态的存在，能够纠正人们认知上的错误，甚至能够挽救生命④，就如阿多尼斯的出现可以说是挽救了约瑟夫，让他在后人类的语境中重新理解自我，重新与世界建立联系。"少年"却似乎与阿多尼斯无关，因为书中已经说明它年事已高，但从另一个角度而言，"少年"一词委实与阿多尼斯紧密相关，因为书中它信任的朋友约瑟夫就是少年。因此通过"阿多尼斯"或"美少年"的名

---

① ［英］菲尔·厄尔：《天空落幕时》，胡雪婷译，中信出版集团 2021 年版，第 150 页。
② ［英］菲尔·厄尔：《天空落幕时》，胡雪婷译，中信出版集团 2021 年版，第 146 页。
③ ［英］菲尔·厄尔：《天空落幕时》，胡雪婷译，中信出版集团 2021 年版，第 269 页。
④ ［美］伊莱恩·斯凯瑞：《美与公正》，卓慧臻译，清华大学出版社 2021 年版，第 24 页。

称，大猩猩与小男孩融为一体，构成了后人类语境中"集体想象"的化身，呼应着肯定伦理中对"我们"的理解。

三 "温柔的举动让他热泪盈眶"："我们"的共同体

在评论界的定义中，《天空落幕时》是一部改编自真实故事的历史小说，此书的真实性在于对战争的描述，虚拟性则在于对约瑟夫和阿多尼斯两位"同命相连"知己的书写。然而，正是小说创作的虚拟性，赋予了作品张力，从后人类的角度彻底否定了霸权，并重新定义了个体与这个"大家共享的世界"之间的联系。故事的结尾，依偎在阿多尼斯的遗体旁，约瑟夫和法雷利夫人相拥而泣，"为了他们失去的东西，为了他们失去的人，但更重要的是，为了他们最终找到的东西"①。约瑟夫不止一次在阿多尼斯面前流泪。当时他因父亲战死而陷入绝望，是阿多尼斯毫无保留的信任，让他热泪盈眶。眼泪是柔软的，有时也被视为脆弱的代名词，仿佛映射出在战争、灾难、流离面前生命的脆弱。然而这脆弱中却蕴含坚韧，正如在小说的最后，承受丧友剧痛的约瑟夫，终于在法雷利夫人面前摘下心中的面具，在她的臂弯里体会到了与阿多尼斯相处的安全感。在肯定伦理中，脆弱和坚韧共同构成"恒久"（endurance），指个体不仅能生存下来，还能持续下去，在发展中构建积极性。②《天空落幕时》书写的是战争，战争中分崩离析的不仅有物质实体还有精神实体，扼杀的是置身灾难中的人们对未来的希望。但是，若细读故事的结尾，会发现失去的是"两种"，即"人和东西"，找到的却为"一种"。③ 这"一种"东西为何，厄尔

---

① ［英］菲尔·厄尔：《天空落幕时》，胡雪婷译，中信出版集团2021年版，第278页。
② Rosi Braidotti and Maria Hlavajova, *Posthuman Glossary*, London: Bloomsbury Publishing, 2018, p. 222.
③ 这种失去"两种"、找到"一种"之意在英文原版措辞中体现得更加明显："… they both cried: for what they had lost, for who they had lost, but most importantly, for what they had finally found" (Phil Earle, *When the Sky Falls*, London: Andersen Press, 2021, p. 304)。其中，说明失去的东西时，用了指"物"的代词"what"和指"人"的代词"who"，但是说明得到的东西时，仅用了指物的代词"what"。

没有明示，却是整本书希望之光的源头，是对希望的肯定。这种肯定意味着反对任何成员拥有霸权地位，强调每个个体都浸润在、内化于普遍生命力搭建的联结之网上。[1]

厄尔是在书写冲突、分裂、霸权的过程中，在所有生命的安全都受到威胁的战争叙事里，将希望播撒于书中对普遍生命力的描写上，文字间迸发出的是对共同体的渴望，并将这样一种在共享的世界中、由人和非人组成的共同体视为消泯灾难、战乱、分裂的希望之光。布拉伊多蒂认为，肯定的希望反映出人们对未来可能性的憧憬，后人类思想之所以能实现积极改变，是因为其重新定义了"个体"与所有人和非人"共享世界"之间的关联。[2] 肯定伦理中定义的新唯物主义哲学反对二元对立，而将所有主体视为一个共同物质的不同模块[3]，而布拉伊多蒂所构建的批判性后人文主义的概念根基，为"新斯宾诺莎主义的一元本体论"。[4] 一元论是布拉伊多蒂为陌生化选取的概念性参照系，其内涵为一个开放、相互关联、多定性和跨物种的生成性的流变，其中的后人类主体超越了人类中心论，而获得了一个"寰球性的空间"。[5] 这种当代一元论认为，物质具有活力和自组织能力，其中的"一"代表"我们以及我们所置身的世界，是一个一体的生命，也即'一'的世界"。[6] 书中的战场和动物园，为两个不同的场域，前者代表对立冲突，后者则象征对"一"的世界的渴望。故事的结尾，阿多尼斯因伤势过重而离去，但是它所代表的能够修正错误的"美"依然存在，视它如父如友的"少年"约瑟夫也已经与自我、与创伤达成和解，因而可以说，阿多尼斯虽然逝去，但"美少年"的集体属性和创

---

[1] Rosi Braidotti, *The Posthuman*, Cambridge & Malden：Polity Press, 2013, p. 193.

[2] Rosi Braidotti, *The Posthuman*, Cambridge & Malden：Polity Press, 2013, p. 193.

[3] Rosi Braidotti and Maria Hlavajova, *Posthuman Glossary*, London：Bloomsbury Publishing, 2018, p. 221.

[4] Rosi Braidotti, "A Theoretical Framework for the Critical Posthumanities", *Theory, Culture & Society*, Vol. 36, No. 6, November 2019, p. 35.

[5] Rosi Braidotti, *The Posthuman*, Cambridge & Malden：Polity Press, 2013, p. 89.

[6] 周伟薇、王峰：《朝向共同体的后人类快乐伦理》，《华东师范大学学报》（哲学社会科学版）2022 年第 3 期。

造力价值却在后人类的语境中延续。

厄尔对战火中动物园的书写，是在对立最激烈处将二元对立陌生化，挑战的是霸权和理所应当的优越感，指向对于集体想象"质"的转变。约瑟夫所寻找的正是这样一种在后人类语境中对自我、对世界认识"质"的飞跃。作为一名阅读障碍症患者，约瑟夫的世界总是被误解。格里斯校长在测试中发现他不是在读书，而是在背书，就断定约瑟夫是作弊者、骗子，无法阅读这件事情是谎言。为此，约瑟夫的皮肉承受了校长手杖的鞭笞，这根名为克拉伦斯的手杖代表校长的权威，以及他基于自我的判断对学生不假思索的惩罚。这一次，救约瑟夫于水火的是法雷利夫人，她不但因自己的迟来向约瑟夫道歉，而且在校长面前将这根鞭笞约瑟夫的克拉伦斯折断。厄尔在书写约瑟夫对此事的内心独白时，重点强调了"得到他人道歉"对于小男孩而言很陌生，正如之前他向阿多尼斯说出的那声"谢谢"，同样也不是他常说的话。

然而，出自法雷利夫人之口的"抱歉"和出自约瑟夫之口的"谢谢"，却昭示着认知上质的转变，即在包括人和非人的普遍生命力的语境中，将视角从个人的"我"转向集体的"我们"的质变。无论是法雷利夫人还是约瑟夫，他们都不再以狭隘的自我为中心来认知世界，而是在与其他生命互动的过程中，理解到事物的复杂性，从而在开放包容的探索中实现自我认知的拓展。那根鞭笞学生的手杖，其名字克拉伦斯（Clarence）也并非厄尔随意而选，而是拥有重要的寓意。这个源自拉丁语的名字，有一层意思为"清除"，正如这根手杖的作用，就是要清除格里斯眼中学生的恶习和错误。然而，克拉伦斯的折断却预示着这种以绝对权威为基础、霸权式"清除"的崩塌，而厄尔希冀在崩塌的废墟中再造的则是开放、包容的共同体，是彻底扬弃消极性、指向动态生成未来的希望。折断克拉伦斯的法雷利夫人带着约瑟夫离开学校，二人以勇敢、正义、坚韧保护着阿多尼斯，澄清着外界论称它攻击伯特的诬陷，向着构建"我们"的共同体而努力。

此处的"我们"并非既成的事实，而是实践的产物，是在动态生成中得来的认知,让人们能够在复杂的差异性共存的当下,将目光转移到那些被忽视的主体身上,在开放包容的共同体中探寻未来的可能性。在后人类批评思想中,一元论与主导或掌控无关,而是指向一种彻底的包容(radical immanence),让人们在应对伤痛和消极性的过程中,将被忽视、被误解、被霸凌的痛楚,转化为联结对世界新的认知,践行更积极、更具创造力的选择。行文至此,不得不承认无法说清谁/什么是小说的中心,是约瑟夫、法雷利夫人、阿多尼斯还是动物园。或许这也并不重要,重要的是他们最终形成了共同物质中的不同变量,能够以彻底的包容对待不同性,将当下看成一个不断生成、动态变化、为创造积极可能性而有所贡献的连续体。在这样一个动态生成的、探寻积极性的当下中,约瑟夫和法雷利夫人在小说结尾时找到的东西,就是对"我们"的理解,以及在探寻希望的跋涉中对共同体的渴望。

结　语

厄尔在小说的扉页引用了英国湖畔诗人乐队的歌词:"我看着你的眼睛,我看见另一个生命和值得品读的心灵","终有一天,属于我们的时刻会到来",歌词中就包含了作者在书中思考的关键词"生命"和"我们"。作者透过约瑟夫的眼睛,让读者看到了超越人类界域、值得品读的生命和心灵。战火中动物园的守护者,在动态生成的当下,实现了由消极向积极的转变,拓展了生命的宽度,在扬弃陈旧思想的过程中,将人类中心主义的优越感陌生化,重新理解了生命之间的平等关系,并在霸权、毁灭、对立的黑暗中找到了前行的希望——"我们"的共同体。面对复杂、多样、多元,却也饱受冲突、战乱、气候变化之苦的21世纪,《天空落幕时》中的后人类书写,体现出如何以肯定、包容、开放的后人类哲学面对不同性,建立生命之间的联系,构建能带来积极可能性的共同体,并启发所有人思考如何从肯定和动态生成的视角看待世界,为共同体的建设做出贡献。

奈恩·诺梅兹与其对新冠的诗意化呈现

基斯·埃利斯*

【摘要】 长久以来,各种自然灾害、沉重的灾难和瘟疫频繁造访地球,它们以不同的行为模式展示着自身的存在,并吸引着作家以不同的文学体裁呈现它们。回顾数年来的活动轨迹,我们发现,飓风给人们预留了一定的时间去预测、观察并去不断地感受它。在此过程中,人们对飓风的了解与日俱增,而诗人对它的了解最深,可以说了如指掌。从一开始,人们就特别重视作家对危险事件的描写,《圣经》中挪亚方舟的故事是对全球性洪灾最有力的宣传,被何塞·马蒂(José Martí)称为"美洲第一诗人"的丽亚·德·埃雷迪亚在《飓风颂》中,就以其杰出的文学才华冷静地向我们展示了大自然那令人望而生畏的力量。当下,我们正经历着一场史无前例的疫情,心中惴惴不安。相较于其他健康危机,新冠的危害程度类似于灾难诗的先锋、智利诗人奈恩·诺梅兹(Naín Nómez)笔下的《荒芜的大地》(Baldío)和他之前的作家艾略特(T. S. Eliot)笔下的《荒原》。

【关键词】 健康危机;灾难诗;《荒芜的大地》;《荒原》

---

* 【作者简介】基斯·埃利斯(Keith Ellis),加拿大多伦多大学荣休教授。他在加拿大多伦多大学(Univeristy of Toronto)教授西班牙语美国文学长达37年,有多部相关研究著述。他最近将有两部关于古巴诗人 Nicolás Guillén 诗歌研究的书出版。

Naín Nómez and the Proper Poetic Treatment of Covid-19

Keith Ellis

Abstract: Throughout the ages, natural disasters, calamities, plagues have been known to pay periodical visits to this planet. The visitors exhibit different forms of behaviour and appeal to different genres. Hurricanes, follow tracks that they have created over the years, allowing time for anticipating, witnessing and sustaining the experience of the hurricane. In that process, people have come to know hurricanes well. Poets are foremost among those people. They know hurricanes to their very souls. From the very beginning, the linkage between writers and dangerous events has been highly prized. The planet-covering flood received fabulous publicity thanks to the accommodation it received in the Bible. And "the first poet of the Americas," José María Heredia (1803—1839), as José Martí called him, demonstrated his unique ability to show calmly the awesome force of nature in his "Ode To The Hurricane" (1822). We are now living through the unusual and distressing experience of a pandemic which we can compare with other health crises and measure to what extent the Chilean poet Naín Nómez places himself with his poem *Baldío* [Waste Land] in the vanguard of the genre of disaster poetry, ahead of T. S. Eliot with his *The Waste Land*.

Key words: Health crisis; Disaster poetry; *Baldío*; *The Waste Land*

Naín Nómez's poem *Baldío* [Waste Land] reached me promptly in Toronto from Santiago de Chile in May 2020, the date of its composition being the 12th of that month. Two months earlier, on March 11, 2020, the often fatal illness caused by the Coronavirus had been declared officially by the World Health Organization to be a pandemic. The near simultaneity of that event and its poetic representation by Nómez speak to the comprehensive preparedness of the author to write his poem. The worsening to the realm of pandemic of the frightening respiratory illness, with its rising numbers of fatalities, which was by then beginning to hold the attention of serious scientists everywhere, carried with it the implication that a corresponding high level of poetry would be required to reflect that engagement of science.

On scrutinizing Nómez's *Baldío* [Waste Land], one observes that the selection of language and devices from which he composes his poem is not greatly different from that to which Gérard Genette and Northrop Frye, for example, were attracted as theorists and compilers. But, as with great poets, Nómez's creative mastery takes him beyond the strictures of such theorists. It enables his capacity to demonstrate to his readers a freedom from some normally observed constraints, and it pulls forward the art of literary theory and literary criticism to cope with his creative work. In fact, it is due to the function of the selected language and devices rather than to theory that it is practicable for us to look for hallmarks of progress in literary endeavour. The critic feels the obligation to go further than Genette and Frye usually go by assessing, for instance, the function of the paratext. ①

By responding to the requirement for an identification of its function within the work and not just classifying a paratext, the writer is stimulated to produce works that the reader will recognize as being built on elements that are useful, meaningful and effective in their deployment. Hence, when we turn to Nómez's poem, we encounter first of all a title, a code that orients us broadly to the world into which the author wishes to thrust us or lead us gently. We immediately notice something odd here. We know this title, *Baldío* [Waste Land], as belonging to a different author, to a different work. Not-

---

① I make this point with regard to Genette in "Before and Beyond Genette: Cuba's Nicolás Guillén and the Empowered Paratext." It applies to Frye as well.

withstanding the difference of language—Spanish and English—the title suggests the sameness of two worlds. Is Nómez proposing to re-create in 2020 T. S. Eliot's famous poem *The Waste Land*, doing something akin to what Jorge Luis Borges's "Pierre Menard, autor del Quijote" aspired, with ultimate futility, to do with Cervantes's *Don Quijote*? The question is further made to seem relevant by the epigraph that governs the whole new work: "I had not thought death had undone so many." This direct quote from the early section, "The Burial of the Dead," of T. S. Eliot's "The Waste Land" coincides with words that occur near the beginning of Nómez's poem ("con algo de pavor" [somewhat terror-struck]). And so we find ourselves, as readers, being nudged to acknowledge a similar past experience, a hellish one, lived and partially survived by humanity.

But in a decisive way, from the first uses of the paratexts (the title, the epigraph and the initial lines), Nómez is doing something that is distinctive, not only in the attractive liveliness and effectiveness of his poetic language and devices, but also in the consummate skill and sense of propriety with which he provides those indispensable features.

Nómez does not try to impose any mythic or religious meaning on the pandemic. He sees it as a social phenomenon that manifests its malevolence with multitudinous effects centrally and with resistant vigour in the medical field. Language, up-to-date with new developments, is placed respectfully at the poetic, metaphorical service of conveying the changes—infections, illnesses, treatments, further treatments, persistent and ubiquitous diagnostic signs, and strenuous curative therapeutic efforts. The awful questions resulting from the bain of scarcity in unequal societies—to whom is hopeful treatment to be administered? whom to let live a while longer? whom to let die unpretentiously? whom to bury? who will bury? —make their critical way into the poem. The tense, existentially consequential function of dialogue enlivens and makes dynamic the character of this social tool in Nómez's

Baldío. The accumulated action has been surpassing the examples of those pandemics with which we were provided at the beginning of the poem in the references to the various genres (poetry, short story, novel and cinema). And the spectacle of the present is still ongoing without our knowing where it will end. Even more, given the early date of his poem's composition, he has been prophetic in his vision of the pandemic from his distant outpost in Chile—a pandemic that is a profound socioeconomic truth of global experience with rich, absorbing content, keeping the reader's mind alert and busy with the metaphorical transports to which it is delightfully submitted, in the formal, aesthetic sense, while it laments the sad, real-life accuracy of the perpetual victims of the world ever since our human society has been organized by the dictates of imperialism. The T. S. Eliot of *The Waste Land* would hardly have been inclined to expend the mental and imaginative energy necessary to contend, however briefly, with such dualities of joy and sorrow; hence the flat dullness of his negative expression. Nómez, however, has brought to his vision the means to convey it to the world with the timely resilience of a battler. Thus enabled, Nómez is self-sufficient, needing no Virgilian or Tiresian or Westonian helper. [1] In fact, Nómez's personal public experience—shared intimately, in Toronto and Ottawa with Juan Carlos García, another eminent Chilean writer, as well as with hundreds of thousands of exiled Chileans, together with some colleagues from different academic institutions in Canada—has provided him with fertile endogenous material for his poem.

As interesting as all this may be as background information, giving a glimpse of the literary time from the point of view of a Spanish American and early signs of its impact on the world, more remarkable for Nómez from a ge-

---

[1] In order of apparent importance for T. S. Eliot, they are Virgil, the epic poet of Rome, Tiresias, an oracle in Greek mythology and literature, and Jessie Weston, a medievalist scholar on the Arthurian legends and Holy Grail traditions.

neric standpoint and its potential usefulness was the claim of a literary invention made by the Honduran writer, Augusto Monterroso. In his collection *Obras completas* (*Yotros cuentos*) [Complete Works (And Other Stories)] of 1959, he offered to the world what he said was the shortest story ever written.①

Monterroso's disquieting story about the existence in reality of a frightening dream, or the reality of a nightmare, consists of its title "El dinosaurio" and one very short sentence: "Cuando despertó, todavía estaba allí." [When he woke up, it was still there.] The reader will have found in these words a familiar ring with the very first sentence of *Baldío* ("Cuando despertó la pandemia todavía seguía ahí" [When he woke up, the pandemic was still there]), as he/she will perhaps have already encountered the Monterroso quotation and studied it in relation to its length. Several interesting studies of the potential of the short story are the following: Mary Louise Pratt's "The Short Story: The Long and the Short of it" (1981) in which she considers some generic factors that may help to distinguish the novel from the short story; Sarah Hardy's "A Poetics of Immediacy: Oral Narrative and the Short Story" (1993); Erminio Neglia's illustrative *To make a long story short* (1989) and *Short Stories and Poems* (2020); Keith Ellis's "Lo épico en la lírica de Pablo Neruda" (1990), whose generic mixture guides us to recognize and endorse the generic trend to the brevity of the short story. And here in Nómez's *Baldío* the futile desire for a nightmare to end is underscored by the allusion to the brevity and the quickness of the genre of the short story.

---

① I know hardly anything about literature in the Chinese and other Eastern languages, for instance, but I believe that, if Monterroso had presumed to include languages such as those in his claim of supreme brevity for his story, he would by now have been superseded or corrected by many users of those signs and symbols by which the Chinese communicate what I understand to be their concise and sometimes enigmatic or cryptic tales.

New light has been thrown on all these considerations regarding the short story genre, and other genres, as they affected both creators and literary critics, by an initiative taken by Nómez in his *Baldío*. From the late 1980s we had been noticing in our seminars at 21 Sussex (the site of the offices and the seminar room of the University of Toronto's Department of Spanish and Portuguese in those years) the tendency of the aforementioned theorists, Gérard Genette and Northrop Frye, to be gatherers of potentially useful literary devices; but that by often refraining from demonstrating or pointing to their dynamic usage it seemed to be quite alright with these theorists if these devices were simply decoratively there or were standing idly by.

Pace and speed are prominent in Nómez's *Waste Land*. In the first five lines we have the slight paraphrase that maintains the brevity and quickness of Monterroso's short story. And still within these first five lines the protagonist of Nómez's poem is further characterized and shown in reaction to his setting with even some added pre-history of the action. All of this is associated with a nightmarish world that is quickly now merged into the real world and its history of plagues and calamities conveyed by the interrelationship of several genres.

If, for example, the Frenchman and the Canadian had given greater thought to the idea of the contribution of the first words, the title and the initial phrases of a literary work, they might have found a way of coming to know the superb and humble Mexican prose writer, Juan Rulfo. They would then almost certainly shortly thereafter have found themselves reciting by heart one or more of the very marvelous openings of his works, beginnings that may very well confirm the title as being in full harmony with the story which it in effect introduces. Consider these opening words from Rulfo's *Pedro Páramo*:

Vine a Comala porque me dijeron que acá vivía mi padre, un tal

Pedro Páramo. Mi madre me lo dijo.

[I came to Comala because they told me that my father, one Pedro Páramo, lived here. It was my mother who told me.]

Having discovered Rulfo and his exemplary mastery of the art of beginning the long or short story in a way that no time is wasted, the reader, at the end of the story, finds that he/she had been favoured with an encapsulation of the action, the tone and the real status of the story's world from the very beginning of the narration. The reader finds too that the rest of the story consists of a series of pleasant reinforcements of this structure: pleasant, not because they fulfill our expectations for social happiness, but because they find ways—sometimes paradoxical, ironic, contradictory, strange or simply delightful—of conforming to what we feel was promised at the beginning. Just when the reader has gone through those normative ropes and has found, for instance, how valuably indicative of a dystopian family life some casually offered subject pronouns can be, this reader comes upon, with its briefest of beginnings, a beginning that augurs, in the case of *Baldío*, the persistent presence of something from which one wants to be relieved.

Nómez takes full advantage of the fact that the normative findings we make about the short story apply also, especially with regard to length and intensity, to poetry. And certainly in *Baldío*, his welcoming of prose works, specifically of the short story, into it, there is ample evidence of his useful incorporation of this genre into his poetry, sometimes by the use of a whole story. Words and phrases such as "mundillo" [little world] and "al fondo de los mares" [at the bottom of the seas] are indicative of our poet's penchant for inclusion, centripetal movement and the global process and dimension. Consonant with this is his regard for pace and the resultant mental liveliness.

When we scrutinize Nómez's generic practice—his pragmatic ceding of power, self-control and autonomy to the genres themselves—we come to notice that the phenomena with which they are engaged are also imbued or endowed with this power, control and autonomy. Herein lies the secret of the aptness of the generic approach that Nómez takes so readily to his *Baldío*.

Nómez's display of knowledge of the contemporary world demonstrates first of all the fact tht that the acquisition of such knowledge is a part of his sense of responsibility as a poet who undertakes to write such a work as his *Baldío*. He seems determined to make this knowledge accessible to his readers. But by what standards should we judge the adequacy of this knowledge? I dare say, as we have implied before, by the criterion of fluency, by the consummate ease with which Nómez has made the language of *Baldío* sparkle, language that includes today's technical terminology, that exceeds the coverage of some of our most trusted dictionaries and places those tools quickly on the path to obsolescence. Nómez has signaled that he is a significant figure in the present trend that perpetuates by replacing. We of the world of the humanities will be grateful to find in this poem such phrases as "cybernetic prosthesis" and "cyberspace" in their true contexts within the communications or health sciences fields, so that we may learn from them. At the same time the modernizing impulse is so pronounced in this poetry that had *Baldío* appeared some months later, and had the precisely appropriate context been found, the clarifying appearance or presence of the term "artificial intelligence algorithms" might have been found here.

Remarkable knowledge is also to be seen to include here developments in the literary field that have had a bearing on culture and on international politics. There are in Nómez's poem allusions such as the one to figures from the comic strips such as Batman and Robin, invented in the U. S. , driven to raging popularity there for their vain, trivial, impossible heroics, and then, like a plague, sent to culturally infect other countries. There are inevitably welcoming allusions to critics who belong to Nómez's generation such as Antonio Skármeta and Manuel Jofré (also a doctorate of 21 Sussex, like the fellow Chilean writers of Nómez's generation already mentioned.)

The most significant of the many instances of literary knowledge displayed in this poem is that of the short story which its author Monterroso claims to be the shortest story ever written. This distinctive literary work and its author's claim are not simply alluded to in Nómez's poem; they play a signal nuclear role within it, serving as linkage to several themes, tightening the thematic structure of the poem, and becoming by its reliably spaced presence a key part of its music. Allusions to Monterroso's story are functioning here, bearing out the paradox that the shortest story can serve as the frame for a story told with splendid elegance from the genre of poetry and with wondrous access to knowledge that is more than encyclopedic. [1]

For example, the associations established in the poem by the phrase "... exiled from everywhere..." illustrate the density of the thematic linkages in the poem. This phrase is first associated with indigenous people as one of several examples of prime victims of the virus (others are the elderly, women, migrants, the poor). But the phrase also has the potential to make connections with various salient points of his poem. He could see the phrase embodied in Monterroso's life of exile, whether economic or political. In the popular imagination, it is easy to find the "everywhere" in the "repúblicas bananas" as Pablo Neruda named them in his famous poem of 1950, "La United Fruit Co." (492 – 3). "Exiled from everywhere" also refers to a wider Latin American and Caribbean problem that is linked to another persistent problem, "unequal distribution" of resources. This has been identified for centuries now as a long-term underlying condition that explains the cause of poverty and the unequal struggle to end it. The phrase is also a reference to the author's own exile and to the crisis surrounding the decision he will have

---

[1] It is important for understanding the paradoxical nature of Monterroso's short story, "El dinosaurio", to know that dinosaurs had died out 65 million years before the appearance of humans, hence the threatening nature of a bad dream become reality evoked in this literary allusion.

made as to whether or not to return to Chile, his native country, that was still within the domain of a constitution that had been brought into being by the brutal Pinochet and when his country's social scientists were still prone to take advice from from experts who were Chicagoans and from other gangsters from everywhere.

Nómez is a beneficiary of the fact that when the light of comparative literature was fading in the west, *Comparative Literature and World Literature* of the Normal University of Beijing appeared to relume that light and make it shine on writers everywhere who deeply recognize and, with appropriate power and subtlety, reveal general connections and comparisons between writers and between genres everywhere (see my article on the glosa genre and another on the poem by Cuba's Nicolás Guillén, "Voy a Wuhan" [I am going to Wuhan]).

The factor of pace or speed of narration or action is often insufficiently taken into account by authors, theorists and critics. This can be the consequence of too rigid an understanding of the generic identity of texts and can even have serious consequences for an author. Some of Eliot's biographers and Eliot himself have revealed that the poet suffered from writer's block, described generally as extreme difficulty in deciding on what to write and how to proceedwith writing. Eliot himself came to see that his solution to this problem was to see a psychiatrist in Lausanne, Switzerland (See Pericles Lewis, "The Waste Land"). Any diagnosis of writer's block that doesn't point primarily to the adoption of a flawed critical approach is almost surely a misdiagnosis.

It is natural to sympathize with anyone who believes that the exercise or development of his talent, especially an extraordinary talent, has been jeopardized by a disabling illness, one that is so difficult to diagnose or treat that he has to seek help from a distant specialist. In those circumstances, perhaps in desperation, rather than declare helplessness, we tend to bring the problem within the range of our understanding and competence, and, in this specific case we can suggest to the complainant, the T. S. Eliot of "The Waste Land", that he do a careful analysis of two texts that have the same title: his own and one by a lesser known author called Naín Nómez from Chile. We are sure that in that careful reading he will find in the latter some keys to his recuperation that incur far less risk and leave him far greater personal control and responsibility than by submitting himself to one of those doctors of the brain from Switzerland or, if he is even less lucky, from Scotland and Canada.①

But we should also try to keep him from getting periodically into the same kind of trouble and ask the following: would not the constant inclination to find himself in "the middle way" (see Michael R. Stevens. "T. S. Eliot's Political 'Middle Way'") also create a disposition to tentativeness that would sooner or later place the patient in an immobile or blocked state? Contrast this situation in which T. S. Eliot has placed himself with the ease of expression or fluency that give the reader the impression that Nómez enjoys aspects of life, that the Chilean may find aspects of life to be sorrowful too, but that among life's joys there is reserved for him the special joy of writing, which comes from a sense of responsibility, of the duty to make his talent useful and that, the greater his own sense of that talent is, the more incumbent it is on him to exercise it. So that this approach gives him a sense of constant connection with a public that keeps him free from feeling cloistered, and immune from such punishments as T. S. Eliot faced for disconnection as staying silent in the face of atrocious agression on what was a constitutional republic.

The epic or narrative form lies so constantly available, deep in the consciousness of the human species, that no elaborate framing is needed to summon up the atmospheric presence of the genre, to let people know that a sto-

---

① The notorious Scottish psychiatrist, Donald Ewan Cameron, who practiced for man years in Canada.

ry is being told. This is what Pablo Neruda achieved with his very succinct "alguna vez" in his poem "Galope muerto" of 1950 (173 – 4). And it is what Naín Nómez magically, with splendid mastery of the art of great literature, brought into being when he took a story, five words in length, and made it serve, buttressed by myriad devices, smoothly, musically integrated, as the marvelously elastic frame for his merged poem and short story about the most devastating pandemic of all time, one that is still with us. Nómez's resplendent, engaging language demonstrates for us and for other poets, as Dante did and as T. S. Eliot did not, that dullness is not a necessary characteristic of what is the representation of a distressing and prolonged experience of the humanity of our continuing time.

In Nómez's poem *Baldío* [Waste Land] we find poetic skill that is not to be found in "The Waste Land". This is so largely because T. S. Eliot does not seem to possess the sensitivity needed to treat the topic, whereas Nómez is capable of summing up a variety of topics in two richly metaphorical lines, such as:

las ovejas negras abandonadas en la cuneta

de la autopista de la globalización

[the black sheep abandoned on the shoulder of globalization's highway].

It is a mark of our good fortune that, in our time, as we live its contradictions and paradoxes, we have beside us a quiet gentleman who was, in every good way, prepared to put into poetry of the highest level, poetry that springs from the healthiest of human sentiments, and the best readings of poetry and the art of poetry. We owe him great gratitude for sharing his exceptional talents with us. [1]

---

[1] Those who recognize champions in the field of education will want to give to 21 Sussex Avenue, on the campus of the University of Toronto, a warm embrace, because this outstanding poem by Dr. Naín Nómez (now Professor Emeritus of the University of Santiago, Chile) overshadows the most known effort of a Nobel prize-winning poet (T. S. Eliot) who had been nurtured at Harvard, Oxford and the Sorbonne.

BIBLIOGRAPHY

Borges, Jorge Luis, "Pierre Menard: autor del Quijote", *Ficciones*, Barcelona: Emecé, 1956, 16 – 22. Print.

Eliot, T. S. , *The Waste Land*, http://shiraz.fars.pnu.ac.ir/portal/file/? 970445/The-Waste-Land-Original.pdf. Web.

Ellis, Keith, "Before and Beyond Genette: Cuba's Nicolás Guillén and the Empowered Paratext", *Comparative Literature and World Literature*, 4, 2 (2019), 1 – 30. Web.

——, "The Glosa: A Genre to be Noticed for Its Constructive Values", *Comparative Literature and World Literature*, 1, 4 (2016), 43 – 57. Web.

——, "Nicolás Guillén, the Cuban Sage, Goes to Wuhan", *Comparative Literature and World Literature*, 5, 1 (2020), 42 – 73. Web.

——, "Lo épico en la lírica de Pablo Neruda", *Hispanic Review*, 58, 3 (Summer 1990), 309 – 324. Web.

Frye, Northrop, "Rhetorical Criticism: Theory of Genres", *Anatomy of Criticism*, Princeton University Press, 1971. Print.

Genette, Gérard, *Paratexts: Thresholds of Interpretation*, Cambridge University Press, 1997. Print.

Gordon, Donald K. , *Los cuentos de Juan Rulfo*, Madrid: Playor S. A. , 1976. Print.

Hardy, Sarah, "A Poetics of Immediacy: Oral Narrative and the Short Story", *Style*, 27, 3, (Penn State 1993), 352 – 58. http://www.jstor.org/stable/42946056. Web.

Lewis, Pericles, "The Waste Land", https://campuspress.yale.edu/modernismlab/the-waste-land/. Web.

Monterroso, Augusto, "El dinosaurio", *Obras completas (Y otros cuentos)*, Anagrama, 2003. Print.

Neglia, Erminio G. , *Short Stories and Poems*, Welland, ON: Soleil, 2020. Print.

——, *To make a long story short*, New York: Senda Nueva de Ediciones, 1989. Print

Neruda, Pablo, *Obras completas*, Vol. I. Buesos Aires: Losada, S. A. , 1957. Print.

Nómez, Naín, *Baldío*, Santiago de Chile: Palabra Editorial, 2020. Print.

——, "Waste Land", Trans. Keith Ellis, *BIM*, 9, 2 (2020), 87 – 91. Print.

Pratt, Mary Louise, "The Short Story: The Long and the Short of it", *Poetics*, 10, 2 – 3 (June 1981), 175 – 194. Print.

Stevens, Michael R. , "T. S. Eliot's Political 'Middle Way'", *Acton Institute* (Religion and Liberty), 9, 5 (June 20, 2010) . Web.

Weston, Jessie L. , *From Ritual to Romance*, Princeton University Press, 1993. Print.

Wood, Cecil G. , *The Creacionismo of Vicente Huidobro*, Fredericton, N. B. : York Press, 1978. Print.

Appendix I

BALDÍO

Naín Nómez

"**Nunca hubiera creído que la muerte se llevara a tantos**"
T. S. Eliot

Cuando despertó la pandemia todavía seguía ahí

y recordó el cuento de Monterroso

con algo de ironía con algo de pavor

Durante los días anteriores tuvo varias pesadillas

pero ninguna comparada con ésta

Como toda persona letrada

rememoró *La peste* de Camus *El año de la peste* de Dafoe

y*En las montañas de la locura* de Lovecraft

en la versión cinematográfica de Carpenter

o los films directamente virales como *Contagio* de Soderbergh

o *Pandemia* nuestra antesala al infierno

aunque por alguna razón

le resonaba con mucha fuerza

El hundimiento del Titanic de Hans Magnus Enzensberger

esa metáfora de la modernidad ostentosa

un barco monstruoso

petrificado en el fondo de los mares

A su juicio la proliferación del virus

expandiéndose por el mundillo de la especie humana

dejando su marca afiebrada en tarjetas monedas mejillas

administrando la vida y la muerte en los hospitales

fuera de la biovigilancia y el control

era solo un aviso de lo que vendría

cuando la utopía de la comunidad inmune

fantaseada por el nuevo sujeto del tecno patriarcado

se convirtiera en el reality show más espectacular de las últimas décadas

un desfile de fantasmas con mascarilla

sin manos sin labios sin lengua sin rostro casi sin piel

los nuevos intocables de una secta invisible

que dejan mensajes en aparatos que nadie escucha

sin cuerpo apenas una prótesis cibernética

apenas una máscara entre otras máscaras

un tapabocas que te obliga a callar

con diferentes diseños para mantener la desigualdad social

más allá de las imágenes cinematográficas

del zorro el jinete enmascarado o el enmascarado de plata

del dúo dinámico batman y robin

fuera del imperio fuera de la performance teatral

apenas un código una casilla en la nube una sombra

no se reúnen con nadie no tienen carne

su domicilio es amazon facebook instagram

una partícula de ser humano consumiéndose a si mismo

en la soledad de un estado de excepción permanente

de cuerpos abducidos atemorizados encapsulados

¿Para siempre?

Cuando despertó pensando en el monstruo

pero también imaginando otro lugar ciudad

otro planeta donde fuéramos todos inmunes

sin cuerpos abyectos y extraños ni fronteras ni muros

si dio cuenta y por el resto de sus días

que el pensamiento no le servía para despertar

fuera de su casa del miedo (al) ajeno

para salir del encierro de su dormitorio

de la segunda dermis con sus guantes esterilizados

el temor a hacernos virales

si tocamos la puerta la basura la bolsa del pan

la saliva que sale de los labios amados

sonidos partículas vivas ventosas que se adhieren

a nuestros pulmones el temor

flotando de una garganta a otra sobrepasando

las barreras migratorias la vigilancia

digital y el flujo del capital

¿O es sólo la metáfora de otro texto mayor?

¿A quiénes dejaremos morir?

¿A los más pobres?

¿A los viejos con sus enfermedades primarias?

¿A las mujeres golpeadas maltratadas asesinadas?

¿A los aborígenes exiliados de todas la tierras?

¿A los inmigrantes hacinados en barrios de la periferia?

¿A los marginales escondidos en sus carpas de cartòn?

¿A los nuevos zombies sin rumbo vagando por las calles solitarias

de las ciudades del mundo?

Despertó y se dio cuenta del espectáculo

de la dramaturgia de la muerte

los caídos ya no pueden ser felices o infelices

ni siquiera tienen ataúd o ceremonia del adiós
se quedan casi sin despedirse en medio de la calle
en medio de las cloacas de los mercados semivacíos
ateridos de frío o sudando por la canícula implacable
bajo el hervor creciente de un sol moribundo
multitudes de cuerpos frotándose unos con otros
de carnes podridas y verduras disecadas
exiliados de pueblos y casas sin hogar ni alimento
espectadores sin ojos de su propia doble agonía
probablemente sorprendidos
por esta oscuridad por este desencuentro
no querido ni anhelado
por este pétalo negro de locura
ya inscrito en los libros sagrados
como un recuerdo de los dioses olvidados
o un tic nervioso de la ciencia
la mesurada y correcta tabla de salvación
de la tragedia planetaria

Despertó y se dijo-en eso estamos ahora-
confinados controlados segmentados vigilados
en fin "normalizados" en la micro república de una habitación
en el umbral del afuera y el adentro
en la prisión blanda del metro y medio de distancia
en los tentáculos acomodaticios pero encubiertos del telecontrol
custodiados desde el ciberespacio
para que sigamos siendo los consumidores dóciles
que soñaron que fuéramos
tele alimentados todos

Estamos

en la batalla de Chile la batalla de Santiago

la batalla del Universo "estamos en una guerra señores"

y hay que ganarla aunque perdamos

varios millones de ¨clientes¨ desbancados del mapa global

invisibilizados en la televisión y los celulares

donde los muertos como antes los desaparecidos

no tienen consistencia

para el espectáculo aséptico de todos los días

somos un número una cantidad una ficha escamoteada

de la vista de parientes y amigos

a perpetuidad

aunque él piensa

no hay ninguna batalla que ganar o perder

el virus es un dinosaurio una pesadilla un sueño

una verdad que siempre estuvo allí

y no tiene la culpa

de nuestra insoportable levedad de existir

de nuestra pretenciosa manera de mirarnos

sin vernos la cara

y de encerrarnos en la pesadez del miedo

para vigilar prohibir castigar

lucha donde Tanatos desplazó a Eros

hasta nuevo aviso

Así es como la tierra se convirtió en una gran cárcel

algunos nos encerramos en los rincones de casas o pernoctamos

en otros lugares donde murallas y techos reducen nuestra mirada anclados a un presente interminable

mientras una multitud de seres extraños sale de las alcantarillas

y vaga por las calles sin rumbo como mutantes exiliados

de las redes las pantallas los medios de comunicación

como residuos en tránsito virus del virus

también eliminados del porvenir

que no está disponible que no les pertenece

¿Qué nos espera?

¿Cuándo será la próxima pandemia?

¿un planeta sin agua ni alimentos el baldío irreversible?

¿la radiación la guerra?¿el frío y el calor recargado?

¿el fin de todas las predicciones

el auto exterminio total?

¿Mutaremos?

Mientras tanto

el día venidero se nos escapa y desaparece

en nuestra sociedad sin orificios

en medio de nuestra disposición al aburrimiento

(midiendo los pasos rumiando el desempleo

acallando los gritos destemplados temiendo el sonido del timbre)

Yo tú nosotros ellas en la jaula invisible monstruos todos

saliendo de la pesadilla convertidos ahora en lo espeluznante

"apretando nuestros ojos sin párpados esperando que llamen a la puerta"

las ovejas negras abandonadas en la cuneta

de la autopista de la globalización

el tumor que se expande el tejido podrido

que se filtra de la tierra una y otra vez
invadiendo los campos y las ciudades
para desandar
el camino de la especie

Appendix II

WASTE LAND
Naín Nómez, translated by Keith Ellis

"I would never have thought that death had taken away so many."
T. S. Eliot

When he woke up the pandemic was still there
and he remembered Monterroso's short story
somewhat ironically somewhat terror struck
In previous days he had suffered several nightmares
but none compared to this one
Like all learned people
he recalled Camus' *The Plague*, Dafoe's *The Plague Years*
and Lovecraft's *At the Mountains of Madness*
in Carpenter's cinematografic version
or virus-centred films like Soderbergh's *Contagion*
or *Pandemic* our ante-room to hell
even though for some reason
he heard resounding powerfully
Hans Magnus Enzensberger's *The Sinking of the Titanic*
that metaphor of ostentatious modernity
a monstruos boat
petrified at the bottom of the seas

In his view the proliferation of the virus
expanding thoughout the little world of the human species
leaving its fevered stamp on business cards coins cheeks

administering life and death in hospitals

apart from the biovigilance and the control

this was only a warning of what would come

when the utopia of an immune community

dreamed up by the new character from the techno patriarchy

would become the most spectacular reality show of recent decades

a parade of masked ghosts

with neither hands nor lips nor tongue nor face almost without skin

the new untouchables of an invisible sect

who leave messages on machines to which no one listens

almost disembodied like a cybernetic prosthesis

barely a mask among other masks

a face shield that forces you to be quiet

with different designs to maintain social inequality

beyond the film clips

of the fox as the masked jockey or the silver masks

of the dynamic duo Batman and Robin

outside of the empire outside of the theatrical performance

barely a barcode a cloud address a shadow

they do not meet with anyone they have no flesh

their real home is amazon facebook instagram

a particle of human being consuming itself

in the solitude of a state of permanent exception

of encapsulated frightened abducted bodies

Forever?

When he woke up thinking of the monster

but also imagining a different place city

a different planet where we would all be immune

without abject and strange bodies or frontiers or walls

he realized and knew for the rest of his days

that thinking was not helping him to awaken

outside of his house out of fear of strangers

to leave the enclosure of his bedroom

of his second skin with its sterilized gloves

our fear of becoming infected with the virus

if we touch the door the garbage the bread bag

the saliva that drips from loved lips

sounds live airborne particles that stick

to our lungs fear

floating from one throat to another passing

the migratory barriers the digital

vigilance and the flow of capital

Or is it only the metaphor for another larger text?

Whom will we let die?

The poorest?

The oldest with their underlying illnesses?

The beaten ill-treated murdered women?

The indigenous peoples exiled from everywhere?

The immigrants stacked together in outlying districts?

The marginal ones hidden in their cardboard tents?

The new aimless zombies wandering the solitary streets

of the world's cities?

He woke up and became aware

of the spectacle of the drama of death

the fallen ones can no longer be happy or unhappy

they can't even have a coffin or a farewell ceremony

   they lie there almost without saying goodbye in the middle of the street

   in the middle of the sewers of the half empty markets

   stiff with cold or sweating through the implacable dog days

   under the intensifying cauldron of a dying sun

   multitudes of corpses rubbing against each other

   with rotted meat and dessicated greens

   exiled from villages and houses with neither hearth nor food

   spectators blind to their own double agony

   probably surprised

   by this darkness by this loss of familiarity

   undesired and unlonged for

   by this black petal of madness

   already inscribed in the sacred books

   like a recollection of forgotten gods

   or a nervous tic of science

   the measured and precise last resort

   of the planetary tragedy

He woke up and said to himself-that's where we are now-

confined controlled segmented surveilled

in fact "normalized" in the micro republic of an apartment

on the threshold of being outside and inside

in the soft prison of a meter and a half of distancing

accommodative in its tentacles but concealed from telecontrol

watched over from cyberspace

so that we might keep on being the docile consumers

who are dreaming that we might be

tele fed all of us

We are
in the battle of Chile the battle of Santiago
the battle of the Universe "Gentlemen we are in a war"
and we must win it even though we lose
several million "clients" busted from the global map
made invisible on television and on cellular phones
where the dead who were previously disappeared
have no substance
for the asceptic spectacle of all our days
we are a number a quantity a code snatched away
from the sight of relatives and friends
in perpetuity
although he thinks
there is no battle to win or lose
the virus is a dinosaur a nightmare a dream
a truth that was always there
and is not to be blamed
for our unbearable levity toward living
for our pretentious way of viewing ourselves
without seeing our faces
and for isolating ourselves within the heavy weight of fear
in order to keep watch prohibit punish
a struggle in which Thanatos displaces Eros
until further notice

That is how planet earth became a huge prison
some of us locked ourselves into the corners of houses or we stayed over-

night

    in other places where walls and roofs reduce our view

    anchored to an interminable present

    while a multitude of strange beings emerge from the sewers

    and wander the directionless streets like mutants

    exiled from the networks the screens the means of communication

    like residues in transit viruses of the virus

    also eliminated from the future

    that is not available that does not belong to them

What now awaits us?

When can we expect the next pandemic?

a planet without water or food the irreversible waste land?

the radiation the war? cold and heat out of balance?

the end of all predictions

total self extermination?

Will we mutate?

Meanwhile

the coming day slips away from us and disappears

in our society that has no orifices

in the midst of our disposition to boredom

(measuring our footsteps contemplating unemployment

quieting out-of-pitch shouts fearing the sound of the bell)

I you we they in the invisible cage all of us monsters

coming out of the nightmare changed now into something ghastly

"squeezing our eyelidless eyes waiting for someone to knock on the door"

the black sheep abandoned on the shoulder

of globalization's highway

the rotted tissue the tumor that expands

that is filtered from the earth time and again

invading fields and cities

to retrace the footsteps of our species

浅议智利诗人艾薇拉·赫尔南德斯[*]

苏利达·马兰比奥

The Insolent Gaze of Chirean Poet Elvira Hernández
Soledad Marambio

When police are blinding protestors on Chile's streets, eyes like poet Elvira Hernández's become more important than ever.

As I write this, Chile is burning. The streets are burning, the monuments, the symbols, and signs of an abusive and unequal system that has been in place since Pinochet's dictatorship. People are saying "no more"; they are taking to the streets even though thegovernment is replying with violence. There have been deaths, wounded. A couple of hundred people have been blinded by police pellets. Amidst all this, graffiti has filled the city's walls. People write their demands, their exhaustion, their poetry.

I can imagine Elvira Hernández (b. 1951, Lebu) reading the walls and also writing, scribing down what she sees in the streets of Santiago. The

---

* 【作者简介】苏利达·马兰比奥（Soledad Marambio），女，纽约城市大学（CUNY）博士，智利诗人和翻译家，现供职于挪威卑尔根大学（University of Bergen）。

原文为评论体，没有摘要、关键词和分节。

smoke, the graffiti, the repression, the people asking, in the thousands, the millions, for a change. Hernández started writing poetry under Pinochet's dictatorship; soon after she was detained by the regime's secret police, which supposedly mistook her for a wanted *guerrillera*. She was released after five days, and not long after that she began writing *La bandera de Chile* (1991; Eng. *The Chilean Flag*, 2019), a collection of poems that would circulate for years by word of mouth, in mimeographed copies and loose pieces of paper. The book, written in 1981, was published ten years later by an Argentine publishing house. It was not until 2010 that the first Chilean edition appeared.

Right before *La bandera de Chile* was written, something broke. More than one thing, really. The country, the people, their language, and their poetic tradition. After the coup d'état, Hernández said in an interview, "you couldn't write as before. It would have been like eating a plate of stale food." The old way of writing, the bombastic Nerudian style with his poet-asprophet voice, was useless after the political violence that the terrorist state imposed on the country. Hernández said that Neruda's majestic metaphors and the lushness of his images couldn't speak to a ravaged country. For her, the model that made more sense after the coup was the one installed by Nicanor Parra's poetry or, as it is called, by his antipoesía. Parra brought the streets, the ugliness, the absurdity, and the small things of daily life to poetry, countering the idea of the poet as a little god, as the creator of new worlds, or as an anointed one entitled to be the voice of everyone.

Parra's dark humor and the everyday language he had brought to poetry were part of the material that Hernández worked with. The rest—and perhaps the more important part—came from the reality around her and her particular way of seeing her surroundings. "I don't have other eyes to see what I saw," she once wrote, but her eyes are sharp and dive deep into reality. She reads the signs of daily life—a flag, a bird, sports, the coming of days and the falling of nights—and creates with them uncanny images charged with what runs deep within us Chileans. She doesn't speak—not often at least—of a place of personal intimacy; her voice is her own and at the same time the voice of the collective: "I never heard 'little god' /never heard 'little me' either. /A small grain of salt that has to go back to its ocean." Hernández is not the prophet-poet that speaks for us; rather, she is one of us, always trying to go back to her ocean, where all of us are, swimming, being waves, foam, fish, floating and trying not to sink. The difference is that Hernández writes her way back. And she started that writing with a flag:

It is not devoted to a single person
    the Chilean flag
it surrenders itself to anyone
    who knows how to seize her.
    the seizing of the flag

Hernández's flag—or the way she sees and portrays the Chilean flag—is one that doesn't have a will or even a distinctive subjectivity. This flag—blue, red, and white—is just a piece of cloth that hangs from a pole and sometimes gets carried by the wind, the same way she is carried by the forces of history. I write "she" because that is what Hernández sees in this flag: a cloth, a bit of fabric that gets treated as women have been treated in Chile and so many other parts of the world too:

The Chilean flag is hanging from two buildings her fabric swells up like an ulcerated belly—falls

        like
    an old tit—
like a circus tent

> with her legs in the air she has a slit in the middle
> little coochie for the air
> a little hole for the ashes of the General O'Higgins
> an eye for the Avenida General Bulnes
> The Chilean flag is on her side
> forgotten

The flag hangs like washcloths on a laundry line, the result of women's work, of hands reddened by soap, friction, and cold water. Instead of flying proud and powerful, this flag swells like a poorly fed stomach and falls like the breast of an old, wasted woman. Yet at the same time, she—the flag/the woman—has to be ready to perform and entertain, to also be a recipient for the ashes of the Men of the Republic, the ones who built what is now being burned by people tired of abuse, of being treated as disposable, forgotten for so long with their cold and fear and hunger. Because even though Hernández wrote *La bandera de Chile* during the 1980s, it can be read as if it were written today. "The Chilean flag is reversible . . . /The Chilean flag is the perfect division," one of the poems says, and, really, what country doesn't have a symbol that can be read so differently depending on where you read it from?

Now we can see two Chiles seizing the flag. One Chile does so from La Moneda, the government house, and involves the smallest and richest part of the country, the one that doesn't want to lose its privileges, the false idea that they are the ones that shape the country. The other Chile is the more populated one; it's the country that has seen public education disappear, resulting in education as a privilege rather than a right; the same country that has to buy basic food on credit and that sees its old people working hard until their last days, trying to survive on the miserable pensions that the neoliberal system has engineered for the country. That Chile is the one now making the Chilean flag swell proud in the air, while people demand a new and more equal order.

It's complicated, and it doesn't make sense, to talk about Hernández's poetry without talking about Chile's reality. She is an enormous poet of the day-today of a country that struggles but stands. Her gaze is always upon it, on its land and also on the sky, when she even has time to stargaze.

> I didn't see the Halley on the first day...
> I didn't see it.
> I didn't see it
> with my head buried in papers
> words without sense, words
> and I missed that black wonder dressed in smoking
> that nocturnal party, that darkish riot, ah for
> doing extra hours and more hours
> collect and recollect money and make
> cash and the fact
> that the world would keep existing for me.

This poem is from *¡Arre! Halley ¡Arre!* (1986; Giddyup, Halley, giddyup!), a collection in which she talks about the Halley's Comet fever that Chile experienced in 1986, the last time this celestial body appeared in the earth's skies. Hernández redirects the reader's eye to what was important then: the comet was crossing the sky while underneath, on land, people were trying to feed themselves and to survive the dictatorship. The poetic voice in the poem is trying to make a living, so she doesn't have time to look at the stars. And she is also too conscious of what is happening around her, a reality too close for her to be able to look away. The last line of the poem reads: "They say that it was like a severed head appearing /without wanting to ever disappear. " Here, the comet becomes the head of a victim of the dictatorship, one of the thousands that disappeared under state terrorism, and Hernández masterfully weaves together the banality of the enthusiasm about a comet—fed by TV and newspapers—and the nuances and horrors of daily life in dictatorial Chile.

Sometimes, the burden she writes about is more vague, almost imperceptible in the daily order of things, like in this poem from *El orden de los días* (1991; The order of days):

> domestic insomnia clouds his days ...
> shirts hung out are lashed bodies
> physics doesn't hold hands with man
> the pots don't fill up just with water
>   this day doesn't end

Again, poverty and hunger are at the center of the poem. Hernández can write about birds she sees from her window, Halley's Comet, a trip, Santiago, but she never stops seeing what is affecting the collective, the ocean she returns to, word by word. She wrote in *Pájaros desde mi ventana* (2018; Birds from my window) that "Poetry is not thematic. /Poetry talks about everything at the same time. /Poetry is a box of surprises. " Hernández's poetry is truly filled with surprises, complex ideas, and the dark places of routine. Running through all this, there is always a deep political consciousness and commitment. She said when writing about the year of the coup d'état: "I suspect that it wouldn't have mattered to know that Goethe advised poets against taking an interest in politics. We were in a region in America where writing and being involved in the Latin American people's struggle was presented as unbreakable. " But what happens when the struggle never ends?

After the dictatorship, the new democratic governments from the center-left coalition and, later, the right dressed Chile up in the shiny clothes of neoliberalism, much like Pinochet had done during his regime. The country became wealthier, but the inequal distribution of riches favored just a few and condemned the rest of Chile to precariousness. Inequality became even more acute than before. So, when struggle doesn't end, poetry like Hernández's becomes always political without sermonizing. It is timeless, dedicated to daily life, its subtleties, its ugliness, and, also, its greatness, like in this poem from *Pájaros desde mi ventana*:

> This morning
> with the morning light
> the *tarabilla* has arrived
> to knock on the eastern window.
>
> We still believe in signs
> and we walk into the day hoping.

This book about birds is—as of now—the most recent one published by this poet whose work was for decades an open secret among readers and writers of poetry. It is also one of her most intimate books. We see what she sees from her window or, rather, windows, because the poems were written over four years and include some of her travels. But with Hernández it is never just about seeing; there is always something more in the images her poetry conveys. For example, we can imagine the eyes that see birds drinking from a drop of water, but those eyes bring us to a further sight. The poet's gaze pictures the birds thinking that they need to transform themselves, to go back to being dinosaurs, bigger, more powerful, ready to fight against what plunders their soil, water, and sky, in short, the Chilean environment.

This same preoccupation is in another poem of this collection:

They are gone, the *queltehues* of Luis Carrera.
To their nook arrived
the electric lawn mowers
the garden lights
the dogs that go down to pee from the high-rises.

They are gone
their elegant frame and
their curtsies.

Hernández's poetry tells us once and again that poetry talks about many things at the same time. It talks about what it sees outside a window, over our heads, in the streets, in the people's stomachs. It also can tell us about Elvira Hernández, who was not born Elvira Hernández but María Teresa Adriasola. She chose her pen name to write poetry and to let Adriasola write literary criticism, but now Hernández has taken over all of her work. It is her, Hernández, whom I think of while reading her poetry. It's Hernández whom I imagine seeing the streets of Santiago burning, writing down what she sees these days, using her eyes once more to register the authority's deafness and violence. Now that the police are deliberately blinding people who protest, eyes like Hernández's, eyes that see deep and can tell others what is happening, are more important than ever.

除恶务尽：铲除白人至上的执念*

法比安·卡诺尔著　艾利森·安德森译

Déchoukaj'：Uprooting the Fetishes of White Supremacy

Fabienne Kanor, trans. Alison Anderson

A writer traces how the murder of George Floyd is continuing to arouse people in cities everywhere, including her own mother in Martinique.

Sa ki ta la rivyè pa ka chayé'y. What belongs to you, river can't carry away. Everyone in the French Antilles, labeled French, has grown up with this saying. It is part and parcel of their beliefs, their customs; it is in their genes. It has fashioned their ways of being, thinking, dreaming, examining history, of triggering or idly waiting for their fate. To grasp how far the saying can go, you must move the words around, and you will conclude that what belongs to you belongs to no one else. The right to own and control your body, your history, your culture, your luck, your economy, and your

---

* 【作者简介】法比安·卡诺尔（Fabienne Kanor），女，作家和电影制作人，在宾夕法尼亚州立大学（Penn State University）教授法国文学、法语语系文学和电影。

本文原文为法语，由艾利森·安德森（Alison Anderson）译为英文。评论体，没有摘要、关键词和分节。

land ought to be a universal principle, a natural human right that no one can attack with impunity or without repercussions. Those who have plundered will be brought to book. Those who have been plundered must have their possessions restored to them. Sooner or later.

The murder of Mr. George Floyd, and the protests that this murder—caught live as it was being committed by a government employee—is continuing to arouse, have given us the opportunity to challenge the Creole folk saying. In cities everywhere, streets have been filled with raised fists, demanding justice and redress. Demanding the respect that is owed but that has been confiscated for centuries. Denouncing and dismantling the machinery of a world built on institutionalized racist practices: an old, old world that has never purged its sin of granting privilege to some and condemning others to timeless suffering.

But *what belongs to you, river can't carry away*. In Antwerp and in Bristol, in Brussels and Pretoria, in Nashville, Richmond, St. Paul, Boston, Washington, and elsewhere, communities whose rights have been scorned have taken to the streets, together with their allies, in order to uproot statues. They have fallen, the fetishes of white supremacy. They too are threatened with death or knocked to the ground, these men of marble, stone, or bronze, heirs of a slave-owning or colonial past and heroes of patchily recorded national sagas that all too often consist of blatant lies.

In Martinique it was Victor Schœlcher, consecrated founding father of the abolition of slavery in all the French colonies and possessions, who drew the wrath of the activists on May 22, the day on which the abolition of slavery is commemorated. In images streamed live online, the execution of the colossus is ritualized. The militants place a rope around his neck. They insult him, flog him, knock him off his pedestal, and kick him repeatedly until the French politician, who died in 1893, expires for good and returns to dust. Schœlcher is virtually a household name in Martinique; it is that omnipresent. It is, notably, the name of a school, a town, a commune, a street, and a public library that has been classified a historical monument. It is the name that generally springs to mind when the question of the second abolition of slavery is discussed. It is the name people know because it is the only one that the official version of History has retained and passed on to them. In Martinique, we don't speak of the independence of human beings but of the abolition of a system. Which presupposes, if we stick to the etymology, the intervention of a subject that wields power (in this case, France) and the passive presence of an inanimate object (slavery).

For my Martinican mother, who returned to her native land upon retirement after forty years of good and faithful service to France, this Schœlcher, whose name she systematically garbles when she says it, is the liberator of her oppressed Black people. My mother ignores the fact that her benefactor, like most of the politicians of his era, approved of the continued possession of the colonies, of the right of France to dispose of lands that did not belong to it, and of the expansion of French cultural values to these occupied territories. She does not know, my mother who left school at the age of fifteen, that the so-called definitive abolition which Schœlcher officially initiated did not in any respect lead to the end of the old world or of capitalism. Compensated for having lost their workforce, the former slave owners, protected by France, continued to prosper, invincible and firmly planted on their pedestals.

My mother, who has never taken to the streets to protest against anything, does not know, either, that for centuries a small number of her people have been fighting against French cultural alienation and the white domination incarnated in the French Antilles by the white Creoles. It was those militants who on May 22 decided to put an end to Schœlcher's legacy, not in order to sully the memory of the Republic, as certain high-ranking politicians hastened to claim, or because they think that the hero with the garbled name accomplished nothing of worth, but because they do not think that particular totem represents them. What they want to honor is the silenced memory of their rebel ancestors: those enslaved men, women, and children who struggled to survive and struggled to break free, with their sweat, their strength, and their faith. What these rebels are demanding, in the end, is to obtain *what belongs to them, that river can't carry away*; it is the right to tell their history in their own way, to tell the story of all the Black warriors who forged that history, the right to teach it in their schools, the right to show it and celebrate it in their public space, and the right to no longer be invisible.

I look at the faces of Schœlcher's uprooters. They speak openly and take responsibility for what they have done. I can see hope in their eyes but exhaustion, too. They have been tired for so long, for as long as this world has refused to change. They are so tired it makes you tired, just talking about it. On June 17, 2020, two weeks after the huge rally held outside the Paris tribunal against racism and police violence in France, the Haitian producer and filmmaker Raoul Peck declared he was "tired of being the one who *has to* make the effort to understand, the effort to explain, the effort to be magnanimous in the face of your 'innocence.'" He was addressing the country of France where he has been living for over fifty years. He was denouncing its "respectable paternalism" and the racism it has failed to own up to, "every bit as brutal and effective" as the one that suffocated George Floyd. Tired of seeing History always going in the same direction, always repeating itself, the director of *Lumumba* and *I Am Not Your Negro* admitted to how disenchanted he is feeling. That morning, before picking up his pen, he had burst into tears.

Raoul Peck's words took me back to June 2017, when I was invited to a conference in Port-au-Prince to hear Angela Davis. It was not a speech she gave, it was a lament. Thinking of her community, with its rights constantly violated, and its bodies that did not die of natural causes, Angela Davis confessed that she, too, was tired. We are tired, she said, of seeing our people get killed, of seeing them die, we are tired of mourning our dead.

I too have felt tired. I too have had tears in my eyes.

We die in Minneapolis because a policeman, a government employee, has the right to kill a Black man in America. We die in Haiti because "the debt of independence" imposed by France paralyzed the economy of the island for over a century. We die in Sierra Leone, in the Democratic Republic of Congo, in Ivory Coast, and elsewhere, because fewer public schools and hospitals are being established there than pillaging multinational corporations. We die in South Africa because the wounds inflicted by apartheid have still not healed. We die unburied in the Sonoran desert and in the depths of the Atlantic because what belongs to everyone—the planet and the right to move about on it freely—belongs only to a handful of privileged people. We will end up dying in Guadeloupe and Martinique, because the soil there, spiked with Kepone, contains enough of the substance to poison generations to come.

To write in the flesh, in the bones of a Black woman, is to give an account of all these deaths, and to try to offer healing to those who remain. It is to be a survivor and to wonder, at every instant, how much a word weighs, in this world. These days, I'm tempted to believe that words don't weigh a thing compared to acts. I have thought that if I could remake myself, could do it all over again, I would learn not to be afraid of dying, I would learn to fight. As a little girl I inherited the virus of inaction. As the child of poor Black immigrant parents, I was scared to death of taking my destiny in my hands, of claiming *what belongs to me and that river can't carry away*. When I was little, French people who were no more French than I was would say to me, "Go back to your country!" When I was little, at the white school where I was the only Black, I meekly put up with the white kids messing my hair and making fun of me. When I was little, I got called "Negro" and "ca-

ca boudin" and "Brillo pad. " When I was little, I wet my panties when it was my turn to raise my hand and express my opinion in front of the whole class. When I was little, I acted as if all the times my freedom had been taken from me didn't matter, as if the other kids, the ones who ruined what belonged to me, had every right to do so.

When I was little, I watched how my father—for all that he was a big man—would bend and bow and scrape, hide his accent and his six-foot-two frame and the color of his skin, hide his language and his honor. I saw him disappear behind his complexes and his fears. When I was little I put up with the smell of bleach my mother brought home from the hospital where she did everything a Black woman without an education or a future can do. She smelled of bleach, but it was as if she smelled dirty. When I was little, I was afraid to answer when people asked me what my mother did. And so I would make myself inconspicuous, I would do and think what white-skinned France expected of me. I said thank you, sorry, excuse me, I don't know, I'm not pretty, I'm not smart, I'm not this enough, I'll never be that enough.... When I was little, I pulled the rug from under my own feet to stand where they wanted me to stand. In Creole, we say *yo* to mean "they. " When I was little, to me this *yo* meant white people. I put this *yo* inside me, and we grew up together.

I am writing to reclaim what belongs to me.

As I watched Mr. George Floyd dying on television, I felt that I had already seen these images. A classic scene, based on familiar dramaturgical elements: on one hand, hatred and impunity. And on the other, force of habit. Force of habit, getting lynched in public, with no one coming to help you. Force of habit, not going to help. What would I have done, what might I have tried, if I'd been on the other side of the screen, among the onlookers? Would I have gone closer, instead of watching, to order the murderer to stand up? "Stand up if you're a man! Stand up!" Would I have risked my hide to save Floyd's? What does "risk my hide" mean? What do you get, for not doing anything?

Cowardice is a contagious disease.

Anger is benign when it works miracles.

I called my father.

I called my mother.

My father, as helpless as Floyd, did not comment on the murder. My mother, for the first time in her life, was indignant: "Too many people have died. There are too many Blacks getting killed by whites. Now they say you have to take a knee to protest, but racism is in the soil and the air they breathe in the United States. It's like the virus, they'll kill anyone, when you're Black they kill you. No! It has to stop!" If she lived in Min neapolis, she would have taken to the streets to uproot them all: every racist policeman in that town and in all the united American states, the racist whites in that town and in all the united American states, every racist on the entire planet. Then my mother stopped talking, because she was angry, and tired, and her knee was hurting her. She'd spent too many years waxing the corridors of France's hospitals. Her legs don't move as quickly as they used to.

I hung up.

Less alone, and prouder. And so, after forty years of services rendered to a homeland that imposed its silence and its heroes on her, my mother had broken her chains. Her no weighed more than any act of abolition, and more than all my words. She had taken Schœlcher's place. My mother, woman of the people, She-People, was now her own totem.

我们的复仇行为会成为孩子的笑柄

菲利普·梅特斯

Our Revenge Will Be the Laughter of Our Children Philip

Philip Metres

What is it about the revolutionary that draws our fascinated attention? Whether one calls it the North of Ireland or Northern Ireland, the Troubles continue to haunt the land and those who lived through them.

Séanna Walsh's face is impassive. That's the first thing you notice about him, after his imposing bulk of a body. It appears he has spent a long time to compose his face, to harden it, until it became hewn, glacial. Beneath it, you sense unplumbable depths. He was just sixteen years old when he went to prison for the first time in 1973, as a Volunteer in the Irish Republican Army, long before his black hair started turning ice-white. During the next twenty-five years, he'd spend over twenty years in serving three sentences, until he was finally released under the terms of the Good Friday Accords.

---

* 【作者简介】菲利普·梅特斯（Philip Metres），约翰·卡罗尔大学英语系教授，和平、公正与人权项目（Peace, Justice, and Human Rights program）主任。

本文原文为评论体，没有摘要、关键词和分节。

Still, Séanna hasn't lost his sense of humor. Our delegation of students and faculty from John Carroll University have just arrived to Belfast from America on an overnight flight, bleary-eyed, and now find ourselves at Malone Lodge Apartments hosting Séanna and his comrade Jim Gibney, prominent activists in the Republican movement, party members of Sinn Fein.

Leaning in on the rickety chair we've set up for him, Séanna asks us, "Have you had any rest yet?"

"None at all," I say, hoping the legs of the chair don't give out underneath him.

"Then you'll get some during this talk," he quips, leaning back.

We laugh, and the ghost of a smile seems to pass over his face. Perhaps he's softened a bit, since I first met him eight years before, but it's hard to tell.

Just behind him the bay window opens up, and the city is spread out below, all the way to the Black Mountain that stands at its far edge.

During the Troubles, that thirty-year descent into political violence that led to the deaths of thousands and tore the country apart, Séanna and Jim believed themselves to be revolutionaries in a war for freedom from British rule. Today, twenty years after the 1998 peace accords, even the name of this country is still contested. For the Protestant Unionists and Loyalists, we are now in Northern Ireland, part of the United Kingdom. For our guests, staunch Republicans, this is the North of Ireland: the last remnant of Eire still under British control. It depends on your point of view, what name you were willing to stand by, or even kill or die for. Séanna was prepared to do all three.

Now, during peacetime, the question is more mundane, and perhaps more difficult: What are you willing to live for?

Since 2011, with the assistance of Raymond Lennon, I've been coordinating study tours on the peace-building and conflict-transformation process in Northern Ireland for John Carroll University, meeting with locals who lived through the tumult of the Troubles and have come out on the other side of violence. Séanna and Jim have been stalwarts of our program, crucial inputs in a complex array of perspectives. I think of them as a pair, since every time I've met them, they've been together.

Perhaps it's because they grew up together in a Catholic enclave of Protestant East Belfast known as "the Short Strand." The little beach. The Short Strand, pronounced here as "strahned," was an island stranded in the middle of a sea of Loyalism, and those who grew up there knew what it meant to look out for your own.

Séanna's large and quiet presence fills the room. When he's handed a cup by one of the students, he frowns. "This tea is cold!"

Karly, the student, blanches, wordless, horrified. She's failed at her first job, making what they call *a spot* of tea. She just couldn't figure out when the electric teapot had come to a boil.

Walsh gets up and heats it up himself, mumbling a half-joke about the service around here.

In the margins of my notebook, I'm scrawling potential titles for the name of our meeting: *Tea with Terrorists*? Victims of IRA violence would call them murderers and worse. Séanna and Jim won't say what they have done, because, twenty years after the peace accords, they still could go to jail if those words or old crimes came to light.

I wonder what it's like to carry those secrets in the plain light of peacetime.

It's not fair to just call them terrorists. Look at them: Séanna and his gray-white hair, looking like someone's tough uncle, Jim and his piercing eyes and stylish frames, resembling a college history professor. They are like all of us, with complicated lives and reasons for what they have done or what they have failed to do.

But the truth is that I'm also a little afraid of them. I know their ferocious commitment; I can see the fierceness in their faces, and also the hurt.

How long does it take for a warrior to come home? In *The Odyssey*, after fighting in a decade-long war, Odysseus takes ten years to get home. In my favorite reading of the epic poem, psychiatrist Jonathan Shay proposes that the journey is a powerful allegory for the painful and circuitous route that every soldier needs to take in order to come home again. Working with veterans at the VA, many of whom struggled with PTSD and other emotional stress from combat, Shay comes to see each episode—from the poppy eaters to his long stay with Circe—as metaphors for the ways that soldiers rely on narcotics or sex to try to numb the pain.

A Republican and lifelong activist who also spent some of the Troubles in prison (despite never having been convicted), Jim Gibney is small and voluble, with intense blue eyes shining through his horn-rimmed glasses. He's the thinker, launching into his narrative of the North as a colonial problem, something that's been going on for "many centuries" but only "became armed in the last fifty years."

"I didn't like prison," Jim admits, as if embarrassed to say it in front of his friend and us. "In essence, though," he pauses, "it was education. Comradeship."

He leans forward, trying to find the words.

"I was transformed from being a boy who wouldn't have read a book to one who was a custodian of books."

When Séanna first went to prison back in 1973 for a failed bank robbery, he was no ordinary criminal seeking easy money. He was funding the Provisional Irish Republican Army. Séanna got involved in the movement when Loyalists killed his friend Patrick McGrory. Because history has a way of repeating itself here, it also happened to be in the same neighborhood that the B-Specials, a particularly vicious arm of the security forces in Northern Ireland, had murdered his grandfather fifty years earlier. All this history within arm's length of where Séanna and Patrick would have played on the streets as children.

In prison, Walsh got an education that his public schooling had never taught him—about Irish history, politics, and language. What began as anger turned into ideology.

"The British couldn't kill the fish," Séanna says, "so they tried to pollute the sea."

By age twenty, Séanna was appointed the IRA commanding officer in the Crumlin Road jail and was considered an old-timer.

As the sides entrenched, the Troubles got uglier—with all sides committing greater and more brutal acts of violence. The IRA and other paramilitary organizations on both sides of the conflict engaged in regular bombing campaigns in which civilians frequently died. They even terrorized their own communities, using kneecappings, banishment, or even disappearance to stop collaborators or criminals from interfering with the struggle. With the complete breakdown of local policing, paramilitaries functioned as law enforcement. If the person's crime were bad, they would get a "kneecapping" —that is, a bullet to the knee. But if the crime was egregious, they'd get a "six pack" —shots to both knees, ankles, and elbows. There were nearly as many kneecapping victims as there were deaths during the Troubles.

At the same time, the Shankill Butchers, a rogue gang affiliated with the Ulster Volunteer Force, terrorized Catholic neighborhoods by randomly torturing and murdering civilians in the late 1970s. Their crimes were among the most shocking of the Troubles. While the IRA could be seen as selecting its attacks against what they deemed were British military targets, the Butchers went further by randomly picking Catholics off the streets and subjecting them to the depths of human cruelty—pulling out teeth, beatings, and cutting throats all the way to the spine.

Ostensibly to restore public order, but also to break the Republican movement, the British government ended the political status of paramilitary prisoners in 1976 through the policy of Criminalization. Then, to crack down on the organizing happening in prison, the British government phased out the use of Crumlin Road jail and the open Nissen huts of Long Kesh prison, replacing them with the H-Blocks of The Maze, isolating the prisoners from one another.

If Criminalization was an attempt to delegitimize paramilitary activity, it only made the paramilitaries resist further. The IRA found new ways to organize and resist. Landing in prison a second time on weapons charges, Séanna participated in the Blanket Protest, begun in 1976 when IRA volunteer Kieran Nugent refused to wear the prison uniform given to him in the H-Block, wrapping himself instead in a blanket. By 1978 three hundred volunteers, including Séanna, had donned the blanket, refusing any accommodation.

"There was no master plan," Séanna says. "Just a young man who resisted."

The IRA prisoners were regularly beaten, even tortured, by guards who saw them as enemies of the state and a threat to their Protestant Unionist community. The No Wash Protest soon followed, when police refused the inmates a towel to dry themselves off. After a fight between an IRA volunteer and a police officer, inmates destroyed their cell furniture in protest of the beating. As a response, the guards removed all furniture, leaving only the blankets and mattresses.

The Dirty Protest ensued. Prisoners refused to leave their cells to shower or to slop their waste buckets out of the window and instead poured them under the door to flood the halls. In retaliation, the guards would push the urine back inside the cells. At some point, prisoners took to wiping their excrement on the walls of their cells. It had a theatrical madness to it, which makes a perverse sense, since it was either the act of men driven crazy or performance artists confronting their audience with an external representation of their condition of oppression. Maggots were everywhere, and the stench was overwhelming. The visiting Archbishop Tomas O Fiaich reported:

> One would hardly allow an animal to remain in such conditions, let alone a human being. The stench and filth in some of the cells, with the remains of rotten food and human excreta scattered around the wall, was almost unbearable. In two of them I was unable to speak for fear of vomiting. Several prisoners complained to me of beatings, of verbal abuse, of additional punishments ... for making complaints, and of degrading searches carried out on the most intimate parts of their naked bodies.

One film taken inside the prison shows two "blanket men" with long black hair and beards and haunted eyes, wrapped in a robelike blanket. They look like replicas of the 1970s images of Jesus. Yet in that same film, two other prisoners smile at the camera, singing or shouting something that we cannot hear. Despite the stench, the archbishop felt that the spirit of the men was high, as he noticed "Irish words, phrases and songs being shouted from cell to cell and then written on each cell wall with the remnants of toothpaste tubes."

In *One Day in My Life*, Republican martyr Bobby Sands writes keenly of the daily torments experienced by the prisoners:

> [The prison guard] stepped beside me, still laughing, and hit me. Within a few seconds, in the midst of white flashes, I fell to the floor as blows rained upon me from every conceivable angle. I was dragged back up again to my feet and thrown like a side of bacon, face downwards on the table. Searching hands pulled at my arms and legs, spreading me like a pelt of leather. Someone had my head pulled back

by the hair while some pervert began probing and poking my anus.

The bitter cold, the stench, the physical and psychological torture of regular beatings, anal cavity searches, and derision were a daily reality for prisoners. But Sands also wrote poignantly of throwing maggots from his cell window onto the yard below to watch the birds gather to feast: "sparrows and starlings, crows and seagulls were my constant companions... my only form of entertainment." He composed *One Day in My Life* in 1979 on bits of toilet paper that were smuggled to the outside—as were all the "comms" (communications) —in a biro pen refill case that he hid in his cheek or anus and then passed secretly to a family visitor to the prison.

Despite the violence he faced in prison, Sands remained spirited. "I am," he wrote near the end of his life, " (even after all the torture) amazed at British logic. Never in eight centuries have they succeeded in breaking the spirit of one man who refused to be broken. They have not dispirited, conquered, nor demoralised my people, nor will they ever."

When British prime minister Margaret Thatcher won election in 1979, she ratcheted up the rhetoric of Criminalization, and the prisoners fought back with a hunger strike in 1980. The strike was for political status but was called off when the prisoners thought they'd won.

Though the British made promises to change the policy in 1980, nothing changed in the prison. So after fierce debate within the Republican movement, another hunger strike began, with Bobby Sands taking the lead position. Other hunger strikers would follow, separated by one-week intervals, to ensure that the pressure would build on Britain.

While in prison, Jim Gibney, in a stroke of genius, decided to put Bobby Sands up for election to the British Parliament in Fermanagh, and a month into his hunger strike, he won. Sands would write in his final diary, begun during the hunger strike: "They won't break me because the desire for freedom, and the freedom of the Irish people, is in my heart. The day will dawn when all the people of Ireland will have the desire for freedom to show. It is then that we will see the rising of the moon. "

It's the soaring rhetoric of a Romantic, a Romantic willing to kill and to die.

In advance of our meeting, Jim told Raymond—our program coordinator and a native of Belfast who appears to be on friendly terms with everyone in this country—that they didn't really want to talk about him again. Bobby Sands. I wondered if it was because it's too hard to keep talking about the past. But the redoubtable Raymond mentions him anyway, along with Séanna's association with the Republican icon and martyr who died after sixty-six days on hunger strike, protesting the lack of political status for IRA volunteers in the prison.

Séanna met Bobby in Long Kesh in 1973. He was sixteen, and Bobby was eighteen. Both were released in 1976, and they "went back into active service," as Séanna calls it. Just a month before, my students and I had been reading Bobby Sands's final diary during the hunger strike, and Séanna is mentioned in the first pages.

"The thing about Bobby," Séanna says, looking into the distance, "was that he was just an ordinary guy. What really brought about the difference was the crucible of the H Blocks," the prison constructed to house and isolate political prisoners.

Séanna pronounces the *H* like "haitch," one of the only ways to distinguish Catholics from Protestants. It became a way for street thugs to test a stranger, to see whether they were worthy of freedom, a beating, or worse. Quite literally, it was said that Loyalists (or was it Republicans? — the story differs depending on the speaker) would carry a piece of paper with an *H* on it and ask their potential victim to pronounce it. That, or say the Hail Mary. Your answer could spare or end your life.

When we first met him seven years ago, when talking about Sands,

Séanna had to wipe away the wetness from his eyes, a sudden thaw, his impassivity cracked. This time he stays far from the hard part, skirting the shores, saying vaguely, "We're living with the legacy of that whole period."

During the strike, enormous pressure came in from the outside—from the Catholic Church, from family members—but Bobby Sands held fast. He had an iron will, total commitment. After seventeen days, he could no longer write in his diary. He kept asking for poetry to read.

Thirty days, forty days, fifty days, Sixty days.

Jim was the last person to see Bobby before he died in the prison hospital, and as he recalls it, his voice softens to a whisper.

Bobby's mother and sister were around his bed when he arrived. Bobby was blind at this point, having lost his sight due to the extreme effects of starvation.

"'Is that you, Jim?' he asked. I said yes. He gave me his hand and I took it. He said, 'Tell the lads I'm hanging in there.'"

Neither of them wants to go farther.

In 1981, after Sands's death, Séanna would become the officer-in-command of the IRA prisoners. He was back in prison for a third time, arrested for possession of rockets in 1988. After the Good Friday Accords allowed for the release of prisoners, he was the IRA representative selected to read the 2005 IRA statement to announce that they had given up the armed struggle in favor of a political one. In the bluish video, you can hear birds singing and a baby crying now and then in the background as Séanna sits in front of a green flag and reads a written statement, his face drawn and his voice direct but almost flat in affect.

I kept wondering about that baby, the life outside the frame of that camera, where someone had to mind a crying child and where birds sing as if there were no war.

It's been said that if the Troubles had been fought by films, the Irish would have beaten Britain long ago. It's true that the movies depicting the Irish struggle have been enormously popular and often artful. Yet it's also true that in the films of the Troubles, the IRA often play the foil. They begin as daring radicals, whose courage and audacity seem attractive and almost mythic, but later they reveal themselves to be cruel beyond any normal human measure. I watched these films with fascination—furious at British oppression and intransigence, in awe of the commitment of the IRA, and repulsed by the lengths they would go for a United Ireland.

In the film *In the Name of the Father* (1993), Gerry Conlon, a petty thief, is convicted of an IRA bombing he didn't commit. Based on actual events, Conlon, his father Giuseppe, and others—known as the Guildford Four and the Maguire Seven—are swept up in a British crackdown after the Guildford pub bombing in 1974. Tortured into false confessions or railroaded by false evidence, all of them wind up in prison for many years. During the film, Conlon becomes infatuated with a fellow prisoner and IRA member, Joe McAndrew, whose charisma, political vision, and muscle seem to be the opposite of his timid milquetoast of a father. McAndrew is a man who can whisper to the baddest Loyalist prisoner that he knows where his family lives and have that man announce to all that McAndrew is all right by him.

However, Conlon's awe changes when he witnesses McAndrew nearly burn the prison warden to death in an act of pure revenge. Watching the film, the viewer is drawn in by McAndrew, with his revolutionary discipline and ability to move people to action, and then sickened by him, as Conlon is later on. The hero, it turns out, is Conlon's sweet and simpering father, whose devotion to his wife and to his cause—writing letters to his British lawyer—demonstrate the durable heroism of ordinary faith.

Even so, what is it about the revolutionary that draws our fascinated attention? Is it the profound courage and single-mindedness of commitment? The ability to stretch oneself beyond the boundaries of normal human morality?

Séanna and Jim. Who's minding whom? Every time I've met one, I've met the other, as if they were two parts of the same person. In the room with us, both men cross their legs, left over right, rhyming. When one stops speaking, the other picks up. Jim gestures with his hands—fingertips touching, then dancing, then, when he stops speaking, crossing them over his chest. When either one stops speaking, he scrolls through his phone, as if he's managing two realities at once.

Jim sets up the colonial context of Ireland, the story of eight hundred years of British oppression, the red-meat-and-potatoes narrative of Republicanism, which led to their being dragged into the "war"—their favored term for the Troubles.

So often, former paramilitaries tell their story as if they were caught in conditions that gave them no choice but to fight. Séanna picks up the thread and turns it in another direction: "I've never felt that I had no choice. I always felt that I was the author of my own destiny."

That's what draws my fascination toward the revolutionary. That, despite holding fiercely onto their narrative of victimization, they choose not to remain passive victims. That in resistance, they become captains of their fate.

Yet at what cost—not only to the victims of their violence, but also to themselves?

In college, when I first got an inkling of the Troubles, I'd been reading the poems of W. B. Yeats in class. Despite the fact that he was part of the Protestant ascendancy, Yeats loved Ireland and the romance of Irish culture and nationalism. Yet something changed in him when, on Easter Sunday in 1916, the Irish Republican Brotherhood rose up and declared a free Irish Republic, taking over the general post office in Dublin and other sites around the country. The uprising, broadly opposed even by the Irish people, was brutally crushed by the British, and nearly all the leaders were executed. The severity of punishment inflamed Irish nationalism and would lead to the War of Independence.

In his poem "Easter 1916," Yeats measures his own fascination-repulsion reaction to the Easter rebels, many of whom he knew personally, in his powerful refrain: "All changed, changed utterly: /A terrible beauty is born." Yeats saw the power of that sacrificial act of revolutionary violence, how it changed so much in his benighted Ireland. It was terrible, in both senses of the term: awe-inspiring and awful. Yet it was also beautiful.

Despite his aristocratic background (which he shared with many of the leaders of the rebellion), Yeats could see that they'd chosen to give up the "meaningless tales" that they'd shared at their social clubs to become their own story. Yet he's haunted by what they've given up in the process of their revolutionary ardor:

> Hearts with one purpose alone
> Through summer and winter seem
> Enchanted to a stone
> To trouble the living stream.
> The horse that comes from the road,
> The rider, the birds that range
> From cloud to tumbling cloud,
> Minute by minute they change;
> A shadow of cloud on the stream
> Changes minute by minute;
> A horse-hoof slides on the brim,
> And a horse plashes within it;
> The long-legged moor-hens dive,
> And hens to moor-cocks call;
> Minute by minute they live:
> The stone's in the midst of all.

> Too long a sacrifice
> Can make a stone of the heart.

Yeats wonders whether the rebels became stones in the living stream, forgoing their essential humanness in this violence. Such sacrifice, the sacrifices that they made to rebel—did it turn their hearts to stone? did they lose their humanity?

This is the question we cannot know, those of us who have not gone into the shadows and risked everything personally and made decisions that could lead to death. But I think of Bobby Sands feeding birds outside his prison cell window with the maggots from his own offal, and of him reading poetry while starving himself to death.

Perhaps it's not fair, director Jim Sheridan's depiction of the revolutionary in *In the Name of the Father*—which is, after all, the usual representation. It reflects bourgeois values. We, well-meaning liberals, pay lip service to resistance but advocate nonviolence from the safety of middle-class privilege, into which we can retreat after the end of any activism. So many of us are simply unable or unwilling to make the sacrifices necessary to make radical political change.

In an interview about the film *The Crying Game*, a stunning film about the Troubles and the possibility of self-transformation, Sinn Fein writer and Republican activist Danny Morrison laments that the film unfairly depicts the IRA. To Morrison, no film had captured their humanity: "Why isn't there a film made which portrays the IRA as flawed . . . but still emerging at the other end with their humanity intact?" The two main characters "are depicted as psychopaths. . . . They are all fanatics. To me, that's unreal." Perhaps he's right. But there's an ache in his wondering, as if that journey back to humanity is a long one.

Morrison himself is known among Irish poetry circles for his notable meeting with Seamus Heaney on a train. In Heaney's telling, Morrison tried to hector Heaney into writing a poem for the prisoners engaging in the Dirty Protest and later the hunger strikes. Heaney refused to cave to the pressure. In "The Flight Path," Heaney writes that Morrison demanded a poem: "'When, for fuck's sake, are you going to write /Something for us?' / 'If I do write something, /Whatever it is, I'll be writing for myself,'" he replied.

Morrison remembers it differently, as a cordial encounter that ended in a handshake: "In *Stepping Stones* [Heaney] says that he felt he was being 'commanded,' and for that reason changed his mind. . . . I find that explanation hard to reconcile with the fact that after our conversation we parted with a handshake; he gave me his address and telephone number and agreed to read the poetry of Bobby Sands," which included criticism of artists and poets for their silence in the face of oppression and which Sinn Féin later published.

Did Heaney exaggerate his rebellion against the rebels, or did Morrison minimize the threatening impact of being approached by a member of the IRA to ask for fealty? We'll never know. We stand in the gulf between the civilian and the warrior, between the poet and the revolutionary.

Back in Belfast, sometimes Jim and Séanna's back-and-forth testimony in our little apartment room feels a little staged, as if they are performing for us. Maybe that's because they keep switching between talking and looking at their phones. There is a rote quality to it, as if they've heard everything the other has said or are acting in a play whose script is not yet completed, the script of Republicanism and its unremitting quest for a United Ireland.

As if to punctuate a previous point, Séanna lifts up his phone to us and says, "I hope you don't think I'm uneducated, scrolling through the phone. I was looking for this picture that someone posted on Facebook." He turns the screen toward us. It's a bus whose route reads "#93 Bobby Sands Street," and it's from Nantes, France.

Raymond comments on the international reach of Bobby Sands, including in Iran. Séanna picks up the idea, noting that Bobby Sands Avenue in Tehran came about when some local revolutionaries put a homemade placard over the sign for Winston Churchill Avenue. Later, the authorities made it official. The street was the site of the British embassy.

"For a while," Séanna said, glee radiating through his usually impassive face, "all correspondence to the British embassy had to be addressed to Bobby Sands Avenue." The British actually built a side street with a new name to create a new address for the embassy, just to avoid the humiliation.

(Later I'd learn that, thirty years before, during the burial of three IRA volunteers in Milltown Cemetery, a rogue Loyalist named Michael Stone attacked the funeral crowd with grenades and pistols. Shrapnel tore into Séanna, who was driven to the hospital in a funeral hearse. He'd never mentioned this attack, in all the years we'd been meeting with him.)

After a pause in the back-and-forth between Séanna and Jim, I begin my question: "You spent over twenty years in prison—"

"—Twenty-one," he interrupts. As if he's counted every day. And keeps counting them.

"What was it like to be released, after such a long time? How did you manage? What was it like to be freed?"

"Have you ever read *L'Étranger*? The novel by Camus? That's how I felt. An outsider."

Séanna squints and looks out into the distance over Divis Mountain when he speaks. *Divis* means "black" in Irish, as the sun falls behind it every night.

"I felt numb. It has dulled somewhat as I've gotten older." He pauses, searching for the words. "In prison, I thought freedom was simple, was easy. It meant being out of prison. But I was naïve. Whenever I came out of prison, I was as dedicated as I was as a sixteen-year-old. But the context has changed. There is no longer an armed struggle. I traveled the length of the country to convince comrades to lay down their arms."

It helped, he said, that he had a strong wife, also a Republican, who raised two daughters while he was in prison. I wonder what they might say, about what it was like to have a husband and father that they barely knew outside of prison, who was absent more than he was present. I wonder what his wife would say about her side of the struggle, what it was like at home.

The Republican movement had a place for him when he got out, which was critical because he couldn't get work otherwise.

In some ways, he's like the several thousand other IRA Volunteers who walked out of prison after years behind bars, blinking in the sudden light of freedom, trying to find their way in the new, post-Troubles reality. They did their national service, as it was called, but so many are the walking wounded, suffering from alcoholism and drug addiction, trying to cope with all kinds of pain. The descendants of Odysseus, not yet in Ithaka. Still trying to get home.

Tony, one of our students, begins a question: "Bobby Sands said that our children's revenge—"

"—Our revenge," Walsh corrects, almost barking, "will be the laughter of our children."

It's important for him that we get things right, that the record is clear. Twenty-one years in prison. Sixty-six days on hunger strike. Our revenge will be the laughter of our children.

Of all the words I've read and heard about Northern Ireland, these are the ones that have haunted me most. Painted prominently on the Bobby Sands mural on the Republican enclave of Falls Road, Sands's words encapsulate the paradox of the Republican struggle, a struggle that has led to much blood in the name of a free and united Ireland.

The struggle, according to Sands, was the means to create a better life for their children. So that their children wouldn't have to live the way that they had to live. Isn't that every parent's wish, that our children be spared our particular hardships? In this land, when so many suffered oppression and violence for so long, that natural parental feeling was even more pronounced. So that their faces might be free from the ice of the Troubles, to laugh or to cry, without fear of what it might mean to open up that way.

Perhaps this is why Séanna keeps moving himself, keeps telling his story—that it may be different for his children, or his children's children.

As I complete this essay, I look up Séanna online to find something I didn't know about him, something that might reveal more of his mystery.

He's on Facebook, I discover, and I click on the link.

In the profile photo, he's sitting in a plush chair, an infant wrapped in a blanket and lying wide-eyed across his arms, with a look of animal seriousness that some babies wear. Right next to them, a vivacious redheaded toddler straddles the back of a couch. He and the toddler squint similarly toward the camera. That's a squint I know, the squint of Séanna thinking, unconsciously disagreeing, with the glare of a world that never seemed to be gentle or fair or free. Yet the shapes of their mouths—it's uncanny—are nearly identical, both parting in a smile.

跨文化与跨媒介研究

迷狂与开悟：论巴塔耶与铃木大拙的关系

张历君*

【摘要】 巴塔耶在1934年结识了后来的爱侣萝荷。也是在这一年，巴塔耶因受风湿病困扰，前往意大利养病。他在这段期间开始接触东方灵修方式。赖守正认为，巴塔耶"因接触东方灵修方式（禅、瑜伽）而有所感悟，故有《内在经验》和《冥想方法》两本书的诞生"。1942年，巴塔耶因染上肺结核而被迫辞去他在法国国家图书馆的职务。他在养病期间，完成《内在经验》。这本书最终在1943年由伽利玛出版社初版。值得注意的是，《内在经验》初版后一年，巴塔耶在1944年2月至4月的日记中，记下了他对铃木大拙著作的阅读心得，并谈及了他对禅宗的理解。这部分日记后来发展为一篇题为《内在经验与禅》的短文，收入1945年初版的《论尼采》一书，成为该书的第三篇附录。本文尝试初步阐明，巴塔耶有关"内在经验"的思考，在何种意义上构成他接受铃木大拙著作和禅学思想的基本条件；并进而点出巴塔耶"超越诗歌"的主张与禅宗诗偈之间相互呼应的关系。

【关键词】 巴塔耶；铃木大拙；内在经验；非知；开悟

---

* 【作者简介】张历君，香港中文大学跨文化研究哲学博士，现为香港中文大学中国语言及文学系客座助理教授，亦为《现代中文学刊》通讯编委、苏州大学海外汉学（中国文学）研究中心成员、香港中文大学图书馆香港文学特藏顾问委员以及香港艺术发展局评审员。研究方向为中国现代文学与思想史、现代中西跨文化关系、文化研究理论等。

Ecstasy and Satori: On the Relation of Georges Bataille and Daisetz Teitaro Suzuki

Lik-kwan Cheung

Abstract: In 1934, Georges Bataille got acquaintance with Laure who became his lover afterwards. That same year, he suffered from the rheumatism and traveled into Italy to recuperate. It was around this period that Bataille began his study of the Eastern spiritual practice. According to a Bataille scholar Shou-Chen Lai's research, Bataille completed his two books L'expérience intérieure and Méthode de meditation on the basis of the inspiration from the Eastern spiritual practice (Zen and Yoga). In 1942, Bataille quitted his position at the Bibliothèque Nationale de France owing to phthisis. He made use of the period of recuperation to finish L'expérience intérieure, which was initially published in 1943 by Gallimard Press. It is noteworthy that Bataille wrote about his reading experience on Daisetz Teitaro Suzuki's works and the understandings on Zen in his diary from February to April in 1944—the year after the first publication of L'expérience intérieure. A part of his diary was later developed into an essay titled as "Inner Experience and Zen," which became Appendix III of his book, Sur Nietzsche (1945). This paper attempts to preliminarily reveal how Bataille's idea of "inner experience" played a major role for his reception of Suzuki's Zen Buddhism. This research will also point out the relation between Bataille's idea of "beyond poetry" and his understandings of Chinese Zen poems.

Key words: Georges Bataille; Daisetz Teitaro Suzuki; Inner experience; Non-knowledge; Satori

让人激动的是，正是巴塔耶（Georges Bataille）——他的名字对于很多读者而言意味着迷狂（extase）的神秘，或是对迷狂体验的非宗教寻求——排除了［……］"在某个集体性实体当中的融合式完成"（如南希［Jean-Luc Nancy］所言）。那是巴塔耶所深深反感的。我们不要忘了，他考虑的与其说是让人忘记（自身在内的）一切迷醉状态，还不如说是一个迫切要求的过程，而这个过程，为了实现自身，开动并外置了一种并不充分且无法取消如此不充分性的生存，一种毁灭内在性和超越性之惯常形式的运动。

——布朗肖（Maurice Blanchot）[①]

一　无头公案

1936年，巴塔耶创办了一份新刊物《无头者》（Acéphale）。这本杂志的第一期只有八页，共收录了两篇文章：一篇是巴塔耶的《神圣的共谋》（"The Sacred Conspiracy"）；另一篇则是克罗索斯基（Pierre Klossowski）关于萨德侯爵（Marquis de Sade）的文章《怪物》（"The Monster"）。[②] 赖守正是这样理解"头者"（Acéphale）一词的意义的："'头'代表的是理性、权威、天主，无头的人指的是鄙视心灵与理性、不再相信天主、不再向权威屈服，任由激情奔放驰骋者。"[③] 马松（André Masson）与巴塔耶商量后，为《无头者》绘画了封面插画——一个无头人身的形像：他既非人亦非神，双脚牢牢立于大地，其私处是死神的头颅，他的肚子里是迷宫，胸前有两颗星星，一手持刀，一手握着燃烧的心脏。[④] 布罗奇（Alastair Brotchie）认为，马松的这幅插

[①] 布朗肖：《不可言明的共通体》，夏可君、尉光吉译，重庆大学出版社2016年版，第13—14页。Maurice Blanchot, *The Unavowable Community*, Trans. Pierre Joris, New York: Station Hill Press, 1988, pp. 7–8.

[②] *Acéphale*, No.1, Jun. 1936, pp. 1–8. Georges Bataille et al., *The Sacred Conspiracy: The Internal Papers of the Secret Society of Acéphale and Lectures to the College of Sociology*, Ed., Marina Galletti and Alastair Brotchie, London: Atlas Press, 2017, pp. 123–129.

[③] 巴代伊（Georges Bataille）：《情色论》，赖守正译注，台北：联经出版公司2012年版，第56页。

[④] Stuart Kendall, *Georges Bataille*, London: Reaktion Books, 2007, p. 129.

画,是对巴塔耶整体思想的有力表达。① 马松的插画明显是对达文西(Leonardo da Vinci)《维特鲁威人》(*L'Uomo Vitruviano*)等文艺复兴时期画作的戏仿。达文西等的画作描绘了人体和谐构造和比例,而马松的插画则提供了这类文艺复兴人体描绘的反观念论版本(anti-idealist version)。马松的插画无疑将巴塔耶思想中那种颠倒的赫耳墨斯主义(reversed hermeticism)道成肉身。"无头者"不单指摆脱了思想的人,更指一个取消了等级制度的、群龙无首的组织(headless organization)。

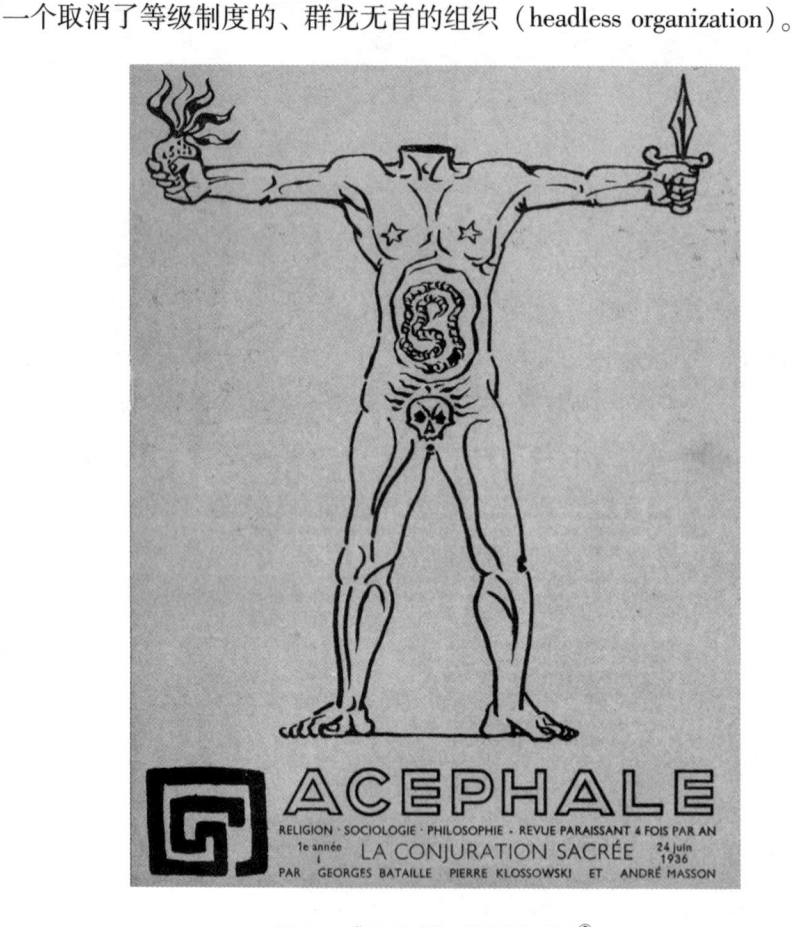

图1 《无头者》创刊号封面[②]

---

① Georges Bataille et al., *Encyclopaedia Acephalica*, London: Atlas Press, 1995, p. 12.
② 插图引自 *Acéphale*, No. 1, June 1936, p. 1。

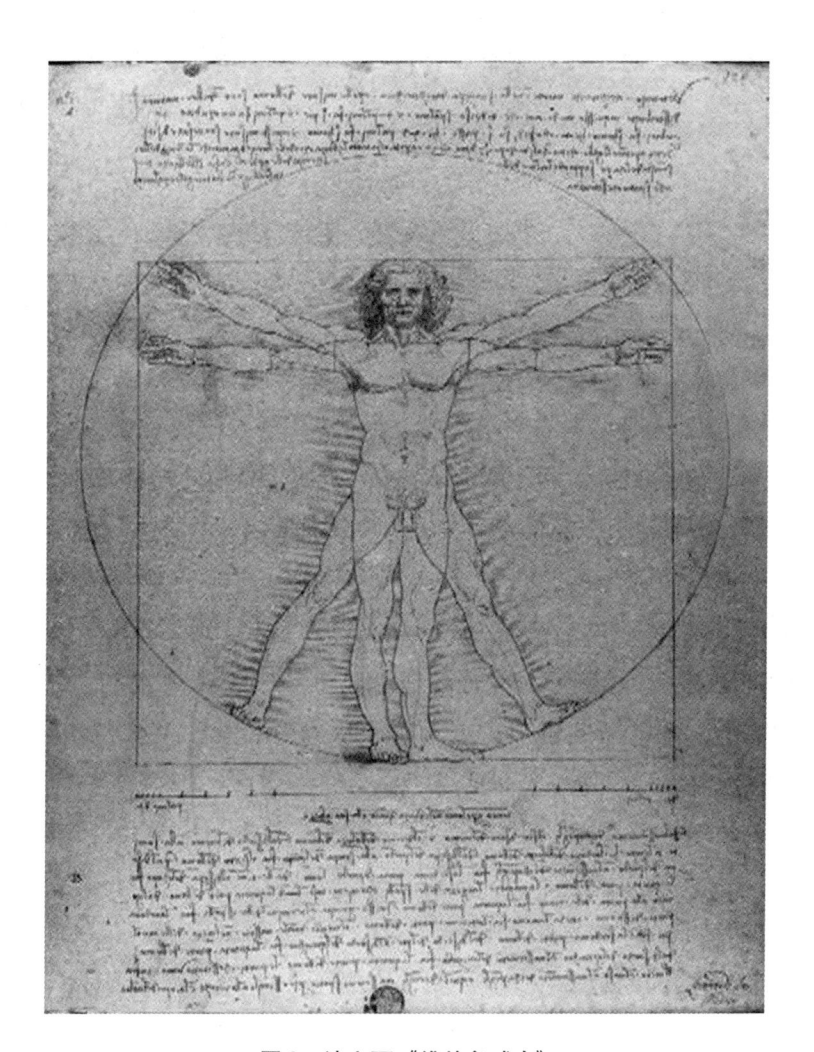

图 2　达文西《维特鲁威人》

马松的插画明显启发了巴塔耶。巴塔耶在《神圣的共谋》中这样写道：

> 在我自己之外，我遇到了一个让我大笑的存在，因为他没有头颅。他也同时让我感到恐怖，因为他是由纯洁和罪恶所构成的；他左手执持钢铁的武器，右手则拿着尤如圣心的火焰。他在同一场爆发中统一了生和死。他不是人，也不是神。他不是我，但大

于我：他的胃是一个迷宫，他在其中迷失了自己，而我也与他一同迷失了自我，我发现自己就是他，换言之，就是怪物。①

巴塔耶认为，人类受到头脑的禁制，犹如囚犯被囚禁于监狱中。唯有摆脱头脑，才能获得解脱和自由。他认为，超越人类的存在不是上帝，因为上帝是禁制一切罪恶的象征，也就是对自由和解脱的否定。如此一来，超越人类的存在应该是对禁制一无所知的纯洁存在。② 而马松的无头者插画显然将巴塔耶的意念清晰地勾勒出来。

1935 年，巴塔耶与布勒东（André Breton）、克罗索斯基、艾吕雅（Paul Éluard）、海涅（Maurice Henie）和佩雷（Benjamin Péret）等为了抵抗法西斯主义，共同组织了"反击"（Contre-Attaque）小组。这个小组又称"革命知识分子战斗联盟"（Union de lutte des intellectuels révolutionnaires）。③ 但巴塔耶很快便对布勒东心生不满。1936 年，巴塔耶辞去了"反击"秘书长的职务。从这个时期开始，他一边创办《无头者》杂志，一边构想成立一个与杂志同名的新型共同体社团。这个社团"更多以宗教而非政治为导向"。④ 无头者小组的核心成员基本上来自"反攻"小组，换言之，与苏瓦里纳（Boris Souvarine）的民主共产主义社（Democratic Communist Circle）是同一个圈子的人脉。无头者小组的部分成员与巴塔耶一起居住在马尔利森林（Marly forest）附近的圣日耳曼昂莱（Saint-Germain-en-Laye），并在此举行会议。⑤ 这个小组在马尔利森林的秘密聚会，后来成为在法国知识界广泛流传的轶事。肯德尔（Stuart Kendall）在《巴塔耶》（*Georges Bataille*）一书

---

① Georges Bataille et al., *The Sacred Conspiracy: The Internal Papers of the Secret Society of Acéphale and Lectures to the College of Sociology*, p. 125.

② Georges Bataille et al., *The Sacred Conspiracy: The Internal Papers of the Secret Society of Acéphale and Lectures to the College of Sociology*, p. 125.

③ 巴代伊（Georges Bataille）：《情色论》，赖守正译注，第 55 页。

④ 肯德尔：《巴塔耶》，姚峰译，北京大学出版社 2018 年版，第 191 页。Stuart Kendall, *Georges Bataille*, p. 129.

⑤ Stuart Kendall, *Georges Bataille*, London: Reaktion, 2007, p. 133.

中这样描述这些秘密聚会的情况：

在圣日耳曼昂莱城外的马尔利森林，阿塞法勒（Acéphale）在每月的月圆之夜集会。之前以便笺通知成员抵达的时间和方式，即何时乘坐哪列火车。他们都在沉默中悄然而至。新加入的成员——巴塔耶称之为"幼虫"——由乔治·安布罗西诺（Georges Ambrosino）作为他们的引导，悄无声息。会议在森林中一棵被闪电劈到的树木旁召开。巴塔耶扮演牧师的角色，橡树就是他的讲坛，以一匹马的头骨作为装饰。与会者歃血为盟，所用的刀类似阿尔法勒人像中的那把。有经验的成员不会和任何人说起他们在这里的所见所为。①

诚如布朗肖所言，"'无头者'（Acéphale）。我相信，它是巴塔耶所唯一看重的团体，多少年来，它仍作为一种极端的可能性，铭刻在他心中"②。四十多年后，克罗索斯基仍对"无头者"念念不忘。他在 1990 年接受雷威（Bernard-Henri Lévy）的访问，便谈到巴塔耶创立"无头者"的目的："创立一种宗教，也就是他想干的。创立一种没有上帝的宗教"③，并详细记述自己亲身经历的马尔利森林的秘密聚会：

[……]我记得在马尔里森林（Marly forest）里面对"雷击树"默祷的场景。[……]仪式很美。大家都产生一种同情心理。当然不是怜悯含义的同情！我们是共享……我们共同参与……[……]我们是二十几人乘火车一直到达……这个车站叫什么名字来着？这是个很漂亮的车站，圣—依—拉—布列台什。我们是

---

① 肯德尔：《巴塔耶》，姚峰译，第 201 页。Stuart Kendall, *Georges Bataille*, p. 135.
② 布朗肖：《不可言明的共通体》，夏可君、尉光吉译，第 23 页。Maurice Blanchot, *The Unavowable Community*, trans. Pierre Joris, p. 13.
③ 雷威（Bernard-Henri Lévy）：《自由的冒险历程：法国知识分子历史之我见》，曼玲、张放译，中央编译出版社 2000 年版，第 168 页。

在晚上到达那里。当时嘱咐大家的是:"您默祷;但要秘密进行!一定什么也不要说出您所感受到的,或想到的东西!"巴塔伊(Georges Bataille)本人没再向我们说更多的东西,他从未告诉过我们这类仪式表示着什么。我能对您说的,就是觉得仪式很美。我记得,那天晚上下着瓢泼大雨,在一棵雷击过的树脚下有一堆硫磺、硝石、树脂点燃的火。一切都是事先安排的。雷击树可能就是"无头兽"(Acéphale)神,就像马松画的那个形象。[1]

克罗索斯基认为,这不是什么"入教的神秘仪式"。[2] 在他的理解中,那棵"雷击树"可能就是巴塔耶和马松二人共同构想的"无头者"。他在忆述中反复强调"沉默"和"默祷"在整个聚会过程中的重要性。这一感受与布朗肖对"无头者的共通体"(The Acéphale Community)的理解不谋而合:"'无头者'一直披着神秘的面纱。那些参与其中的人并不确定自己是其中的一份子。他们从不提起,或者,其言语的继承者都持有一种仍坚定地维持着的审慎。以'无头者'的名义出版的文字并没有揭示这个团体的范围,只有几句稍有提及,但许久之后也还让那些写下它们的人深感震惊。共通体的每个成员不仅是整个的共通体,更是诸存在之整体的激烈的、失调的、爆烈的、无力的化身,这些存在倾向于完好地生存,结果得到了它们已提前坠入其中的虚无(néant)。每个成员只有通过分离的绝对(l'absolu),才能形成团体;而分离需要肯定自身,以便打破关系,直至生成关系,一种悖谬的、甚至无意义的关系,因为这是同排除一切关系的其他绝对(l'autres absolu)建立的绝对的关系。"[3] 克罗索斯基在聚会回忆中所强调的"沉默"和"默祷",相当重要。巴塔耶正是透过"沉默",打

---

[1] 雷威(Bernard-Henri Lévy):《自由的冒险历程:法国知识分子历史之我见》,曼玲、张放译,中央编译出版社2000年版,第169页。

[2] 雷威(Bernard-Henri Lévy):《自由的冒险历程:法国知识分子历史之我见》,曼玲、张放译,中央编译出版社2000年版,第170页。

[3] 布朗肖:《不可言明的共通体》,夏可君、尉光吉译,第23—24页。Maurice Blanchot, *The Unavowable Community*, trans. Pierre Joris, pp. 13 – 14.

破成员在日常生活中所形成的既有关系，并借此重新在聚会中生成另一种"悖谬的、甚至无意义的关系"。这也是布朗肖所谓的"同排除一切关系的其他绝对（l'autres absolu）建立的绝对的关系"。

二　内在经验

1934 年，巴塔耶与第一任妻子席薇雅（Sylvia Maklés）分居。席薇雅几年后与拉康（Jacques Lacan）结婚，成了拉康的第二任妻子。巴塔耶在 1934 年同年结识了后来的爱侣萝荷（Laure）。萝荷原名克莱特·佩尼奥（Colette Peignot），当时仍然是苏瓦里纳的女友。也是在这一年，巴塔耶因受风湿病困扰，前往意大利养病。他亦在这段期间开始接触东方灵修方式。赖守正认为，巴塔耶"因接触东方灵修方式（禅、瑜伽）而有所感悟，故有《内在经验》（*L'expérience intérieure*）和《冥想方法》（*Méthode de méditation*）两本书的诞生"。[①]

1936 年，正当巴塔耶构想"无头者"社团的时候，他和萝荷正式结为情侣。按照肯德尔的考证，萝荷并未成为"无头者"的核心成员，应该将她视为社团边缘的影子人物。[②] 无论如何，萝荷肯定是巴塔耶这个时期的重要伴侣。1938 年，萝荷因肺病不幸去世。[③] 巴塔耶后来撰写了悼念文章《萝荷的一生》（"Vie de Laure"）。他在文章中这样形容萝荷："萝荷的一生带有部分放荡的气息。[……] 萝荷的美只为伯乐展现。我从没看过像她这样不易妥协、内心纯净、也不摆架子的人。对她而言，任何事都显而易见。[……] 大家总说她的名字之于我，就像她哥哥所言，是巴黎活力之泉源，我想确实如此。她象征着纯洁、自负中又带点谦逊。"[④] 在萝荷的葬礼上，巴塔耶在棺木盖

[①] 巴代伊（Georges Bataille）：《情色论》，赖守正译注，第 54—55、57 页。
[②] Stuart Kendall, *Georges Bataille*, p. 134.
[③] 巴代伊（Georges Bataille）：《情色论》，赖守正译注，第 57 页。
[④] 转引自巴代伊（Georges Bataille）《情色论》，赖守正译注，第 55 页。Laure（Colette）Peignot, *Laure: The Collected Writings*, trans. Jeanine Herman, San Francisco: City Lights Books, 1995, pp. 235, 237, 238.

上前，将威廉·布莱克（William Blake）的《天堂与地狱的婚姻》（The Marriage of Heaven and Hell）放进萝荷的棺材。

巴塔耶在萝荷死后，翻阅她留下来的笔记，他开始意识到自己失去的一切。[①] 他在萝荷去世后的几个月里，精进了自己的冥想修行。他阅读并实验瑜伽修持，全身心投入修习濒死大乐的法门。[②] 这一切都成为他几年后写作《内在经验》一书的前行准备。1942年，巴塔耶因染上肺结核而被迫辞去他在法国国家图书馆的职务。他在养病期间，完成《内在经验》。这本书最终在1943年由伽利玛（Gallimard）出版社初版发行。[③] 巴塔耶时年四十四岁，这是第一本在封面上正式署上他个人名字的专著。[④]

然而，诚如肯德尔所言，"实际上，称《内在体验》（Inner Experience）为一本书是很勉强的，它是作者个人经验的记录，其文本如作者经验一般杂乱无章。第二部分——《折磨》（'Torture'）——直接记录了作者的思想发生滋长的过程；行文会被记忆和引证打断，被对话和引语打断；不断变化的笔调、语域，甚至文体：诗歌会扰乱哲学的诗意散文"[⑤]。程小牧亦指出，巴塔耶本人称他自己在《内在经验》所展现的这种驳杂不纯的文体为"记叙"（récit），其实就是他"平时写下的思想笔记的集合"。[⑥] 巴塔耶这种独特的写作风格，其实是与他有关"没有上帝的宗教"的思考方向紧密联系起来的。

1954年，巴塔耶增订再版《内在经验》。他在这个再版本中，将

---

① 转引自巴代伊（Georges Bataille）《情色论》，赖守正译注，第55页。Laure（Colette）Peignot, Laure: The Collected Writings, trans. Jeanine Herman, San Francisco: City Lights Books, 1995, p. 146.

② 转引自巴代伊（Georges Bataille）《情色论》，赖守正译注，第55页。Laure（Colette）Peignot, Laure: The Collected Writings, trans. Jeanine Herman, San Francisco: City Lights Books, 1995, p. 148.

③ 巴代伊（Georges Bataille）：《情色论》，赖守正译注，第58页。

④ Georges Bataille, Inner Experience, trans. Stuart Kendall, Albany: State University of New York Press, 2014, p. vii.

⑤ 肯德尔：《巴塔耶》，姚峰译，第242页。Stuart Kendall, Georges Bataille, p. 162.

⑥ 程小牧：《译者前言》，载巴塔耶（Georges Bataille）《内在经验》，程小牧译，生活·读书·新知三联书店2017年版，第13页。

《内在经验》和《冥想方法》合成一册，并加上《1953年附言》（"Post-Scriptum 1953"）一文。增订再版的《内在经验》被列入一个五卷本丛书的出版计划里。这套丛书总题为《非神学大全》（*La Somme athéologique*）。这个总题明显是对圣托马斯·阿奎那（St. Thomas Aquinas）的经典名著《神学大全》（*Summa Theologica*）的戏仿。① 在巴塔耶生前，这个五卷本丛书的出版计划，最终只真正完成了第一卷《内在经验》，其余四卷均未完成编辑或撰写工作。

然而，"非神学"（athéologie）却肯定是巴塔耶后期提出的一个重要概念。1957年初版的《情色论》（*L'Érotisme*）虽然没有被纳入《非神学大全》的丛书出版计划中，但巴塔耶却将该书第一章题为《内在经验中的情色》（"L'érotisme dans l'expérience intérieure"），并在文中尝试初步探讨他的"非神学"研究方法与内在经验的关系：

> ［……］学者从外面发言，像解剖学家谈论大脑一样。
> ［……］<u>我则是从内部讨论宗教，如同神学家谈论神学一般。</u>
>
> 没错，神学家谈的是<u>基督神学</u>。而我要谈的宗教，不同于天主教，并非<u>单一种</u>宗教。它可能是<u>宗教</u>，但它从一开始就非某一特定宗教。我要谈的不是某一特定的祭仪或教条，也非某特定宗教团体，而是所有宗教所面临的问题：就像神学家处理神学问题，我将这些问题当作自己的课题。不过我不谈基督宗教。若非基督宗教也是宗教的一种，我会对它退避三舍。这点可从本书以情色为主题可以清楚看出。情色的发展既然在各方面均无法自外于宗教，反对情色的基督宗教谴责了大多数的宗教。就某层意义而言，基督宗教可能是最不宗教的宗教。
>
> ［……］

---

① Stuart Kendall ed., *The Unfinished System of Nonknowledge*, Minneapolis and London: University of Minnesota Press, 2001, pp. xi - xii. Stuart Kendall, *Georges Bataille*, pp. 189 - 190.

如此一来，我谈论宗教时，就可以不像宗教史的老师一样，只将婆罗门神当作众多神祇中的一个：我会把自己当作是婆罗门神本身。但是，我并非婆罗门神，我什么也不是。我必须追求某种没有传统、没有仪式，既没有人引导也没有任何阻碍的孤独经验。在本书中我要描述的经验不涉及任何信仰；本质上，我想传达内在经验：一种在我看来不属于任何宗教的宗教经验。①

巴塔耶讲得很清楚："内在经验"其实是一种"不属于任何宗教的宗教经验"。他并明确指出，自己会以跟宗教史的老师不一样的方式讨论宗教。譬如，他不会像宗教史的老师那样，将婆罗门神视为神祇。恰恰相反，他"会把自己当作是婆罗门神本身"。但他同时也清醒认识到，自己"并非婆罗门神"，他这个研究者"什么也不是"。他这样做的原因，是要从自己的内在经验入手，重新接近和把握宗教经验，也就是他所谓的"从内部讨论宗教"。在这个意义上，他是在从事类似"神学"的研究，而非学究式的宗教史研究。但另一方面，他也并非"神学家"，因为他所探讨的，并非单一种"基督神学"，而是要"追求某种没有传统、没有仪式，既没有人引导也没有任何阻碍的孤独经验"。

诚如程小牧所言，"'非神学'并不是'反神学'，而是以类似神秘主义的方式探寻一种无上帝的极限。与外部世界密切相联的'经验'一词，被限定于内部精神世界，借助'内在经验'这一奇特的概念，巴塔耶试图发现经验主体和认知客体在最炽热状态中的融合，在一种语言不能限定其界限的未知中，探索人的可能性的极限、非逻辑或非语言所达到的交流"②。有趣的是，巴塔耶尝试将"情色"也纳入他所提出的"非神学"研究领域里，并将"情色"直接理解为"内在经验"。他尝试在"情色"之中，了悟经验主体与认知客体融合为一

---

① 巴代伊：《情色论》，赖守正译注，第 86、87—88 页。Georges Bataille, *L'Érotisme*, Paris: Les Éditions de Minuit, 2011, pp. 35 - 36, 37.
② 程小牧：《译者前言》，载巴塔耶（Georges Bataille）《内在经验》，程小牧译，第 12 页。

的状态，并借此迫近语言所无法明确限定或界定的"非知"（non-savoir），亲证人类可能性的极限。如此一来，我们才能明白，他为什么会在《情色论》第一章的开端这样界定"情色"：

> 情色是人类<u>内在</u>生命的面貌之一；我们往往不了解这点。人类不断地向<u>外</u>寻找欲望对象，但是这个欲望对象响应的还是欲望的<u>内在性</u>。对欲望对象的选择，永远视欲望主体的个人品味而定。即使大多数人相中同一个美女，其关键通常还是在于她身上难以掌握的面貌，而非客观的质量。如果她无法激起我们内心的共鸣，根本无法迫使我们青睐她。简而言之，即使人类的选择基本上大同小异，但还是与动物有所不同：人类的选择牵涉到人类特有、复杂无比的内在活动。①

对于巴塔耶来说，"情色"是人类内在生命的重要面向。"情色"产生于欲望对象在欲望主体内心激起共鸣的刹那。因此，如果不从"内在经验"的路径入手，我们根本无法把握和接近"情色"本身。

三　超越诗歌

巴塔耶在《内在经验》第一部分的开端，是这样界定"内在经验"与"神秘经验"之间的关系的：

> 我所说的<u>内在经验</u>是通常被称之为<u>神秘经验</u>的东西：迷狂或陶醉状态，至少是沉思的激情状态。我较少关注人们至今都坚持的"忏悔式"经验，无论是怎样的忏悔，而更多关注一种纯粹的、无羁的甚至是本源的经验。这是我之所以不喜欢<u>神秘</u>一词的原因。②

---

① 巴代伊：《情色论》，赖守正译注，第86、87—88页。Georges Bataille, *L'Érotisme*, p. 33.
② 巴塔耶：《内在经验》，程小牧译，第25页。Georges Bataille, *Inner Experience*, trans. Stuart Kendall, p. 9.

巴塔耶讲得很清楚:"内在经验"指的就是"迷狂或陶醉状态"。这种状态通常被称为"神秘经验"。然而,他却不喜欢以"神秘"一词来命名这些经验,因为他所关注的,更多是"一种纯粹的、无羁的甚至是本源的经验",而非与"神秘"一词相关的宗教信仰。

巴塔耶认为,"教条化的预设给经验设置了不恰当的限制",而他真正想做的则是,"让经验无限制地自由通行,而不是引到一个预先设定的结局上"。① 所以他尝试提出"非知"的原则,借此点明他所探究的"经验"及其与"宗教信仰"的分别:

> 但产生于非知的这种经验确实存在。它并非不可言喻,如果我们谈论它,也并不违背它,但说到知的问题,经验甚至会避开仍存在于头脑中的答案。经验什么也不启示,不能建立信仰,也不能从信仰出发。②

换言之,由非知所产生的经验,并非完全不可说,但头脑和"知"所预设的"答案",却肯定无法把握这种非知的经验,因为"经验是在狂热和焦虑中提出(验证)的问题,即一个人对他的存在知道些什么"。人在狂热中,无论获得了怎样的领悟,都无法将这种"领悟"转化为以下的宣称:"我看见了这个,我所见的就是这样。"他甚至也不能说:"我看见了上帝、万物的绝对或本质。"而他唯一能说的,是"我所见的脱离了理智"。③ 非知的经验既与启示和信仰无关,亦与理智和头脑无关,它是对"迷狂或陶醉状态"的纯粹把握和领悟。

如此一来,我们可以重新回到上一节所提及的《内在经验》的文

---

① 巴塔耶:《内在经验》,程小牧译,第25页。Georges Bataille, *Inner Experience*, trans. Stuart Kendall, p. 9.

② 巴塔耶:《内在经验》,程小牧译,第26页。Georges Bataille, *Inner Experience*, trans. Stuart Kendall, p. 9.

③ 巴塔耶:《内在经验》,程小牧译,第26页。Georges Bataille, *Inner Experience*, trans. Stuart Kendall, pp. 9 – 10.

体问题。为何这本书会采取一种杂糅思辨、叙事和诗歌等不同文体的书写方式？答案明显是，因为巴塔耶唯有借助这种独特的"记叙"混合文体，才能勉强接近"非知"的经验。而《内在经验》初版时，其腰封上印着的，恰恰就是"超越诗歌"（Beyond Poetry）。① 肯德尔认为，"巴塔耶将此书定位于诗歌之外，也就是认为这本书超越了那些超现实主义者笔下无足轻重的文学。他也暗示诗歌只是过程中的工具——众多工具中的一件——在此过程中，经验本身是唯一的价值"②。我们应怎样理解一种以达至"一种纯粹的、无羁的甚至是本源的经验"为目标的诗歌写作？要回答这个问题，我们需要将目光转向一位巴塔耶研究者甚少提及的人物：铃木大拙。

巴塔耶在1944年2月至4月的日记中，谈及了他对禅宗的理解。这部分日记后来发展为一篇题为《内在经验与禅》（"Inner Experience and Zen"）的短文，被收入1945年初版的《论尼采》（*Sur Nietzsche*）一书，成为该书的第三篇附录。这篇两页的附录，只有开篇第一段简介禅宗的文字，是由巴塔耶撰写的。文章的其余部分几乎都是对铃木大拙著作的摘录。③ 巴塔耶文章的重点，是追问"何谓开悟经验"。他是这样理解"悟"的：

> 禅修的基础是打坐冥想，但它的唯一目的却只是达至一种可称之为悟（悟り）的启悟时刻。没有任何易于把握的方法保证我们能开悟。悟是出其不意的扰乱、突如其来的契机，它让某些意料之外的陌生感得以释放出来。④

巴塔耶所理解的"悟"，显然就是他念兹在兹的"非知"经验。

---

① Georges Bataille, *Inner Experience*, trans. Stuart Kendall, p. 210.
② 肯德尔：《巴塔耶》，姚峰译，第252页。Stuart Kendall, *Georges Bataille*, p. 168.
③ Georges Bataille, *On Nietzsche*, trans. Stuart Kendall, Albany: State University of New York Press, 2015, pp. 171-172.
④ Georges Bataille, *On Nietzsche*, trans. Stuart Kendall, Albany: State University of New York Press, 2015, p. 171.

按照肯德尔的考证，巴塔耶阅读的铃木大拙著作，是1944年出版的《禅学论丛》(*Essais sur le bouddhisme zen*) 的法文译本。铃木大拙原本以英文写成《禅学论丛》，题为*Essays in Zen Buddhism*（三卷本）。① 巴塔耶在文章中摘录的其中一个重要段落，是铃木大拙对日常生活中各种开悟契机的直接描述：

> 开眼悟道的机会随处可见。机会随手可得，在听一种无声之声或难解之言的时候，在观察一朵花开的当口，或在失足跌倒、卷起窗帘、使扇扇风等等日常琐事的当中。所有这一切，悉皆足以唤醒个人的内在意识(inner sense)。显然是一种微不足道的事情，但它对于心灵却有无限的效用，实非吾人的想象所可企及。②

值得注意的是，巴塔耶在摘录上述段落时，只抄录了前半段有关各种日常琐事的描述，却省略了后半段有关"内在意识"(inner sense) 的描象讨论。然而，铃木大拙后半段有关"内在意识"的讨论，却相当接近巴塔耶自己有关"内在经验"的论述。

此外，巴塔耶也注意到铃木氏对禅偈的分析。巴塔耶说："禅的表达往往披上诗歌形式的外衣。"③ 他随后摘录的是宋朝杨亿居士（字大年）的诗偈：

> 八角磨盘空里走，金毛狮子变作狗。

---

① Georges Bataille, *On Nietzsche*, trans. Stuart Kendall, Albany: State University of New York Press, 2015, pp. 285–286.

② 铃木大拙:《铃木大拙禅论集之一：自性自见》，徐进夫译，海南出版社2017年版，第161页。Daisetz Teitaro Suzuki, *Essays In Zen Buddhism: First Series*, London: Rider & Company, 1958, p. 245.

③ Georges Bataille, *On Nietzsche*, trans. Stuart Kendall, p. 172.

拟欲将身北斗藏，须应合掌南辰后。①

巴塔耶没有摘录整首诗偈，他只摘抄了后两句偈语。他似乎很喜欢这类禅宗悖论。他在文章的草稿中，还摘抄了傅大士另一首悖论式的诗偈：②

空手把锄头，步行骑水牛。
人从桥上过，桥流水不流。③

他同样只摘抄了这首诗偈的后两句。

巴塔耶没有对这些他摘抄的诗偈留下任何解释。我们如今已无法猜测，巴塔耶在阅读这些诗偈时，究竟领悟了什么。但可以肯定的是，这些巴塔耶曾经摘抄过的禅偈，应该相当接近他所主张的"超越诗歌"（beyond poetry）的理念。④ 而更为确定的是，他一定有读过以下一段铃木大拙对禅宗悖论的解释：

> 禅在它的矛盾反语方面，较之其他神秘教义要具体得多，后者只限于与生命、上帝或世间有关的一般陈述，而禅则将它的矛盾肯定推展到日常生活的每一个细节之中。它毫不迟疑地否定吾人最最熟知的经验事实。"我在这里写作，但我一个字也没有写。你也许正在展读这篇文章，然而世间却没有一个人在读。我既盲

---

① 铃木大拙：《铃木大拙禅论集之一：自性自见》，徐进夫译，第165页。Daisetz Teitaro Suzuki, *Essays In Zen Buddhism: First Series*, p. 250.
② Georges Bataille, *On Nietzsche*, trans. Stuart Kendall, pp. 285–286.
③ 铃木大拙：《铃木大拙禅论集之一：自性自见》，徐进夫译，第185页。Daisetz Teitaro Suzuki, *Essays In Zen Buddhism: First Series*, p. 272.
④ McCormick 曾在她2020年完成的硕士论文中探讨了巴塔耶与铃木大拙的关系。这篇论文应该是现时有关这个论题唯一的专题研究。可惜的是，McCormick 的论文没有进一步讨论巴塔耶"超越诗歌"的主张及其对禅宗诗偈的阅读。详见 Lucy Elizabeth McCormick, *Silent transmission: The influence of Buddhist traditions on Georges Bataille's "La pratique de la joie devant la mort"*, MPhil (R) thesis. Glasgow: University of Glasgow, 2020.

且聋,但每一种颜色和声音我都看到听到。"①

巴塔耶在读到这段文字中铃木大拙对基督教神秘主义的批评时,大概也会不期然会心一笑罢。

---

① 铃木大拙:《铃木大拙禅论集之一:自性自见》,徐进夫译,第 186 页。Daisetz Teitaro Suzuki, *Essays In Zen Buddhism: First Series*, p. 273.

框内的时间
——法斯宾德电影姿势研究

林晓萍[*]

【摘要】《恐惧吞噬灵魂》是德国新电影运动的主力之一赖纳·维尔纳·法斯宾德1970年代风格转型之作。法斯宾德在其中以其独特的电影姿势,把个体存在于此时此刻正在发生的状态悬置于银幕的画框之中,使其摆脱道德秩序与权力的书写规定,重归自然随性的姿势。法斯宾德对个体存在当下性的呈现,既是阿甘本意义上的姿势的复归,也是其生命范式的实践。

【关键词】 时间;存在;画框;姿势

Time in the Frame-A Study of Fassbinder's Film Gestures
Xiaoping Lin

Abstract: *Angst essen Seele auf* (*Fear Eats the Soul*) is a work of transformation of style by Rainer Werner Fassbinder, one of the mainstays of the New German Cinema movement in the 1970s. In it, Fassbinder, with his unique cinematic pose, suspends the state of individual existence as being

---

* 【作者简介】林晓萍,女,北京外国语大学文学博士,中山大学外国语学院德语系助理教授,主要研究方向为德语语言文学理论与文化学研究。

there and being-in-the-world in the frame of the screen, freeing it from the written prescriptions of moral order and power and returning it to the gesture. Fassbinder's presentation of the presence of individual existence is both a return to the gesture in Agamben's sense and a practice of his paradigm of life.

Key words: Time; Presence; Frame; Gesture

作为德国新电影运动的主力同时也是其中最极端和最个性的导演, 赖纳·维尔纳·法斯宾德（Rainer Werner Fassbinder）以其对真实的艺术呈现, 对战后德国电影乃至世界电影导演艺术理论带来深远影响。《法斯宾德论电影》《法斯宾德的世界》等都对法斯宾德的艺术风格、导演理论等问题进行深入研究。尤其他在1970年代尝试的好莱坞式德国电影叙事方式, 使其在"真实"与"艺术"间直接实现巧妙的平衡。他对"真实"的呈现很明显承袭布莱希特"离间效果"剧场传统, 但同时又以通俗剧（Melodrama）的形式, 实现细腻的情感描摹甚至耸动到无以复加的视觉奇观。那么他的这种风格与手法是为了实现对社会传统价值观的批判, 并为弱势群体伸张正义吗？本文选取法斯宾德1970年代风格转变十分明显的《恐惧吞噬灵魂》为例, 从其视觉结构入手, 以影片构图为出发点, 尝试阐释电影的结尾, 最后说明法斯宾德的电影诗学中的创作目的——电影姿势。

一 故事张力与视觉结构张力的矛盾

法斯宾德从《四季商人》（*Händler der vier Jahreszeiten*, 1971/72）开始, 到70年代中期, 不断尝试情节剧剧作, 以期拍摄一部德国式的、具有社会批判意义的好莱坞电影。[1] 这种风格转向的一个重要原

---

[1] Thomas Elsaesser, *Rainer Werner Fassbinder*, Berlin: Bertz und Fischer Verlag, 2001, pp. 436 - 455. 法斯宾德在其访谈中明确表明自身在这一时期的创作意图。参见 Robert Fischer, *Fassbinder über Fassbinder: Die ungekürzten Interviews*, Frankfurt am Main: Verlag der Autoren, 2004, pp. 273 - 300。

因是：道格拉斯·赛克（Douglas Sirk）1950 年代电影对法斯宾德的影响。法斯宾德认为可以像赛克一样，通过情节剧的形式在情感层面影响并争取更多的观众群体，同时表达自身的社会政治立场。上映于 1974 年的电影《恐惧吞噬灵魂》（*Angst essen Seele auf*）正是体现法斯宾德对赛克电影的接受，表达其自身创作意图和形成其独特的创作风格的典型影片。这部在 1973 年 9 月份仅用了四个星期完成拍摄的通俗剧（Melodrama），极为难得地采用了十分温情的叙事方式，讲述了一位身处社会底层、以打扫清洁为生的德国老妇人艾米，与一位来德国务工的年轻摩洛哥劳工阿里（Ali）之间的爱情故事。单从情节上看，本片与赛克的剧情片《深锁春光一院愁》（*All that Heaven allows*, 1956）的故事结构十分相似，但是不少研究对于法斯宾德在《恐惧吞噬灵魂》中所表达的政治立场一直莫衷一是。[1] 比如朱迪·迈恩（Judith Mayne）、托马斯·施比科博尔（Thomas Spijkerboer）与詹姆斯·C. 富兰克林（James C. Franklin）在关于《恐惧吞噬灵魂》的影评中指出，这部电影展示了在经济与社会剥削存在的情况下，个体的爱情关系以及个人幸福是不可企及的。[2] 克里斯蒂安·布拉德·托玛森（Christian Braad Thomsen）则强调，法斯宾德在这部电影中并没有将社会体制的不合理结构作为批判重点，其重中之重在于人作为个体的责任。[3] 争论的焦点在于对影片结尾情节的阐释：影片以一个固定镜头结尾，艾米坐在阿里的病床前哭泣。但是这个悬而未决的结尾意味着两人的爱情最终未能战胜外界的攻讦，还是说此处的停顿暗示着两人光明的未来？但是简单地将情节归为悲剧或者喜剧，均会导致阐释的悖论：如果将艾米与阿里二人的爱情理解为悲剧，又以此为出发点，将这部电影看作法斯宾德对社会秩序的批判，那这就与

---

[1] Thomas Elsaesser, *New German cinema: A history*, Basingstoke: Rutgers University Press, 1989, pp. 56 – 60.

[2] Judith Mayne, "Method and Message: Forms of Communication in Fassbinder's Angst Essen Seele Auf", *Film/Literature Quarterly*, Salisbury, Md. Vol. 7, Jan. 1, 1979, pp. 182 – 200.

[3] Christian Braad Thomsen, "Rainer Werner Fassbinder. Leben und Werk eines maßlosen Genies", *Medienwissenschaft: Rezensionen*, Vol. 11, No. 1, 1994, pp. 186 – 188.

影片后三分之一两人旅行回归之后被邻居、朋友、同事、家庭接纳的剧情相悖。而如果将两人的爱情冠以美好的期许，然后认为这是法斯宾德对个体的期待与希望，相较于结尾处两人悬而未决状态下灰暗的冷感色调未免难以令人信服。

这种矛盾点可以概括为影片故事张力结构与视觉结构的矛盾：

1. 开端：艾米进入酒吧，与阿里相识，与阿里共舞（00：00—08：54）

2. 冲突：阿里送艾米回家，留宿，与艾米相知（08：54—22：31）

3. 冲突：艾米的爱情受到外界的质疑与反对，但两人仍决定成婚（22：31—36：11）

4. 冲突：两人与阿拉伯工友共同庆祝，并向家人宣布婚讯，遭遇极力反对与唾骂（36：11—46：06）

5. 冲突：阿里被杂货店老板驱逐，艾米被同事嫌弃排挤，阿里的聚会被邻居举报，邻里极尽所能排挤二人（46：06—59：58）

6. 高潮：艾米与阿里在露天酒馆中遭遇服务员与其他客人的尖锐敌意，崩溃大哭（59：58—01：03：09）

7. 结局：艾米与阿里旅行归来，与杂货店老板、邻居以及家人关系恢复（01：03：09—01：09：55）

8. 结局：艾米与阿里渐行渐远（01：09：55—01：25：24）

9. 结局：艾米与阿里在酒吧共舞，阿里病重住院（01：25：24—01：33：07）

与电影故事张力结构变化相反的是故事的视觉结构变化。法斯宾德在故事高潮部分很明显放缓了影片的视觉张力结构，不仅减少了对空间纵深感的刻画，而且放慢了影片的镜头切换速度与剪辑节奏。反而在故事的结尾处，法斯宾德不仅极大地强调影片视觉空间的纵深，还在完成空间转换的同时，加速视觉重心的转移，因而张力十足。

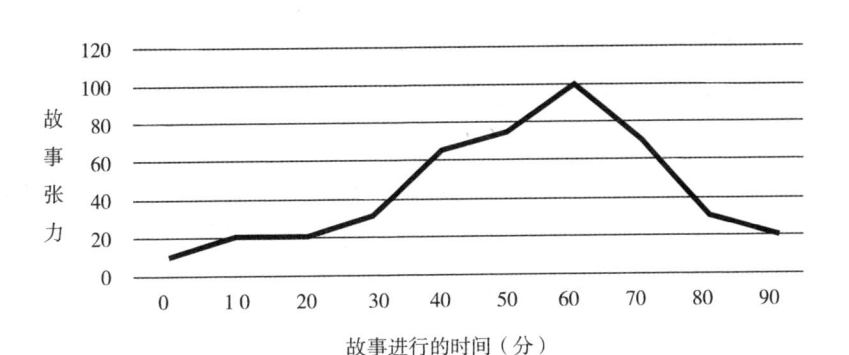

图 1　故事张力结构图

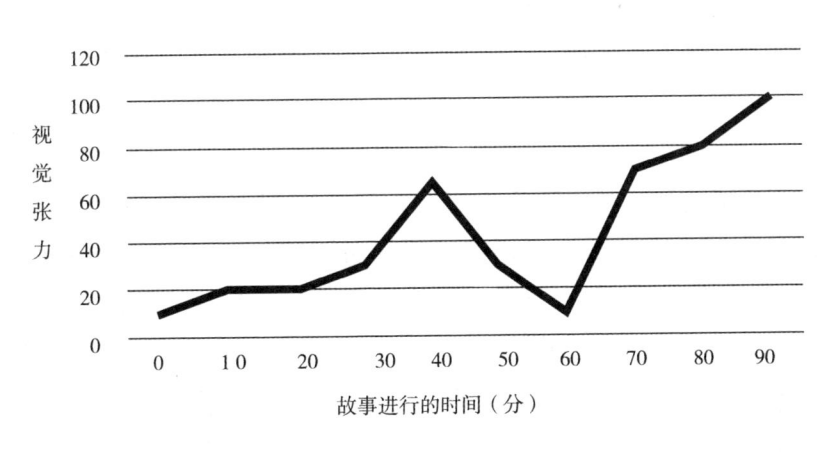

图 2　视觉结构图

所以说单独从情节的角度出发，容易陷入将电影简化成文本的窠臼之中，其实无法完善地阐释法斯宾德的创作意图以及其电影中的叙事策略。罗伯特·麦基（Robert Mckee）在他的《故事：材质·结构·风格和银幕剧作的原理》（*Story. Substance，Stracture，Style and the Principles of Screenwriting*，2010）中曾经以《银翼杀手》作比，来阐述电影独立于文学之外的主要特征：

如果我们拿出《银翼杀手》中的一个单一画面，让世界上最优秀的小说大师用语言来创造出那一构图，他将会写出连篇累牍的文字而且永远也不可能捕捉到其精髓。而那仅仅是在观众体验中流淌的成千上万的复杂意象之一。①

产生于故事情节上的争论如果无法从情节本身解决，那就有必要回归电影作为独立艺术表现形式本身，将其视觉母题、观众对影片的接受以及导演本身对这种接受的操纵作为考察对象，然后再进一步推导法斯宾德的创作意图。欧文·潘诺夫斯基（Erwin Panofsky）在《电影中的风格和媒介》中对这一问题也做出如下阐述：

> 观众在电影院座位虽然也是固定的，但只是肉体上的固定，作为一种审美体验的主体，并不固定。在审美上说，观众始终在运动，正如观众眼前的空间也在运动。②

不论法斯宾德在《恐惧吞噬灵魂》中究竟要对社会秩序进行批判，还是对个体提出要求，都只能通过电影这一视听媒介来实现。"电影并不像传统图像一样呈现一种现象，而是展现一种理论、意识形态、观点。这些则意味着现象。因此，电影并不讲故事，而是生产一个事件，并赋予这个事件以画面：电影生产故事。"③ 如果电影不仅仅是叙述一个已经发生的故事，而是指生产故事的过程，那么影片如何生产故事并为之赋予何种画面，将是本文讨论的核心与重点。

二 禁锢画框中的开放性

《恐惧吞噬灵魂》中重复出现的一个视觉母题即是无处不在的框。

---

① ［美］罗伯特·麦基：《故事——材质·结构·风格和银幕剧作的原理》，周铁东译，天津人民出版社2014年版，第393页。
② ［美］欧文·潘诺夫斯基：《电影中的风格和媒介》，李恒基译，载杨远婴主编《电影理论读本》，北京联合出版公司2017年版，第51页。
③ Gesten Vilém Flusser, *Versuch einer Phänomenologie*, Frankfurt am Main: Fischer Verlag, 1994, pp. 119–124.

故事高潮部分，艾米与阿里孤零零地在雨中对坐，两人一直紧握双手，姿势不曾发生大的变动。而远处酒馆中的服务员与客人则是以一种十分固定的姿态出现在由竖向线条构成的封闭画框之中。

图3　雨中对坐

然后影片在呈现出双方互相对峙的空间位置之后，直接将重心转到艾米与阿里之间，同时以过肩镜头将门框中的服务员与客人纳入两人的对话，从而将双方置于同一个空间语境范围内。镜头虽然在艾米与阿里的对话展开之前，就已经通过远景交代了两人所处的纵深空间（酒馆露天场地），但是当镜头拉进之后，重心完全聚焦在艾米与阿里身上，之后随着两人的对话不断切换视角，环绕在二人周围。这就把原本有纵深的、开放的背景空间压缩，构成一个狭小的封闭平面。艾米与阿里的窘境跃然图上。而对面看似为封闭的画框构图，服务员与客人在艾米与阿里的语境之中很明显带有对他们两人的敌意，但实际上这些人并不具有明显倾向性的面部表情，只呈现出一种观察者的姿势。这种观察的指涉对象是艾米与阿里。这就在故事与视觉之间构成

— 179 —

图 4　酒馆服务员和顾客们的观察

明显的矛盾：从情节上讲，阿里与艾米两人在开放的空间之中，他们是观察服务员与客人的主体；但是从视觉符号上讲，服务员与客人们才是观察的主体，阿里与艾米反而是呈现在平面之上的客体。因此，门框在此时代表的绝不是封闭和禁锢，而是在双方之间构建成互相指涉的意义开放状态。这也就能解释为什么艾米与阿里对服务员和客人的姿势有不同的解读：阿里的阐释——所有人都在看，是对观察这一姿势的描述；而艾米从自身的视角出发，对观察这一行为进行观察之后，经过反思，认为所有人都在嫉妒他们。而回到服务员和客人们作为观察者的视角就会发现，影片本身并未对"观察"这一姿势进行价值倾向的解读：法斯宾德镜头下的人物均在以一种十分剧场化的僵硬姿势"观察"他人，也"观察"自己。框型构图在法斯宾德手中一方面强调和框定观察对象，另一方面则以这种自我指涉的方式，生成不确定性与开放性。

三 画框中时间的持存

《恐惧吞噬灵魂》在故事结尾处达到了影片视觉张力的高峰：通过阿里发病的酒吧与医院病房之间的跳切，法斯宾德十分干脆地缩短了影片叙事的时间。此时，"呈现"艾米与阿里的存在状态取代第三人称视角的"叙述"成为影片的中心。影片完成跳切之后，艾米与医生被直接置于病房门构成的画框之中。此时摄影机聚焦在二人旁边等高的镜子上。随后镜头缓慢向左平行移动，给了床上的阿里一个近景特写，然后快速切换到艾米与医生的半身镜头。

图5 病房中艾米与医生

位于近景的艾米呈现出十分坚毅的神态，这表明她至少认为自己完全可以掌控事态的发展。而处于灭点之上的阿里则十分渺小脆弱。随后艾米主动走向阿里，医生离开，镜头向镜子推进，再一次通过固定机位构成近似于定格镜头的画面，将艾米与阿里一同捕捉到镜子里。然后镜头直接剪切至医生关门离去。尽管这段影片中镜头不断变焦、移动，法斯宾德都试图将艾米与阿里呈现在同一画框之中。

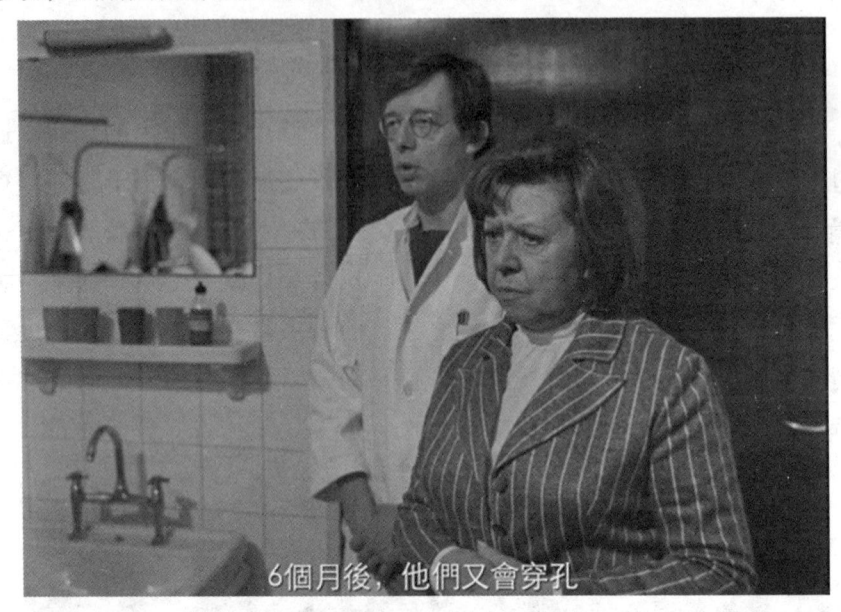

图6 镜子里的阿里

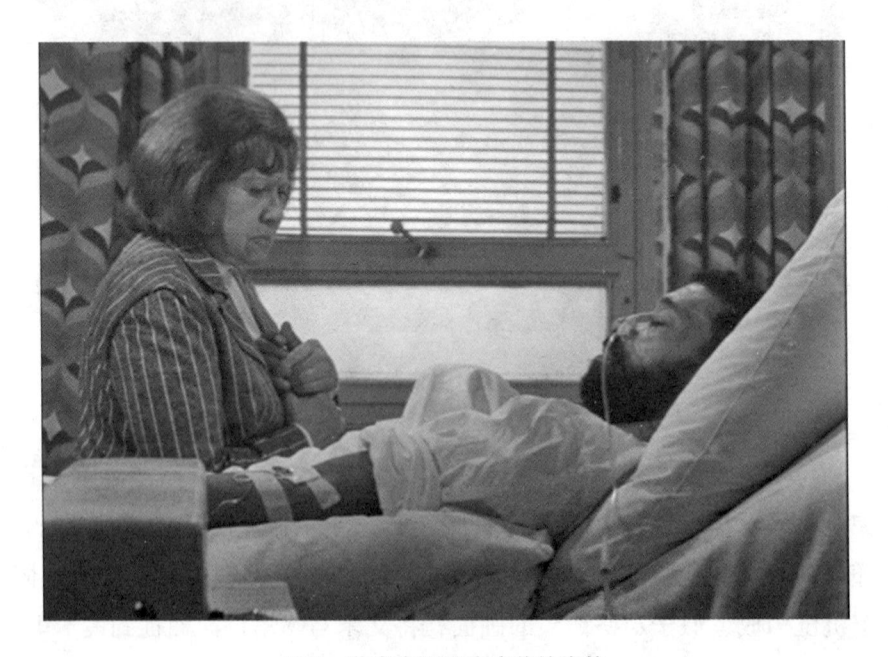

图7 艾米在阿里病床前的姿势

这种被观察的状态随着镜头切换和移动的速度,在影片的最后一幕达到视觉张力的顶点。艾米低头看着病床上的阿里,背景是明亮刺眼的窗户。随后她伤心哭泣,背景音乐响起了《四季商人》(*Händler der vier Jahreszeiten*,1971/72)中为主角汉斯所配的曲子《渺小的爱情》(*Die kleine Liebe*)。此时艾米虽然有扭头的动作,画面的时间看似也随着这首忧伤的小调开始流转,但是直至画面淡出,框中两人的状态均未发生变化。法斯宾德在对人物进行框定裁切的同时,完全消除了画面的纵深。虽然窗帘选用了暖色调,但是处于背光状态下的垂直褶皱,与顺光状态中百褶窗的横线构成交织密集的监禁状态。法斯宾德虽然在此处给了一个窗户的画面,但取消了窗户外的世界,这就让窗户这一意象失去对外部世界的呈现,进而形成自我指涉的闭环。在此过程中,镜头随着艾米走到阿里的床前,通过变焦的方式,将这个固定镜头之中的艾米与阿里完全框定,最终形成一个趋近于定格镜头的画面。艾米与阿里最终被投掷于这个被裁切的画布之上,成为观众"观看"的对象。法斯宾德通过持续的画面与空间,将个体存在的时间性"表达出来"。[①]

这种趋近于定格镜头的画框表达的不是戛然而止的未完成状态,而是在呈现艾米与阿里存在正在发生的过程:艾米知道医生所言皆是事实,她无比担忧阿里的健康;但是艾米同样也知道她与阿里要继续生活,她绝不可能像赛克电影中的主角凯丽一样直接躲在孤立时间的象牙塔之中,而是必须直面其存在的当下时刻。但是阿里究竟会不会真的回到她身边,她还能像以前一样重新成为阿里的灵魂伴侣吗?两人还能在一起面对邻里、同事与朋友的冷嘲热讽、明枪暗箭吗?艾米呈现出来的哀伤既是对阿里的心疼与担忧,也是顾影自怜:她在反思自我存在的状态之中意识到了自身存在状态的不确定性。她对二人过去的回忆与反思,对当下阿里暂时回归的开心与对他身体状况的担忧,对二人未来的迷茫,以一种运动的影像方式共存于这个固定画框之中。在这个平面

---

① [法]贝尔纳·斯蒂格勒:《技术与时间3:电影的时间与存在之痛的问题》,方尔平译,译林出版社2012年版,第41页。

画布之上，过去、当下和未来以不确定性的状态得以持存。这种持存的时间，与赛克电影中那种被裁切出来的、孤立的、乌托邦式的凝固时间完全不同。它是开放的，且因其不确定性反而成为自由的时间。

四 持存的时间与法斯宾德电影之中的摄影姿势

德勒兹在他的《运动—影像》一书中谈及电影的场面调度时，提出如下论述：

> 如果说整体是不确定的话，那是因为它具有开放性，具有不断发生改变的属性，或者说会突然之间呈现出新的状态，简言之，能够绵延（dauern）的属性。①

影片结尾处的镜头呈现出来的时间具有德勒兹意义上绵延的属性，是一种"连续的当下时刻，与之前和之后有明显外部关系的时间流，这其中，过去是以已经存在的当下，将来以将要到来的当下时刻显现出来的"。② 画框所起到的作用就不仅仅是把艾米与阿里作为对象框定起来，同时还能够将观众放到观察者的位置。观影过程与画框之内存在的发生，在意识层面融合成同一个事件。这就在观众与艾米和阿里之间形成了一个阐释对话的空间。画框中艾米与阿里的时间，是观众作为个体对自身存在时间的外在化。这段持存的时间是观众借由法斯宾德之镜头，使自己成为第三者的过程。这种对自身存在与反思的过程，正是亨利·伯格森在《创造进化论》中提到的"摄影机机制"（das Verfahren der Kinematographie）：

> 我们不是把自己放在事物内部本质之上，而是将自我放置于

---

① Gilles Deleuze, *Das Bewegungs-Bild: Kino I*, Frankfurt am Main: Suhrkamp, 1998, p. 24.
② Gilles Deleuze, *Das Zeit-Bild: Kino II*, Frankfurt am Main: Suhrkamp, 1999, p. 346.

事物之外，以便人为地重构事物的变化。从某种程度上讲，我们是把从眼前略过的现实拍摄成快照，而又因为这些快照能够表达现实的特性，所以我们只需要顺着一种抽象的、同质的、不可见的、基于认知机制的变化，将其串联起来。其目的在于模仿这种变化自身的特性。感知、知觉、语言等运作机制都是如此。无论我们是要思考变化亦或是表达变化，还是说要感知变化——我们都要启动我们内在的摄影机制。因此可以将上述论断做如下概括：我们的日常思维模式就是摄影机模式。[1]

影片的画面是观众认知机制的媒介。观众在观看这个片段之时，借由剧中人物的视角，观看被摄影机呈现出来的当下。被观众感知和反思的这个"当下"，并不是一段已经被叙述的、属于过去和他者的时间，而是其自身存在的当下。这就极有可能让观众在观影的过程中越出故事情节的桎梏，产生相应的离间效果。正如法斯宾德自己在论述《恐惧吞噬灵魂》时所说的那样："他们有可能，甚或不得不从这故事中抽离，但这对本片并无害处，反倒有益于他们自身的现实——我认为这是根本之道。影片必须在某一时刻不成为影片，必须不成为故事，而是开始活起来，使你问道：我和我的人生又是如何光景？"[2]所以艾米与阿里的存在虽然被法斯宾德呈现在一个相对封闭的画框之内，但是画框之中持存的时间，并不是凝滞的当下，而是跟随艾米对自我当下存在的反思以及观众在时间客体化之下对自身存在的观照，不断生成新的意义和可能性的时间。

所以法斯宾德镜头下的画框构图，在呈现时间的维度上，具有两种层面的认知功能。第一，画框极大程度上取消了场景的空间纵深，在减弱人物空间属性的同时，造成了极大的压迫感和禁锢感。而且场景中的人物是自愿进入这种桎梏状态之中的，这就更强调了个体所面

---

[1] Henri Bergson, *Schöpferische Entwicklung*, Jena: Eugen Diederichs, 1912, p. 309.
[2] ［德］莱纳·维尔纳·法斯宾德：《法斯宾德论电影》，林芳如译，人民文学出版社2004年版，第53页。

临的困境与绝望：他或者她无法也不愿摆脱这种困境——因为这种困境是存在本身的枷锁，是生活本身。法斯宾德呈现在观众面前的，不是某个特定的虚构的故事中某个特殊的虚构人物所经历的过去，而是对存在正在发生这一事件的叙述。因而画框正是将时间客体化的前提条件。第二，画框作为对取景范围的再框定与再筛选，是法斯宾德对意识的第一记忆、第二记忆和第三记忆之间进行剪辑的结果。他运用固定画框，并将镜头固定，从而融合了人物和观众双方对当下时间的体验，消解导演通过镜头以及剪辑的作用对这段被摄时间赋予的意义。观众在此刻虽然可能无法与剧中的人物产生共情，但是能够与人物同时反思自我的存在方式。框内的时间，并不是从时间流之中单独攫取的、孤立的过去，而是正在发生的当下，是过去与未来在当下的显现，是时间的绵延。所以说法斯宾德的"画框"呈现出来的其实是存在以开放的整体性呈现自我的过程。雅克·奥蒙（Jacques Aumont）在《电影导演的电影理论》（Les théories des cinéastes，2002）中论述法斯宾德的电影乌托邦时认为，法斯宾德的电影重点是：

> 帮助观众更能承受这个世界，但它并不是要观众接受那份疏离，而是要看见它，一旦电影达到这个理想，观众便获得进一步的解放，他将会获得更像是一个拥有历史意识或是社会意识的主体。[1]

法斯宾德正是用十分克制且冷静的镜头呈现生活本身，并给予观众反思自身存在的可能性。电影从这个角度上讲，就不仅仅是对现实的再现，而且是对观众个体视点的解放。而法斯宾德将存在发生的过程以电影的形式表现出来这一事实，也说明他的出发点是个体是可以认识和把握其自身的存在状态的。

因而，《恐惧吞噬灵魂》的结局绝不能被看作"爱情"的"悲

---

[1] ［法］雅克·奥蒙：《电影导演的电影理论》，蔡文晟译，武汉大学出版社2019年版，第223页。

剧"，法斯宾德的创作意图也完全不能简化为对社会边缘人的刻画以及对社会规训的批判。虽然电影本身离不开叙事，但是法斯宾德并没有像威廉·弗卢赛尔（Vilém Flusser）所认为的那样，以上帝的姿态凌驾于历史与时间之上，通过肆无忌惮的剪辑与粘贴，操纵故事的时间，影响观众的感知与认知过程。[1] 观众也没有像弗卢赛尔所警告的那样，被设定为被动哺喂信息和故事的银幕奴隶，作为电影作者的法斯宾德亦没有想要在电影中传达"超验"信息[2]，而是对现实通过画框进行遴选之后进行一种自然的呈现。这种呈现的过程从这个角度上讲，其实是弗卢赛尔对"摄影的姿势"（die Geste des Fotografierens）的定义。在弗卢赛尔看来，摄影的机制中，被拍摄的人其实并不被看作一个现实的人，而是被当作"对我来说"存在的对象来看，这就意味着，艾米与阿里对于观众来说是一种现象。这种机制依赖于一种在弗卢赛尔看来十分人性化的特质："将我们自己从观察者的角色中解放出来，将之只作为环境的一个部分来观察。"[3] 在弗卢赛尔看来，个体认知的过程与摄影的过程具有一致性：在摄影的过程中，摄影师不仅将自身独立于被观察的对象之外，对其进行观察，而且还在反思该对象在此时此刻向摄影师敞开自我的方式。这个过程一方面包括对摄影对象的遴选，另一方面包括反思。而这种反思不仅表现在摄影师对存在发生的一种呈现，还包括摄影师对自身意图的思考，也就是对自身存在的反思。这种笛卡儿式的怀疑论，正是法斯宾德的手法。他以门、窗等封闭画框对现实进行遴选，然后在"如实"地呈现角色作为个体其存在发生在此时此刻的过程。而观众在感知画面的同时，由于导演的离间手法，完全可以跳脱出导演编制的故事梦幻，在银幕之外，与导演一同反思自我的存在方式。

所以说法斯宾德实际上以电影的手段实现了弗卢赛尔的摄影的姿

---

[1] Vilém Flusser, *Kommunikologie weiter denken: Die Bochumer Vorlesungen*, Frankfurt am Main: Fischer Taschenbuch, 2009, pp. 173 – 175.

[2] Vilém Flusser, *Kommunikologie*, Mannheim: Bollmann, 1996, pp. 205 – 207.

[3] Vilém Flusser, *Gesten: Versuch einer Phänomenologie*, Frankfurt am Main: Fischer Verlag, 1994, p. 105.

势。诚然,构成《恐惧吞噬灵魂》故事主体与情节冲突的部分,并不是个体的生存困境,而是亲密关系中的权力与剥削关系,以及他人即地狱的社会秩序异化的现状。但是构成电影视觉张力的则是法斯宾德对个体生存现状的呈现与反思。这种通过"门"这种封闭画框达成的极简的现实主义手法,以呈现存在发生过程的形式,使得观众"看见"生活本身,并开始正视和反思。这正是电影区别于文学与戏剧形式的本质。而且观众的反思,虽然不一定就意味着个体能够对自己的生存状态做出相应的改变(当然,法斯宾德也没有相应的期待),但是这种不带电影作者操纵的、被解放的视角已然可以看作法斯宾德的政治诉求:他在电影之中呈现的是个体的另一种存在可能。由此引发的观众对自身存在的思考,绝非对当时西德政治的逃离和冷眼旁观,也绝非其自身乌托邦幻想的自娱自乐,而是对生活本身的关注。按照法斯宾德自己的说法,"我关心的是,看本片的观众能检视他们内心深处的感觉。使得,这正是我拍这部片子(指的是《爱比死更冷》,1967)所关切的,除此无他。我认为这比我将警察呈现成巨大的压迫者要更具政治性——或者说,在政治意味上更尖锐、活泼"[1]。法斯宾德在《恐惧吞噬灵魂》中所做的,并不是将电影作为有目的的手段或者无手段的目的,来批判和书写他对社会的定义与看法,而是将电影作为手段本身,呈现个体存在正在发生的过程。他的电影在这个意义上既不是演员内在生命的自我表达,也不是封闭式的叙事行为,本身不具有导向性目的,而是将生命的意义悬置于画框之中,既拒绝让存在服从道德秩序的审判,也拒绝让其臣服于权力脚下。因此,法斯宾德的电影构建出来的是一种悬而未决的"空"的状态,生命在这种自然随性的姿势下,重新获得神圣性,找回了阿甘本在《关于姿势的笔记》(1978)中所说的西方资产阶级早在19世纪末就已经丧失了的"姿势"。[2] 法斯宾德正是借由电影实现他的生命政治范式,艾米在阿里床前低泣的姿势也毫无疑问地实现了他的诗意时刻。

---

[1] [德]莱纳·维尔纳·法斯宾德:《法斯宾德论电影》,林芳如译,人民文学出版社2004年版,第33页。

[2] Giorgio Agamben, *Mittel ohne Zweck: Noten zur Politik*, Berlin: Diaphanes Verlag, 2001, p. 52.

种族、历史和身体：展演中的人性[*]

马修·谢诺达

Race, History, and the Body: Humanity on Display

Matthew Shenoda

Standing before a museum exhibit of a mummified five-year-old "Purchased in Egypt in 1895," a father holding the hand of his four-year-old considers ways to alter the narratives intended for museum visitors.

One Saturday afternoon in November I found myself near Chicago's Hyde Park neighborhood with my wife and daughter and decided to take a walk around the University of Chicago's campus. My daughter was then just a couple months shy of turning five, taken to proudly proclaim that she was four and a half! After running around the quad at the U of C making sculptures of sticks and fallen leaves, we stumbled on the Oriental Institute and a bit reluctantly decided to enter.

As we walked in, we discovered that, as is common with certain muse-

---

[*]【作者简介】马修·谢诺达（Matthew Shenoda），罗德岛设计学院（Rhode Island School of Design）文学艺术教授，非洲诗歌图书基金（African Poetry Book Fund）的创始编辑。

本文原文为评论体，没有摘要、关键词和分节。

ums, the entrance had no formal fee but a posted rate for "suggested donations." Knowing what we might expect in a museum like this, my wife and I looked at one another with a smirk and with a mutual understanding that our people had donated enough to such enterprises; we walked in, wallets intact.

As we entered the museum we walked through the writing tablets of ancient Mesopotamia, awed by the incredible evolution of script, the way that fables, etched into rock, were used as lessons for schoolchildren, lessons to help them locate themselves in the historical trajectory that led to the moment of their childhoods.

Before long we came upon the Egyptian exhibit. I began by looking at a set of scrolls examining the Demotic and the Coptic script with intimate familiarity, taking note of the odd description under one Coptic script that stated, "These are the names of the 12 apostles that could have been used for religious devotion, or perhaps for magic ritual." Magic ritual, I thought? What an odd choice of language. Having spent my life steeped in the Coptic Church and her theology, I was quite sure that the use of this particular text had nothing to do with "magic ritual," whatever that might have meant. But perhaps what we call prayer, our colonizers see as magic. Surely, my people would have wished for some magic in the moment that our culture was being robbed and stripped of all its artifacts and their proper meanings.

I shrugged and continued looking at the exhibits. Within earshot I heard an eager undergraduate student (no doubt enrolled in a course on Egyptology) explain to a couple, old enough to have been his parents, the detailed intricacies of ancient Egyptian culture. His recitation and sense of conviction was all too familiar, textbook; an insistent yet distant sense of understanding, an equanimous assuredness that lacked any cultural intimacy. That moment gave me a distinct sense of disconnect; here we were, three Egyptians standing not five feet away from him, but how would he have known? We moderns are rarely connected to our ancestors; such a connection would make for far too complex a reality than most care to make, and it would certainly call into question how we might interact with all the artifacts that lay before us. There was a clean (or not so clean) line between us that separated the gaze from the gazed upon. So often, it seems, we go on in this way, severing history, dividing the body amongst itself and calling the past past.

Then, with my daughter's hand in mine, we turned a corner and found ourselves standing before the body of a young boy; a five-and-a-half-year-old boy, according to the description on the case. Here he was, mummified at such a tender age having suffered an early death, and we were told nothing of him, save his age, an age that they claimed they could narrow down to the month. Like my daughter, on the cusp of a birthday, the museum label claimed the half-year, a familiarity that made it seem as if he was known, as if his birth and life were known. And as I stood before this body, I could not help but think what heart wrench this must have been for his family and community, for what we know for certain is that no matter what the era, what the locale, what the circumstances, the death of a five-year-old is a significant and life-altering event; it is a time of mourning, deep mourning.

As I stared at his body sitting before me in a glass case in Chicago, lying on display in a manner anathema to the traditions of our people, past or present, I tried to contain the hurt and anger I felt in front of my daughter. Then, I read the small inscription on the case that stated: "Purchased in Egypt in 1895." I was immediately struck by the use of the term "purchased," an exclamation not only of ownership but of a sense of "legality." The typical term for museum antiquities is "acquired"; though an imperfect and problematic term, it leaves room for the truth, a space in understanding the colonial relationships between people and power and those people and things "acquired." But here we are purchased, bought, legally owned. And I stood there a bit speechless beside her, struck at how she and this boy were almost exactly the same size, how in a different moment, this nameless boy on display could have been her. I sat silently, trying to figure out how to explain this to her. Trying to figure out how his parents, who lost him at such a young age and took such care in preserving his body, as was the tradition, would feel if they saw him now, thousands of miles from home, disrupted from his eternal resting place in the cold, sterile rooms of an American university. I took solace only in knowing how our people view the spirit and tried to tell my daughter, not about colonialism and the theft of our culture—she knew some of the truth of this, even at that age—but what I tried to do instead was to explain to her that the boy before us was not really him, not the fullness of him, anyway; that they took his body from its intended place but could not capture his spirit from that place, which had long since departed. Had long since been freed.

We stood before that case for a while, she looking at it with curiosity, me largely silent and thinking that there was something terribly wrong about this, terribly wrong about the normalization of bodies in cases, even as an attempt to educate. There was a truth missing there, a fundamental dishonesty in that experience which drives me to want to see a different world for my children. I began to wonder what alternatives we might have. We cannot upend history, but God knows we can face it. And in that moment I thought, what might a replica of this boy's body feel like, as opposed to his actual body? How might this entire experience shift if we were to alter the narratives intended for museum viewers? What might change if we told this story in its fullness, if the museumgoer was immersed in the pain and reality of history? If the display were not a display, but an experience, a calling, an implication? What if we, honestly, linked the past to the present? What if every viewer had to face the truth?

I stood still for a long moment in my thoughts, with my daughter's hand in mine. All the while, students were walking around pontificating on this and that, looking at this body as if it were an object, a thing. As if this were not a child once full of life and breath. How easily the contexts we create shape our memory. As if his family and community had not mourned and prayed fervently as they laid him to rest, as if his grave was not robbed by the hands of thieves, as if he wasn't stolen from his home, as if to say, all these years later, we still own you, the story of you. As if to say that anyone who finds this peculiar is the peculiar one, because there is only one way to see the world. And in the end, all I could think was:

It is difficult to trust people who have little respect for human life.

And so here we are, now, in this moment, race, history, and the body, our bodies, consistently implicated in all that we do. And here we are in this moment where we are taught the only way to find full safety and comfort for our bodies is to sever our mind from body, to sever our spirit from body, to sever our histories from our bodies. To say, the past is past. To say, I accept. I accept that this is not my son's body in a glass case, because after all he's not *really* my son. To say all the ritual, all the song, all the belief, all the sweat, all the prayer that has culminated and shaped itself into these remnants of culture that lie before us is a distant thing, is an antiquated thing, is a thing for a time not our own. And in the end, all I can think is:

It is difficult to trust people who have little respect for human life.

让文字发声：作为集体转换的索克语翻译*

麦克斯·桑切斯著　温迪·考尔译

Giving Voice to Words: Translation as Collective Transformation in Zoque

Mikeas Sánchez, trans. Wendy Call

For Indigenous writers, language serves as a unifying element in the struggle to defend lands and life. Here, Zoque writer Mikeas Sánchez reflects on translation as "thinking with the heart, listening to the invisible, and collectively dreaming."

In my language, Zoque, poetry is present in our most solemn rituals, such as the call for rain, dances to ask for abundant harvests, prayers to the mountains, and to heal the sick. We also make use of poetry in our community's most important moments: births, marriage proposals, weddings, and funerals. The Zoque language holds our essential, ancestral knowledge of cuisine, medicine, oral tradition, and community practices.

---

* 【作者简介】麦克斯·桑切斯（Mikeas Sánchez），女，土著索克诗人、翻译家、教育工作者、社会活动家。

本文由温迪·考尔（Wendy Call）翻译和改编为英文，原文为评论体，没有摘要、关键词和分节。

My paternal grandfather was a well-known curandero or healer. He inherited the gift of poetic language and used it in his traditional medicine. Zoque poetry comes from this soul-healing song. Illnesses manifest in our physical bodies, but their origin is spiritual. People often fall ill from *espanto* (shock), sadness, fear, hatred, or shame. To cure children suffering from *espanto*, for example, we identify the specific location where the soul left their body, take them back to that place, and gently beat their feet with sprigs of *cocohuite* (San José flower) and basil. As the family walks with the child suffering from *espanto*, they recite a prayer, speaking to the soul and imploring it to return to the body.

I learned about poetry through these healing practices. My grandfather didn't teach me deliberately, but neither did he hide it from me, so I memorized some of the verses. The healing chants and the prayers to the mountains have the same rhythm and musicality. Only later did I connect these chants to poetry on the page.

Creating bilingual poetry, in both Zoque and Spanish, has been challenging because I am an autodidact—as are most of the Indigenous writers in Abya Yala. I learned the grammar of my Native language through my writing practice, not through my schooling. I began writing bilingually in Zoque and Spanish in 2003; since then, I have published six books. Each of those six is different in its grammatical usage of Zoque because, during those years, changes in spelling, even changes in linguistic conventions, occurred. I have adapted because I want my language to be heard, to be embodied in literature.

In Mexico, there still isn't literacy in Indigenous languages. This is a problem for minoritized languages like Zoque. The number of speakers is fewer and fewer as these languages are displaced by Spanish, the hegemonic language. The Mexican state has not defined a comprehensive policy requiring literacy education of all children in the languages of their grandparents. At the same time, online social networks and other digital platforms force language displacement toward Spanish or English. Writing is a way of positioning a minoritized language to be recognized by its own speakers, rather than waiting for acknowledgment from the nation-state through laws and institutions.

Our Zoque writing goes beyond the straightforward concept of single authorship, toward recognizing the community as guardians of collective wisdom. A single author may garner prestige and even fame, but how does the author's community benefit? When the community feels not only represented but also an active part of the writing, there is recognition of both individual potential and collective, oral tradition.

When we detach ourselves from individuality, we can aspire to collectivity. In this collectivity is the tremendous chorus of nature and the dream that seems to be our own but that, in fact, affects the entire community. Listening with the heart is essential in this era of individualism, in which we seem to listen only to ourselves—an endless echo that deafens us. Listening with the heart also means listening to the trees, to the river, to the ants, and to the cicadas—all of whom have their own voices.

I am from an agricultural village established more than three thousand years ago in the territory inhabited by the ancient Olmec people—the oldest culture of Mesoamerica. My village is located in a special place: the headwaters of a watershed. It rains nearly year-round, which sustains abundant trees, rivers, streams, waterfalls, and natural springs. It is a green community that has the misfortune of being located on the foothills of an active volcano and surrounded by oil and mineral reserves. Our lands are very valuable, not for the natural resources that I just mentioned, but for their spiritual richness. They are home to the guardians (both male and female) of the forests; the rivers are protected by Nä'a'yomo, female energies that protect the waters; the Chichonal Volcano is inhabited by Piokpatzyuwe. Language has been a unifying element in the struggle to defend our lands and life. The ancient wisdom that we have inherited from oral tradition requires that we respect Nasakopajk, or Mother/Father Earth.

Our grandmothers and grandfathers taught us to listen with our hearts, to listen to nature, to our dreams. For Zoque people, listening is a very particular process, done through the heart, not the mind. My mother would say, "I have a concern in my heart," and then something would happen. My father would see that red mold was growing in the corners, and he would say, "Someone is going to die soon." Sadly, that would happen. My great-uncle once dreamed that Piokpatzyuwe, the guardian of the Chichonal Volcano, invited him to a birthday celebration on March 28, 1982. Then, on that day, the volcano erupted.

We Zoques sometimes have dreams that are not connected to the person who had the dream but rather to others in that person's family or community. For example, one man in our community dreamed that the guardian spirit of Atziki Mountain, which was threatened by a Canadian mining company, appeared and asked him not to damage the mountain. When the man woke up, he told the community leaders about the dream, and they organized themselves to prevent the miners from delivering more equipment to the planned mining site. The collective dream is a connection with our ancestry, and so we Zoques have the custom of talking about our dreams before they are erased from our memory. Through this listening process, a person can be cured of fear, sadness, and hopelessness.

Translation is important because it offers the chance to teach readers to think from their hearts and to collectively dream. Translation provides an alternative to a modernity that ignores nature's voices, that lacks the words to name them. That sort of communication lies beyond the linguistic resources of language, beyond its capacity to offer vital energy. My Spanish translations of my Zoque poems seek a way out of silence. They include words that cannot be translated into Spanish because there are no comparable Spanish words. Translation is not about something as simple as words; rather, it is about thinking. It is thinking with the heart, listening to the invisible, and collectively dreaming something that gives the words' essence a permanence in the world, different from what can be described in Spanish. There is no way for Spanish to label a philosophy of life that asks permission of the trees before cutting them down, or someone who asks permission before taking a step on the earth because invisible energies inhabit those particular spaces.

Translation makes it possible to give voice to words, a voice that becomes action and meaning, purpose and transformation. To think of translation as the innate ability of humans to communicate with others implies not only the ability to learn new words but also to learn another way of being human—capable of communicating with a tree, a river, a mountain. That is impossible without naming. That which isn't named doesn't exist. For this reason, we must preserve the energetic power of the Indigenous names of the villages, the mountains, the rivers. I say Nasakobajk, which is Mother/Father Earth; I say Tzawi'kotzäjk, and it is the Mountain Shaped Like a Monkey. But "monkey-shaped mountain" isn't Tzawi'kotzäjk. Tzawi'kotzäjk has its own history, its own voice, its own energy that is invoked through the simple fact of speaking its name.

Poetry is an act of linguistic resistance, a struggle to position our Native language in public, academic, and artistic spaces. Previously, we were obliged to speak in low voices because our language was a source of shame. No one taught us to love our Native languages—far from it. We have had to do that on our own, to find ourselves again, because we were lost in the hugeness of the world. Poetry has been a light amidst darkness.

中国与世界

【晚清民国中西知识交互中的现代性】专题

《新文化辞书》试释*

李欧梵著　杨明晨译

【摘要】 1923年商务印书馆出版了由唐敬杲主编、十一位学者共同参与撰写的《新文化辞书》，该书作为一部在五四新文化运动脉络中出现的百科全书巨著，其意义远不止于工具书的实用性，更是知识分子在新文化建构事业中面向大众读者的"新知"生产实践。书中词条的类别划分、具体选择与整体编排结构，折射出撰写者译介西学、取道日本并且以中国知识经验与之碰撞的复杂思想图谱。占有最大比例的宗教—哲学类词条和茅盾编写的文学类词条是展示当时思想史生态的典型部分，其中具体引介的名家、概念、流派等词条案例反映了编者的不同倾向，而总体上又呈现出一种平衡不同意识形态冲突、开放包容的世界主义姿态。

【关键词】《新文化辞书》；新知；宗教—哲学；茅盾

---

* 【作者简介】李欧梵，香港中文大学冼为坚中国文化讲座教授，哈佛大学荣休教授，中央研究院院士，主要研究领域为现代文学及文化研究、现代小说和中国电影。

【译者简介】杨明晨，女，香港中文大学文化及宗教研究系哲学博士，北京师范大学文学院比较文学与世界文学研究所讲师，主要研究领域为20世纪中英美文学文化关系、文化研究理论。

本文的英文原稿标题为"Xinwenhua cishu (An Encyclopedic Dictionary of New Knowledge): An Exploratory Reading"，2019年刊发于2019年梅嘉乐等编选的纪念瓦格纳先生的论文集中。Leo Ou-fan, "Xinwenhua cishu (An Encyclopedic Dictionary of New Knowledge): An Exploratory Reading", in Barbara Mittler, Joachim & Natascha Gentz, and Catherine Vance Yeh, eds., China and the World-the World and China: Essays in Honor of Rudolf G. Wagner, Gossenberg OSTASIEN Verlag, 2019, Vol. 3, pp. 41 – 54.

Xinwenhua cishu（An Encyclopedic Dictionary of New Knowledge）: An Exploratory Reading

Leo Ou-fan Lee. trans. Mingchen Yang

Abstract: *Xinwenhua cishu*, which was chiefly edited by Tang Jinggao and completed by a group of eleven modern Chinese intellectuals, was published by the Commercial Press in 1923. As an encyclopedic dictionary in the context of May Fourth Movement of New Culture, the significance of *Xinwenhua cishu* was not merely of practical use like a toolbook, but more became a practice of "new knowledge" production aimed at the general public for the purpose of enlightenment project. The category, selection and structure of entries in the book demonstrated the landscape of how Chinese intellectuals re-translate/rewrote Western sources on the basis of Japanese reference. The areas of Philosophy-religion and literature highlighted the intellectual communication in the early 1920s — the former occupied the commanding share of entries and the latter was in charge of the famous writer Mao Dun. They included abundant entries on celebrities, concepts and schools which reflected authors' different attitudes, and overall presented the spirit of openness and cosmopolitanism through balancing the conflicting ideological trends in China in the 1920s.

Key words: *Xinwenhua cishu*; New knowledge; Philosophy-religion; Mao Dun

我谨以此文献给鲁道夫·瓦格纳（Rudolph Wagner），以示对他给予我学术启发和指导的莫大感激。是鲁道夫多年前第一次向我提起了《新文化辞书》（英文缩写为 EDNK）这部特殊的书籍，他在一次研究之旅中发现了它。鲁道夫当时含蓄地请我一定要取来阅读这本辞书，因为它代表了"新文化运动"的一个标志性成就。但像往常一样，我未能及时回应他的这一请求。直到去年，鲁道夫和他夫人叶凯蒂（Catherine Vance Yeh）到访香港，并多住了一段时间，他送给我一个很即时的礼物，即他最近与米连娜（Milena Doleželova-Velingerová）合编的《万国新知中文百科全书（1870—1930）》[*Chinese Encyclopaedias of New Global Knowledge（1870—1930）*]论文集。这好像提醒我是时候加入这场学术大冒险了，我感觉我再也没有任何理由推脱。因此我忠实地追随了梅嘉乐（Barbara Mittler）在为该论文集和中文版读本撰稿时所表现出的先锋性研究①，我也投入《新文化辞书》这一特殊的巨著中去（共两册，1107页，附加157页中文和英文索引）。以下是我的一个初步报告，其中不免吸收了不少梅嘉乐的发现和洞见。

一 中国的启蒙事业

关于这部著作，我的第一印象是它应该是中国经由日本对另一部百科全书的翻译，它本身是一部对西方资源的再译或重写之作。② 但随着我阅读的展开，我开始意识到，书中许多与中国相关的内容[例如，它列出了杜威（John Dewey）在中国讲学的城市]，其实显示出有一位"作者"或一个作者群在有意识地将多种信息来源和撰述整合在一起。在此意义上就百科全书而言，这应当被视作一种原创性的工作。作为商务印书馆回应五四新文化运动的一次出版投资，这部百科全书

---

① Barbara Mittler, "China 'New' Encyclopaedias and Their Readers", in Doleželová-Velingerová, Milena and Wagner, eds., *Chinese Encyclopaedias of New Global Knowledge（1870—1930）: Changing Ways of Thought*, Rudolf G. Heidelberg & New York: Springer, 2014, pp. 399-424；梅嘉乐：《"为人人所必需的有用新知"？》，载陈平原、米列娜编《近代中国的百科辞书》，北京大学出版社2007年版，第193—207页。

② 台湾学者陈建守后来在他的研究中也的确印证了我的想法。他经过对《新文化辞书》中759项词条的一一检视，发现整部辞书的词条至少来源于两部日本辞书，分别是《日本百科大辞典》和《哲学大辞典》。他认为这两部日本大辞典给了《新文化辞书》词条选择的灵感，其中《哲学大辞典》对《新文化辞书》的词条内容叙写有重要影响。参看陈建守《竞逐新文化——〈新文化辞书〉的编纂工程与思想图景》，《中央研究院近代史研究所集刊》（台湾）第112期。

出现得如此及时,且意义重大。①

该书的中文和英文标题表现出一种细微但显而易见的差别:在中文原文中,这是一部有关"新文化"的著作,因此直接指向提倡新文化的五四运动;而英文标题却用了"新知"(New Knowledge)一语,该词在思想史谱系中可以追溯到清末"新学",指的是宣称实用目的的西学,因此很大程度上其本质和意图都是实用主义的。那么,在多大程度上这部新百科全书辞典不同于其他更早出版的"实用性"辞典或百科全书?其中文标题使用的"新文化"是否等同于五四之际出现的"新知"?在该书的序言中,主编唐敬杲声称,正是近些年的新文化运动才改变了中国的阅读图景,因此有必要生产面向大众的新知。"凡从前博学深思之士所能具备的学问,自今以后,一般民众,没有不应该加以修习。"② 因此介绍这套新知的明确目的就是教育一般阅读大众的思想。《新文化辞书》作为新式教育机构中教科书和学术著作的一个补充性读物出版,这与商务印书馆明确的出版议程相一致。在此意义上,《新文化辞书》已被视为一项启蒙的事业。③

《新文化辞书》中"新知"的主体内容基本上完全来源于西方——不过佛教部分是个明显的例外,尽管佛教最初也是外国的事物。正如梅嘉乐所声称、我也十分赞同的一点,这部辞书的理想读者应当可以同等程度地自如运用中文和英文,因为《新文化辞书》中的词条都是按英文字母表的顺序组织,在很多词条中列出的参考书目也大多是英文、德文或法文。这一知识水平当然已经超出了当时普通读者的能力水平。但如果我们从编者的角度出发去接触这部巨著,那么它的内容

---

① 众所周知,王云五在1921—1930年在商务印书馆担任主编和编译所所长,他所从事的最有雄心的事业是出版了多部辞典、百科全书以及陆续有超过一千种书籍面世的"万有文库"。王云五或许在背后也为《新文化辞书》提供了帮助。

② 唐敬杲:《新文化辞书叙言》,载唐敬杲编《新文化辞书》,商务印书馆1923年版,第1—2页。我使用的是香港中文大学图书馆2015年获得的再版版本。

③ 我不想涉入有关五四运动应当被命名为"中国文艺复兴"还是"中国启蒙运动"的论争。余英时教授认为两者都不是,但在我看来,"启蒙"一语在中国词源学中包括明确的教育含义,也因此与五四时期商务印书馆和其他出版社的各种出版事业相关联。

看上去似乎有意设计得尽可能"博大精深",以此给读者一种西方"新知"的深度感和博大感,这种知识已经超越了晚清"西学"仅仅对实用性的关注。《新文化辞书》采用了现代白话文,切合五四时期的出版状况,以此令一般读者容易理解。

因此我不愿将《新文化辞书》仅仅视为一部参考书,而更愿把它看作在那个关键历史时刻生产出来的一部重要文化记录,它记载了当时高层次的知识秩序。与此同时,我发现自己采用了一个有利的后世读者的位置,可具备一种后见之明。在定位这部巨著的"历史性"时,我不禁发现它有许多"漏洞"(loopholes),因此我将"在场"(书里有什么)和"缺席"(书中本应有但缺失的部分)都考虑在内。我的阅读仅仅是开放这个"文本"(text),并将其置于当时的文化与历史脉络的一个初步尝试。我非常欢迎读者批评指正,因为我的观点只基于有限的研究,它只是尝试性、推测性的。

在我看来,《新文化辞书》是一项来自商务印书馆十一位编者的集体事业。梅嘉乐已经确认了他们中大部分人的背景[①]。主编唐敬杲是商务印书馆编辑部富有经验的工作人员,他可能是将《新文化辞书》汇总起来的主要人物,另外协助他的十位编辑仅仅以"校订者"的身份出现在书的内页上。唐曾在日本接受教育,1915年加入商务印书馆担任编辑。他也是《现代外国名人辞典》和《综合日汉大辞典》的编辑,还与另外一位编辑何崧龄一起参与编辑了一部早些时候的百科全书——《日用百科全书》。唐敬杲可能翻译了日本樋口龙峡所作的《近代思想解剖》(《近代思想の解剖》)[②],我有理由相信唐在辞书中的组织原则以及一些西方现代思想家的词条至少部分地来源于这部日本著作。

唐敬杲总体负责《新文化辞书》,每位编辑都被指定负责与他们

[①] 梅嘉乐:《"为人人所必需的有用新知"?》,载陈平原、米列娜编《近代中国的百科辞书》,北京大学出版社2007年版,第193—213页。

[②] 该书的第一个中文本在1921年出版,编者被归为商务印书馆编译部;但日后1974年台湾出版的再版将作者归为唐敬杲。我们需要更多的研究来比较日本文本《近代思想の解剖》、中译本以及《新文化辞书》中的相关词条以确定它们之间的关联。我感谢当年香港中文大学的同事崔文东教授关于该书的研究帮助。

的知识专长大概相近的领域和词条。唐敬杲在叙言中列出了十二个值得整理的词条类别：政治、宗教、经济、法律、社会、哲学、文艺、美术、心理、伦理、教育以及自然科学。对我来说具有诱惑力的工作是推测编者们在创作这本书时的劳动分工——谁具体负责哪一类别？从可获得的传记资料来看①，我尝试列出下表：

　　—唐敬杲：总论，哲学
　　—李希贤：经济［翻译了拉法格（Paul Lafargue）的《财产进化论》］
　　—何崧龄：马克思主义经济学与唯物论（《日用百科全书》的编辑）
　　—沈雁冰：文艺，美术
　　—周昌寿：自然科学（物理）
　　—陈承泽：语言学
　　—范寿康：哲学，教育
　　—黄士复：佛教（《综合英汉大辞典》的编辑）
　　—黄访书：英语
　　—郑贞文：自然科学（化学）
　　—顾寿白：人类学，生理学，医药学

　　以上列表可以表明商务印书馆在其全盛时期可谓贤才会聚。尽管除了茅盾（沈雁冰）外，大部分名字都不如五四知识分子和作家那样为人熟知。可以说，他们在中国的启蒙任务中扮演的实是葛兰西所说的"有机知识分子"。他们有着明显相似的教育背景：大多数都曾在日本受过教育，也懂得包括日语在内的一些外语。我们可以合理地假设，即使不说大部分词条都复制或摘录自日本，那也至少可以说有一

---

① 这些材料摘选自多处来源，我感谢崔文东教授和我的研究助理赵杰锋，他们在查找资料上提供了珍贵的帮助。但是我没办法列出所有这些编者写作或翻译的著作，其中有一些在王云五主编的"万有文库"系列中出版。

些词条是基于日本资源基础之上而形成的。查出这些词条自然会花费大量时间和精力，我们主要想表达的是，这一集体性纲要展现出了一种学问与专业知识的视野广度，促使《新文化辞书》形成的集体努力代表了出版史上的一个全盛时期。事实上，在五四时期再也没有其他这类成果出现。

二　宗教、哲学与思潮

正如梅嘉乐所注意到的，哲学与思想的内容在词条中占有绝对比例，除此之外或许也应该加上宗教。最长的词条是佛教（共63页，每页22行，大概660字，另外还有14页关于释迦牟尼的词条），其他宗教没有如此详尽的解释，基督教有10页，伊斯兰教有5页。为什么佛教应该获得如此慷慨的篇幅，而基督教没有呢？唐敬杲在序言所谓"叙述务求详尽"的原则之下，为这种做法进行辩护："虽然对于材料底选择，十分严格；但是一经认为确实有用的材料，便不惜穷原竟委，为详尽的叙述。即如佛教一条，我们必定要把佛教底意义，佛教底教理，理想，佛教底分派，佛教底流传，以及佛教各宗底宗义，沿革等等，为组织的、一丝不漏的叙述，务使读者毫不费力，对于佛教得到一个确切的完全的概念。"[①] 佛教这一长长的词条的确忠实于编者的要求，那些深奥的概念都得到了清晰的解释，不同派别教义的划分也以相对简单易懂的语言来描述。将之通读一遍像是读了一本虽短却完整的书。这一词条很有可能是由黄士复所作，他当时可能正在为另一部著作搜集资料，这部著作后来以《佛教概论》为名在1933年由商务印书馆出版。黄士复的这两项工作有共通的方法和组织结构。

虽然如此，我们还是很难同意，这一外国宗教（尽管它已经中国化了）因为是"有用的"，便值得如此广泛的篇幅。在多大程度上佛

[①] 唐敬杲：《新文化辞书叙言》，载唐敬杲编《新文化辞书》，商务印书馆1923年版，第3—4页。

教可以被证明是"新知"或者服务于五四时期的新文化事业呢？我们只能从其时流行的"人间佛教"中找到一个背景性的因素，不仅像太虚、弘一（李叔同）这类人物广受欢迎，而且不少跨越不同意识形态领域的著名知识分子，如梁启超、鲁迅、瞿秋白等都在他们的写作中使用佛教术语和概念。或许《新文化辞书》的编者们已经考虑到有必要针对这一文化现象提供一些知识上的实质内容。

在哲学领域，亨利·柏格森（Henri Bergson，1859—1941）是篇幅最长、内容最广泛的人物词条。柏格森大概是欧洲20世纪早期最流行的哲学家，他曾受到讲学社（由梁启超带头组织）邀请访问中国，但最终没有实现。张东荪、李石岑、瞿秋白以及其他众多不同意识形态的知识分子，都曾出于各自目的，发现柏格森观点的启发之处。在《新文化辞书》的词条中，柏格森的主要概念——"持续"（durée），"物质与记忆"（matiére et mèmoire），"创化论"（l'evolution créatrice）都得到了清晰、充分的讨论［但没有生命冲动（élan vital）的概念］。另外一位当代德国哲学家杜里舒（Hans Driesch，1867—1941）获得了与柏格森同样的篇幅，他在1922年确实访问了中国，关于他的词条似乎是因为他的到访才补充上去的（因为这些书页是作为额外页嵌到辞书264页中的）。另外两位访华者伯特兰·罗素（Bertrand，1872—1970）和泰戈尔（Tagore，1861—1941）分别有9页和5页。美国实用主义哲学家、也是胡适的老师约翰·杜威（John Dewey，1859—1952），仅有两页篇幅。尽管杜威在中国受到欢迎，但他在《新文化辞书》中的简短待遇只能表明编者们没有重视杜威和美国实用主义哲学。但是，杜威在他的一次讲座中曾介绍过他的美国同事威廉·詹姆斯（William James，1842—1910）的著作，詹姆斯既是哲学家又是心理学家，他在《新文化辞书》中却占了5页。

很显然，当时中国名气最大的三位当代哲学家是柏格森、杜里舒和罗素。还有一位当代德国哲学家威廉·冯特（Wilhelm Wundt，1832—1920），尽管他现在已经不为人熟知，但也曾在辞书中获得7页篇幅的详细介绍。冯特像杜里舒一样，也是20世纪之交从自然科学转向哲学研究的学者。另外一位在辞书中被充分叙述的人物是鲁道夫·倭铿（Rudolph Eucken，1846—1926），他是杜里舒的老师。尽管倭铿的传记词条只有 2 页半，但他的思想却在"新理想主义"（Neo-idealism）条目下被广泛探讨（有 4 页）。倭铿最具开创性的观点"人生观"（Lebensanschaungen）对 1923 年著名的"科学与人生观"论战有所影响，张君劢及其他学者在论战中系统阐述了倭铿的观点，这场论战也即所说的"科玄论战"。①

因此我们可以注意到《新文化辞书》哲学词条所具有的两个特点：德国哲学具有优势地位；强调与当时中国的关联。新文化运动的中心动力之一便是希望及时了解并追赶上西方（特别是欧洲）的最新思潮，一项关于"新知"的事业也必须满足当时知识分子的这一需求。这或许就是《新文化辞书》的编者们在选择以及决定词条长度的过程中主要关心的问题。

除了上述所提到的人物外，还有一些现代欧陆主要的哲学家也在辞书中获得了相应关注：黑格尔（Hegel）8 页，尼采（Nietzsche）8 页（也是被嵌入 696 页中的），莱布尼茨（Leibnitz）6 页，费希特（Fichte）5 页，笛卡儿（Descartes）4 页，卢梭（Rousseau）4 页，康德（Kant）4 页，斯宾诺莎（Spinoza）3 页，叔本华（Schopenhauer）2 页半。在古代哲学家中，占有最大份额的是苏格拉底，有 15 页；相比之下，柏拉图只有 7 页；而亚里士多德尽管在政治、伦理以及美学方面的著作都比苏格拉底具有更持久的价值，他也只占 2 页半。其他一些古希腊哲学人物和学派也包括其中，这或许是为了使读者充分了解西方思想的源头而提供足够的知识，由此实现百科全书的功能。

《新文化辞书》中还有许多哲学概念的词条，比如唯心论和观念论（都对应英文"idealism"，两个词条总共 12 页）、唯物论（Materi-

---

① 彭小妍：《人生观与欧亚后启蒙论述》，载彭小妍编《文化翻译与文本脉络》，台湾："中央研究院"中国文哲研究所 2013 年版，第 221—268 页。我也要感谢当年香港中文大学的同事张历君教授有关这场论战和柏格森在中国的研究，他的研究成果集中体现在他 2020 年出版的专著《瞿秋白与跨文化现代性》（香港中文大学出版社）中。

alism，6页）、经验说（Empiricism，3页）、实用主义（pragmatism，4页半）、实证论（positivism，2页）。康德（Kant）占有4页篇幅，而新康德主义（Neo-Kantianism）占了6页。人文主义（英国人文主义现象）仅获得可怜的2页篇幅，或许是因为这个概念过于宽泛和抽象。另外一些概念说得相当晦涩，如实验法学说（Experientialism，法学研究中的概念）、后天说（Aposteriorism）、同性神教（Homoiotheism）（指印度古代宗教）。不同的是，一些带有意识形态意味的概念（例如英文词汇中以"ism"做后缀的词）就会获得更广泛的关注（可以参见下文）。

如果黄士复是佛教部分的撰稿人，那么哲学词条或许应当归于范寿康和主编唐敬杲。范毕业于东京帝国大学教育哲学专业，1923年他一回国便加入商务印书馆做编辑。他还编过一本教育辞典，之后成为一位著名哲学教授，出版著作涉猎广泛，包括有关柏拉图和亚里士多德的书。后来几年，范成为有名的教授，在安徽大学和中山大学执教，1947年他移居到台湾并成为"国立"台湾大学哲学系主任。[①]

再看辞书中的其他领域和学科——经济、政治、法律、社会学、自然科学，这些词条尽管总体上不如哲学和宗教内容详尽，但也同样全面广泛。由于我知识和训练有限，我只能在此举出些有代表性的例子。

卡尔·马克思的传记词条很简短（有1页半），但他的思想却被分散在不同的词条中得到充分介绍，如"科学社会主义"（Scientific Socialism）、"唯物论"（Materialism）、"唯物史观"（Materialistic Conception of History）、"剩余价值说"（Theory of Surplus Value）等。马克思似乎更多地被视为一位哲学家和经济学思想家而非革命者。这部分内容也许与其中一位编者何崧龄有关，何似乎是一位马克思主义经济学专家，并且为一本1926年出版的关于马克思唯物观的书撰写了三篇有分

[①] 范寿康的生平资料参考自"武汉大学百年名典"系列中出版的范寿康《中国哲学史通论》作者简介。参见范寿康《中国哲学史通论》，武汉大学出版社2008年版，作者简介页。

量的专业文章。①

列宁的传记词条有些独特（列宁被拼作 Nicholai Lenine，有 4 页），它十分详尽地叙述了列宁的生平，以及他在 1917 年 10 月那场惊天动地的布尔什维克革命活动；后面又以英文翻译了一份列宁著作的长书单，这一书单占了一整页半。② 另外，列宁的革命思想还在"布尔札维主义"（Bolshevism，即今天通常译作的布尔什维克主义）的词条下得到讨论（有 6 页），写作者在列宁对马克思主义的思想继承问题上做出了既支持又反对的平衡观点。该词条尽管将"无产阶级专政"引为马克思的观点，但又引用了反布尔什维克一派的立场，指出马克思和恩格斯承认革命的失败，因此《共产党宣言》应当仅仅被视作一个历史的文书。③

在政治意识形态领域，最长的词条是无政府主义哲学家克鲁泡特金（Kropotkin）。克鲁泡特金有 19 页的大量解释，盖过了另一位俄国无政府主义者巴枯宁，他仅有两页半的篇幅。这不仅显示出，在当时中国克鲁泡特金无政府主义的名号比马克思和列宁更受欢迎，而且也表明编者们认为他的观点更有思想价值。除了自 1910 年代早期就已经在中国流行的无政府主义外，我们还发现"社会主义"（Socialism）与"修正派社会主义"（Revisionism）的词条。事实上，马克思在社会主义的词条最后也再次被提及（有 6 页），这一词条还包括了欧文（Robert Owen）、圣西门（Saint Simon）、傅立叶（Fourier）、布兰克（Louis Blanc）、蒲鲁东（Proudhon）、劳特伯丘斯（Bodbertus）和拉萨尔（Lassalle），其中大部分都是乌托邦社会主义者。具有社会主义倾向的文化人士，如莫里斯（William Morris）和拉斯金（John Ruskin）也被包含其中（前者 2 页半，后者 2 页）。在修正派社会主义中，尤其是伯恩斯坦（Eduard Bernstein）和工团主义（Syndicalism）的理论分别占了将近 5 页和 4 页。我越读越意识到，马克思主义革命思想主流

---

① 中华学艺社：《唯物史观研究》，商务印书馆 1926 年版。
② 唐敬杲：《新文化辞书》卷二，商务印书馆 1923 年版，第 561—565 页。
③ 唐敬杲：《新文化辞书》卷一，商务印书馆 1923 年版，第 71 页。

并没有主导《新文化辞书》，取而代之的是，编者们好像倾向于提供各类塑造世界的西方思想。

更令人讶异的是编者多少表现出对达尔文和达尔文主义的冷待（共4页半）。社会达尔文主义令人意外地没有被解释，这也是极罕见的一个未被关注到的当代重要"主义"的例子——甚至在推广这一概念的斯宾塞（Herbert Spenser）的简短词条中也没有出现。另一方面，我们发现了另一个与之分开的"进化论"（Evolutionism）词条。进化论的概念可以归因于达尔文和拉马克（Lamarck）两人，但是后者在另一个"拉马克的进化论"（Lamarckism）词条中获得更多作为早期先锋者的赞誉。在学术谱系中与拉马克相并列的人物威廉·莱尔（William Lyell）并没有被提及，而达尔文与鲁迅都读过莱尔三卷本的《地质学原理》（*Principles of Geology*），鲁迅是在南京矿路学堂将之作为教科书，与赫胥黎的《天演论》（*Evolution and Ethics*）一书一起读的。

在心理学领域，威廉·詹姆斯正流行并被容纳其中，但弗洛伊德和他的精神分析理论却过时"出局"了，尽管商务印书馆的另一出版物《东方杂志》在1910年代中期曾首次介绍了弗洛伊德以及他对梦的解析。另一方面，社会活动家和女性主义者艾伦·凯（Ellen Key）有7页篇幅，反映了她的观点在中国大为流行。社会学领域中，涂尔干（Emile Durkeim）被收录，但韦伯（Max Weber）和西美尔（Georg Simmel）没有，他们两位也是德国社会学奠基人，其著作最早系统地阐述了有关现代性的社会和心理病症。取代他们的是：我们可以发现美国社会学家富兰克林·吉丁斯（Franklin Giddings）的名字，他对社会学的主要贡献主要由《社会学原理》（*The Principles of Sociology*）等一些导论式教科书构成，《社会学原理》曾被翻译为包括中文在内的多种语言。在历史研究领域，兰克（Leopold Ranke）被收录在内，而狄尔泰（Wilhelm Dilthey）没有。《新文化辞书》中还有大量经济理论词条，特别是古典经济学（如亚当·斯密、李嘉图等）。关于"资本主义"的词条虽然简短（只有2页）但十分重要，因为它标识出了帝国主义和军国主义的联结，并且最后下了结论："所以略为有些同情心的人，就不惜为'社会主义'，'共产主义'等大声疾呼。"①

在自然科学领域，爱因斯坦和他的相对论涉及两个简短词条，但辞书对爱因斯坦修订牛顿万有引力定律、将时空作为相对而非绝对概念的科学突破，做出了有力解释。不过，爱因斯坦的赞助人兼朋友、同时也是量子理论的奠基人普朗克（Max Planck），却在书中消失不见。另外，开普勒（Kepler）、伽利略（Galileo）、牛顿等早期科学巨匠也在一些简短的词条中得到适当介绍。

上述例子有助于表明，尽管《新文化辞书》涉猎广泛，但它绝不是一个"客观"的、包罗万象的资料汇编，编者对于收录什么、不收录什么有他们自己的观点。辞书遗漏掉一些现代思想的奠基人物，部分原因也许是编者在商务印书馆图书馆中所使用的参考资料的问题（包括来自日本和英国的不同百科全书）。因为我们已经没有商务印书馆图书馆的藏书资源（它在1931年日本空袭中被烧毁了），我们只能猜测这些参考资料的性质和常规质量。从《新文化辞书》的总体内容来看，似乎德国与英国的名称概念占据了词条的主导，但它们也许是从日本获得或翻译而来。在《新文化辞书叙言》的结尾，主编特别感谢周昌寿提供了珍贵的材料，这可能是指自然科学领域，因为周是一位物理学家，1920年至1945年在商务印书馆编辑部工作，1937年在主管自然科学著作的汇编时被任命为自然科学部门的负责人，之后还撰写了有关量子力学和相对论的独立卷著。②

以我的考察，《新文化辞书》似乎并没有一个明确的政治立场，我们仅偶尔可在其用语和词条长度中，觉察到某种意识形态的同情。这似乎反映了《新文化辞书》编者和商务印书馆的一般脾性，他们或许可以被视作中国20世纪20年代的温和派，试图在相互冲突的意识形态浪潮中平衡掌舵。商务印书馆之所以在商业上成功，正是因为它

---

① 唐敬杲：《新文化辞书》卷一，商务印书馆1923年版，第157页。
② 周寿昌的生平资料及在商务印书馆的工作参考自陈应年所写的文章《周昌寿在商务》。参看陈应年《周昌寿在商务》，载王涛等编《商务印书馆一百一十年》，商务印书馆2009年版，第222—224页。

坚持折中的态度,《新文化辞书》也不例外。

三 茅盾与文学

追随梅嘉乐的例子,我想在本文余下的部分聚焦一个我可以宣称拥有些专业知识的领域——文学,估测一下茅盾对《新文化辞书》的贡献以及他自己的文学兴趣所在。

茅盾是《小说月报》的编辑,这是《新文化辞书》出版之际商务印书馆一份重要期刊。众所周知,茅盾在1921年刚被指任为编辑,就立刻将这一期刊改组为"新文学"的代言。他只为这份期刊做了三年编辑(1921—1923),这段时间恰巧赶上《新文化辞书》项目。他的自传和回忆录描述了其在商务印书馆编译所英文部工作时的环境、以及他与几位编辑的相熟情况。[1] 因为《新文化辞书》没有专攻文艺的其他编辑,因此可以安全地假定茅盾全面负责这一领域的所有词条。的确,茅盾一些早期的文学兴趣,如他对托尔斯泰的热情、对自然主义的矛盾态度,以及对"新浪漫主义"(见下文)的支持,全部都在《新文化辞书》中有所体现。

从茅盾自己文学兴趣的视角出发,我的探索从查看他"自然主义"的词条开始(共8页,其中有2页系缺页),因为茅盾不久之前刚写作了《自然主义与中国现代小说》这篇著名文章,茅盾对这一文学思潮和方法的了解令我印象深刻。这一词条的主要来源是勃兰兑斯(Georg Brandes)里程碑式的著作《十九世纪欧洲文学主流》(*Main Currents in 19th-century Literature*),这本书在当时有中文节译,茅盾自己对文学进化的理解应该也来源于此书。文学的进化观呈现出一种线性发展的趋势,分为几个代表性范式:从古典主义到浪漫主义,再往后到19世纪的写实主义和自然主义。在自然主义的词条中,茅盾着力处理了写实主义与自然主义的差异与相似,并且最后得出结论,认为它们在很

---

[1] 茅盾:《我走过的道路(上)》,人民文学出版社1981年版,第102—136页。

大程度上是相交叉的。追随勃兰兑斯的观点，茅盾追溯了从华兹华斯到左拉的自然主义渊源。当法国自然主义作为对象征主义和神秘主义的反拨而占据历史上风时，茅盾及时注意到这一思潮的重要贡献，特别是其中被视作写实主义/自然主义早期阶段代表人物的福楼拜，以及后期阶段的著名人物左拉和莫泊桑。① 我们还可以发现额外三页从哲学、伦理学、教育三方面讨论自然主义的内容，这或许是主编唐敬杲介入的结果。② 相较于"自然主义"，"写实主义"的词条只有2页半，另外有对巴尔扎克和福楼拜的简短探讨（前者有2页，后者1页半），后者的小说《包法利夫人》被看作自然主义的先驱之作。狄更斯作为两位最受喜爱的英国小说家之一（另外一位是萨克雷，辞书中没有他的词条），获得2页半的篇幅待遇。托尔斯泰有7页（与只有1页的陀思妥耶夫斯基形成对比），对他讨论更多的是其道德哲学和基督教思想，而非小说。

"浪漫主义"有7页的历史叙述，包括从英国浪漫主义运动起始，到德、法、意、俄各国的发展流变。有趣的是，它有一个部分是"道德及实际生活上的浪漫主义"，集中讲施莱尔马赫（Schleiermarcher）。另一相关的文学思潮是"新浪漫主义"（Neo-Romanticism），茅盾明显受其影响。在《新文化辞书》中，有4页致力于详尽解释这一术语，它被视为对科学主义信仰的反拨。如果说写实主义和自然主义展示的是人生的外在现实，那么描写神秘"灵魂觉醒"（Réveil de l'âme "awakening of the soul"）的文学就是新浪漫主义的范畴。像他的同代人一样，茅盾也是从日本批评家厨川白村的著作中了解到一术语，特别是《近代文学十讲》一书，而厨川白村则转而引自西蒙斯（Arthur Simons）的《象征主义运动》（*The Symbolist Movement*）。③ 茅盾似乎在

---

① 唐敬杲：《新文化辞书》卷一，商务印书馆1923年版，第661页。
② 《近代思想解剖》第十章《自然主义之思潮》中的情况也是如此，这本书可能是唐敬杲对一部日本著作的翻译（参第207页脚注②)。该章开头讨论了哲学、伦理学和教育等方面的自然主义。
③ Bonnie McDougall, *The Introduction of Western Literary Theory into Modern China*, 1919—1925, Tokyo: The Center for East Asian Cultural Studies, 1971. 杜博妮在第三章《浪漫主义与新浪漫主义》（"Romanticism and Neo-Romanticism"）中给出了详尽的解释。

两端之间摇摆不定,一方面是他直接倡导的写实主义与自然主义(这两个术语在他的叙述中常常混淆);另一方面他又为象征主义和新浪漫主义这种更前卫的艺术现象所吸引。因此他花了4页篇幅在象征主义的词条上,从中将象征主义分为文学、绘画和音乐三种表现形式。在文学方面,他引用了马拉美(Mallarmé)、梅特林克(Maeterlinck)、豪普特曼(Hauptmann)、赫尔曼(Sudermann)、德默尔(Dehmel);在绘画方面,他将之等同于印象主义;在音乐方面,代表人物是瓦格纳(Wagner)而不是德彪西(Debussy)和早些时候的勋伯格(Schoenberg)。这种模糊又多少有点奇怪的理解可显示出,茅盾对他自己竭力追赶的最新潮流并不很明了。①

在文学词条中,一个最明显的缺席者是波德莱尔,他的名字在中国绝对不会不为人知,事实上,他是被翻译得最多的欧洲诗人之一。为何波德莱尔会被忽视是个谜。一个可能的猜测是茅盾从来不热衷于现代诗歌,因为他依赖于写实主义—自然主义—新浪漫主义这一文学进化发展的线索,他似乎并不确定新浪漫主义的潮流是否会被现代主义接替而成为过去。茅盾的纲目似乎回避了整个欧洲现代主义光谱:不仅像克林姆(Klimt)、马蒂斯(Matisse)、毕加索、夏加尔(Chagall)、康定斯基(Kandinsky)这些现代艺术大师没有获得任何叙述(正如梵高和高更的情况一样),而且乔伊斯、卡夫卡、普鲁斯特、T. S. 艾略特、托马斯曼的名字也消失不见或仅仅被提及一下。现代音乐也是同样的情况[马勒(Mahlner)、勋伯格(Schoenberg)、斯特拉文斯基(Stravinsky)都没有被提及]。的确,"现代主义"(modernism)、"先锋派"(avant-garde)以及就此而论的"现代性"(modernity),这些术语在《新文化辞书》中都无处可见,尽管有一些对不同艺术流派的简短介绍,如表现主义(2页)、未来主义(1页)和象征主义(3页)。

---

① 如果我们将《新文化辞书》中的现代欧洲文学词条,与茅盾之后为青年读者设计的《西洋文学通论》(世界书局1933年版)一书相比较,我们可以看到更详尽的讨论,不仅关于自然主义的各种著作,也包括之后发生的思潮(第九章),有关未来主义的讨论也令人印象深刻。在所有五四作家中,茅盾和郁达夫也许是最了解西方文学的。

诚然，尽管茅盾希望在《小说月报》的"小说新潮"栏及时追踪欧洲文学的最新潮流，但这些现代作家和艺术家都是其时文艺界的新兴之秀，或许因此还未受编者注意。

虽然那些我们现在认为是重要现代主义者的名字在《新文化辞书》中消失不见，但不少冷门作家却可以从中找到他们的位置。如法国诗人和小说家朱莲（Claude Theuriet）、英国诗人詹姆斯·汤普森（James Thompson）、古希腊诗人泰门（Timon）都在其中。著名法国作家司汤达在他的原名"培尔"（Marie Henri Beyle）之下有一个词条。著名俄国作家契诃夫（Chekhov）拼作"Tchehoff"，只有一页的篇幅就被打发了。我读得越多越意识到，考虑到整项辞书计划在哲学上的份量，茅盾对其做出的贡献是有限的，整本辞书的质量并不均匀。当然，这是我自己的一种偏见，无论文学词条有什么优点和弱点，我们都必须感谢茅盾的贡献。它们因作为那个时代阅读盛宴的一部分索引而变得格外有价值——我们可以了解到五四作家和读者在西方文学中读什么以及希望读些什么。他们贪婪的胃口和兴趣的多样性昭示着开放和世界主义的精神，相较于他们，生活在信息饱和时代的我们并没有表现得更好。

结　论

《新文化辞书》的出版实现了商业上的成功，这可以从一年后（1924）的再版看出来。但读者的实际使用状况我们就只能依凭想象揣测了。当然，我将之视为一个思想史文本的策略容易引发争论，其他人或许会发现更多适合于百科全书辞典的有用信息。尽管书的设计与结构安排不容许更加详尽的阐述空间（佛教除外），总体风格由展示和叙述构成而不是深度分析，但我仍然觉得，我越是一页页地来回穿梭，越可以发现大量"隐藏的宝贝"。

当时的普通读者如何阅读它或使用它是一个只能推测的事，但似乎可以想见，至少对于受过较好教育的读者来说，《新文化辞书》的写作风格对他们而言应无困难。编者们达成了"高深学问底通俗化"的目标，他们"以最平坦最显明的文辞叙述出来，使人人都能够很容易的了解"，"竭力的避除烦冗"，"应用最经济的结构，最简单的辞句"，从而"使读者以最小的努力，获得最高的效率"。① 但是，最后一个愿望或许很难实现：读者能否以最小的努力获得最高的效率取决于他的教育背景，这是个难以说清的问题。若要找到一个词条，读者需要同时知道它在源语言中的名称和它的中文翻译/音译名。如果读者不知道名称和术语而又想查验它该怎么办？我试着使用中文索引，但事实证明它并不高效。不管是当时还是现在的理想读者，都必须具备足够的知识水平。就此程度而言，我认为辞书的大部分读者是受过良好教育并且渴望获得西方"新知"的人。我也认为，即使当时最见多识广、受教育水平最高的读者，在面对这样丰富的"陌生"材料时，也会畏怯迷茫。至今我还没有从五四领导者那里发现《新文化辞书》的相关印证。

《新文化辞书》的编者的确有他们自己的思想偏好，与五四领导者十分不同。胡适提倡的杜威，陈独秀提倡的拉非耶特（Lafayette）、拉马克（Lamarck）、圣西门、傅立叶，李大钊提倡的列宁，这些人物没有一个占据重要的篇幅。相反，正如前述所注意到的，编者们似乎认为现代德国哲学家更具有思想的重要性，甚至严复首次介绍到中国的社会和政治思想家（斯宾塞、赫胥黎、J. S. 密尔、孟德斯鸠）与其对比之下也相形见绌。像狄德罗的《百科全书》（*Encyclopédie*）一样，《新文化辞书》并不仅仅是呈现"新知"，而更是以一种新的方式组织"新知"，以此服务于一个目的——开拓一般大众的思想视野。不过《新文化辞书》的编者们，在试图促使一般读者接受这些西方新知识的过程中，也有意无意地提高了他们自己的知识水平。一批数量惊人的学术知识被浓缩在这部两卷本的著作中，对于一个日后像我这样的学者而言，尽管有些吹毛求疵，但还是深深为其折服。阅读这本知识书籍是一次深获教益、富有成果的经历。

---

① 唐敬杲：《新文化辞书叙言》，载唐敬杲编《新文化辞书》，商务印书馆1923年版，第4页。

震惊、祛魅与规训：晚清大众媒介中的火车经验书写（1902—1911）

张春田　韩雨薇[*]

【摘要】 作为工业文明的重要标志，火车在很长一段时间内兼具新奇危险与文明进步两方面的意涵。从19世纪初火车诞生之初，人类对其复杂微妙的情感就在不断地交织酝酿：既忍受着嘈杂的轰鸣与令人心惊的震颤，同时享受着运输及移动的便利。"火车"的现代性在中国的兴起和发展，牵涉中国人交往方式、时空感受与道德伦理的激烈变迁。本文通过整理和分析1902—1911年间大众媒介中与火车有关的一些文本，揭示晚清社会文化转型中火车所扮演的多重角色，从震惊、祛魅与规训三个角度，透析火车书写的多重性及其意义。

【关键词】 晚清；火车；现代性；震惊；规训

---

[*]【作者简介】张春田，华东师范大学中文系副教授、语文教育研究中心研究员，主要研究方向为中国现当代文学、中国近现代思想与学术、文化理论与批评、都市文化与视觉文化、情感理论。

韩雨薇，女，华东师范大学思勉人文高等研究院科研助理。

【基金项目】本文为中央高校基本科研业务费项目、2021年华东师范大学青年预研究项目"抒情传统与中国近代文学转型"（项目编号：43800 - 20101 - 222253）阶段性成果。

Shock, Disenchantment and Discipline: Train Experience Writing in the Mass Media of the Late Qing Dynasty, 1902—1911

Chuntian Zhang, Yuwei Han

Abstract: As an important symbol of industrial civilization, the meaning of train is full of contradictions for a long time, which represents novel, dangerous and civilized progress. Since the train appeared for the first time in the early 19th century, it involved complex and nuanced experiences and feelings. People not only endure the noisy roar and the frightening tremor, but also enjoy the convenience of transportation and mobility. The rise and development of "modernity of train" in China involves the drastic changes of the way of communication, the feeling of time and space, and the moral ethics of the Chinese people. This paper explores some train-related texts in the mass media between 1902 and 1911, and reveals the multiple roles played by trains in the social and cultural transformation of the late Qing Dynasty. From the perspectives of shock, disenchantment and discipline, this paper analyzes the multiple and significance of the writing of train in some genre.

Key words: Train; Modernity; Shock; Disenchantment; Discipline

1890 年，在伦敦出任驻英二等参赞的黄遵宪以乐府古题"今别离"写下吟咏火车的诗句："今日舟与车，并力生离愁。明知须臾景，不许稍绸缪。钟声一及时，顷刻不少留。虽有万钧柁，动如绕指柔"，热情地赞扬这新式交通工具迅猛的运行速度。然而火车的出现及其影响，却不仅像他诗里描述的这般简单。

火车是工业革命最重要的成果之一，在西方，火车可谓维多利亚时代的象征。时至今日，火车已成为现代性最为显著的隐喻。火车发明之初，伴随其运行的轰隆声，人们的心情是复杂的：迷恋、惊奇或是恐惧兼有，时空感受因之发生急剧变革，争论更是不曾止息。这些争论正是"火车"作为现代性象征,杂糅了种种矛盾的外在显现。火车挟带一股势不可当的力量介入晚清社会,并逐渐重新定义社会秩序。本文在梳理晚清最后十年(1902—1911)报纸期刊上有关火车文本的基础上,尝试解读火车与晚清新文化之间的复杂关系。

无论是从现代性角度去解读火车这一器物,还是探究火车究竟如何影响世界的现代化进程,火车是一个理想的切入口。[①] 本文重点探讨从火车所引发"震惊",整个社会对其采取恐惧敌视的态度,到人们主动去理解、迎合"火车"这一象征进步发展的事物,再到火车被接纳之后如何规训与改变人们的生活方式与世界观的过程。当然,这三种状态在历史中并非线性排列,但是从材料中大体可见"震惊—祛魅—规训"这样的变化。从敌视到将其内化为一种现代生活不可或缺的生活方式,机器与人之间的相互磨合生发出人们笔下丰富各样的现代性经验书写和反思。

一 "惊魂与轮进"——火车与"震惊"体验

弗洛伊德首先将"震惊"引入了精神分析中,最初用来形容人的精神系统能量不足以将外部的兴奋约束住,而产生精神系统保护层被突破的状况。[②] 其实,人类世界的工业化进程一直都是一个伴随着"震惊"的过程。火车作为新事物出现在晚清社会时,给人带来的超负荷的兴奋,不仅来自对先进技术的惊喜与崇拜,也同样不乏对其运行之高速和汽笛之刺耳的惊惶。机器与人类的作用从来都不全是愉快的体验,与机器相处的过程伴随着种种难以忍受的痛苦,19世纪欧洲医学界产生了许多与铁路、火车相关的病理名词,诸如"铁路脊椎"

[①] 香港中文大学李思逸博士在其2020年出版的新著《铁路现代性:晚清至民国的时空体验与文化想象》中,分别从"铁路的命名"、"铁路视觉图像"、"回归物"、"孙中山的'铁路梦'"、"铁路旅行"以及"车厢界限及陌生人问题"等方面对火车与现代性经验进行了论述,具有参考性。

[②] [奥]西格蒙德·弗洛伊德:《弗洛伊德后期著作选》,林尘等译,上海译文出版社1986年版,第10页。

"铁路休克"[①] 等。相当长一段时间里，火车的轰鸣声、令人无法忍受的震动以及惨烈的交通事故给人带来不可逆转的身心创伤。中国人甫一接触火车，这种惊喜与惊惧交织的"震惊"体验便常常出现在当时人们笔下。譬如1905年《国粹学报》上的一首诗《火车中望都城诸山》就写到诗人乘火车时的体验：

晓月下芦沟，行入坐山胫。出郭未五里，巉岩峙万岭。
拔地形莺翔，竟天势马骋。玉泉颇蜿蜒，锦屏独修整。
岩去奇若失，峰来美先逞。堪霞鹤背晴，初阳雁边炯。
西山百枝干，下盘十万井。遥知登高人，俯见田棱棱。
千仞青巑岏，秋色压我顶。西风吹枯山，野火烧乱梗。
车行迅风飘，惊魂与轮迸。挥手谢山神，遥见飞鸟影。

有趣的是诗人在火车这一极具现代性的空间内"挥手谢山神"，将现代世界的"火车"与古典世界的"山神"并置，可以想见流连于"山神"与"飞鸟"世界中的前现代诗人在高速运行的火车上会有怎样的"震惊"之感，而"挥手谢山神"更像是现代世界取代古典世界的进化论式隐喻。当然，并非所有的震惊体验都是这样饱含诗意的，在1910年第3期《江宁实业杂志》刊载一则《搭京汉火车者须知》，为防旅客被火车汽笛声惊吓摔伤，铁路局将火车的汽笛改成了极具古典特色的"铜铃"：

向来京汉铁路定章，凡搭客上下车辆，均以鸣笛为号，但汽笛一鸣，搭客上下不免慌张，诚恐有跌伤毙命情事。刻由铁路南局改订新章，上下车辆以铜铃为号，于五分钟以前先行摇铃，俾搭客小心上下以免危险。

[①] 关于铁路病理学，参考 [德] 沃尔夫冈·希弗尔布施《铁道之旅：19世纪空间与时间的工业化》第7章与第9章的详细论述。

> 汽笛声猛不隄防便吃一惊,虽胆壮者且然,况老妪、幼孩、病夫、愚子之为胆怯者乎,鸣铃为号,洵属佳便,凡各火车均当以此为法。

与马鸣声相比,汽笛声分贝更大且毫无征兆,从冰冷的机械中发出,这没有生命的噪声不仅仅是因为音量,更主要是因为其"陌生"而对人具有相当大的震慑力。"汽笛"作为一种现代产物,它发出的声音似乎天然就与"现代性"概念联系在一起。这种异质、恐怖而现代的新事物出现,具有可怕的杀伤力①,在人们面对传统与现代的冲击而不知所措之时甚至足以致人死地,而铜铃的替换则弥补了人们面对现代性巨大断裂时的心理间隙。

当然,最让人"震惊"的还是诸如火车相撞这样的意外事故。以1908年5月5日《新闻报》上这条火车撞击伤人的新闻为例:

> 前日正太火车由太原开行,行不数里,忽有材料车迎面而来,彼此均未预为招呼,致骤不及避,迎头互撞,致死二人,伤五六人,凡车中人均大受惊,恐正太火车在初开之时已屡有失事,今行之既久,尚有如此疏忽之举,该站长及司机几人诚不得辞其咎也。

如果说《火车中望都城诸山》中火车的速度催生出的还可能是一种"惊喜",那么这同样的速度在相撞之时便足以使人产生"惊恐"之情,陌生未知的机器在肇祸之后给人类带来的是巨大的恐慌。英国作家查尔斯·狄更斯曾经在1865年6月9日遇到一场铁路事故,虽然他成功逃离车厢,但这恐怖的回忆使他永远留下了"铁路休克"的症状。后来,弗洛伊德创造了"铁路焦虑"这个新的术语,用来指火车脱轨引发的恐惧和由于火车震动而激起的性冲动及其他相关的精神状态。② 铁路

---

① 关于"汽笛"更加详尽论,参见吴雪杉《汽笛响了:阶级视角下的声音与时间》,《美术研究》2016年第5期。

② 张杰:《火车的文化政治学》,中国社会科学出版社2018年版,第13页。

引发的种种疾病一度成为医学界十分关注的课题。赫伯特·W. 佩奇在《外科与法医学视角下没有明显机械损伤或者神经冲击的脊柱与脊髓伤害》中指出，在街上被马车碾过的人与铁路事故的受害者相比，铁路事故存在着巨大的恐惧和惊慌的元素，而马车事故中是没有的："每次铁道碰撞事件，哪怕没人身体受伤，都足以对心智造成非常严重的后果，也足以成为一种手段，能够从惊骇当中，也仅仅从惊骇当中，引起一种崩溃的状态。"[1] 在中国，火车引入之前就有康有为等写文章提及火车，普及国外的新式交通工具，中国的乘客往往会先在文字和图片中见识火车，再真正地乘坐火车，大多火车乘客早已具有足够的心理准备，单单乘坐火车已不太可能造成所谓的"休克"与"创伤"。因此与英国的情形不同，乘火车引发的身心疾病在晚清报刊中几乎不见记载。当然，这"震惊"依然不容小觑，火车失事造成的创伤依然占据公共话语领域中相当重要一部分内容，成为当时人们谈论火车的重要话语资源。分析文本资料，可以看到"碾毙""撞杀""轧毙"这样的字眼频繁出现，意外事故的书写构成了清末火车叙事的重要部分。

随着火车进入中国后逐步普及，震惊之感渐趋消弭。图1展示了"意外事故"类信息逐年出现的数量在当年文本总数中所占比例，折线代表的比例在后五年逐年下行，大致上能够说明在后期火车失事带来的"震惊"感在人群中的关注度渐趋减弱，"火车失事"一类的信息正在一点点淡出人们的视野。

二 从"断非中国所能仿行"到"亦奇妙矣哉"

火车引入中国除了带给人们"震惊"之感，同时伴随着中国广大乡土社会对"火车"妖魔化的想象。莫言《檀香刑》写高密东北乡农

---

[1] ［德］沃尔夫冈·希弗尔布施：《铁道之旅：19世纪空间与时间的工业化》，金毅译，上海人民出版社2018年版，第209页。

图 1

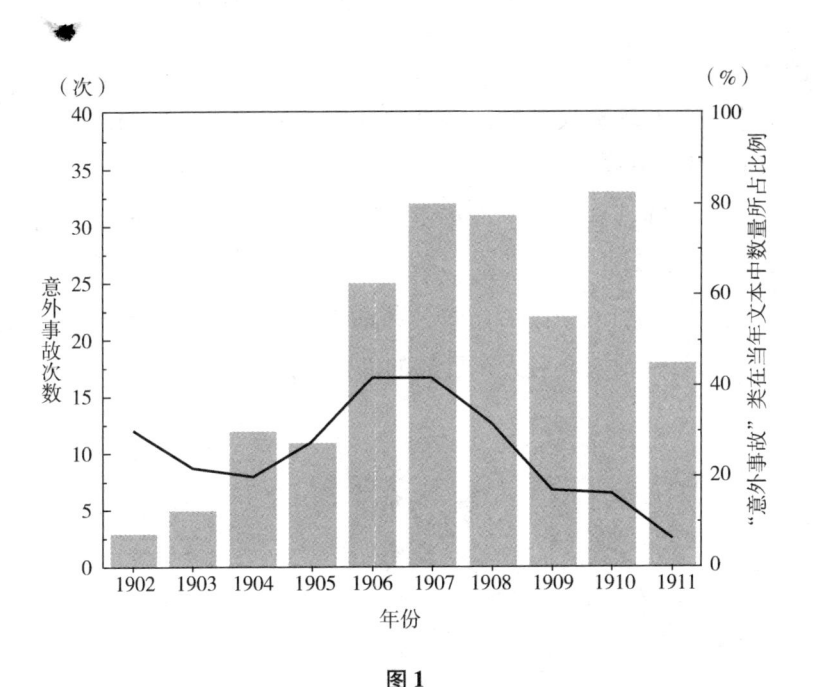

说明：统计数据基于"晚清全国报刊索引"数据库中 1902—1911 年间"火车"词条相关的文本，下文数据来源相同，不再标注。

民参加义和团，起因就是德国胶济铁路的铺设，群众之间流传着可怕的传说："德国人把中国男人的辫子，压在了铁路下面。一根铁轨下，压着一条辫子。一根辫子就是一个灵魂，一个灵魂就是一个身强力壮的男人。那火车，是一块纯然的生铁造成，有千万斤的重量，一不喝水，二不吃草，如何在地上跑？不但跑，而且还跑得飞快？"[1] 人们的担忧并非只是杞人忧天：恐惧感在官方世界同样普遍。1880 年，直隶提督刘铭传进京上奏，提议修筑铁路，而跟随郭嵩焘出使外洋的刘锡鸿言辞激烈地提出 25 条理由反对兴修铁路，认为铁路的铺设惊扰了中国的山川神灵，"火车实西洋利器，而断非中国所能仿行也。"[2] 刘锡鸿的观点具有代表性，体现出面对火车这一陌生事物时过激的自我

---

[1] 莫言：《檀香刑》，作家出版社 2001 年版，第 190 页。
[2] 关于晚清兴修铁路时刘锡鸿与刘铭传的相关争论，参见李文耀《中国铁路变革论：19、20 世纪铁路与中国社会、经济的发展》，中国铁道出版社 2005 年版，第 10—12 页。

保护。

大众媒介在塑造火车的公众形象时也具有不可磨灭的影响。对十年间（1902—1911）报刊杂志上"火车"文本种类分布进行统计，可以发现这十年间报刊杂志上火车意外事故的相关新闻报道条数占到了文本总数的19.44%（见图2），仅次于报刊上的火车时刻表，"火车失事"成为火车引入中国后当时公共话语领域中讨论最多的问题，数量上充分表明中国人面对火车事故的创伤与焦虑。

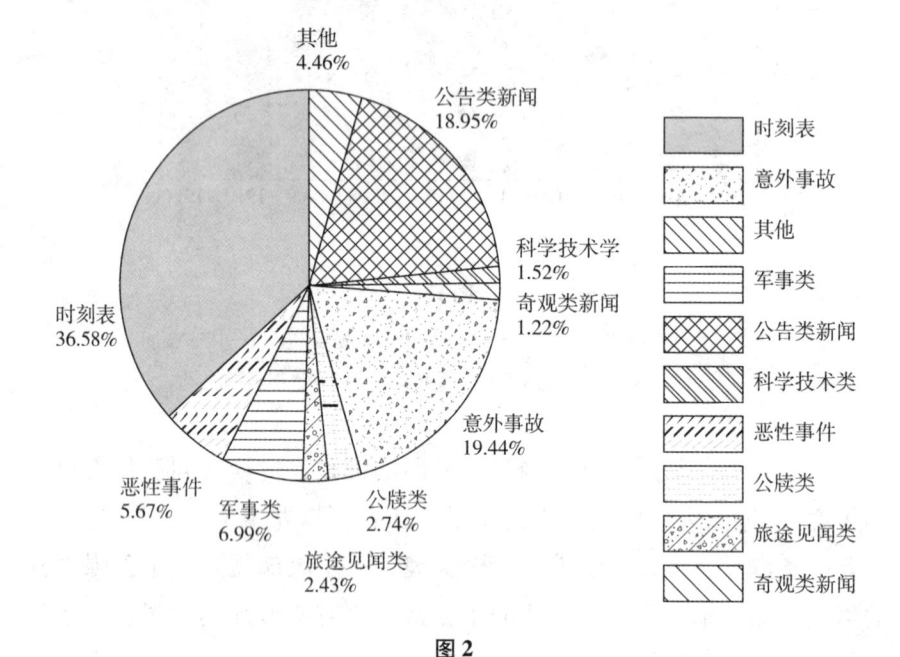

图2

以十年间意外事故报道数量及所占比例最高峰的1907年为例，在此列举1907年上半年火车意外事故的新闻标题，见表1。

表1　　　　　　1907年上半年火车意外事故新闻标题

标题	出处	日期
火车相撞伤人	《新闻报》	1907－1－1
火车失事原因	《新闻报》	1907－1－4
纪火车遇险	《新闻报》	1907－1－4

续表

标题	出处	日期
欧境火车失事	《时报》	1907 - 1 - 7
火车被毁	《新闻报》	1907 - 1 - 30
火车失火	《时报》	1907 - 1 - 31
萍醴火车失事	《新闻报》	1907 - 3 - 4
火车忽炸	《新闻报》	1907 - 5 - 9
沪宁铁路火车出轨	《时报》	1907 - 5 - 22

新闻媒介如此密集地对火车意外事故进行报道，有意或无意间形塑并深化了"火车"在受众群体心目中恐怖的印象。使得人们脑海中"妖魔化"的火车形象在这些报道中被一遍遍强化。传播学理论中有框架学说，认为新闻媒体有设置议题的功能，媒介的报道行为塑造着受众对事物的认知框架。戈夫曼认为，所谓框架，就是人们用来阐释外在客观世界的心理模式，或指在某个特定时间用来理解社会境遇的一套特定的期望，所有我们对于现实生活经验的归纳、结构与阐释都依赖于一定的框架。[①] 报纸新闻对火车失事大量报道，与此同时却很少出现火车速度快、运输便利这样的积极性文字，这很大程度上可以归结于大众媒介渴望吸引读者、倾向于呈现意外事故，致力于对受众造成感官刺激以牟利的固有局限。大众传播媒介的这一局限相当程度上构建了人们理解"火车"这样一种新鲜事物的方式：危险大过便捷，速度的背后蕴含失控的可能。当然十年间关于"火车"的文本还有很多其他内容，但无论在数量还是典型性上都远无法与"意外事故"报道相提并论。媒介一点点强化着人们对火车的"妖魔化"想象，而作为媒介议题的"火车"便以这样的方式影响着晚清社会对"现代"的认知。

固然火车的背后蕴含无限的危险与未知，然而"火车一响，黄金

[①] 关于框架理论，参见陈堂发《新闻媒体与微观政治——传媒在政府政策过程中的作用研究》，复旦大学出版社2008年版，第61页。

万两",有识之士同样明白火车于经济发展的重要作用,譬如 1903 年胶埠火车通车,《新闻报》称"青岛商务之兴可拭目而待矣"。这期间报刊中出现了不少科普文章,造成了祛魅的效果,极大程度上疏解了保守势力对社会发展需求的阻碍。1910 年《铁路界》第 1 期署名杨日新的一篇文章热情洋溢地介绍了火车上的无线通信技术:

> 火轮船之能利用无线电信,夫人而知之,岂知今则火车亦可利用无线电信矣。谓予不信,请征诸美国,美国阿哈马市之幽尔盎巴西灰枯铁道会社其工场中有电器技师欺米热拿博士者,初造一机械,利用无线电信,虽远距离之间亦能使其信号铃应手而鸣。今日之新发明即基于是,后氏又造一无线电信之发信所,可自由移动,并造一无线电信用之贮电池车,凡自发电所至,贮电池车之通信如进止退返,皆能如命,不爽毫厘。嗣复累经实验,遂造出一信号车,其主要部为青铜箱,前面嵌以圆镜,车顶立感电针一枝,旁以技师一人司之。欲促其在旁技师注意,即由发信所传电波于感电针而箱中之电球即发赤光旋转而附于箱外之铜锣亦随之而鸣。后氏又多移此感电针于机关车发信,所有命令则虽无信号车,而所传之电,亦可直达于机关车,而机关车之进止退返皆可以无线电信指导之矣。嘻!亦奇妙矣哉!
> ......

文章详细介绍火车通信的整套流程,极具现代科学的严谨态度,以现代媒体传播手段普及工业文明新知识。通过科普,晚清民众从与火车的纠葛中第一次大规模习演了一套现代科学的思维模式,逐渐破除对工业文明的妖魔化幻想。

三 "专载之车"与"必设法改良"

福柯曾指出,从修道会继承而来的时间表有效地实现了对"活动"的控制。时间表的三个主要方法——规定节奏、安排活动、调节重复周期——不久就应用于学校、工厂和医院中。① 而火车严格遵守时刻表的机制与修道会甚至是监狱的模式如出一辙。以1909年10月9日《新闻报》刊登的沪杭火车开行时刻表为例，时刻表刊明从上海开往闸口的三班火车分别于上午八点三十分、十二点整、下午三点三十分发车，三班车到达终点站闸口的时间分别为上午十一点二十分，下午二点五十六分、五点五十一分。火车时刻表的出现很大程度上改变了晚清国人的时间观念。时间表对于中国社会来说还是陌生的事物，以时辰、刻为单位的计时方式被时、分这样更加精确的单位取代，这种服务于工业化环境的计时方式无形中加快了生活节奏，干支纪年的循环时间观被时刻表的线性发展观念逐步取代。而且无一例外地，同一份报纸中，火车时刻表的文字排布比其他新闻信息要更为密集，给人紧张、压抑之感，不知不觉被快节奏规训。因此阅读火车开行时刻表更容易产生古典社会里很难出现的，关于时间的紧迫感与焦虑感。张杰认为，这种压迫感使人性越来越呈现出一种机器特征，亦即马克思之"异化"。② 这无疑是一种现代性征候。正如伊格尔顿所说："如果我研究铁路时刻表不是为了发现一次列车，而是为了刺激我对于现代生活的速度和复杂性的一般思考，那么就可以说，我在将其读作文学。"③ 将火车时刻表读作文学当然夸张，但火车引入中国之后，的确在相当程度上影响中国人的生活习惯与观念，精确的"守时"成为现代生活的基本素质。

空间方面看，火车给人带来的空间观念的冲击在于等级车厢的空间区分及车厢空间切分造成的空间领属感，即每一个人都有自己的位置，而每一个位置都有一个人，乘客原则上不允许在不同等级的车厢间流动。《时报》1910年8月21日刊登一则译自西报的纪事：

---

① [法] 米歇尔·福柯：《规训与惩罚》，刘北成、杨远婴译，生活·读书·新知三联书店2003年版，第169页。
② 张杰：《火车的文化政治学》，中国社会科学出版社2018年版，第97页。
③ [英] 特里·伊格尔顿：《二十世纪西方文学理论》，伍晓明译，陕西师范大学出版社1987年版，第10页。

中国与世界

> 近日有一西女从中国北地来，拟乘火车晋省。余适与同行上车，寻得二等小房一间，方欲坐，不意该房有一中国贵族妇人先在行李仆从充满一室，此外尚有一客。余等入车后，该太太口中呶呶，似大不满意者。须臾，随口痰吐，并吸纸烟将车内作践不堪。余起寻管车人，未得，因告之车站长以此间无特别专载西人之车，辞之。嗣后，又有一西人偕其妇上车，盖新婚旅行者，该西人亦有烟癖，于是一室之中西人吸雪茄，华妇吸纸烟，吞云吐雾，烟气满车，不意此西人无意中竟将雪茄烟灰坠落中国太太衣上，太太大怒，跃起，骤以臂钏击西人头额，并抓伤其面。西妇在旁见其夫被殴，上前助战，遂与太太扭作一团。太太仆人闻訾逃开。殴毕，太太即唤仆人至证明，并未先行动手，迨车至济南，即诉之抚院，并延律师为辩护。此事若非有西国旅客为作证，西人必反受辱于华妇矣。

作者（为欧洲人）的书写耐人寻味："余适与同行上车，寻得二等小房一间，方欲坐，不意该房有一中国贵族妇人先在行李仆从充满一室"，字里行间充斥着一丝微妙的敌意，不料妇人同样"口中呶呶，似大不满意者"。空间的入侵与争夺似乎在车厢内悄然展开。随后作者不堪忍受，寻找车站长，却得知没有"专载西人之车"，可见在此之前中国有列车为西方人设专用车厢。火车车厢的奥妙之处在于，它将之前永远不会有什么接触的陌生人安排在同一个封闭空间内，如陈建华所言，在这样一个陌生而公共的空间内，来自五湖四海的各色人等如何相识相知相斥相斗？新的面相学交际学如何产生？空间在现代人际关系及其价值塑造中扮演了什么角色？[1] 车厢的空间划分无疑遵循一种现代化的规训机制，福柯认为，纪律的设立要从对人的空间分配入手，在封闭的空间内实行单元定位或分割原则，并把有几种不同用途的空间加以分类。[2] 火车车厢空间划分的纪律性自然地延伸到车

---

[1] 陈建华：《文以载车——民国火车小传》，商务印书馆2018年版，第207页。
[2] ［法］米歇尔·福柯：《规训与惩罚》，刘北成、杨远婴译，生活·读书·新知三联书店2003年版，第160—161页。

外，形成了现代社会公共空间内人际交往的基本模式。

关于规则的知识是规则意识的重要部分，时空观念的转变作为一套"知识性"思维模式逐渐发展形成旅客的规则意识，《时报》1911年8月5日刊登一则《乘淞沪火车之五煞》，最后一点作者写道："无我①于某日自炮台湾乘车至申，车轮方始转动，适糊涂老爷乘四人肩舆飞奔而来，距车站约百数十武站长遥见之则大□②，停车，糊涂老爷竟得以从容上车，阔煞！"这位老爷虽已误车，却能使站长停车等候其上车，作者暗讽其"阔煞"，表达不满，当时乘客秉持应当服从火车时刻表的规则意识大约可窥一二。

另一方面，乘客对自己购买车票后所拥有的权利也有了更加明晰的认识。1910年3月6日，《时报》发表一篇署名N的乘客的"抱怨"，指责由浙至沪的末次火车晚点：

> 每闻人言，每日下午末次由浙来沪之火车无一日不差时刻者，少则一二点钟，多至四五点钟不等，我以为是必过言。昨日天甚暖，余有事返杭，且薄衣矣，继思假令今日而车又差时夜风天寒不如仍厚衣为是，至淞暖甚，颇自懊悔，及下午四十四分钟至车站候浙来车，久之不至，风甚大，过一刻不来，甚异之。过二刻仍不来，更异之，至三刻四刻而仍不来，日间天既暖，人尽衣薄衣，至是在月台上吹风，一点钟人尽瑟瑟抖，于是有骂者，有号寒者，有取衣加身者，中年尚可支持，老少甚苦之，伫立既久，不但号寒，而且啼饥静以睹之，几为一般难以当时。我虽未能一一询问，然因是而归家病者谅必非鲜，呜呼！我旅客何辜，而必受此荼毒耶？彼公司何心，而必以此心戏弄旅客耶？假今机关车不能速驶，则时刻表不妨展缓，譬如云：四点四十四分到淞者不妨直云五点五十五分或六点六十六分或七点七十七分，省得客人

---

① "无我"为作者自称。
② "□"表示该处字迹脱漏。

立在月台上受苦。呜呼！彼公司中人而尚有人心尚□□护旅客性命，则必设法改良，不然我为此言可谓非圣诲法。

冷曰：圣之极至于杀人不用刀，贤之极至于杀人不见血。呜呼！余不欲言。

这篇带有投诉性质的文章感情激烈，痛斥火车晚点"戏弄旅客"。"譬如云：四点四十四分到淞者不妨直云五点五十五分或六点六十六分或七点七十七分，省得客人立在月台上受苦"一句，得理不饶人的控诉背后可见时间规则意识已经深入乘客内心，火车时刻表规训了乘客的时间观念，但同时乘客也会反过来要求火车的准点，要求铁路公司平等地遵守规则，这无疑是一种现代人的心理诉求和精神状态。同年8月《时报》一名作者写文章请求火车站派巡警于车站附近，防止车夫不按规定，刁难旅客的事情发生，这已经是对铁路公司服务规章相当细化的要求。

晚清的铁轨引进中国不仅规训了作为乘客的民众的时间观念、空间观念与规则意识，使人们的素质面向现代化社会演进；而且，民众的"受规约"同时制约着铁路公司发展出一套完善的运营体系，在这种相互作用之间，具有现代精神的消费者与商业组织正逐渐孕育而生。

结　语

作为"器物"的"火车"与晚清现代性经验问题早已不是一个新鲜的话题。本文在系统整理1902—1911年报纸杂志中的"火车"文本基础上，以历时性的视角处理"火车"与现代性诸问题，从震惊、祛魅与规训三个阶段考察火车与晚清中国社会之间的相互作用，无论是孤立文本的微观举证，还是图表数据的宏观展现，文本的材料都大体在一个时间维度内，支撑着整篇文章的论述。通过这样一条脉络，我们从一个不太一样的角度来理解"火车"与晚清现代性问题，通过报刊上关于"火车"的文本，梳理了从"震惊"体验到消弭"震惊"、再从"妖魔化"到祛除"妖魔化"、从熟人社会的集体无意识到现代性制度规约与规则意识建立的整个过程。我们得以通过"火车"这一"新式"交通工具管窥晚清中国的"现代性"面孔。

想象中的文化雅集：作为民国上海媒介文化景观的"咖啡"与"茶"

韩竺媛[*]

【摘要】 20世纪二三十年代，咖啡馆受到许多上海文化知识分子的青睐，成为他们进行社交聚会的首选场所。同时，中国人传统的饮茶习惯被重新赋予了现代的内涵，并催生了在民国文化精英中盛行的"茶话会"，这是中国文人雅集传统与欧洲沙龙文化的结合。随着与"咖啡"和"茶"相关的文化雅集被延伸到了大众报刊中，"咖啡"和"茶"成为当时流行文艺思潮中重要的文化符号，《申报》上的"珈琲座"专栏和《文艺茶话》杂志是其中最具代表性的两个例子。通过征集聚焦现代文艺的文章，文化精英们可以在一个想象中的公共文化空间中参与另一种形式的聚会，这对于他们集体主义认同感的产生至关重要。"咖啡"和"茶"容纳了多层次的文化现代性想象，并成为一部分上海文化知识分子试图主导文艺美学取向的象征性"文化资本"。

【关键词】 雅集；珈琲座；文艺茶话；公共空间；文化资本

---

[*]【作者简介】韩竺媛，女，香港中文大学文化研究学系博士，研究领域为近现代中国媒介文化、文艺现代性、性别研究、知识生产与接受。

Imaginary Genteel Gatherings: "Coffee" and "Tea" as Cultural Landscape within Popular Media in Republican Shanghai

Zhuyuan Han

Abstract: In the 1920s and 1930s, cafes were favored by many intellectuals and became their preferred venue for social gatherings in Shanghai. At the same time, the traditional Chinese habit of tea drinking was reconfigured with modern connotations, facilitating the flourishment of "tea party" among Republican cultural elites, which embodied a combination of the Chinese literati tradition of genteel gathering and European salon culture. When genteel gatherings related to "coffee" and "tea" were extended to the popular press, "coffee" and "tea" represented important cultural symbols within the popular literary trend at that time, and the "Coffee Seat" column in *Shenbao* and the literary journal *Literature and Tea Party on Art* are two of the most representative examples. By soliciting essays focusing on modern literature and art, a particular group of cultural elites were able to engage in another form of genteel gathering in an imagined public cultural sphere that is crucial to the emergence of their collective subjectivity. In this sense, "coffee" and "tea" accommodated multiple layers of imagination of cultural modernity and functioned as the "symbolic cultural capital" for some Shanghai intellectuals who endeavored to dominate the aesthetic taste of modern Chinese literature and art.

Key words: Genteel gathering; Coffee seat; Literature and Art Tea Talk; Public sphere; Cultural capital

前　言

1936年2月15日,《六艺》创刊号刊登了著名漫画家鲁少飞的一幅素描漫画,题目为《文坛茶话图》,漫画下方的文字介绍了茶话会的参与者都有哪些人。坐在主位上的是邵洵美，坐在他左手边的是茅盾，而右手边则是郁达夫，嘴里叼着雪茄的男子林语堂坐在老舍旁边，张资平则坐在冰心和白薇身边，其他参会者还有洪深、傅东华、鲁迅、巴金、郑振铎、杜衡、张天翼、鲁彦、施蛰存、凌叔华、穆时英、刘呐鸥等文艺界知名人士。这幅漫画描绘了20世纪30年代中国最有名的一批文化知识分子齐聚一堂的场景，尽管他们分属不同的文学和艺术流派，彼此之间的共处却依旧传递出一种和谐而高雅的氛围。虽然鲁少飞的漫画只是一幅虚构的作品，但它确实在某种程度上捕捉到了当时的社会现实，因为在20世纪二三十年代，与喝茶和喝咖啡有关的文化聚会盛行于上海的知识分子群体之间，茶馆和咖啡馆也是这些知识分子经常光顾的地方，是他们进行社交和文艺对话的理想场所。这些以文艺为主题的集聚，在某种意义上是中国士大夫"雅集"传统的现代传承。

图1[①]

---

① 鲁少飞:《文坛茶话图》,《六艺》1931年第1期。

"雅集"传统在中国社会有着悠久的历史，曾对文人文化的形成产生过巨大的影响。通过追溯先秦至北宋时期中国古代文人雅集的诞生与发展谱系，胡建君指出，到了北宋，雅集的形式与内涵已趋于成熟，尤以苏轼等一批著名文人在西园举办的"西园聚会"为代表。[①]他的分析表明，雅集是中国文人文化生活的重要组成部分，而诸如"西园聚会"的名词逐渐成为文化想象的重要标志，推动了各种文学著作和艺术作品的产生。栾梅健在特别关注现代时期的同时，也从南社这一现代文学社团形成的角度研究了中国文人的聚会活动。他探讨了南社成员如何继承文人雅集的悠久传统，同时为其注入了现代内涵。他认为，南社的集体性是由传统雅集的变革性仪式产生的。[②] 同样，在审视中国现代文学社团的发展时，贺麦晓（Michel Hockx）注意到了传统雅集习俗在此间的延续以及它与中国现代文学实践之间密切的联系。[③] 此外，费冬梅的研究也提及了 20 世纪初中国知识分子的文化集聚现象，虽然她更关注沙龙文化如何从欧洲传入并日趋盛行，但也简要地追溯了雅集文化在中国历史上的演变，以及它如何影响现代文人的文化生活。[④] 另一方面，彭丽君关注到了民国时期知识分子与喝咖啡相关的文化体验，她研究了饮用咖啡和踏足咖啡馆如何帮助青年知识分子产生自我认同，以及咖啡馆是如何在 20 世纪 20 年代的上海成为满足中国知识分子对现代性想象的空间的。[⑤] 胡悦晗则在他的文章中指出，在民国时期的上海，茶馆和咖啡馆与餐厅一起，共同成为知识分子发展社交网络和产生集体认同的主要场所。[⑥]

---

① 胡建君：《我有嘉宾：西园雅集与宋代文人生活》，上海锦绣文章出版社 2012 年版，第 8—15 页。
② 栾梅健：《民间的文人雅集：南社研究》，东方出版中心 2006 年版，第 33 页。
③ Michel Hockx, *Questions of Style: Literary Societies and Literary Journals in Modern China: 1911—1937*, Leiden, Boston: Brill, 2003.
④ 费冬梅：《沙龙——一种新都市文化与文学生产（1917—1937）》，北京大学出版社 2016 年版。
⑤ Laikwan Pang, "The Collective Subjectivity of Chinese Intellectuals and Their Café Culture in Republican Shanghai", *Inter-Asia Cultural Studies*, Vol. 7, No. 1, 2006, pp. 24–42.
⑥ 胡悦晗：《茶社、酒楼与咖啡馆：民国时期上海知识群体的休闲生活（1927—1937）》，《衡阳师范学院学报》2015 年第 2 期。

多位学者都关注到了文化雅集与中国知识分子集体性之形成的关系,以及喝茶或喝咖啡如何构成知识分子重要的文化体验。然而,无论是将知识分子的文化雅集和身份认同感的形成,与蕴含在他们文化实践中的茶和咖啡文化相结合进行研究,还是对大众报刊中以"茶"和"咖啡"为主要标志的文化集聚的研究,都尚未引起学界足够的关注。本文通过审视中国文化知识分子参与同喝茶与喝咖啡有关的文化集聚,以及他们在大众报刊中呈现的作为现实公共空间中文化雅集的延伸的文艺实践,探讨"咖啡"和"茶"如何容纳多层次的文化现代性想象,并成为一部分上海文化知识分子试图主导文艺美学取向的象征性"文化资本"。

一 上海的咖啡馆与茶馆作为文化雅集的场所

(一) 现代茶馆中的文化雅集

中国传统文人在社会活动方面与城市中的公共场所形成了密切的互动关系,这些场所包括茶馆、酒楼和妓院——即所谓的"三楼"。根据叶中强的说法,在中国古代,"三楼"有一种代偿性的社会功能,它使文人能够暂时脱离正统的社会规则。文人们在这些地方聚会,结交朋友,形成一个相互认同和认可的集体。[①] 雅集为文人提供了获得精神解放的机会,而"三楼"文化作为雅集传统的重要补充,完善了文人士大夫的文化体系。清末时期,"三楼"对于居住在上海租界内的中国传统文人重新融入现代性社会有着不可替代的重要性,它们将这些来自全国各地的陌生人聚集在他们所熟悉的公共空间,从而帮助他们建立了新的社会网络。然而,伴随着新的城市空间的扩张所形成的一个前所未有的现代消费空间,强烈冲击了中国传统文人的情感与文化价值体系,他们逐渐与"三楼"所构建的传统士人文化空间产生了疏离感。[②]

[①] 叶中强:《民国上海的"城市空间"与文人转型》,《史林》2009 年第 6 期。
[②] 在他的文章中,叶中强详细讨论了上海城市中具有现代社会功能的建筑,如电影院、西餐厅、咖啡馆等的发展,如何削弱了传统"三楼"的意义,并进一步影响了上海文人的文化活动和身份建构。详见叶中强《民国上海的"城市空间"与文人转型》,《史林》2009 年第 6 期。

同时，文人之间的传统集聚也受到了一些西方文化理念的影响。

茶馆作为"三楼"之一，在清末民初经历了一系列的自我革新，以适应城市化的快速推进。上海的一些茶馆正努力摆脱现代茶馆作为赌徒、娼妓聚集场所的恶名，试图重拾古代文人在茶馆内集聚时产生的风雅之趣，其中最具代表性的是一家名为"文明雅集"的茶馆。"文明雅集"位于上海二路，由俞达夫所经营。俞达夫是一位画家，曾师从著名的绘画大师任伯年。与其他许多简陋粗鄙的茶馆不同，"文明雅集"总是干净整洁，茶馆内部摆放着精致的茶具，墙面上装饰着典雅的山水人物画，因此吸引了众多文人雅士前来。这些人时常聚集在茶馆里作诗、画画，讨论历史和时事，遵循着他们的前人在旧时组织雅集的仪式惯例。由孙玉声、陈夔龙、王均卿等一批文化名流所牵头组建的"萍社"，是常集聚在"文明雅集"内最有名的文人团体。[1]

上海的现代化茶馆在当时知识分子的文化聚会中也十分盛行。"新雅茶室"（以下简称"新雅"）是一个颇具代表性的经历了现代化改革的茶馆。它位于四川北路，于1927年开业，茶馆内部以火车座椅作为装潢，不仅具有传统茶馆的功能，还提供粤菜和西餐。"新雅"现代化而高雅的环境吸引了众多文化名人，尽管他们具备着不同的文化意识形态背景，但都渴望能有一个优雅的场所与志同道合的朋友聚会。鲁迅曾在1930年2月1日的一篇日记中写到，他与冯雪峰、沈端先、王馥泉等左翼知识分子，在"新雅"参加了由大江书铺创办人陈望道为筹办《文艺研究》杂志所准备的招待宴。[2] 曹聚仁在他的回忆录中也回忆说，他在文化界的很多老朋友都曾在"新雅"举办聚会和休闲活动。[3] 据胡山源所述，唯美派作家林徽因和周扬常在"新雅"

---

[1] 相关信息来自吴承联《旧上海茶馆酒楼》，华东师范大学出版社1989年版，第39—42页。
[2] 鲁迅：《鲁迅全集·第十六卷》，人民文学出版社2005年版，第181页。
[3] 曹聚仁：《上海春秋》，生活·读书·新知三联书店2007年版，第305页。

聚会,那里是当时众多"马路文人"的大本营。① 邵洵美作为一位热衷于社交的颓废唯美主义派作家,当他得知"新雅"内经常有一大批文人聚会时,便急不可待地从很远的地方赶来拜访,他的彬彬有礼与博学多才成功赢得了那些文人的欢迎,因而得以受邀参与他们的聚会。② 此外,茅盾每周一都会在"新雅"主持"月曜会",上海的许多青年作家都会前来参与。在"月曜会"上,与会者会就时事交换意见,并接受来自茅盾的文学指导。③ 随后,"新雅"成为文人和艺术家在工作之余时常聚集的地方,并为他们提供了相互结识和扩大交际圈的平台,这些人当中也包括那些从海外归来的钟情于西式社交模式的知识分子。④

(二) 文化知识分子们在咖啡馆的聚会

当咖啡馆因其为人们提供想象和体验西方现代性的特质而逐渐在上海流行起来时,其所蕴含的社交功能也吸引了文化知识分子们的关注。咖啡馆文化于18世纪和19世纪在欧洲发展至顶峰,并孕育了一种独特的社交文化。当年轻的卡尔·马克思于19世纪40年代初次到访巴黎时,他参加了于巴黎咖啡馆内举行的工匠聚会,并注意到人们去咖啡馆并不只是为了喝酒或吃饭,而是咖啡馆中所具备的形成社团组织的可能性,以及它对不同谈话内容与思想的包容性深深吸引着公众。⑤ 作为"巴黎社会网络的主要环道"(a primary circuit for Parisian social networks),咖啡馆里发生的各种对话和仪式催生了政治革命和不同的现代意识形态,包括法国大革命,以及共产主义、社会主义、波希米亚主义和无政府主义思想。⑥ 巴黎的咖啡馆最初是为精英服务

---

① 胡山源:《文坛管窥:和我有过往来的文人》,上海古籍出版社2000年版,第57页。
② 林淇:《海上才子:邵洵美传》,上海人民出版社2002年版,第32—33页。
③ 端木蕻良:《文学巨星陨落了——怀念茅盾先生》,《北京日报》1981年4月9日。
④ 施蛰存:《文坛漫忆丛书:散文丙选》,黑龙江人民出版社1998年版,第72页。
⑤ W. Scott Haine, *The World of the Paris Café: Sociability among the French Working Class, 1789—1914*, Baltimore: Johns Hopkins University Press, 1998, p. 1.
⑥ W. Scott Haine, *The World of the Paris Café: Sociability among the French Working Class, 1789—1914*, Baltimore: Johns Hopkins University Press, 1998, p. 2.

的，而后逐渐发展成为政治化的公共讨论空间，"各行各业最英勇、最机智的首脑人物齐聚一堂"（the most gallant and wittiest heads of every estate come together）。① 聚集在咖啡馆的人们能够开展各式各样的谈话而免受国家层面的监视和干预。欧洲咖啡馆内的交际与文明秩序吸引了渴望在现代拥有一个雅集场所的中国文化知识分子，特别是那些对西方异国情调格外着迷的人。张若谷，一位曾经留学法国的自由派海派文人，在他的文章中将咖啡馆视为现代城市生活的象征。他曾回忆起他和朋友们在一家名为巴尔干半岛的咖啡馆里讨论文学与文化问题的时光：

> 记得在今年四月一日的下午，傅彦长，田汉，朱应鹏与我，在那里坐过整个半天。我们每人面前放着一大杯的华沙珈琲，……大家说说笑笑，从"片莱希基"谈到文学艺术时事，要人，民族，世界，各种问题上去②。

在张若谷看来，上海的中产阶级之所以迷恋逛咖啡馆，是因为它提供了一个可以与朋友进行长时间交谈的地方，这是一种生活的意趣。③ 1927 年春天，张若谷在上海遇到了他的日本朋友，从他们那里得知，他们对东方人未能拥有类似于文艺俱乐部的咖啡馆而感到不满意，这促使张若谷开始设想建立一种属于中国人自己的"文艺咖啡馆"。④ 张若谷的主张得到了文艺界的支持，因许多咖啡馆在当时被贬低为过于粗俗，无法满足文人的高雅品位。⑤ 事实上，尽管 20 世纪二三十年代，在上海很难觅得张若谷所构想的那种咖啡馆，但是有许多

---

① James Van Horn Melton, *The Rise of the Public in Enlightenment Europe*, Cambridge: Cambridge University Press, 2001, p. 243.
② 张若谷：《珈琲座谈》，上海真美善书店 1929 年版，第 3—4 页。
③ 张若谷：《现代都会生活的象征》，转引自王敏、魏兵兵、江文君等《近代上海城市公共空间（1843—1949）》，上海辞书出版社 2011 年版，第 219 页。
④ 张若谷：《珈琲》，《申报》1927 年 11 月 4 日。
⑤ 陈尹嬿：《民初上海咖啡馆与都市作家》，《中国饮食文化》2009 年第 1 期。

外国人开办的咖啡馆能够满足他的心愿——DD's 咖啡馆就是其中之一。DD's 是一家俄罗斯风格的咖啡馆,因供应来自俄罗斯、华沙和瓦纳的咖啡而闻名。从 20 世纪 20 年代末到 40 年代,它曾举办过大量新文人的聚会,经常光顾 DD's 的有欧阳予倩、洪深、徐悲鸿、徐志摩、郁达夫、叶灵凤、施蛰存、聂耳、蔡楚生等著名作家、画家、戏剧家、音乐家和电影导演。[1]

1928 年,一位笔名慎之的作家发表了一篇题为《上海咖啡》的文章,其中提到位于四川北路的一家名为"上海咖啡"的咖啡馆,并声称他在这家咖啡馆遇到了许多文学和文化名人,包括鲁迅、郁达夫、叶灵凤、孟超等,这些人中的一些正在进行颇具深意的谈话,另一些人则只是静静地坐在那里思考哲学问题。[2] 这位作者陶醉于咖啡馆内的气氛,并将其定义为"文化天堂",期盼读者能注意到它的存在。然而,五天后,郁达夫在《语丝》杂志上发表了一篇题为《革命广告》的文章,愤怒地反驳了慎之在文章所写的内容。他否定了自己与上海咖啡馆的关系,并批评了当前知识分子对"革命"概念的迷信。[3] 在同一期杂志上,鲁迅也对慎之的文章进行了嘲讽,宣布他从来没有去过这样的咖啡馆,并且鄙视它的装腔作势。他甚至指出,咖啡馆的本质是资产阶级的。[4] 鲁迅的文章后来被选入他的全集,标题是《革命咖啡店》,讽刺了一些文化名人将"咖啡"与"革命"等同起来的虚伪行为。[5] 似乎在郁达夫和鲁迅看来,"咖啡"的概念与小资产阶级情调和资本主义商业化密不可分,因此与无产阶级色彩的"革命"一词不相容,甚至是矛盾的。

实际上,上海的咖啡馆不仅对那些崇尚新文学和城市文化的文人充满吸引力(如新感觉派作家),它也吸引着倡导无产阶级文艺的

---

[1] 叶中强:《上海社会与文人生活:1843—1945》,上海辞书出版社 2010 年版,第 292—293 页。
[2] 慎之:《上海珈琲》,《申报》1928 年 8 月 8 日。
[3] 郁达夫:《革命广告》,《语丝》1928 年第 4 期。
[4] 鲁迅:《鲁迅附记》,《语丝》1928 年第 4 期。
[5] 鲁迅:《鲁迅全集·第四卷》,人民文学出版社 2005 年版,第 117—119 页。

"左翼"文人。例如,前文所提到的DD's见证了"左翼"文化和中国电影业之间最初的互动。据著名"左翼"剧作家夏衍回忆,他曾与上海明星影片公司经理之一的周剑云以及另外两位朋友钱杏邨和郑伯奇,于1932年夏天在DD's咖啡馆会面,讨论邀请一些"新文艺工作者"担任公司编剧的相关事宜。[1] 此外,位于四川北路的"公啡"咖啡馆在20世纪20年代末国民政府对"左翼"人士实施严酷的"白色恐怖"迫害期间,曾多次接待过"左翼"知识分子的定期聚会。由于"公啡"的主人是犹太人,又是外国人常去的,因而不会引起警察的监视。[2] "公啡"也是"左联"诞生的摇篮。1929年10月中旬,"左联"的第一次筹备会议在"公啡"咖啡馆二楼举行,鲁迅、夏衍、郑伯奇、冯乃超、蒋光慈、柔石、冯雪峰等12位成员参加了会议。此后,每周都会有筹备会议在"公啡"持续举行。[3] 其他"左翼"文化团体也喜欢在"公啡"召开会议,例如,沈端先于1930年秋冬之际在"公啡"召集主持了"左翼戏剧家联盟"的第一次党团会议。[4]

二 "咖啡"与"茶"作为大众媒介中重要的文化符号

(一)《申报》的"珈琲座"栏目

当进步的知识分子前往上海的咖啡馆参加文化聚会时,他们与同一聚会中的参与者分享相似的审美理想和文学品味,从而实现了自我认同并建构着自我形象。后来,一群现代主义的文化知识分子因沉醉于咖啡馆雅集自带的高雅氛围和异国情调,将这种聚会延伸到了大众报刊的版面上。

1928年8月6日,《申报》"艺术界"专栏的责编朱应鹏发表了一

---

[1] 夏衍:《懒寻旧梦录》,生活·读书·新知三联书店2006年版,第153—154页。
[2] 杨纤如:《左翼作家在上海艺大》,载中国社会科学院文学研究所、《左联回忆录》编辑组编《左联回忆录》,知识产权出版社2010年版,第78页。
[3] 夏衍:《懒寻旧梦录》,第98—99页。
[4] 赵铭彝:《左翼戏剧家联盟是怎样组成的》,《新文学史料》1978年第1期。

篇短文,介绍了"艺术界"附属的全新专栏"珈琲座"① 的设立。在为该栏目所作的介绍词中,朱应鹏这样写道:

> 从本月起,本刊辟出这样一块小小园地,设立了一个珈琲座,为读者诸君随便聚谈之所,无论谈文艺也好,谈见闻也好,谈社会问题也好,谈一切都好,总之,无所不谈,希望同志们有闲空的时候,不妨随时入座,无不竭诚欢迎。②

在"珈琲座"专栏成立之时,上海文艺界的都市异国情调浪潮已经达到了高潮,欧洲沙龙文化在其中起到举足轻重的作用。"沙龙"最早出现于欧洲的文艺复兴时期,文人们聚集在一起,就音乐和诗歌等话题进行文明的交谈。同时,它也是一个由作家主导的创作和传播文学作品的重要公共空间。在 18 世纪中叶之前,"沙龙"一词通常被用来指代王室和贵族家庭中的客厅,后来它被定义为"一个更适度的房间,在这里,个人在相对亲密的基础上进行社交"(a more modest room where individuals socialized on a relatively intimate basis)。③沙龙文化在法国,特别是在巴黎,发展出了更为精致的形式,并于 1740 年至 1780 年间到达顶峰。④法国大革命后,"沙龙"一词开始用来指代社交聚会,它相对独立于国家政策法规的约束,体现了启蒙运动公共领域的鲜明特色。

沙龙文化在 19 世纪末和 20 世纪初随着西方先进知识的传入而被引入中国。其间,被洋务派选派出国的中国留学生也在归国后带回了

---

① 晚清民国时期,"咖啡"和"珈琲"都被用作英文 Coffee 一词的中译名,"咖啡"一词最早于 19 世纪 40 年代出现于魏源的《海国图志》,1915 年由中华书局出版的《中华大字典》收入了"咖啡"二字,此后"咖啡"逐渐被确定为 Coffee 的正式译名,"珈琲"一词则借用了日语的译法,常用于 20 世纪 20—30 年代上海的多家日本咖啡馆名字中,同时也被大量海派文学家采用。详见柯伶蓁《咖啡与近代上海》,硕士学位论文,台湾师范大学,2011 年,第 14—16 页。
② 应鹏:《开幕词》,《申报》1928 年 8 月 6 日。
③ James Van Horn Melton, *The Rise of the Public in Enlightenment Europe*, p. 198.
④ James Van Horn Melton, *The Rise of the Public in Enlightenment Europe*, p. 205.

全新的西方文化理念。陈季同是福州船政局于1877年派出的35名海外留学生之一，他在法国留学期间深深地沉浸于法国的沙龙文化之中。陈季同曾受邀参加法国的许多沙龙，参与讨论各种与法国和中国有关的文化议题，他的幽默和智慧给许多法国作家留下了深刻的印象。[①] 在他的一篇文章中，陈季同如实地分享了他在巴黎咖啡馆参加沙龙的经历：

> 客厅里坐满了坐客。谈话，欢笑，看各地各种言语的报纸，互相讲传每日的新闻议论着，没有一点不自然的样子，但是也没有什么神秘。你不必去倾听，虽则如此，但你仍旧可以闻见一切。而且，也有互相讨论交换印象与思想的，一种相互的得益，只在一瞬霎间产生的。[②]

沙龙文化很快受到了许多其他包括张若谷、曾朴、李金发等现代主义文人的欢迎，他们崇尚法国的浪漫主义和巴黎的异国情调，且大多是曾在法国主修文学或艺术的留学生。[③] 在这些文人对法国文学艺术经典的热情推介下，上海咖啡馆内的文化雅集大多沾染了巴黎沙龙的光环。若干好友聚在一起，在咖啡馆里一边品尝咖啡，一边进行文艺相关的闲谈，在大多数情况下，这些文化知识分子的咖啡馆雅集都是出于对法国文艺沙龙的推崇和刻意模仿。

---

① 黄兴涛：《近代中西文化交流史上不应被遗忘的人物——陈季同其人其书》，《中国文化研究》2002年夏之卷。
② 陈季同：《巴黎的咖啡店》，载张若谷《异国情调》，世界书局1929年版，第4页。
③ 张若谷和李金发都曾在法国或法语国家学习，前者在比利时鲁汶天主教大学主修社会学和哲学，后者在法国第戎国家美术学院主修雕塑，二人都曾对法国文学和艺术进行了全面细致的介绍。例如，张的《异国情调》一书于1926年出版，他在书中介绍了法国文化的许多方面，并表达了他对这些文化的赞美，李曾在《人间世》第18期上发表了一篇题为"法国的文艺客厅"的文章，讨论了法国沙龙文化的特点，并呼吁在中国推行。虽然曾朴自己没有去过法国，但他从陈季同那里得到了关于法国文学的指导，并将法国沙龙视为西方异国情调的象征。详见费冬梅《沙龙：一种新都市文化与文学生产（1917—1937）》，第18页；陈尹嫄《民初上海咖啡馆与都市作家》，第90页。

中国与世界

前文所提及的"珈琲座"开幕词中,朱应鹏明确表示"珈琲座"专栏就如同现实中的咖啡座,大家可以在这里自由地就任何问题交换意见,因而可以推断出,"珈琲座"栏目的设置旨在延续咖啡馆内有关文艺创作的对话和聚会。法国沙龙文化在上海的流行,使咖啡馆逐渐成为一个显著的公共空间,并且作为作家和艺术家举办文艺沙龙的理想场所而存在。正如发生在咖啡馆内的现实雅集尤其热衷于讨论流行的文艺思想一样,在"珈琲座"专栏上征集的大多数短文都是关于文学和艺术的时兴话题。该专栏上发表的文章中,有很大一部分是关于文艺界的最新活动,以及对外国艺术概念和理论的译介。例如,1928年9月21日,一位名叫紫因的作者在专栏上发表了一篇短文,在文章中,他/她讨论了日本现代主义小说家小泉八云对英国著名作家乔治·梅里笛斯(George Meredith)文学风格的评价,希望这位在国内受到冷落的文学家能够得到关注。[1] 同年12月8日,"重"发表的一篇文章介绍了最近在德国发现的歌德画集,说明歌德不仅是一位杰出的诗人,同时也是一位杰出的画家。[2] 一个月后,一位名为"郑重"的投稿人发表了另一篇题为《一位在法国的亚美利加作家》的文章,介绍了"求利安·格莲"(Julian Green),一位在法国文坛大放异彩的美裔作家的成长经历。[3] 1929年2月21日,瑞麟为该专栏写了一篇文章,讨论维克多·雨果的代表作《欧那尼》(*Ernani*),同时介绍了几个重要的西方文学艺术概念,如浪漫主义和古典戏剧的"三一律"原则。[4] 此外,该专栏还时常刊登各种文艺活动的时间和地点的广告,上海剧院的公演信息,以及现代派作家,特别是新感觉派作家的新文学作品的出版消息。

那些经常光顾并聚集在上海咖啡馆的作家和艺术家,同时也是"珈琲座"专栏的主要撰稿人,该专栏由此成了展示他们审美趣味和

---

[1] 紫因:《小泉八云对梅里笛斯的意见》,《申报》1928年9月21日。
[2] 重:《歌德画集的发现》,《申报》1928年12月8日。
[3] 郑重:《一位在法国的亚美利加作家》,《申报》1929年1月9日。
[4] 瑞麟:《谈欧那尼》,《申报》1929年2月21日。

取向的窗口。因此,"珈琲座"可以被视为一个由现实延伸到报刊版面上的想象中的文艺聚会,可与在咖啡馆中实际存在的文化雅集媲美。在那些渴望法国文化氛围的文艺分子的设想中,报纸上的"珈琲座"专栏,与城市中的咖啡座类似,是一个想象中的场所的象征,使他们得以在一个公共空间中相互交流、交换意见。① 启蒙时期的欧洲沙龙以其交流属性为核心,非常重视通过不断交流思想和见闻而形成的集体认同,同时,沙龙中的对话往往是异质而平等的。② 在"珈琲座"栏目中,也可以发现这样的特点。它包含了大量有关现代文学和艺术的各方面话题,而且被选中刊发的文章没有任何意义上的高低之分——不管作家是否有名,是否富有,或是否处于相对较高的社会阶层。该专栏体现了现代派文人对以咖啡馆聚会为中心的西方沙龙文化所构成的现代都市生活复杂性的文化想象,并且作为这些文人之间的一个想象的交流空间而发挥着独特的作用。而另一方面,"珈琲座"专栏也在一定程度上继承了其欧洲沙龙的排他性特征。欧洲的沙龙通常有着固定的参与者,外来者要融入其中并不容易,除非他们能得到沙龙成员认识且信任的人介绍。③ 同样的,"珈琲座"专栏的作者往往被限制在一批特定的人群中,这些人的名字反复出现在版面上。

张若谷是"珈琲座"专栏最热心的撰稿人之一。1929年,他的专著《珈琲座谈》由上海真美善书局出版,书名直接取自该专栏,并收录了他在"珈琲座"上发表的一些文章,与该专栏有着相同的文艺内涵和取向。早在"珈琲座"设立之前,张若谷便已因常在"珈琲座"所属的"艺术界"专栏上发表与文艺相关的文章而闻名。在《珈琲座谈》的序言中,他对编辑朱应鹏表示感谢,因为朱应鹏主持"艺术界"栏目的三年内,始终大力鼓励文学艺术评论的发表,从而为上海

---

① 陈硕文:《上海三十年代都会文艺中的巴黎情调(1927—1937)》,博士学位论文,台湾政治大学,2008年,第118页。
② James Van Horn Melton, *The Rise of the Public in Enlightenment Europe*, pp. 202–206.
③ James Van Horn Melton, *The Rise of the Public in Enlightenment Europe*, p. 206.

文艺界的信息交流提供了一个重要的场所。① 随后,张若谷对新设立的"珈琲座"栏目表示欣喜,并提到了他坐在真正的咖啡座上与亲密的朋友进行闲聊的愉快经历,暗示该栏目将是延续他和他自己的老相识的聚会仪式的一个理想场所:

> 除了坐写字间,到书店渔猎之外,空闲的时间,差不多都在霞飞路一带的咖啡店中消磨过去。我只爱同几个知己的朋友,黄昏时分坐在咖啡座里谈话,这种享乐似乎要比绞尽脑汁作纸上谈话来得省力而且自由。而且谈话的乐趣,只能在私契朋友聚晤获得,这绝不能普度众生,尤其是像在咖啡座谈话的这一件事。②

张若谷认为,咖啡座的谈话所带来的高雅气氛和精神上的满足,是无法脱离特定的小群体的。他强调在咖啡座谈话中密友存在的重要性,从而树立起了在咖啡座所聚集的文人身份的区别。尽管"珈琲座"专栏声称向《申报》的所有读者征集文章,但实际上,它只是吸引了那些格外关心现代主义文艺思想,并热衷于接受法国沙龙文化的人,而这些人中的大多数都已经是彼此的熟人。因此,该专栏最终只是扩大了一群特定文人的文化影响力。在这个意义上,"咖啡"成为"珈琲座"专栏中一个重要的文化隐喻,象征着报刊版面上一种想象中的文化雅集的独特性。

(二)"茶话会"与《文艺茶话》杂志

19世纪末20世纪初,欧洲的"茶会"(又称"茶话会")文化传入中国,与本土的饮茶习俗相互影响,为与饮茶有关的传统雅集注入了异国元素。古时中国的"茶会"也称"茶宴",文人雅士们以佳茗宴请好友宾客,吟诗作赋,畅谈古今,其历史最早可追溯至西晋时期,而到了唐宋时期,茶会之风在文人和宫廷中盛行,涌现出大量描写集

---

① 张若谷:《珈琲·序》,第4—5页。
② 张若谷:《珈琲座谈·序》,第6页。

会品茶情形的诗词作品。① 唐代书法家颜真卿在担任浙江湖州刺史期间，就曾邀请陆士修、张荐等友人参与茶会，众人一边啜茶一边共同创作了一篇题为《五言月夜啜茶联句》的联句诗。清末民初，在西方文化的冲击下，"茶会"被赋予了新一层现代内涵。中国首任驻英大使郭嵩焘的翻译张德彝，在他的日记集《随使英俄记》中记录了他在1878 年春夏之交在伦敦和巴黎参加几次"茶会"的经历，他甚至对这些会议的频率有所抱怨："昼夜赴茶会应酬，疲惫不堪。"② 张德彝的日记反映了中国人与现代意义上的"茶会"早期的接触。从他的表述中可以看出，当时中国人已开始用传统的"茶会"一词来指代西方语境中的"聚会"和"沙龙"的概念。

另一个相关的例子是陈秋苹于19 世纪末为新成立的神交社（后更名为"南社"）所撰写的介绍词："本社性质，略似前辈诗文雅集，而含欧美茶会之风。"③ 可见，南社成员认为，古代的文人雅集与当时的西方文化精英所推崇的"茶会"乃内涵不同的两种聚会形式。焕然一新的"茶会"概念，很快受到众多拥护西方新知的中国文化知识分子的欢迎。在20 世纪10 年代"沙龙"一词传入中国之前，知识分子一直使用"茶会"来指代文人的聚会。④ 尽管后来"沙龙"一词在上海文艺界盛行，被用于指代文人间的文化雅集，但仍有一批文化知识分子倾向于采用"茶会"一词来称呼他们的聚会活动，因其富有更深厚的中国本土文化元素。这批知识分子所组建的文化社团名为"文艺茶话"，其成员大多是艺术家与作家。"文艺茶话社"成员曾活跃于20 世纪30 年代初上海文艺界，其成立宗旨与成员的聚集活动具有"中西/新旧"并存的特点——同时结合古代中国文人的"雅集"传统与西方"沙龙"文化。且不同于当时流行的"咖啡馆"聚会，其标榜的"以

---

① 陈文华：《我国古代的茶会茶宴》，《农业考古》2003 年第13 期。
② 参见方维规《欧洲"沙龙"小史》，《中国图书评论》2016 年第6 期。
③ 陈去病：《神交社例言》，转引自栾梅健《民间的文人雅集：南社研究》，第33 页。
④ 梁启超和胡适的书信与日记都记录了"茶会"，并赋予其现代含义。详见费冬梅《沙龙：一种新都市文化与文学生产（1917—1937）》，第17 页。

茶会友"颇具古典意味，主要成员既有来自带怀旧文学色彩的"南社"成员，也有推崇欧洲现代主义文艺的文艺家。

"文艺茶话"的社团活动最早是由美术家兼文学家孙福熙倡导的，他在担任《中华日报》的文学副刊《小贡献》的主编时，曾提出关于"星期日我们做什么"的讨论，引出了"文艺茶话"的成立动机：

> 我们学校生活的人，一到星期日，觉得很无聊，没有事可做，没有地方可走，要想不作无益之事，而利用了这无用的时间，我们提出了"文艺茶话"的组织。①

孙福熙提到，徐仲年对自己的答复是提议模仿法国的沙龙，发起茶话会。②"文艺茶话"的第一次聚会是在孙福熙家中举行的，孙的妻子刘雪亚担任茶话会的主持人，参与这次聚会的有陈抱一、华林、徐仲年、孙春苔等，众人既发表演讲，又分享趣闻，其间还有音乐伴奏，气氛十分快乐融洽，并且还商定了往后每周日都举行一次这样的文艺茶话。③ 茶话社的第二次聚会是在位于上海四川北路的"新雅茶室"举行的，后来，《时事新报·青光》出版了一期名为"一星期茶会"的特刊，此后，茶话会的每次聚会都会提前在印刷媒体上公布。④ 在第七次会议后，"文艺茶话"推出了自己的刊物《文艺茶话》，最早期的编辑之一章衣萍在创刊号上说明了办刊的目的：

> 我们要口里的文艺茶话有点成绩，所以我们刊行这个小小的文艺茶话，这是我们同人的自由表现的唯一场所……我们也希望能引起全国或全世界的文艺朋友的注意，接受或领悟我们的一些

---

① 孙福熙：《说到"文艺茶话"》，《人间世》1936年第1期。
② 孙福熙：《说到"文艺茶话"》，《人间世》1936年第1期。
③ 孙福熙：《说到"文艺茶话"》，《人间世》1936年第1期。
④ 费冬梅：《沙龙：一种新都市文化与文学生产（1917—1937）》，第28—29页。

自由表现的文艺趣味。①

作为综合性文艺月刊的《文艺茶话》于1932年8月15日由孙福熙创刊于上海，由文艺茶话出版发行，主编章衣萍、徐仲年、华林、孙福熙、汪亚尘等都是"文艺茶话"的核心成员，也是《文艺茶话》最主要的撰稿人。据章衣萍介绍，创办刊物的目的是将茶话会的聚会活动实体化，将其从现实中的聚会转化为杂志上的文字。这样一来，"文艺茶话"不仅能够对其团体活动进行翔实的记录，还能在文艺界进行大规模的宣传，从而扩大其美学原则和理念的影响。章衣萍描绘了茶话会轻松而优雅的氛围，与会者可以在夕阳下或于明月和清风中品茶、享用各式甜点，悠然自得地谈论文学和艺术：

> 文艺茶话并不是专为了狼吞虎咽，海上有所"狼虎会"，听说是专门为了吃的。吃饭几十碗，喝酒几十斤，那都是英雄们的勾当。我们惭愧没有那样的能力。在斜阳西下的当儿，或者是在明月和清风底下，我们喝一两杯茶，尝几片点心，有的人说一两个故事，有的人说几件笑话，有的人绘一两幅漫画，我们不必正襟危坐地谈文艺，那是大学教授们的好本领，我们的文艺空气，流露于不知不觉的谈笑中，正如行云流水，动静自如。我们都是一些忙人，是思想的劳动者，有职业的。我们平常的生活总太干燥太机械了。只有文艺茶话能给予我们的舒适，安乐，快心。它是一种高尚而有裨于知识或感情的消遣。②

此外，章衣萍声称，茶话会的本质是包容的，欢迎每一个喜欢文学和艺术的人，无论他或她推崇怎样的文学艺术思潮和流派：

---

① 章衣萍：《谈谈文艺茶话》，《文艺茶话》1932年第1期。
② 章衣萍：《谈谈文艺茶话》，《文艺茶话》1932年第1期。

我们没有一定的仪式，用不着对谁静默三分钟或五分钟；我们也没有一定的信条，任你是古典主义也罢，浪漫或自然主义者也罢，什么什么主义者都罢，只要你爱好文艺，总是来者不拒的。①

尽管"文艺茶话"的文化雅集与西方的沙龙有许多相似之处，但该社团的名称取自"茶话会"，强调"茶"的概念，与异国的"咖啡"相比更注重中国的文化传统。饮茶深受"文艺茶话"成员们的赞赏，通过这种方式，他们试图构建一种与以喝咖啡为中心的咖啡座聚会的异国情调截然不同的高雅文化氛围。在用"纯粹"和"自由"来形容文艺茶话会时，章衣萍提到了王羲之笔下的《兰亭集序》和李白所记述的《春夜宴桃李园序》，以及伦敦的文学俱乐部和法国的沙龙。这表明，"文艺茶话"认为他们的聚会既仿效中国历史上长期存在的文人雅集传统，同时也借鉴了西方的沙龙文化。华林在介绍文艺茶话时，将茶和咖啡作了比较：

> 东方名茶，亦世界佳品，较西方之"佳妃"，其味淡而清……中国素有"品茗"之雅集，不过佳妃浓而艳，富刺激性，此二佳品，亦可代表东西文化之不同也。②

在华林看来，"茶"和"咖啡"一淡一浓的迥异口味，印证了东西文化之间的差异。他没有采用常见的"咖啡"的译法，而是发明了一个新词，即佳妃，并注入了独特的中国文化特征。此外，他不仅提到了中国以喝茶为特征的优雅聚会的传统，暗示了茶话会组织的深层文化根源，还解释了"文艺茶话"的活动深受西欧文艺聚会的启发，如意大利和法国的博物馆和艺术馆举办的活动。因此，他希望经过茶

---

① 章衣萍：《谈谈文艺茶话》，《文艺茶话》1932 年第 1 期。
② 华林：《文艺茶话》，《文艺茶话》1932 年第 1 期。

话会的努力，文学和艺术的风气也能在中国盛行。

就如同"新雅"吸收了传统茶馆以及现代咖啡馆和西餐厅的元素来实现自我转型一样，"文艺茶话"的聚会也强调了中国传统雅集和欧洲沙龙的聚会仪式的结合，该组织将自己定义为一个以共同审美趣味为基础的文学和艺术协会，试图通过"喝茶"的方式将文人联系起来，而"茶"长期以来一直被视为中国传统文人文化聚会的一个重要构成因素。据 Bret Hinsch 的研究，到了唐代，茶已经取代了酒，成为士大夫们享受文化活动时最喜爱的饮品，而宋代的文人则以优雅和富有内涵为由推崇饮茶，认为饮酒过于普通，甚至是平庸。[1] 许多著名的诗人，如白居易，在与友人聚会谈论文学时都钟情于品茶，还会就不同种类的茶的优点和最佳的泡茶方法进行辩论。当茶在士大夫阶层中流行开来时，其所被赋予的高雅与精致的文化内涵被中国的文化精英普遍接受，成为彰显文人及上流阶级独特社会地位的重要文化标志。因此，文人之间自然更倾向于将饮茶作为强调优越文化身份的主要活动。茶在一个强调个体品质的社会，成了实现自我表达的重要媒介，[2] 完美契合文人雅集的内在本质，即传统文人对情感寄托和相互认同的追求。即使到了近代，茶馆的名声曾经历过恶化，但面对外来的"咖啡文化"的冲击，许多文化精英仍坚持喝茶，"喝茶""品茶"也由此成为彰显个人本土文化精神的象征，如鲁迅与周作人兄弟二人都曾表示过自己对于茶的喜爱以及对于咖啡的不屑一顾，他们甚至在茶的种类和泡茶的方式方面都有特定的坚持与偏好。[3]

在他刊登于《文艺茶话》的一篇文章中，徐仲年提倡一种"惟情的人生观"，认为每个人都应该努力解放他/她的"自我"，人们的生

---

[1] Bret Hinsch, *The Rise of Tea Culture in China: The Invention of the Individual*, Rowman & Littlefield, 2015, p. 23.

[2] Bret Hinsch, *The Rise of Tea Culture in China: The Invention of the Individual*, Rowman & Littlefield, 2015, p. 10.

[3] 详见鲁迅《喝茶》,《申报》1933 年 10 月 2 日, 第 5 页; 周作人《关于苦茶》, 贾平凹等编《上午咖啡下午茶》, 团结出版社 2008 年版, 第 107 页。

活应该以美来装饰，表明了强烈的西方美学与哲学倾向。① 徐仲年和华林都曾在法国主修文学艺术，熟悉浪漫主义，作为主要撰稿人，他们的审美取向深深影响了《文艺茶话》的气质。然而，与"珈琲座"栏目竭力鼓吹异国情调不同，《文艺茶话》欢迎新旧文化知识分子，无论他们属于哪个流派，但向该杂志投稿的作家都坚持一个共同的原则：他们都向往一种倡导爱与美的人生价值观，着迷于那些传递抒情和审美情感的文学艺术作品。② 值得注意的是，章衣萍在《文艺茶话》第一期的开场白里将文艺茶话定义为"一种高尚而有裨于知识或感情的消遣"。华林也声称创立茶话会的目的是提倡一种"文艺之高尚娱乐"，努力纠正现有的低劣和有辱人格的消遣方式，如赌博和吸烟。③ 可见，茶话会的成员正在努力完善中国社会的娱乐环境，而他们组织的茶话会以及创办的杂志可被视为实现其目标的尝试。正如贺麦晓所言，该团体建构了一个温文尔雅的集体形象。④ 他们将自己塑造成先进文化理想的代表生产者，定义了文化精英之间共同认可的文学和艺术品味，《文艺茶话》可以被视为他们建立一系列审美原则的手段，并且试图在引领文艺界的未来发展方面起到主导作用。

（三）印刷媒介中的"想象的共同体"与象征性文化资本

在"珈琲座"栏目中，"咖啡"投射出城市文人对咖啡馆内盛行的沙龙文化所体现的法国异国情调的赞美和想象，但在"文艺茶话会"的设想中，"茶"发挥了纽带作用，通过它，其成员能够在吸收西方基本的现代文化影响的同时，与文人雅集的悠久传统建立互动关系，显示出他们对动荡的社会转型中逐渐衰落的文人传统的怀念。虽然"咖啡"和"茶"作为两个重要的文化符号，体现了文化知识分子

---

① 徐仲年：《情与美》，《文艺茶话》1932 年第 1 期。
② 陈硕文：《上海三十年代都会文艺中的巴黎情调（1927—1937）》，博士学位论文，台湾政治大学，2008 年，第 131 页。
③ 华林：《文艺茶话》，《文艺茶话》1932 年第 1 期。
④ Michel Hockx, "Gentility in a Shanghai Literary Salon of the 1930s", in Daria Berg and Chloë Starr, eds., *The Quest of Gentility in China: Negotiation beyond Gender and Class*, London, New York: Routledge, 2007, p. 67.

对中国文化现代性的不同层面的积极贡献,但两者都体现了一种特殊的、有别于其他庸俗大众文化的高雅文化品位。在讨论现代欧洲民族意识的起源时,本尼迪克特·安德森强调了印刷资本主义的发展在培养人们对"民族"的认识方面所发挥的重要作用。他认为,资本主义与印刷技术相结合,奠定了民族意识产生的基础。[1] 书籍和报纸等印刷媒体为人们提供了一种认同感,当他们意识到自己与无数陌生人共享一种同质的印刷语言时,报纸上公布的时间和日期使他们意识到自己与数百万人生活在同一个时间段内,他们以前从未见过这些人,但能够通过想象力感知他们的存在。这构成了现代民族主义诞生的关键性根源。因此,安德森将通过民族主义团结起来的国家定义为"想象的共同体":"资本主义、印刷科技与人类语言宿命的多样性这三者的重合,使得一个新形式的想象的共同体成为可能。"[2] 类似的,在中国社会的变革时代,现代印刷媒介的出现为城市空间中分散的知识分子的形成提供了一个平台,就像茶馆和咖啡馆等公共空间作为社会性的场所一样。通过参与报纸和文学期刊中与"茶"和"咖啡"有关的话语建构,并且用诸如"友人""密友"等词强调亲密情感关系对于专栏或杂志的重要性,一大批上海的文化知识分子成功地将志同道合的人聚集在同一个"想象中的阅读和写作共同体"中。当"咖啡"和"茶"作为重要的文化符号在大众媒介的帮助下被传播时,它们也巩固了一群城市文化精英之间的集体主体性和自我认同。

此外,"珈琲座"专栏和《文艺茶话》所体现的文化实践也反映了城市知识分子在文化生产和知识建设领域重拾权威的野心。这些知识分子正在努力合法化他们重新定义"咖啡"和"茶"中所蕴含的文学和艺术内涵的资格。这与皮埃尔·布尔迪厄提出的"文化资本"的概念相一致。布尔迪厄认为,资本有三种体现形式,而文化资本是其

---

[1] [美]本尼迪克特·安德森:《想象的共同体——民族主义的起源与散布》,吴叡人译,上海人民出版社2011年版,第38—47页。

[2] [美]本尼迪克特·安德森:《想象的共同体——民族主义的起源与散布》,吴叡人译,上海人民出版社2011年版,第45页。

中之一。与经济资本这种最常见的资本存在相比，文化资本是作为象征资本而起作用的，即"人们并不承认文化资本是一种资本，而只承认它是一种合法的能力，只认为它是一种能得到社会承认（也许是误认）的权威"。① 当"珈琲座"专栏和《文艺茶话》的编辑们向有兴趣的作家征集稿件时，他们在"咖啡"或"茶"的象征性术语下召唤起了一个文人群体，该群体中的每个人都精通文艺创作，并且渴望高雅艺术品位的发展和普及。通过这种方式，他们也能够赢得支撑他们建立声誉的"文化资本"，从而实现集体形象的构建，这表明在中国社会现代化时期，当知识分子面临严重的身份危机，并寻求获得文化权威的替代来源时，树立一种高尚的审美理想便变得意义重大。

结　语

尤尔根·哈贝马斯提出，作为现代资本主义社会核心特征的公共空间于18世纪在西欧出现，在这个领域中，一种新的公共意见概念得以形成。相隔甚远的人们在公共领域中被联系起来并进行公开讨论，在那里他们得以积极与他人交流思想和分享观点。公共领域既可以是有形的——在画室、咖啡馆和沙龙举行面对面的聚会，也可以是由印刷媒体构建的——书籍、小册子和报纸在受教育阶层中的流通。② 查尔斯·泰勒进一步说明，公共领域是一种共同空间，可以分为两类——"有专门议题的公共空间"和"元议题的公共空间"或"非地方性的公共空间"。③ "有专门议题的公共空间"指的是有形的空间，如沙龙、酒馆、广场、街道和学校，它们通常包含了基于同一主题组织公众的地方集会。另一方面，"元议题的公共空间"指的是由报纸、

---

① ［法］皮埃尔·布尔迪厄：《文化资本与炼金术：布尔迪厄访谈录》，包亚明译，上海人民出版社1997年版，第196页。

② ［德］尤尔根·哈贝马斯：《公共领域的结构转型》，曹卫东、王晓珏等译，学林出版社1999年版，第1—31页。

③ ［加］查尔斯·泰勒：《现代社会想象》，林曼红译，译林出版社2014年版，第75—76页。

杂志和书籍等公共媒体形成的无形和想象的共同体，它通过一种共同的理解将分散在不同地区的陌生人组织起来，这是现代社会想象形成的重要组成因素。

民国上海的茶馆和咖啡馆是现代文化知识分子实现社交的"有专门议题的共同空间"，因为它们都主持着聚会活动，通过这些活动对文学著作和最新的艺术趋势进行民间对话。正是在这些文化聚会中，共同的审美趣味在特定的文人群体中形成，并与他们经常出入的公共空间形成互动关系。[1] 当他们借助报纸和大众刊物的版面，在公共空间中宣传自己的文学艺术活动，并吸引更多具有类似审美取向的人加入时，他们成功地创造了一个"元主题性公共空间"，可以说是印刷媒体中的"想象的聚会"，并将他们的文化影响力扩大到更大的范围。尽管他们宣称他们没有为实际和虚拟聚会的潜在参与者设定特定的标准，但这仍然意味着他们的娱乐是一种排他性的消遣，只是为了满足一小部分城市文化精英的需要，他们自称"有闲阶层"。[2] 在这个意义上，他们能够获得所谓的"文化资本"。据布尔迪厄所述，文化资本在物质和媒体中被客观化，如文学、绘画、纪念碑等，它能够因其"物以稀为贵"的价值而为其拥有者带来利润，是"在阶级划分的社会中所保障的利润份额"。[3] 因此，通过将"茶"和"咖啡"文化与"珈琲座"专栏和《文艺茶话》杂志中的文化实践塑造得精致而高雅，中国的文化精英们试图主张他们在中国文艺现代化发展方面的主导地位，从而将自身与大众区分开来。

---

[1] 陈硕文：《上海三十年代都会文艺中的巴黎情调（1927—1937）》，博士学位论文，台湾政治大学，2008年，第120页。

[2] 详见胡悦晗《生活的逻辑：城市日常世界中的民国知识人（1927—1937）》，社会科学文献出版社2018年版，第164—178页；胡悦晗《茶社、酒楼与咖啡馆：民国时期上海知识群体的休闲生活（1927—1937）》，第115—122页。

[3] ［加］皮埃尔·布尔迪厄：《文化资本与炼金术：布尔迪厄》，包亚明译，上海人民出版社1997年版，第196页。

世界文学创作

我们约会吧!
一部关于婚恋网站的独幕剧

罗伯特·肯·戴维斯-昂蒂亚诺著　朱萍译[*]

【说明】

本剧可由 4 到 8 名演员演出,时间约为 40 分钟。主要布景极简。主角摩西·佩迪多的位置在舞台前方中央,他面对观众坐在一张小电脑桌前。桌上的电脑显示器要足够低(可以用一台笔记本电脑),这样观众才能看到他的脸。舞台前方左侧放着一个黑色大框架(大约 1.8 米×1.5 米),像一个画框。框内有一个屏幕,可以用来投射图像。演员也可以坐在框架内屏幕前方。在这个框架里出现的东西就是摩西在他的电脑屏幕上看到的东西。

---

[*]【作者简介】罗伯特·肯·戴维斯-昂蒂亚诺博士(Robert Con Davis-Undiano),美国俄克拉荷马大学校长教授(Presidential Professor)和纽斯塔特教授(Neustadt Professor),2019 年,戴维斯-昂蒂亚诺博士被列入俄克拉荷马高等教育名人堂。他著作丰富,最新学术论著是《混血儿回家!塑造和声明墨西哥裔美国人身份》(*Mestizos, Come Home! Making and Claiming Mexican American Identity*)。
【译者简介】朱萍女博士,美国俄克拉荷马大学中国现当代文学副教授,著有《二十世纪中国文学与文化中的性别》(*Gender and Subjectivities in Twentieth-Century Chinese Literature and Culture*),编著过学术集《中国特色的女性主义》(*Feminisms with Chinese Characteristics*)等。

【内容梗概】

离婚四年之后,摩西决定写一部关于 Meet Up! 婚恋网站的剧本。为了积累生动的剧本素材,他在 Meet Up! 上结识了好几位网友并采访他们。

在第一幕中,摩西分别跟科拉贝拉、南茜、妓女安琪和他的心理医生玛丽亚聊天。后来他被科拉贝拉迷住了,幻想着与她发展亲密关系。可她却没有赴两人的线下之约。摩西一度怀疑自己是不是爱上了一个数码假人。最后,他发现他的生活经历与虚拟世界的黑暗现实是冲突的。这个约会网站上的经历促使他思考自我以及在社交应用程序的新领域中出现的新的可能性。

这部剧的核心问题是关于社区的问题:在一个碎片化的数字环境中,社区在多大程度上是可能的。当人与人面对面的接触减少时,亲密关系在多大程度上是可能的?最后,数字通信是如何重新划分人类互动的界限的?

【演员表】
(共需4到8名演员)

摩西·佩迪多:45岁左右的男性剧作家,他在婚恋网站 Meet Up! 上为自己的下一个剧本收集素材。

科拉贝拉·罗德里格斯:婚恋网站的一位女性使用者,45岁左右。

安琪·史密斯:一个在 Meet Up! 上招揽生意的妓女。

玛丽亚·古兹曼医生:摩西的心理治疗师和女闺密。

南茜·威尔金斯:一名 Meet Up! 婚恋网站的女性用户。

克雷格:一名 Meet Up! 婚恋网站的男性用户。

格雷格:一名 Meet Up! 婚恋网站的男性用户。

安娜·拉米雷斯：摩西在 Meet Up！碰到的第一位约会对象。

第一幕

布景：摩西坐在舞台前方中央的一个小桌前，桌上放着一个电脑。舞台前方左侧是一个长 1.8 米、宽 1.5 米的黑色大屏幕。屏幕上显示的和摩西在电脑屏幕上看到的内容一样。观众入场时大屏幕上打出的是 Meet Up！网站的广告词："Meet Up！约会吧！恋爱吧！配对吧！马上注册网站找寻你的另一半。月费优惠。别让幸福为你等待！"

时间：晚上 7 时。

摩西

要保存？见鬼了！（他开始打字。）好吧，现在行了吧？（停顿。）傻电脑，这还不够简单吗？我打字，你上传，然后别人可以看到我写的话。好吧好吧，最后一次！（他又开始打字，这时科拉贝拉在框架中出现。）

科拉贝拉

嘿，摩西，你还记得我吗？

摩西

当然记得。你是……

科拉贝拉

科拉贝拉。

摩西

科拉贝拉，对啊，我没忘。你好啊。

科拉贝拉

你还在写那个关于婚恋网站的剧本，对吧？我希望我上回跟你分享的经历对你有用。（她清了清嗓子）我今天心情不太好，想找个人陪我说说话。

摩西

一定奉陪，我正好还欠你一个人情。

科拉贝拉

你不欠我的，不过……

摩西

你没在网上和别的男人聊天吗？

科拉贝拉

我聊了。不过……有一个男人在我说话的时候嘴里总是叼着一个潜水呼吸器，他看起来有点神经兮兮的。一到他要说话的时候他就把那个潜水呼吸器从嘴里取出来。我实在没法跟他聊……

摩西

没人愿意跟这种人聊天。

科拉贝拉

还有一个老男人一边跟我聊天一边摸自己的裤裆。

摩西

他有病吧？

科拉贝拉

他说起话来声音颤巍巍的，而且他总是东看西看，好像在屏幕上找什么东西，可他却从不看我。有一天晚上他咳出了好多血，有一滴血落到了摄像头的镜片上，他的影像瞬间就蒙上了一层红晕。

摩西

他死了吗？

科拉贝拉

他说不出话来，我看到他仆倒在显示器上。一分钟以后他的影像从红色变成了漆黑一片。从此他就杳无音信。他可能真的死了。

摩西

你当时没打电话求助吗？

科拉贝拉

我不知道他是死是活啊。我隔着电脑能做什么呢？你没有遇到过奇怪的事情吗？

摩西

我也遇到过一些……上周我就碰到一件让人毛骨悚然的事情……

科拉贝拉

快讲来听听。要不然感觉又像是你在采访我一样。

摩西

（摩西说话的时候科拉贝拉离开了框架，两个中年男人走了进来。他们都脸色苍白，穿着同款的黑衣服，留着同款的黑发。他们并肩坐着，戴着相配带链子的牛角眼镜。克雷格的眼镜挂在胸前。摩西走到框架前同他们说话。）你们知道我在写一个关于婚恋网站的剧本，是吧？

克雷格

（他坐在屏幕的左边，说话时声音洪亮。）当然了，老弟。我们都会被你写进剧本里！

摩西

我可从没这么说过，不过我想了解一些你们在 Meet Up! 网站上的经历。你们在那儿交到过朋友吗？

克雷格

交朋友？当然了，老弟。我在 Meet Up! 上遇到了我的爱人格雷格，他现在就坐在我的旁边。我们在一起两年了。格雷格，快来打个招呼。（他边说话边用左手打招呼，格雷格的左手和他的左手绑在一起，也一模一样地晃动起来。）

摩西

你觉得 Meet Up! 是一个交朋友的好地方吗？

克雷格

哦，天呐，当然了！它是个讨人喜欢的网站。你在照片库中看到那个让你特别心动的人，你不由自主地爱上他，并且你在网站上就能了解他的一切。还能比这更棒吗？（他伸手过去小心翼翼地把格雷格的眼镜戴好。）

摩西

你不觉得 Meet Up！太强调外表和肤浅的细节了吗？

克雷格

哪里有？在 Meet Up！上没有任何冗余的信息。老弟，你有没有发现心灵是个诡谲的东西？如果我们期待太多的答案，我们就只会失望。在 Meet Up！我瞬间就看到了我理想人生伴侣的信息。从那时起我和他就一起生活在红尘天堂之中。

摩西

格雷格，你对在 Meet Up！遇到克雷格有什么想法？

克雷格

他好爱这个网站！爱极了！（他凑过去吻了一下格雷格的脸颊。）他这辈子从来没有这么快乐过。

摩西

我很高兴听你这么说。格雷格，你喜欢这个网站的什么方面呢？

克雷格

他喜欢的就是 Meet Up！让他找到了他的一生挚爱！我们太幸福了！

摩西

格雷格，你同意吗？

克雷格

（他伸出双臂，格雷格的双臂也跟着伸了出去。）他当然同意了，双手赞成！Meet Up！使他美梦成真，他从此每分每秒都被爱包围着。

摩西

我可以直接听格雷格说吗？

克雷格

你的要求是对的！格雷格有一个珍贵的关于他光辉一生的故事，那是一个古老的有情人终成眷属的故事。他的故事和我的故事不一样，那里有坚持、爱和宽容。（他在自己胸前画了个十字。）

摩西

谢谢你,不过我还是想听他自己说。格雷格,你能来回答吗?

克雷格

天呐!你太好笑了。没人比格雷格更会表达了,我就因为这点爱他,爱死了。

摩西

我都不知道你在干嘛……

克雷格

格雷格有自己的风格,我当然每分每秒都尊重他的风格。

摩西

我觉得他无法回答我的问题。

克雷格

好吧好吧,但是谁应该来回答问题呢?摩西·佩迪多先生,您是写剧本的,一定有偷窥人心的癖好,您不认为我们都在争取一个窥探生命秘密的机会吗?(他又侧过身亲了格雷格一口,但是两人差点从椅子上滑了下去。)

摩西

(在克雷格努力把格雷格拽回椅子上的时候。)我同意你说的,可是我还是想跟格雷格说话。

克雷格

佩迪多先生,你已经跟他聊了很久了,现在到了说再见的时候了。再见吧!我觉得格雷格已经累了,他睁着眼睛在睡觉呢,我也有点困了。(克雷格和格雷格同时挥手说再见离开了框架。科拉贝拉迅速回来。)

科拉贝拉

他们俩上 Meet Up!是为了让别人羡慕他们的美丽人生吧。

摩西

(轻笑一声。)是啊,我曾经在格雷格仍然能说话的时候跟他们聊过一次,他们都激动得很,抢着告诉我他们那星期一起买菜或者洗车的事情——这些小事都让他们快乐。

（停顿。）

不好意思，有个我的采访对象想跟我连线，我得先接这个电话。

科拉贝拉

可我正聊得兴起呢。

摩西

我也希望我们能继续聊下去，我马上就回来，再见。（科拉贝拉离开框架。他开始打字。安琪走进框架。她穿着紧身牛仔裤和低胸上衣。）

安琪

嘿，摩西！你是第一个花钱请我聊在婚恋网站工作经历的嫖客。你的剧本写得怎么样了？

摩西

还挺顺利。

安琪

你能帮我个忙吗？当你跟你的朋友说起我的时候，告诉他们我的座右铭：我有七十种方法让一个男人觉得满意。第一种是拥抱，这个免费，最后一种是69式。

摩西

（笑。）这听起来很诱人。我会帮你宣传的。

安琪

我也可以让你满意，在你家或者我家都行。第一次打七折。（她看了看手表。）还剩下一分钟免费时间，之后的时间开始收费，你还记得吧？

摩西

当然记得。最后一个问题：Meet Up! 的座右铭是"约会吧！恋爱吧！配对吧！"你觉得人们在 Meet Up! 实现了这些目标吗？婚恋网站对亲密关系的作用是正面的还是负面的？

安琪

（笑。）你问我这个问题？

摩西

是的，你来回答看看。

安琪

我不知道对别人怎样，但是 Meet Up! 对我来说是一个完美的平台。我的顾客只需要知道我的长相和工作时间，还有就是我比他们的女人更开放。

摩西

你不担心他们的其他女人吗？

安琪

那些女人已经和这些男人长相厮守了，相看两厌了。在 Meet Up! 上我可以赢她们一次吧？时间到了。如果你想善待自己，就给我打电话吧。

摩西

（笑。）好的，再见。（安琪离开。）

玛丽亚

（玛丽亚出现在框架里，她坐在一个高脚椅子上。）你现在有空吗？我需要改一下你下周预约的时间。

摩西

嘿，心理医生，你不让你的秘书做这些事吗？

玛丽亚

她休假去了，也许是永久休假。你可以下周一来吗？老时间。

摩西

没问题。我为什么没有在 Meet Up! 网站上得到更多的回复呢？我刚刚同一个妓女和一个有点抑郁的朋友聊了聊。我需要接触更多种人。

玛丽亚

我跟你说过，如果你不回答那些私人的问题而且只给别人看你二十年前的照片和兴趣爱好的话，别人就懒得理你。你真的还玩滑板吗？另外，你有一张照片只拍了你的头顶。

摩西

我曾经玩过滑板。那张头顶的照片不是很有艺术色彩吗？

玛丽亚

摩西，如果你想要更多的互动，你必须显得真诚，不然你什么也得不到。你不需要变得真诚，只需要显得真诚。人们不喜欢虚假的东西，那只会让他们觉得紧张。

摩西

好吧，下周一见。（玛丽亚离开屏幕。一秒钟以后摩西靠在椅背上，右手插在裤兜里。）她骂我的时候可真性感。（他闭上眼睛，手在裤裆里蠕动。）

南茜

（南茜出现在框架中。）嘿，你有空跟我说话吗？

摩西

（迅速从裤裆中抽出手。）我忙着呢，南茜。你可以等等吗？

南茜

我们一周没说过话了，我想告诉你上周五发生的事。

摩西

（他开始打字，她出现在舞台左前方的框架中。）好吧，我听着呢。等我拿个笔记本。

南茜

唉，威廉比网上看起来老得多，也胖得多。他网上的照片肯定是二十年前拍的。

摩西

我早就看穿他了。他必须好好想想怎么变得真诚。人们不喜欢虚假的东西。那些东西很容易就会被戳穿。

南茜

他很健谈，也很有趣。他有厉害的一面（轻笑。），他也是个不错的聆听者。

摩西

他第一次约会就想上床吗？

南茜

是啊。

摩西

你怎么办呢？

南茜

我就吊着他的兴致。我跟他说如果我们发展下去就能做更多事，他懂的。

摩西

你还对网上什么别的人有兴趣吗？

南茜

有一些，不过他们不是太年轻就是太老。那些处于年龄中间层的男人都去哪儿了？

摩西

大多数人都结着婚呢。他们在四五十岁的时候离婚，然后找个更年轻的老婆。

南茜

等他们的年轻老婆为了更年轻的男人甩掉他们的时候他们才上婚恋网站。

摩西

你有没有想过注销 Meet Up! 的账号，到现实生活中去找个伴？或者干脆单着？

南茜

我一直都这么想。我不喜欢在网站上看别人的头像，这让我觉得筋疲力尽。

摩西

就像在车展看车或者在狗狗大会看狗一样。

南茜

我恨不得马上离开 Meet Up！，不过我没时间去酒吧和俱乐部，只有在网站上我才能同时看到几百个男人。所以我现在进退两难——你可得把这个记下来。

摩西

好，我可能会把你写进剧本里，你的角色名叫"南茜"。你如果看到这个名字就知道你被我写进剧本了。

[灯光转暗]
[第一幕结束]

第二幕

布景：摩西坐在舞台前方中央的电脑前。框架仍放在舞台前方左侧。

时间：第二天晚上 7 点。

科拉贝拉

（她站到框架中。）嘿，你有空吗？我们能好好聊聊吗？你不做笔记的那种聊天。你昨天那么草率地就把我打发了。

摩西

当然。你还好吗？

科拉贝拉

你想知道上 Meet Up！，有没有让我觉得快乐。（停顿。）你快乐吗？

摩西

这个嘛……我是个社区大学的老师——这就是我职业的顶点了。我写的剧本从来不赚钱。我的血压有点高。我有白内障。我跑步的时候膝盖会发烫。我也开始谢顶了。不过我还行。为什么问这个问题？

科拉贝拉

你上次采访我之后，我遇到了一个非常糟糕的情况，我一生中最糟糕的情况，我……

摩西

告诉我吧。

科拉贝拉

我甚至想过要结束这一切。我在健身器上挂了一个绞索，在下面放了一把椅子。我知道现在这么说听起来很好笑。

摩西

老天啊，我可笑不出来。发生了什么事？

科拉贝拉

那天和你聊 Meet Up! 触动了我。我意识到我的全部生活就是一个肤浅的约会游戏！内容只有晚餐、咖啡和调情。这不是我在人生这个阶段所要的东西。我这么说可能听起来有点傲娇，但我觉得我值得拥有更好的生活。

摩西

到底是什么让你崩溃了呢？

科拉贝拉

不知道为什么，去年我满 45 岁以后，我就不再把幸福当作美好生活的餐后甜点了。

（停顿。）

我不知道我应该怎么生活。

摩西

我懂。在这阶段人生似乎应该有一套新的规则，可是我们却还没有搞清楚是什么规则。你为什么居然想到在你的健身器上挂起了绞索？（他压抑着笑声。）

科拉贝拉

好吧，这个场面很好笑对吧！我的理想和我的生活总是大相径庭，这种落差让我崩溃。

摩西

你现在还想自杀吗？

科拉贝拉

奇怪的是自杀的感觉已经没有那么强烈了。在我跌入谷底的时候，我也释放了一些东西，就像河流一样，全都一去不复返了。

摩西

我记得有位哲学家说过，你需要在桌子上放一把枪，才能进行一次诚恳的对话。

科拉贝拉

是的，也许自杀的想法对我来说就是在桌子上放一把枪。

摩西

现在你的想法改变了吗？

科拉贝拉

嗯。我不想再看网站上的预制约会资料了。我想更加用心地生活，我想把生活逼到一个角落里，看看它到底给我些什么。

摩西

你可能会遇到一个人，他可能再次激发起你生命的火花。

科拉贝拉

一个灵魂伴侣吗？是的，也许世界上有那么几个人会跟你完全合拍。但这是一个小概率事件。

摩西

在 Meet Up！上我没有看到这种事情，我不知道其他地方有没有。

科拉贝拉

这种事情不可能在 Meet Up！上发生。灵魂伴侣之间需要假以时日才能彼此了解，变得心意相通。

摩西

你确定你说的不是愚蠢的小说和电影吗？

科拉贝拉

我曾经有过灵魂伴侣，否则我也会对此持怀疑态度的。

摩西

你觉得你和前夫是灵魂伴侣吗？

科拉贝拉

嗯,(停顿一下。)一开始我是这么觉得的,但很快我们就互相掐架了。两人关系越来越坏,我们都越来越愤怒。性生活是第一个消失的,然后我们就不再努力了。

摩西

如果一开始这么好,你们为什么要停止努力?

科拉贝拉

这个问题我已经问过自己很多次了。(停顿。)我们都很固执,也弄不清楚我们哪里出了问题,或者说是否真的出了什么问题。

摩西

怎么会弄不清呢?

科拉贝拉

我不确定是不是每个人在结婚一段时间后都过着这么糟糕而孤独的生活。也许这就是我应该过的生活?谁知道呢?世界上没有一本人生的指南手册。

摩西

你们还有了孩子。

科拉贝拉

三个。我爱他们,就像我从未爱过任何东西一样。但他们却成为问题的一部分。

摩西

为什么呢?

科拉贝拉

孩子们让人很容易把所有醒着的时间都集中在他们身上。你必须时刻看着以免他们被车撞到或被人抱走。

摩西

然后呢?

科拉贝拉

然后你就忘记了你生命中别的部分正在枯萎和死亡。

摩西

所以你从没有一个真正的灵魂伴侣？

科拉贝拉

我有过，但那人不是托马斯。（她停顿了一下，清了清嗓子。）在我和托马斯分手的前一年，我和另一个男人有了关系。

摩西

外遇？你有过外遇？

科拉贝拉

有过一次奇遇。

摩西

这就是你离婚的原因吗？

科拉贝拉

并非如此。我在一家建筑公司工作了十年，他是那里的一名建筑师，比我年轻四岁，皮肤黝黑，光头，留着胡子。他说话很温和。他有一种怪癖，每隔十秒钟眼睛就会猛眨一阵子。

摩西

你是不是有一天醒来发现自己已经爱上了他？

科拉贝拉

算是吧。我们总是和团队一起吃午饭，去年起我们开始两个人吃午餐，然后我们开始编造理由来共进更多的午餐。

摩西

然后你们就上床了？

科拉贝拉

他想这样做，但我是天主教徒，我坚持认为如果我们不发生性关系就没有犯错。

摩西

是什么改变了你的想法？

科拉贝拉

有一天晚上，约会以后他开车送我回家，我们不知不觉就开到了他的公寓。

摩西

就这样突然发生了性关系？

科拉贝拉

是的，在他的咖啡桌上。但这对我来说有点突兀。毕竟我已经很久没有被人碰过了，突然越过这条线的感觉并不好。而且我还是一个天主教徒。

摩西

那你做了什么？

科拉贝拉

第二天，我事后吃了一颗避孕药以防万一，（她以天主教的方式行了个礼。）辞掉了工作，并在城里的另一个地方找到了一份工作。

摩西

天哪，我能说"反应过度"吗？你的反应有点……呃……呃……天主教徒！甩掉那个人让你感觉好点了吗？

科拉贝拉

一开始我觉得我做得对，但几个月后我意识到我失去了一个灵魂伴侣，我越来越觉得自己很懦弱。

摩西

为什么？你只是在搞外遇而已啊？

科拉贝拉

我和罗伯托的关系很特别，我俩在每个可能的层面上都心心相印，但我没有勇气去正视这种关系。

摩西

但是外遇的新奇感不是让一切看起来都很美好吗？

科拉贝拉

我知道，我并没有那么天真。但我们之间有更多的东西，一些罕见的东西，我应该给我和他一个机会。我还能说什么呢？我当时没有那么做。

摩西

如果你在 Meet Up! 上遇到那样的人，你还会做出不同的决定吗？

科拉贝拉

像这样的事情在 Meet Up! 上是不会发生的！那里虽然人来人往，但也没有什么事情真的发生。

（停顿。）

如果你不介意的话，我想问你一件让你痛苦的事情。

摩西

哦，这么说你知道那件事。当时报纸上也登了，所以我猜这地区大多数人都知道这件事。

（停顿。）

我仍然感觉很糟糕。这本来可以避免的。

科拉贝拉

你能告诉我发生了什么吗？

摩西

（停顿。）那是一起鲁莽的事故，本可以避免的。

（当他走到舞台前方右侧时，其他的灯都熄灭了，而舞台前方右侧的灯亮了起来，照着一张沙发，安娜坐在上面。她是个很有魅力的中年妇女。）

晚餐，现在我们在我家。这个夜晚再完美不过了。

安娜

你可以给我点赞，因为我看穿了你糟糕的资料。Meet Up! 说你仍然是一个滑板运动员，鬼才信。

摩西

好吧！好吧！也许我有点马虎了。

安娜

是有一点点，但很可爱。

摩西

我给你带了些礼物作为补偿。

（他把手伸进一个袋子里拿出一些软糖，递给安娜。）吃了这个，你就会记得我的 Meet Up！资料特别棒。

安娜

（她笑着吃软糖。）你让我感觉像个孩子。我十几岁起就没有吃过软糖了。

摩西

（他拿出一根大麻点燃。）这东西应该会加速你的逆生长。（他自己抽了几口大麻，然后递给安娜。）

安娜

哦，天哪！（她倒在沙发上。）这东西太上头。

（她气喘吁吁地倒下，似乎有点失控。）

你可能得让我留下过夜了。

摩西

好吧，既然你这么说了，我也正好希望如此！

（他说话的时候，安娜似乎在沙发上睡着了。）

也许我们发展得有点快，但我们早就是成年人了，Meet Up！让我们看到彼此很相配。只要你觉得可以就留下吧。

（停顿。）

你会留下来吧？

安娜

（她似乎睡着了。）嗯。我不确定我可不可以……

摩西

（他又吸了几口大麻。）这一切都太完美了。也许离婚不是那么糟糕的事情。你感觉还好吗？

（停顿。他走到沙发前，轻轻地摇晃着安娜。）

我们很合拍，对吗？（他再次摇晃她，然后把他的耳朵贴在她胸前。）这到底是怎么回事！？没有心跳！

（他惊恐地站起来。）

安娜，安娜！醒醒吧！我觉得大事不妙了！醒醒，否则我要打911

了！安娜，醒醒！安娜！安娜！

（他愣在原地，一个明亮的红灯开始在整个舞台上快速闪烁，并能听到远处的警笛声。十秒钟后，舞台变暗，当灯光再次出现时，科拉贝拉回到背景框中，而摩西坐在他的电脑桌前。）

科拉贝拉
哦，天哪。你和她第一次约会她就死了，难以置信。

摩西
救护车很快就到了，警察也都来了。没过多久，房间里挤满了穿黑衣服的人，其中一个人宣布她死了。

科拉贝拉
所以她的心脏有问题？

摩西
后来我从她的孩子那里得知她有心脏病和低血压，她的血压很容易就会降到零。

科拉贝拉
大麻可以要她的命？

摩西
当她的神经快速兴奋时，她的血压消失了，一切生命体征都瞬间停止了。她在几分钟内就去世了。

科拉贝拉
你事先并不知道……

摩西
我们刚认识不久，我对她没什么了解。后来她的兄弟们来了，在院子里对我咆哮。她的孩子们在葬礼上看到我时哭了。

科拉贝拉
我不知道你怎么才能避免这场悲剧的发生。

摩西
我本可以不那么做的，如果我真的了解她，我也一定不会那么做。

科拉贝拉

但你刚认识她……

摩西

这就是让我后悔的地方。约会网站诱使我们认为我们和陌生人之间已经很亲密。而当我们表现得好像我们真的了解一个我们刚认识的人时,我们其实是在玩火。

这是很荒谬的。

科拉贝拉

我明白你的意思。

摩西

如果我真的了解她,我会保护她,那么她现在还活着。

科拉贝拉

你为什么要告诉我这些?

摩西

你问我的,我相信你。

科拉贝拉

我也相信你。你愿意走出 Meet Up! 的世界,而且你会倾听,这很重要。

摩西

我只是在写一个剧本,试图理解发生在安娜身上的事情……

科拉贝拉

不,你是想看看我们周围的世界正在发生什么。

摩西

我认为我自己在感情关系中不善言辞,但也许这部剧能说出些什么东西来。我会好好写的。

科拉贝拉

你一定会写出一个好剧本的。

摩西

我想见见你。我们明天可以一起喝咖啡吗?

科拉贝拉

呃，呃，我可以考虑一下吗？

摩西

是的。（他用手指默默地数到三。）时间到了。

科拉贝拉

（她笑了。）我试试，明天下午两点在蓝山咖啡馆？如果你看见一个穿着黑色毛衣一脸惊恐的女人，那就是我。我会表现得很情绪化。

摩西

那个脸上带着充满希望的微笑的人就是我。

［灯光转暗］

［第二幕结束］

第三幕

布景：摩西坐在他的位于舞台前方中央的电脑桌前，看起来垂头丧气。框架在舞台前方左侧的同一位置。

时间：一周以后，下午5点。

摩西

（在电脑上和玛丽亚聊天。）我在那里多坐了一个小时，她不可能看不见我。后来我确信她不会来了，可是在我走回家之前，我还折回去查看了四次。我太沮丧了，连公交车都没坐。

玛丽亚

这是我经常从在网上找伴侣的病人那里听到的一个故事。你认识她很久了吗？

摩西

我认识了她大约一个月的时间。她给我提供剧本的材料。然后有一天晚上我们突然感到彼此的距离很近。

玛丽亚

然后呢？

摩西

然后她就这样消失了，好像她从来没有出现过一样。

玛丽亚

没有任何解释或事先的警告吗？

摩西

仿佛有人关上了开关，我怎么都无法再联系上她了。

玛丽亚

我很抱歉，摩西，但你需要让她离开，她从来没有存在过。

摩西

你在说什么啊？

玛丽亚

她是一个假人，这是网上约会的一个常见的陷阱。

摩西

我们谈到了守护爱情的意义。我们谈到了抚养孩子，我们谈了我们分别做过什么错事。这些东西是编不出来的！

玛丽亚

当然可以编出来！人们总是在网上互相撒谎。她显然对你撒了好多的谎。

摩西

你在说什么啊？她怎么会不存在呢？

玛丽亚

她可能是一个逼真的电脑程序。她可能是一个正在与一个编剧合作的女演员。她可能正计划着去搞到你的信用卡。当她什么都没得到时，她就断了和你的联系。

（停顿。）我很抱歉。

摩西

哦，我的天啊！

玛丽亚

你需要向前看。

摩西

科拉贝拉很坦率、很真实。她信任我,我们在很多很多方面都有共鸣。我已经不再是为写剧本才找她了,我想和她共度更多的时间。

玛丽亚

真实?摩西,听听你自己说的话吧!你已经爱上了一个数字幻影,而现在你还想延长痛苦的时间?这有点令人毛骨悚然。别再继续自慰了。

摩西

我的直觉告诉我,你说得不对。

玛丽亚

听着,我希望我的宠物能活得更久,我希望房价不要那么高,我希望多吃巧克力不会让我变胖,我也希望恋人之间不要互相欺骗。但这些都在发生。有那么一丝丝的可能我也许错了,你的那个朋友也许跟你幻想的一样。不过你要抓着那么一丝丝可能性吗?

摩西

我只是需要知道真相。

[灯光转暗]

[第三幕结束]

第四幕

布景:摩西坐在蓝山咖啡馆的一张桌子旁,他和科拉贝拉第一次就约在这里。他打开了他的笔记本电脑开始打字。大框架仍放在舞台前方左侧。

时间:一周之后,晚上 7 点。

摩西

（他面对观众坐在舞台前方中央，望向咖啡店的窗外。这里有低浅的咖啡店的噪音——人们的交谈声，杯子的碰撞声。他边打字边说话。）我不知道你是否愿意和我在这家咖啡馆见面。但我希望你收到了我的信息后会来这里。

（停顿。）

做一个主动的人并不容易。我现在坐在这里，就像在繁忙的道路上开着车而我的导航仪刚刚死机了。（在他说话的时候，玛丽亚出现在框架中。）

（停顿。）

你好！

玛丽亚

你好！你还在等着和数字幻影约会吗？

摩西

我现在在一家咖啡馆，她还没有出现。（当他说话时，科拉贝拉在他身后神不知鬼不觉地走了进来，坐到了舞台左后方的一张桌前。）

玛丽亚

你已经不是在收集剧本素材了。你几乎不认识她，但你却在为她冒险。

摩西

我对她有点了解，而且我想要了解更多。我的名字是摩西，对吧？

玛丽亚

是啊。

摩西

你还记得《圣经》中的摩西死前发生了什么吗？

玛丽亚

你在说《申命记》吗？

摩西

是的，在摩西死前，上帝带他到皮斯加山顶去看应许之地。上帝

— 285 —

只让他看了一眼他一直在寻找的东西。这是一个很好的预告，是对未来的广告。

玛丽亚
好吧，你想说什么？

摩西
我的意思是科拉贝拉就是我的皮斯加愿景。我在真实的时间里瞥见了我想要的东西，那是真正的互动和关怀。这些真实的东西是可以丢失的。

玛丽亚
那么你是否认为 Meet Up! 网站让你变得麻木和愚蠢？

摩西
当然了。我知道我已经学会了快速翻阅人们的资料。我知道我开始对那些长着疣子或痘痘的脸蛋不耐烦，对那些太胖或太瘦的人不耐烦，对长得不漂亮或者不爱笑的人也不耐烦。（他说这话的时候，科拉贝拉站起来，开始朝咖啡馆门口走去。）

玛丽亚
如果你已经想通了，你为什么还在咖啡馆等她？

摩西
我也不确定，但我想我需要冒一次险。（这时科拉贝拉停了下来，但她没有转过身。）

玛丽亚
冒险来面对现实生活中的负面后果？

摩西
是的。我已经厌倦没有什么可以失去的感觉，因为这意味着我什么也得不到。

（这时科拉贝拉转过身来，再次坐回桌子前。）

玛丽亚
如果科拉贝拉现在就在咖啡馆里，你会对她说什么？

摩西

我有太多话对她说了。我会告诉她,她不需要完美。我们不需要完美。我肯定是搞砸了。我害怕自己的阴暗面,而且我经常骗自己。但是,有缺陷和搞砸了也没关系,反正我们要为自己想要的东西而努力。

玛丽亚

我希望你能亲口对她说这些话。

摩西

我也希望。如今亲身的经验变得越来越稀少了,在 Meet Up! 上更少!

玛丽亚

那里的一切都那么诱人和虚假。

摩西

此时此刻我想和她在一起。我们也许会失去一切,但也会得到一些有价值的东西。(这时科拉贝拉站起来,慢慢地走向摩西。)

玛丽亚

好吧,我的朋友。你已经主动把脖子伸出去等候命运的处置了。别忘了告诉我你的脖子碰到了什么。(她离开了框架。)

摩西

(他站着,没有转身。科拉贝拉转身朝门走去。停顿片刻以后,她又转身向他走去。当她离他大约一米多时,他慢慢转向她。)科拉贝拉?

科拉贝拉

摩西?

[灯光转暗]

[第四幕结束]

[全剧终]

飞蚊症

詹妮·斯卡拉格斯著　徐燕译[*]

> 安娜，一名自怨自艾的希腊裔美国人，巫婆，德国特工。工作任务？去往危机重重的希腊阻止人们自杀。

自从姐姐预知了父母的死，有一点就很清楚了——她不是一个普通的十岁小孩。安娜用蜡笔画了一幅画，画中的母亲满脸是血，浑身伤口。左边画着一双鞋和一辆正往外喷火的燃烧的汽车。她说将有不好的事情发生。

一周后是我五岁的生日。那天，警察局凶杀科和洛杉矶法医处的官员们把天使之冠公路的一段封锁起来调查我母亲尸体的案子。很难判定她是被推出车外的还是自己跳下车的。父亲的脸已经"烧得无法辨认"。他的车子在46.5英里标志牌附近五百英尺下的山谷里被发现了。车子行驶失控，冲出路缘，掉进浓密的灌木丛里爆炸了。

我沉浸在失去双亲的悲痛中不能自拔，祖父带我们迁居到欧洲，希望我能够忘掉悲伤。祖父有希腊和德国血统，最不希望我们去美国。我们的童年是在斯图亚特附近的乌尔巴赫度过的。那里的夏天，有时

---

[*]【作者简介】詹妮·斯卡拉格斯（Gianni Skaragas），希腊籍小说家，编剧，其英文作品经常出现在美国各类文学期刊上。他是富布莱特访问学者，目前是希腊国家剧院剧作家，即将完成一部短篇小说集。

候太阳光照进葡萄园的角度，让我看到许多动人心魄的绿色光斑，这些美丽的光斑能让我忘却周遭的一切。

我比任何时候都更怀念父母。于是总设法逃避现实去沉浸在我自己的世界。

迁居德国丝毫没能减少我的丧亲之痛，而姐姐却在双亲坟上的蔷薇花还没凋谢时就把他们忘记了，我不知道那个时候这两件事情哪一个更让我意外。

安娜完全变了一个人。她为能预知未来而非常自豪，她以为能够预知故事的结局就能够有一个不凡庸的人生。每当事实证明她预言准确，她就会眯起双眼，暗淡的眼神透着冷漠。她用目空一切的腔调说话，觉得自己像个天使，因为还能忍耐凡俗的我们。

安娜不相信人性，只关注事态的推进。情感对一个耽于预测人生未来变故的人来说是无足轻重的。

安娜通过画画预知未来。多年以来她画了许多画，其中最令人难忘的画作有：燃烧的灌木丛、特雷莫尔之战、9·11恐怖袭击、本拉登之死、希望：是的，我们可以，不，我们不能、本拉登的二次死亡、阿拉伯的冬天等，这一系列的作品在当时就如同她的性格一样显得非常含义不明。

跟一个自得其乐的不合群者一起长大，这种感觉是很奇特的。姐姐有一颗良善的心，更有一颗坚定的头脑。她拒绝跟外界交流，这恐怕只有圣人或是在梦中才能够办到。

安娜不想结交任何朋友。七年级的时候，她的同学们虽然才十二岁，却都知道不要去招惹她。安娜只要看一眼他们的鞋子就会让他们心惊胆战。

"有个人会被车撞，那人当然不是我。"她说，像新闻播报员那样肯定，脸上泛出愉快的红光。

她那令人吃惊的预言使得人人都怀疑她是个巫婆。没人知道她所知道的。三个身着黑色西装的男子来到我们家，祖父刚把他们迎进门，他们还没开口说话，安娜就说"是的"。

世界文学创作

其中一位名叫汉斯，高鼻梁，厚眼睑，指关节上长着绒毛。他思忖着问道，"你说'是的'是什么意思？"

"是的，我愿意为德国安全部门工作。"安娜忍住笑，抿着嘴回答道，"噢，顺便说一下，有人要当爸爸了，汉斯，这人当然不是我。"

"安吉拉·默克尔要派你去希腊？"

我本想表示关心的，话说出口却像是要吵架。让安娜去左班①的国度，这真是个问题。因为她讨厌希腊的一切。在她看来，希腊就是混乱的代名词。她认为希腊人就是魔鬼派来破坏上帝的造物的。希腊人想要一个社会主义国家，却又不愿意为之买单。欧盟本该让这帮懒惰又自负的废物破产。

"你就把这当作是总理送给你的毕业礼物吧。"

"默克尔派一架虎式武装直升机送我们去希腊，就为了庆祝我毕业？你信吗？"

竟然指望我姐姐用不一样的沟通方式来获取重要信息，我不清楚这到底是德国特工部门谁的主意，但是在过去的四年里，安娜已经成了默克尔的心腹。总理称呼她时用的是她的教名多萝西娅，好像她是家人或是爱宠。安娜爱默克尔，是因为她总能为别人着想，而且热衷钻研国政。她相信，默克尔能成为卓越的领导人是因为有一颗忧国忧民的心。她觉得默克尔在政坛不俗的表现就像一个政治成绩斐然的修理工，而不像一个政客，前者因为修理工作而浑身是劲儿，后者因为能够决策而沾沾自喜。

尽管没有挑明，我却能感觉到安娜把默克尔当姐姐一样爱戴。而默克尔关心多萝西娅就像关心自己一样。对安娜来说，总理证明了安静矜持的女性能够实事求是，也能未雨绸缪，而且总能抓住问题的根本，她们这种对现实的感知来自对人性弱点的敏锐洞察。

---

① 左班，出自希腊作家尼克斯·卡赞扎基（1883—1957）的小说《希腊人左班》。左班是克里特岛上的一个放荡不羁精力充沛的年迈矿工，"我"是一个怀抱高远理想却理性压抑的年少书呆子。两人偶然邂逅、结伴同行。左班引领着"我"重新思索生命，体验跟他过去截然不同的生活。卡赞扎基的作品还包括《基督的最后诱惑》《奥德修纪现代续篇》《自由与死亡》等。

"希腊连妓女都联合起来了,这很让你反感吧?"

"说什么呢!我很自豪自己是希腊人。"

"你是美籍德国希腊人。"

"斯塔姆,我的血管里流的可是希腊人的血。闭上你的嘴,享受生活吧。"

"你到底还有什么瞒着我?"

"有人会喜欢上这里的,这人当然不是我。"

飞行途中,汉斯忍不住告诉我这次的任务非常关键。他已经是三个孩子的父亲了。

"我们经济强大,这对我们朋友的生存来说却很不妙。"他好像马上就后悔这样说。汉斯最讨厌说话用形容词。"我们把银行的存款拿来贷给希腊这样的国家,促使他们来消费我们的产品,然后我们的公司又把这些钱存到我们的银行。希腊已经陷入二战以来最严重的财政危机。四分之三的希腊人希望留在欧盟,却又明白身不由己。这么说吧,我们应该帮帮希腊。"

"你在担心什么?"

"过去三年里希腊自杀的人数呈直线上升。而每一个自杀者背后都有二十来个想自杀的人。"

"可怜的人哪,"安娜说,"为什么日子难过就自杀呢?"

"这我没法回答,但是情况很不妙。"

"这跟安娜有什么关系?"

"她能知道谁有自杀的想法。她能帮助我们找出并阻止这些人自杀。"

希腊情报局长马可是个坚强正直的人,看上去大概四十来岁。就这个年龄来说,他算帅的,腹部微凸,方下巴,金褐色的眼睛透着好奇,抽动的嘴角使他看上去显得滑稽。他手里拿着一只马克杯去倒水,杯子上印着一行字,"欧盟希望所有成员国都能履行义务"。

"那么这个夏天你们要在这里过啰?"他说。

安娜拼命地点头。她久久地盯着他看,不知不觉地露出了笑容。

当他的视线落在她身上的那一刻，好像她也在看着自己，并且意识到之前认识的男人都不算什么。

"你要我们待多久都行。"

我转过头用德语对她说，"有人想撩汉，这人当然不是我"。

她转向马克说，"我需要一个自杀者名单，还有他们的鞋子"。

"你要他们的鞋子？为什么？"

"这个你别管。"

她觉得她无须多说。他觉得她应该听他差遣。两人都很强势。

那天晚上她来问我该穿什么衣服去同马克共进晚餐。他带她去雅典最好的饭店就餐。饭后他用信用卡买单的时候，安娜说典型的希腊人都是靠信用卡和借贷过日子的。马可表示自己从不拖欠还贷，她应该抛开成见。

夏天将尽，他们决定结婚。那年晚些时候，安娜向我透露说，她在第一眼看到对方鞋子的时候就知道自己会嫁给这个梦中情人。

接下来的几个月里，安娜常常感觉视线模糊，然后又开始偏头痛。有时候雅典城上空云层低垂，让人看不清前路，也看不清来路。过去和未来之间空空如也，只有一种因为过于压抑的胃部不适感。这种感觉让夜空都感觉窒息。空气中满是防腐木制品和刨花板燃烧散出的烟尘，那是从成千上万只壁炉里排放出来的。这种新型御寒燃料征税甚高。

又一户家庭失业；领取免费食物的队伍越来越长；政府最新的债务可持续性评估报告。满眼都是不祥的兆头，却看不见一个人。在姐姐的视线里，人们看起来就像朦胧而漫无目的漂浮的潦草字迹，等她定睛去看时，却都害羞地闪开了。

"你应该去看看医生。"

"别担心，亲爱的。"她一边读着《法兰克福汇报》一边回答说，"这叫飞蚊症，并不真实的。"停下来啜了一口咖啡，又说道，"只不过是眼球玻璃体的一些细胞而已"。

我望向窗外，看到无家可归的人们挤在街对面的避难所里，那似乎是安娜刻意视而不见的地方。"安娜，那些人都是真实存在的。"我说。

她急忙否定说，"那只是飞蚊症投放到我视网膜上的影子"。她叹了口气，为我不体谅她而着恼。

巫婆安娜不只是乐善好施，她还相信自己能解决希腊的所有问题。在过去的一年里，她挽救了大概九十九人免于自杀。她认为自己是成功的，因为没有介入那些人的生活。她不允许他人的悲剧将自己裹挟其中。

安娜从来不看人的眼睛，只要瞥一眼他们的鞋子，其命运似乎就会从鞋跟或是鞋带孔里向她显现出来。

"除了将来你就不考虑别的吗？"

"我不知道。除了过去你就不考虑别的吗？"

我鄙视她，她的话就跟她的情感一样空洞。

"那我们在这里做什么？"我说着走出咖啡屋。

"我也不知道。"

姐姐的工作好像从没出过差错，但是上个月她却只能瞧瞧形形色色的脸和鞋子，看看是否能感知到什么。她不知道要找什么，只知道自己越来越没把握。

"你应该高兴，自杀率差不多降到零了。这都是你的功劳。"

"我不能生孩子，"她几乎哽咽道，"我去看过医生，医生说基本上没希望。"

我还没来得及说点什么，她的目光越过我的肩膀就突然怔住了。一家关闭的商店橱窗上挂着一幅中年男子的肖像画，旁边贴着许多便利贴和纸条，上面写着鼓励人们伸出援手的话。

"就是他，"她眯眼盯着那幅画，沮丧地说，"我应该救他的。"

"这不可能。"

"你不懂。我能感觉到。"

我读了几条用希腊文写的留言，告诉她说，"安娜，他不是自杀的，他是死于一氧化碳中毒"。

那天，有什么东西离开了安娜的大脑。接下来的一个月她把自己锁在房间里，整天躺在床上，心情犹如空气中的烟雾。多年以来她头一次开始梦见父母亲。

安娜试图让我相信没事了，但是我很清楚，这幅男子肖像画对她产生了深远的影响。从他的眼睛里，安娜前所未有地看清楚了自己的灵魂。从那一刻开始她对一切都不那么确定了，并且惊异地发现自己并不能明白这一切，那是一种深深的无助感。

她不明白为什么很多她本来可以做到的事情却没有去做，为什么真真切切的事实她却视而不见了。有什么东西在她身上慢慢消失了，从前闪耀着激情的双眼现在露出绝望的神色，飞蚊症不只遮蔽了她的双眼，甚至已经遮蔽了她的灵魂。生命只剩下模糊的感觉，就像遥远的天空上飞机飞过的声音。

我意识到我很爱姐姐安娜。每当她的鞋带散开，我就会帮她系上鞋带打上结，这已经成了我俩的习惯。有时我会半夜里醒来查看她的鞋带是否系好。

我爱姐姐，我简直要感激她没有告诉我母亲曾经试图阻止父亲把车开出路缘。小时候我却那么恨她。我爱姐姐，因为她生了一个左班一样的儿子——她说这是上帝送给她的礼物，使她重获光明。

又一个左班过着自己的日子，迎接生活赐予的一切。

安娜开始失去她的特异功能。生活最擅长用最无情的隐喻教训人。生活喜欢盲目的画家、瞎眼的先知、跛脚的外科医生；喜欢音乐家遭受听力损伤的折磨，喜欢负债累累的左班住在断电的房子里被火盆里的烟气呛得透不过气来。

终于，安娜的天赋异禀彻底消失了。一天醒来，她做了一件从未想到的事情：她开始读小说了。姐姐再也猜不到故事的结局。

诗二首

沙西拉·沙里芙著　程文译　*

离别

非洲的一个地方
我妈妈在照料
她已故母亲的蓝花楹。

经过一条冰冻的河
我父亲喝着冷茶
黎明静悄悄，寒冬凛冽。

有一天你会知道
什么是真正的离别
而又痛苦地连在一起。

今天我们放飞了王师傅做的黑金鱼风筝；
风筝获了奖，但他还是在胡同房子里
积满灰尘的角落用锈刀劈竹子。

＊【作者简介】沙西拉·沙里芙（Shahilla Shariff），女，出生于肯尼亚，现为加拿大籍，从1993年起住在香港。诗作《离别》（*Apart*）入围2013年布里德波特奖（Bridport Prize）。

湖面上阳光斑斑点点。
雕梁画栋的凉亭边，
二胡的心痛纠缠着清风。

我们穿过一座木桥，
荷花的水墓
被云隙洒下的阳光点亮。

手提包

在我房子的一个角落
我对你的记忆胜过
茶花盛开的黎明
在你的白墙红瓦的平房外面，
杂花生树，群鸟啁啾。

我本来要披上开司米披肩，
它的刺绣环绕
一片雨季的绿，
乡村，食物，聊天，祖先，
我们的肤色，
但是他们用它覆盖你的棺木。

所以我拿来了肯加布——
琥珀、檀香油、麝香——
它有你历史的芬芳
而我看到一个幻象
洪波涌起的大海和失落的海岸，
而不是脱线的雨季布匹
带有涡旋花纹

在红木衣橱的背面
扎起你的旧沙丽。

我拿来了手提袋,
猎豹的强光和非洲的太阳
像我的悲哀和你的年华一样嵌入。

诗四首[*]

玛荷莉·亚葛辛著　程文译

4

我只想写他们，
讲述他们的蛮勇，
他们穿越地中海航道的航行。

带着鎏金的祈祷书

我只想说说他们
仿佛每样东西都被爱的手势触碰过

说一说西班牙裔犹太人
他们簪着罂粟花漂泊
妙语如花的旅人

---

[*]【作者简介】玛荷莉·亚葛辛（Marjorie Agosín），女，著名诗人，鲁埃拉·雷默·斯雷纳讲席教授，在威勒斯里学院讲授拉丁美洲研究。著有近五十部著作，包括诗歌、回忆录和散文，近期所获奖项包括哈佛医学院授予的弗里茨·雷德里奇奖。她的第一部小说《我住在蝴蝶山》三月份由西蒙与舒斯特出版。

选自《白色岛屿》（*Las islas blancas*）手稿，原文为西班牙语，中文译者译自杰奎琳·南菲托（Jacqueline Nanfito）翻译的英语版本。杰奎琳·南菲托是凯斯西保留地大学现代语言文学系西班牙语副教授，讲授课程包括拉丁美洲文学与文化、少数族裔研究、妇女与性别研究。

从一座岛屿到另一座，
从世界一角到另一角落。

在声声耳语中
只有一支歌，
记忆的声音。
不可抗拒的信仰柔弱的声音。

134

我离开了白色岛屿和我在那里所爱的
像一个人离开一幢空屋
门上有裂纹
窗像破碎的心

我离开白色岛屿就像一个人向大海之光
道别

我没有收集石子或海贝
我只是离开一缕芬芳
我的皮肤涂抹着声音

我没有回头看
我不怕被变成石头

我只是远离大海航行
玫瑰岛的芬芳
在我的披肩里

白色岛屿的犹太人远航，远航。

162

村庄已在沙丘间消失
曾经在山林间筑巢的鸟群
已选择其他航线

大城市被抛弃，空旷而裸露

再也没有遗留的国家和边界

地理消融
回家甚至比每一次离别
更不确定

她找到了自己的房子
有蓝色门的那一幢
驱散鬼魂

那幢房子留住了树荫

围绕房屋的杏树依旧迎接春天到来
不
她回到了自己的国度
回到那幢房子阳台摇曳如纤腰的曲线
回到太阳东升西落的确定性
回到大海变化无穷的节奏

而她决定等待生活，在它的重重门槛之间

赞美耐心等待太阳的第一批种子
把太阳亲吻的衣服晒出去收回来
读泛黄报纸上的过时新闻

用玫瑰水冲洗人行道
等待逝者回归
把活着的让进门
用茉莉花和苹果泡茶
让自己沉浸在白鹭的歌里

或是沿着古老的小径徘徊

她回家了
仿佛回到一个宇宙
她点亮了所有的灯
就像等待旧爱的人。

170

只有大海，
围住白昼的光。
夕阳如同神圣的花瓣
只有大海和它剥去了任何刺耳之物的服饰
只有精确海浪的节奏
像我们体内携带的世界之脉搏

只有大海永恒黎明的
一切节奏的携带者
而夜如此广大就像对挚爱者之记忆的
躯体

只有大海
和我一起旅行穿越借来的国度
穿越编造的踪迹
大海像一支梦游的乐队

像保险箱存放神秘与一切挚爱的

沉默服装只有大海
它庄严的气度在我体内
在你体内
像一个故事编造出来然后又拆穿
像唤醒陆地的露珠
只有大海
它夏季的香味
造访我们

就像轻柔的爱抚斜倚着鸟群旁边的
光线，符号的星座
只有大海声之线束
丰沛的历史
水之梦。

书 评

"等级制度"与"宇宙种族"
——评戴维斯-昂蒂亚诺《归乡吧,梅斯蒂索人!》

张艺莹*

在世界多民族共存的今日,少数族裔问题得到了越来越多学者、研究者的重视,而对民族历史与现实的梳理便是这一问题绕不过的一环。乌拉圭作家加莱阿诺(Eduardo Galeano)曾指出,民族历史若被遗忘"会导致文化的断层,和对国家过去与现实的难以理解"。[①] 而加莱阿诺所言"断层"的直接指向,则是美洲梅斯蒂索民族群体的文化现状。自16世纪征服时期,美洲历史便具有了双重层面,即"征服者"的历史与"被征服者"的历史。而这"被征服者",先是美洲原住民印第安人,后逐渐演变为混血族群"梅斯蒂索人"。以美国的混血族裔情况而论,在原始扩张的时期,开拓美国的殖民者将印第安人及其混血后裔"从土地上赶走、使他们沦为奴隶、劫掠以及迫害等等"。[②] 这种状况一直持续到19世纪,而它为混血族群造成的影响在现今的美国社会仍有余韵。长久以来,混血族裔群体被迫"融入"他者文化以换取生存资源,而这间接导致了其本民族历史文化的断裂与

---

* 【作者简介】张艺莹,女,北京师范大学文学博士,四川大学外国语学院助理研究员,研究方向为西班牙语言文学、欧洲早期汉学。

① Eduardo Galeano, *El libro de los abrazos*, Siglo XXI Editores, 2001, p. 90.

② [苏] 阿·符·叶菲莫夫:《美国史纲》,庚生译,生活·读书·新知三联书店1972年版,第75页。

书评

社会空间的缺失。这一状况一直为各族裔所抗议，近年来也得到了美洲研究学者越来越多的关注，美籍墨裔族群的生存状况也随之重新被研究者广泛讨论。墨裔群体人口在美国的占比在21世纪初便已超过百分之十，其受教育程度却普遍低下，"失学率四倍于白人""生活在社会的下层"[1]，而这只是其社会资源匮乏的一个侧面。美籍墨裔群体的权利问题将怎样得到改善与解决？对于这一问题，美国俄克拉荷马大学奇卡诺学者罗伯特·孔·戴维斯-昂蒂亚诺（Robert Con Davis-Undiano）教授于其新作《归乡吧，梅斯蒂索人！》（*Mestizos*, *Come Home*！）中试图以历史与现实的多个视角提出见解。

戴维斯-昂蒂亚诺教授作为俄克拉荷马大学英文系资深教授，兼任重要刊物《今日世界文学》社长，多年致力于美国拉丁混血族裔文学文化研究并著作颇丰、成果显著，曾获俄克拉荷马州西语文艺协会2017年"最杰出文学艺术家"荣誉。在其于2016年出版的专著《归乡吧，梅斯蒂索人！》中，作者以文学人类学视角，试图从美洲历史文献中挖掘墨裔美国人群体在美国社会中享有资源不均现状的根源，将美国现存的"等级制度"话语体系与梅斯蒂索群体在美洲大陆的历史渊源相联系，呼吁奇卡诺群体（以及美洲各国的少数族裔）寻回、认同、继续发扬自己的独特民族文化。同时，作为一部优秀的少数族裔研究著作，本书突破了传统奇卡诺作家的"族裔文学研究"单线脉络，以一种更为宏观的视域，交叉联结原始文化遗产、民族文学运动、少数族裔文化反向影响等因素，使得梅斯蒂索族群的文学与文化、历史与现实相勾连、相呼应。由此，民族的历史根源不至被时代发展所遗忘，而是能够在当下的社会环境中找到借古明今、重焕生机的突破方式。

《归乡吧，梅斯蒂索人！》一书分为三辑，分别论述西班牙殖民文化对美洲大陆的影响、当代梅斯蒂索社群建构、奇卡诺文学成果。作者先以殖民时期的西班牙文学、绘画等"文化遗产"入手，探究欧洲

---

[1] 姬虹：《假如美国没有了墨西哥裔人》，《世界知识》2004年第18期。

文化如何促成在美洲绵延数世纪的"纯血"/"混血"二元"等级制度";再通过当代混血族裔群体中的"土地""节庆""混血艺术"等文化概念探寻梅斯蒂索人对民族身份的重构;最后论回文学领域,由当代的奇卡诺作家作品、文学文化研究等成果,提出混血族裔在美国社会中的发展前景与可能性。

本书中出现的一系列指向民族身份的集合名词是在阅读过程中理解作者主张的关键。戴维斯-昂蒂亚诺在书中对"梅斯蒂索""混血""奇卡诺"等族裔概念做出了创造性的阐发与重构。首先是本书标题中的"梅斯蒂索人"("mestizos"),为西班牙语词汇,原义指拉丁美洲原住民与西班牙人的混血群体,在中文中译为"梅斯蒂索人"、"美斯第索人"或"印欧混血种",后词义扩展到可形容广义的"混血种人"。[1] 在美洲殖民时期,"殖民国家妇女没有大批迁入,所以殖民者常娶印第安妇女为妻"。[2] 由于天花等疾病的肆虐、宗教裁判所的排斥,印第安原住民大量死亡,新出现的混血族群便代替原住民,成为与美洲白人相对立的"他者"。若论拉丁美洲的混血族群种类,则内部分类繁多,而"奇卡诺"("墨裔美籍族群"的别称)则是拉美"梅斯蒂索人"总称的一个庞大分支。一方面,本书所使用的原始资料集中于奇卡诺族群,集中于西班牙殖民者在北美洲统治时期所作画作、墨西哥民族的历史传说、墨裔在美国的生存现状概述、墨裔文学文化成果四部分。以墨裔族群为关注中心,是本书的出发点与落脚点。而另一方面,作者同样强调,奇卡诺民族运动将推进全美洲("the A-mericas")为"梅斯蒂索"民族身份与群体利益的奋斗:"美洲的其他种族与人种群体——无论是社区外的部落住民,还是亚裔、中东裔,或其他居民——都有需要被寻回、被认同的历史和故事。"因此,概念"梅斯蒂索人"在本书中被作者赋予了狭义与广义两层指称——狭义上,梅斯蒂索运动在本书中为奇卡诺民族运动所代表、展现(正如

---

[1] 引自大英百科全书在线网站"mestizo"词条 https://www.britannica.com/topic/mestizo,原句为"any person of mixed blood"。

[2] 吕德胜:《拉丁美洲的混血种人》,《拉丁美洲研究》1980年第2期。

书评

本书的副标题——"创造并宣示墨裔美籍的身份");广义上,它则回归本义的所指范畴,指美洲的所有印欧混血族裔。虽则本书所主要探讨的是美籍墨裔的民族历史与现实,但这也是美洲混血族群的处境缩影。而对奇卡诺民族问题的追根溯源,无疑也对厘清美洲乃至世界各国族裔问题有极强的启示与借鉴意义。

本书的亮点在于作者在追溯历史、整理文学文化资料的基础上,极具创新性地提出了三大独创概念。全书开篇,作者便提出"等级制度"("casta system"[①])名词。这一概念在以往的奇卡诺文化研究中未被涉足,是作者对梅斯蒂索民族文化研究的学术推进。此概念出现于引论(Introduction)部分,作者将其定义为"一种根据肤色划分的社会秩序,旨在标明与西班牙人的种族身份的区分,促进了人种身份和先定的社会阶层概念的建立"。对于这一"等级制度"的提出,作者的切入点在于本书中一幅编号为"1.1"的18世纪佚名画作。该图收藏于墨西哥特波佐特兰市(Tepotzotlán, Mexico)的总督辖区国家博物馆(El Museo Nacional del Virreinato),展现的是殖民统治时期西班牙殖民者所设置的根据人种划分的社会身份层级。画布被分为十六个区域,依次展现"高低"等级分明的混血人种类型,每一类型都被"赋予"独特的族群名称类别。例如,女性的拉丁美洲原住民(即"土著"/"印第安人")与西班牙男性所生的人种被称为"印欧混血种",而后,印欧混血种男性与西班牙女性的混血种被命名为"卡斯蒂索人"(castizo),而若卡斯蒂索男性继续与西班牙女性生育,则他们的后裔便可回归为"西班牙人",即通过连续两代与西班牙种族通婚"洗净"土著血统。而若是混血种族内部之间的通婚育子,他们的"种族"将会变得越来越"低劣",不再拥有寻回"西班牙人"身份的

[①] 本概念的提出颇具兴味。"casta"为西语词汇,意为"血统"/"等级",对应英语中的"caste"一词。而"system"为英语词汇,意为"制度"/"系统"。英语中本已存在"caste system"词组,意为"阶级制度"。而本书中概念"casta system"反复出现,想必不是作者笔误,而是赋予其全新寓意,即一个由前半是西语、后半是英语单词构成的概念,或可暗示"'说西语的梅斯蒂索文化'与'说英语的白人文化'的对接"。

机会，这代表着他们在社会资源上的匮乏将一直持续。作者认为，现今美国社会中的"等级制度"正是承继于图中所示的来自欧洲大陆的18世纪殖民规划体系。这一体系中所传递的信息是，接近"白种人"血统的族群拥有越高的社会"身份"，而各混血族裔会处在越来越低的社会阶层中。这不仅是梅斯蒂索人遭受不公待遇的源头，也是少数族裔在美国的生存现状。通过比对该图信息与墨裔民族生态，我们不难察觉出历史与现实一些侧面的极大相似。例如，20世纪，美国主流话语因国内墨裔人口的庞大数目产生恐慌，一些白人作家重拾"种族论"，如彼得·布里姆罗（Peter Brimelow）在《怪异的国家：有关美国移民灾难的常识》（*Alien Nation：Common Sense About America's Immigration Disaster*）中宣称美国将"毁灭"于墨裔移民之手、亨廷顿在其著作《我们是谁：对美国国家认同的挑战》（*Who Are We? The Challenges Of America's National Identity*）中提及墨裔的"拒绝融入"将最终"造成一个强大国家的灭亡"。可见，现今时代下少数族裔所面临的实质问题与话语霸权，一定程度上确实带有"历史传承"。

而另一方面，随着时代发展，梅斯蒂索旧有文化的被压制并不能阻碍他们创造新的民族文化。在《归乡吧，梅斯蒂索人!》的第二辑，作者便以墨裔群体现代标志——五月五日节（Cinco de mayo）、亡灵节（The day of the dead）、低底盘车（lowrider cars）为例，指出奇卡诺群体正在逐渐重塑社会，原本只为墨裔群体所体现出的民族特有文化渐渐成为全美现象。上述民族文化能够对美国白人群体产生影响，除去梅斯蒂索文化自身的活力与吸引力外，混血族裔的庞大人口带来的推动力居功至伟。如作者所说，"拉丁裔社群拥有五千万人民，（它带来的）变革是迅捷的，而拉丁族群的人口数量提升也代表着美国故事的新篇章"。新的民族文化被创造、梅斯蒂索文化与白人文化相对话，社会上的种族群体间逐渐开始了沟通与进一步混合的进程，而这一社会进步，启发奇卡诺学者们提出了又一设想——"宇宙种族"（"la raza cósmica"）。"宇宙种族"概念在《归乡吧，梅斯蒂索人!》一书中为作者所提及，是本书的又一突破点。此概念受作者的"民族文学同僚"所影响而产生，最初由墨西哥作家何塞·瓦斯康塞洛斯（José Vasconcelos Calderón）在同名著作《宇宙种族》（*La Raza Cósmica*）中提出。这一概念认为，人种混合增速与增幅的加大会带来跨族裔话语混合，混血种会成为"多数"而脱离"边缘"。这一"宇宙种族"概念提出后便经格洛丽亚·安扎杜尔（Gloria Anzaldúa）、阿亚·德拉托雷（Victor Raúl Haya de la Torre）等墨裔作家多次引申，在《归乡吧，梅斯蒂索人!》中得到戴维斯－昂蒂亚诺的运用。"宇宙种族"设想是梅斯蒂索人对白人进行的一次"反向编码"，具有明确的未来指向性——日益扩大的移民与跨民族通婚群体必然使得"人种"界限在不远的将来沦为空泛概念，因此在观念上及早放下狭隘的民族隔阂成为一种需要甚至必要。

在本书的第三辑，作者的论述回归文学层面，为读者整理出奇卡诺民族文学运动的主要发展脉络与重要作品。奇卡诺文学是奇卡诺民族运动的重要一环，作家们着眼于墨裔所面临的文化侵略、历史问题、种族与身份问题，通过描绘墨裔美籍群体的生活经历与精神现状，呼吁梅斯蒂索人的精神团结与民族文化传承。作者提及一系列奇卡诺文学的典范之作，如19世纪运动早期的标志性文学作品《我是华金》（Yo soy Joaquin），20世纪六七十年代"奇卡诺文艺复兴"运动的托马斯·里维拉（Tomás Rivera）、罗道夫·贡萨雷斯（Rodolfo González）、鲁道夫·阿纳亚（Rudolfo Anaya），再到后来的桑德拉·希斯内罗斯（Sandra Cisneros）、德米特亚·马丁内斯（Demetria Martínez）、丹尼斯·查韦斯（Denise Chávez）。作家们声势浩大，呼吁平等社会权利的文学运动如火如荼。一方面，民族文学作品体现族裔群体的生活环境与精神状态、反映民众群体遭遇的问题、促进民族精神的团结。而另一方面，在生活方式上，人口众多的梅斯蒂索人在现今历史时期应如何保持团结、为维护民族文化与族裔尊严继续奋斗？对于这一问题，作者提出本书第三个独创概念——"雷索拉纳"（"resolana"）模式。"Resolana"概念是作者对族裔文学文化研究的又一贡献。此西班牙语词汇意为"背风向阳的地方"，在本书中则指"新墨西哥州的市民集会地点，市民们在一处面阳的墙下聚集、分享信息、倾吐遇到的困难"。由此，作为一个咨询信息和发现问题的中间站，"雷索拉纳"模式能够帮助墨裔居民打破从前只有少数受过高等教育的群体所能接触到的信息的限制，达到一种影响力和信息连通的新层面，从而极大地提升族群的整体社会地位。这一模式的提出对梅斯蒂索民族身份的寻回有重要意义，具有团结一个地域内的混血种族裔的效用，可促进梅斯蒂索人内部的信息交互与资源共享，进而带动群体社会实力与社会地位的提升，为族群获取更大的内在能量。

　　戴维斯－昂蒂亚诺教授为何这样关心梅斯蒂索人的权利问题？这是个人动因与社会责任感的完美结合。自其墨籍祖辈"归乡美国"、定居亚利桑那州，至今已有三代，而这"归乡之旅"、这民族身份的寻回常使他的复杂感慨溢出纸背（当然，其祖辈的"归乡"指返回到奇卡诺世代生长、后被殖民者驱赶出的故土；而本书所指的"归乡"则侧重于精神上的"族裔魂"之回归）。混血族裔的身份使得他更加了解本民族的发展走向与生存现状，因此在呼吁进一步的族裔平等措施方面有着极大的热诚与信念。同时，本书的书名《归乡吧，梅斯蒂索人！》（*Mestizos, Come home!*）有一定可能受到其（同样是美籍墨裔的）好友鲁道夫·阿纳亚之影响，后者于2011年发表呼吁奇卡诺平等权利的族裔小说《兰迪·洛佩兹还乡》（*Randy Lopez Goes Home*）。与其他奇卡诺作家不同，戴维斯－昂蒂亚诺没有选择文学创作，而是通过学术创作来推进族裔权益的发展。本书通过依次展开的三部分，进行了由历史到现实、从发现问题到试图解决问题的圆满闭环，为世界少数族裔研究提供了较为科学可信的理论指导与未来指引。奇卡诺民族运动已进行百余年、取得了一定进展与成果，但另一方面，墨裔群体的应有权益在现今的美国社会仍需不懈争取，这也是本书的主旨——一边面向过去、一边指向未来，通过整理出民族的历史与现实，指引民族发展的道路。本书一经问世，便得到了评论界的关注与好评，如《科尔库斯评论》（*Kirkus Review*）将其形容为一部"有视野、有洞察力、有信服力的分析作品"，以尼尔·福莱（Neil Foley）、德米特亚·马丁

书评

内斯（Demetria Martinez）、里拉·阿斯库（Rilla Askew）为首的多位美国作家也多次公开表明对这本著作的认同。历史指向现实，现实又指向未来。民族平等是全世界人民的共同呼声，而这就要求我们更加重视民族历史与民族文化。以历史文化为力量源泉，不仅奇卡诺群体将继续为民族复兴与社会公平而努力，这一努力也会贡献于世界民族发展历程。当今世界是个互联互通的整体，交通运输与科技水平的发展使得侨居、迁居群体日益壮大，这就意味着"生活在他乡"的"少数族群"之壮大。因此，梳理并探讨梅斯蒂索问题不仅是对某一民族历史的交代，不仅是面向过去的研究，更具有极强的现实意义。"他山之石，可以攻玉。"本书作为世界少数族裔研究的最新成果，是创新性与传承性的结合，定能为今后的族裔研究提供借鉴与启发。

原书信息：Robert Con Davis-Undiano, *Mestizos, Come Home!*, Norman: University of Oklahoma Press, 2017。

征稿启事

《今日世界文学》强调全球化与世界视野,旨在推动跨区域、跨语言、跨媒介、跨学科的文学研究,兼顾理论批判与案例分析,关注中国文学与世界文学的联系。本刊在主要发表学术论文以外,也涉及文学文化评论、书评、作家访谈及少量文学创作,诚邀相关领域的海内外学者同人不吝赐稿,欢迎青年学者和在读博士生积极投稿。以下是集刊常设栏目和征稿要求。

1. 常设栏目
1) 世界文学理论研究
2) 区域文学研究
3) 跨文化与跨媒介研究
4) 中国(文学)与世界
5) 世界文学创作
6) 书评/访谈

2. 基本要求
1) 来稿坚持正确的政治导向,学风文风端正,学术规范严谨。
2) 来稿须为原创,未在其他期刊、书籍或网络上公开发表。
3) 来稿文字及图片不涉及国家和企业秘密及其他与著作权有关的侵权问题。
4) 来稿语言为中文或英文,论文需提供中英文题目和中英文摘要。

5）来稿字数

学术论文：8000—20000（中文）/6000—15000（英文）

文学与文化评论：4000—6000（中文）/3000—5000（英文）

书评：4000—6000（中文）/3000—5000（英文）

文学创作：仅接受诗歌、短篇小说和独幕剧。

3. 其他事项

1）征稿时间。本刊长期接受投稿，审稿周期为2—3个月。

2）投稿方式。以WORD电子稿形式发送至邮箱：globallt@bnu.edu.cn，来稿请注明"姓名-《今日世界文学》投稿"。

3）来稿请在最后一页附以个人联系方式（电话、地址、邮编）。

4）如稿件刊发，谨寄送样刊2本，并敬奉相应稿酬。

5）论文格式规范。参看附件。

Call for Paper

In the view of globalization and cosmopolitanism, *GLT* encourages literary studies that cross the limits of regions, languages, media or disciplines. Through theoretical analysis and case studies, *GLT* aims at reflecting on the values of Chinese literature in the world system. *GLT* publishes scholarly research and a small proportion of literary/cultural reviews, book reviews, writer interviews and literary works. It welcomes submissions of original articles and reviews that contribute to the field of comparative literature and world literature. Followed please find the submission guidelines.

1. Journal Columns

1) Theory of World Literature

2) Regional Literature and Area Studies

3) Transcultural and Transmedia Studies

4) China (Chinese Literature) and the World

5) World Literary Works

6) Book Review or Interview

2. Guidelines and Requirements

1）Manuscripts must be original and unpublished. Texts and pictures do not involve copyright infringement.

2）Only Chinese or English writing is accepted.

3）Only electronic submission will be considered. Please send your article as a Microsoft Word document to globallt@ bnu. edu. cn, with the email subject as "Name-Submission to *GLT*".

4）A separate page is supposed to be attached detailing your contact information (tel. number, address, postcode).

5）If the manuscript is published, 2 sample journals will be sent and the remuneration will be paid.

6）Manuscript Length：

scholarly articles：8000—20000 Chinese characters/6000—15000 English words.

literary and cultural review：4000—6000 Chinese characters/3000—5000 English words.

Book Review：4000—6000 Chinese characters/3000—5000 English words.

literary works：only poem, short story or one-act play is acceptable.

7）Please use our Style Sheet in preparing your manuscript for submission.

附件：　　　　　　　　　论文格式规范
Style Sheet

1. 论文需包含标题、摘要、关键词、作者署名及简介、正文、注释。

Scholarly articles should include the title, abstract, key words, author name, author's basic information, the body text and footnotes.

2. 作者署名置于标题之下，如有多位作者，用逗号隔开；作者简介置于篇首页底部，包括姓名、性别、学历、供职机构单位、职称、职务、研究领域。

Author's name is supposed to appear below the title. If there are more than one authors, commas are needed to separate different names.

Author's basic information should cover name, gender, education background, work institution, position, research field, all of which are set at the end of the first page.

3. 注释、引用采取当页脚注形式，需包括作者、著述名称、出版社、时间、页码等信息，具体范例如下：

Footnotes should be used exclusively at the end of each page to acknowledge your sources and citations. A footnote should include the author, title, publisher, publication year, page number of the work cited. Specific examples are shown as follows：

1) 专著（Book）

注明作者、书名、出版社、出版时间、页码；中文参考文献出版地为内地出版社的不需要标注出版地，内地以外的出版地（中国香港、中国澳门、中国台湾等）应在出版社前标注出版地，外文参考文献需在出版社前标注出版地。（Indicate the author, title, publisher, publication year and page number of the book cited. The Place of publication that sites beyond the borders of mailand China is required marked.）

例如：

陈惇：《跨越与会通：比较文学外国文学文选》，江西教育出版社2002年版，第1页。

For example：

David Damrosch, *What is World Literature?*, Princeton & Oxford：Oxford University Press, 2003, p. 1.

2) 译著（A translation work）

注明作者国别、作者、译者、书名、出版社、出版时间、页码。（Indicate the nation and name of original author, name of translator, title, publisher, publication year and page number of the translation work cited.）

例如：

［英］雷蒙·威廉斯：《文化与社会：1780—1950》，高晓玲译，商务印书馆 2018 年版，第 1 页。

For example：

Mo Yan, *Red Sorghum*, trans. Howard Goldblatt, New York：Viking, 1993, p. 1.

3）文集论文（A work in an anthology）

注明引用论文的作者、论文名称、文集编者、文集名称、出版社、出版时间、页码。（Indicate the author and title of a work in an anthology; indicate the editor, title, publisher, publication year and page number of the anthology. ）

例如：

刘禾：《跨文化研究的语言文体》，宋伟杰译，载许宝强、袁伟《语言与翻译的政治》，中央编译出版社 2000 年版，第 1 页。

For example：

Peter Osborne, "Philosophy after Theory：Transdisciplinarity and the new", in *Theory after "theory"*, ed. , Jane Elliot and Derek Attridge, London & New York：Routledge, 2011, p. 1.

4）期刊论文（A Journal article）

注明著者、文章名、期刊名、年卷期。（Indicate the author, title, journal, issue number and page number of the journal article cited. ）

例如：

刘洪涛：《中国当代文学海外传播的回顾与前瞻》，《南方文坛》2021 年第 2 期。

For example：

Jing Tsu, "New Area Studies and Languages on the Move", *PMLA*, Vol. 126, No. 3, May 2011, p. 693.

5）网络文章（Web publications）

注明著者（如果有）、文章名、网站、刊发时间。［Indicate the author (if any), publication title, website and publication year/month/date.]

例如：

《刘慈欣担任中国作协科幻文学委员会主任》，https://www.sohu.com/a/528629015_100117963，2022年3月9日。

For Example：

"Pulitzer Prize Board Announces New Book Category", https://www.pulitzer.org/news/pulitzer-prize-board-announces-new-book-category, June 23, 2022.